Echoes of Extinction

By

D. Ward Cornell

This is a work of fiction. Names, characters, places, and incidents are either the product of the author's imagination or used fictitiously. Any resemblances to actual persons, living or dead, events or locales is entirely coincidental.

Copyright © 2023 by D. Ward Cornell
ISBN: 9798366223461

All rights reserved. In accordance with the United States Copyright Act of 1976, the scanning, uploading and electronic sharing of any part of this book without the permission of the author constitutes unlawful piracy and theft of the author's intellectual property. If you would like to use material from this book (other than for review purposes), prior written permission must be obtained by contacting the author at dw.cornell@kahakaicg.com. Thank you for your support of the author's rights.

TABLE OF CONTENTS

CHAPTER 1: DISCOVERY 1
CHAPTER 2: VERIFICATION 22
CHAPTER 3: POWER 41
CHAPTER 4: GRAVITY 60
CHAPTER 5: CELEBRITY 78
CHAPTER 6: DEMONSTRATIONS 95
CHAPTER 7: CRISIS 109
CHAPTER 8: AFTERMATH 132
CHAPTER 9: PROOF OF CONCEPT 151
CHAPTER 10: SURVIVORS 177
CHAPTER 11: DECEPTION 195
CHAPTER 12: CHRISTMAS 213
CHAPTER 13: PRODUCTION 228
CHAPTER 14: ACCELERATION 252
CHAPTER 15: PLATFORM 280
CHAPTER 16: DELIVERY 301
CHAPTER 17: REVERSAL 322
CHAPTER 18: RECOVERY 341
CHAPTER 19: CREWS 358
CHAPTER 20: CONFRONTATION 382
EPILOGUE 405
AFTERWORD 414
COMING SOON 419
ABOUT THE AUTHOR 434
OTHER BOOKS by D. WARD CORNELL 434

CHAPTER 1: DISCOVERY

[07.12.2034] PENTAGON, WASHINGTON D. C.

Have you ever had one of those days where you wake up, or snap back from a daydream, with an epiphany? Where in an instant you realize nothing is what you thought it was. Where you see everything through a different lens?

Well, I have. Twice, in fact. The first was in Afghanistan, my second tour, at the very end.

...

[08.26.2021] I woke up in a fog, face down on the ground, head pounding, frantic action all around me. I tried to get up, but my arms and legs weren't fully under my control. Then a familiar voice cut through the buzzing in my ears. "Wimberly, get the hell up." It was Mac.

Hands grabbed me and pulled me up as the distinctive crack of a high-power sniper rifle brought me back to myself. I knew that rifle and knew its owner. Some poor fool had just bought the farm because Alex never missed.

"What happened?" I blurted out.

"IED. People down, a lot of them."

I recognized that voice, too. It was Ty. Now on my feet and fully back in the moment, we ran and ducked behind a barrier. That's when the epiphany came. In ten years, the only thing people would remember about Afghanistan was Abbey Gate and America's disastrous withdrawal. This whole misadventure had been for nothing. But even as the thought went through my mind, I knew it wasn't true. Three of the best friends I would ever make just rescued me: master mechanic Mackenzie Stone (Mac), munitions expert Tyrell Mosely (Ty), and marksman extraordinaire Alexandra Reyes (Alex).

...

[07.12.2034] We all left the military shortly after we got home. Eight years later, they all joined me in my new venture. But now, twelve years after Abbey Gate, I sit across the table from Secretary of Defense Alaster McDaniels and the head of the Joint Chiefs of Staff, Admiral

Nelson Sloan, and for the first time realize the new Manhattan-like Project we've been working on for the better part of the last year is being run by Xerox copies of the people that put me at Abbey Gate years ago. How did I let this happen? I suppose I'll have to go back to the beginning in order to explain.

Day 1
[08.09.2033] OPERATIONS CENTER, FULL CYCLE SOLAR, INC.

The day started with my normal routine, up early, then a five-mile run in the cool, mountain shadows of the western Arizona dawn. Most days, some of the guys join me. Today, it was just Mac and Ty. It was in the low 80s this morning, humidity only 8%, which reminded Ty of a similar morning run in the Afghan mountains. Needless to say, there were a lot of *do you remember when's*. All good memories. We rarely talk about the other ones.

Now in the office, my head is buried in operations reports. Our company, Full Cycle Solar (FCS), is an electricity provider. We provide 24/365 base-line electric power. We use a novel power-generation technology that I developed as part of my PhD work at Cal Tech after I got out of the military. The idea is simple, a variation on the traditional Solar Concentration approach, in which hundreds of mirrors concentrate sunlight on a collector which is used to heat molten salt. The salt is then used to drive a steam generator. Dozens of huge concentration stations have popped up around the world and they all come with environmental impact issues.

My idea was different, modular. We place a five-meter-wide multifaceted lens assembly above an insulated column of molten salt that's been placed in the ground. Each day the lens collects enough sunlight to super-heat the molten salt, enough that it can run a twenty-kilowatt steam generator for twenty-six hours. Each little generation unit, which we refer to as a well, is standalone and only costs about $1,200 per kilowatt to build. From a distance, each generator looks like a little mushroom sticking up out of the ground. Two plus years in, we have five hundred units built. Plant output is ten megawatts, constant day and night. We have enough land to put in twenty thousand units, which will bring us up to four hundred megawatts over the next ten years. Not bad for an ex-army grunt.

The squawk of my two-way radio brings me back to the moment.
"Wimberly."
"Hey, boss. We've got problems up at Well #8."

"And a bright good morning to you too, Gabe."

My gibe gets a laugh from operations manager Gabriel Wilson.

"The salt temperature is dropping. Preliminary scans suggest a failure within its lens."

"How? Was there an earthquake or something?"

"I don't know. I'm planning to send a team up to look at it. But I know you prefer to take things like this on your own."

"What evidence do you have that it's a lens failure?"

"The first clue was a temperature alarm. The sun's been on it for ten minutes with no corresponding temperature increase. The security camera image isn't definitive, but it shows some foreign materials that shouldn't be there."

"You think someone damaged it?"

"Looks more like something hit it."

"OK. Ask Alex to meet me on the helipad."

...

Well #8 is two miles southeast of the operations center, on the other side of the ridge. By air it's ten minutes away, by jeep twenty. All the roads on our property are gravel. The only exception is the paved main road out to the highway. That's the reason I got the helicopter. I'd learned to fly when I was a teenager, taught by the guy that sprayed the family vineyards, so why not?

As we approach the ridge, Alex points. "Something's happened over there. See the way the cactuses have been mowed down? And all the displaced rock?"

I envy Alex's eyesight. Maybe it's part of the whole sharpshooter thing.

"Looks like a giant skid mark," I reply.

"Something has obviously crashed there."

"Obvious?" I ask.

"Kai, you're so blind. Maybe I should get a license to fly this thing."

To most of the world, I'm Kyle Wimberly. To my former squad, it's Wimberly, boss, or Kai, the latter originating from a Hawaiian kid in the platoon on the first tour. Sadly, he was one of our unit's casualties—an incredibly friendly and generous kid who tried to win the Taliban over with aloha.

"Number eight is just over the ridge. I can probably see it if you go a little higher."

I hate burning the extra fuel. But thinking about the kid, Keone, makes me want to do something nice for Alex.

"What the hell is that?"

Alex is pointing again. I'm squinting.

"Looks like a shipping container to me," she adds. "Well, a stylish one anyway."

I finally see what she's pointing at, a long metallic object nestled up against the solar lens frame above Well #8. I'd initially thought the glistening I was seeing came from the lens.

"Looks more like a giant metal cigar to me," I offer.

"You've got a point there, boss." Then, moments later, "Oh, the lens is really messed up. Total scrap job."

To see this for myself, I bring the helicopter in to a hover. "Total scrap job," I echo. "Thankfully, the landing pad's clear. I'm going to set her down."

"It looks like there are people on the far side of your metal cigar," Alex says with excitement. "I'm going in weapons hot."

We settle on the pad, and I start the shutdown procedure. But Alex is out the door before the rotors slow much.

A minute passes before it's safe for me to leave the helicopter unattended. Not having heard any shots yet, I know Alex has the trespassers under control. So, I take the thirty-second detour around the lens to see the extent of the damage. The glass and broken facet assemblies on the ground tell the entire story.

My inner self wants to curse this intruder. But truth be told, I doubt this happened intentionally. Nonetheless, the generator powered by this unit needs to be shut down to preserve the heat in the salt. It can hold the heat thirty to sixty days before the salt solidifies. But, if that happens, it will take about the same amount of time to reliquefy the salt.

"Wimberly, I need you over here! You've got to see this."

The urgency in Alex's voice and her use of my real name is a throwback to Afghanistan, triggering an immediate response. Every other thought discarded, I turn and run toward her as if our lives depended upon it. The shortest path to Alex is around the near end of the metallic object. As I get closer, I note it looks more rectangular than I thought while approaching in the helicopter. I also notice the stub wings and tail stabilizer I hadn't seen from the air. Is this an experimental plane of some sort that crash landed?

After cresting the aircraft's stern, I see something I never thought I'd see—two humanoid beings laid out on the ground, apparently dead. Even more astonishing, I see Alex helping a third toward the aircraft's hatch.

"Kai, come help me. He's heavy and claims to be a messenger from another world."

"An alien that speaks English?"

"I'm pretty sure it wasn't Russian," she sasses back. "Now come help me. He's heavier than he looks."

"Where are we taking him?" I ask, as I give the stranger the visual once over that I gave every Afghan back in the day. This creature is humanoid—two arms, two legs, hands, feet, head—but truly alien. I fight the immediate revulsion of the gray green skin and giant fish eyes as I take more of him in. That's when I see his leg. Compound fracture—flesh, bone, and blood. Neither the texture of its waxy flesh, nor the color of its thin, brown blood look human. Regardless, I saw enough wounds like this in the field to know the urgency of medical care. "We need to get him to a hospital."

"No," the alien says, speaking for the first time. "I have equipment in my shuttle."

"This is worse than anything the two of us can fix, no matter how good the equipment," I argue back.

"No. The authorities cannot learn of my presence yet. Your world is in grave danger, and we are here to help you. But it is too soon to contact the authorities."

With no time to argue, I grab his other arm, then nod to Alex. The short little alien is surprisingly heavy, but the two of us carry him to the shuttle's hatch. We set him down as he guides me through the opening procedure, but as the hatch opens, a shiver passes over me. Do I really want to enter this ship?

"Come on, Kai. We don't have much time."

I take a deep breath, then step in so we can lift him up over the threshold. The shuttle is dark inside, illuminated only by light coming in through the hatch. But what I see isn't very impressive. In fact, it's just plain creepy—three sofas and nothing else. All my Afghan spider-senses scream danger, but on the count of three, Alex and I lift him over the threshold, anyway.

Moments later, the alien makes a guttural sound that makes my skin crawl, and the shuttle comes to life. Equipment and control panels of every type simply materialize out of nowhere, some just floating there in front of the sofas. The shock is so thorough that I almost lose my grip on our extraterrestrial visitor.

"Holoprojections," the alien says, then points to one. "Help me get over there."

With care not to touch anything in the now crowded space, Alex and I maneuver him into place.

"Do you have a name?" Alex asks.

"To'Kana, captain of this vessel and commander of our mission."

He reaches out and manipulates some controls on a panel that materialized as soon as we got him seated on the sofa. Moments later, he visibly relaxes.

"There's still time," he whispers. Then his oversized intelligent eyes lift to Alex. "My crew were killed in the crash. The auto-doc could do nothing for them. But it can still save me. The procedure will take nine of your hours. Please exit so I can begin. It would be better for you not to watch the auto-doc work."

I look at Alex, then, catching her eye, shoot a glance at the hatch. She blinks her right eye in return, then I stand and point toward the exit. "We'll keep a guard posted, so no one bothers you. Then in nine hours, I'll be back."

"Good. There are things we need to discuss." As I turn to go, he asks, "Do you have a name, human?"

"I'm Kyle. She's Alex. I own the land here and the equipment your ship damaged on arrival."

"Thank you, Kyle and Alex. Please keep my presence here a secret."

I nod. "Until we speak again."

Once out and the hatch closed, I ask, "What do you think?"

"An alien that speaks English...." Alex's voice trails off for a second. "I didn't see that coming. But he sure does not look human and the tech in his shuttle doesn't either."

"Agreed, but how much trouble will we be in if we don't tell the authorities?"

Alex reaches out and touches my arm. "Kai, I think you need to call Justin. This is his domain. He'll have a clearer idea about how to handle it. But don't tell him we have an alien until he's right here outside the hatch. He won't come if you do."

HEADQUARTERS RUNWAY

The sound of Justin's Gulfstream 800 (G800) coming over the mountains catches my attention. The sight of the plane takes me back to the first time we met. Captain Justin Wicks, Air Force pilot, flew one of the giant C130s that were the lifeblood of the Afghanistan mission.

They brought in supplies, refueled helicopters and fighters in flight, ran rescue missions, and carried the injured to Germany.

What I didn't find out until later is that his family was rich. I mean, like, super rich. His father, one of Wall Streets' legends, almost disowned Justin when he signed on with the Air Force after 9/11. He already had a commercial license to fly his father's Gulfstream 5.

He retired from the Air Force at the end of 2020, so was spared the embarrassment of Abbey Gate. I met him on a mission where he was flying, and my team was his cargo. Despite the age gap, he took Alex on a couple of dates. It didn't really work for either of them, but as Alex's protector of sorts, I got to know Justin pretty well.

For all the crap he got from his father while he was in the Air Force, they welcomed Justin back with open arms and a partnership offer—half a million a year, plus a target annual bonus of a full million. Who can imagine such a thing? Even more shocking, he turned it down, wanting to start a business of his own.

His idea was apparently good, because his father bankrolled it. That was just over ten years ago. Since then, Justin's net worth has grown to exceed his father's, and he's the one I went to see when it became clear my PhD work could be an electric power game-changer.

The sound of the G800's engines powering down brings me back to the moment. It's time to go get my business partner. As I pull up in my Jeep, the door on the G800 snaps open. Seconds later, the stairs fold down. A minute after that, Justin steps up to the doorway and waves.

"Kyle, it's been a while, my friend. I was starting to think this operation was getting boring."

"Well, it's not boring today."

As Justin starts down the stairs, his co-pilot and girlfriend, Jill, steps into the doorway. She waves and gives me a wink. I return the wave and in truth have trouble tearing my eyes away from her. Even in a flight suit, she looks hot. Seconds later, Justin steps off the stairway and Jill starts her way down.

Justin approaches, hand extended. "Jill's going to supervise the refueling and replenishment, then head over to operations to complete the paperwork. I've only got five hours, so let's get after it."

We both hop into the Jeep, and as soon as we leave the runway, Justin starts, "So there's a problem at Well #8. One so important I needed to come down, and so confidential I had to come down on faith."

"Yeah. It could affect the value of the business, so I thought you needed to see it with your own eyes."

I keep my eyes on the road, so can't see Justin's expression. But the fidgeting in the passenger's seat is enough to convince me that my principal investor is appropriately worried.

"I put a lot of faith in you, Kyle, when I contributed the land to your company," Justin reminds. "You told me that your containment method was foolproof. Do you know yet how it failed?"

"That's not the problem."

"Then what the hell is!" Justin explodes.

"Something fell out of the sky and hit the lens assembly on Well #8. We've had to shut it down to preserve the heat. That gives us thirty-to-sixty days to get the assembly repaired before its salt reservoir freezes."

"I presume you have a back-up plan."

"Worst case, we trash the lens assembly and replace it with the new one that just came in for Well #51."

Justin groans, "Twenty thousand and a two-month delay…"

I can all but hear the gears crunching away at the new information. Then he snaps out of it. "So, this isn't about the well; it's about the thing that fell out of the sky."

"It is."

"And it only damaged the lens on Well #8?"

I laugh. "Sorry, I didn't intend this to be a guessing game. An aircraft of some sort crash landed and hit the lens assembly on Well #8. We didn't find out about it until sunrise, when the well didn't start heating. When I came up to investigate, I found this… thing. Two people aboard were seriously injured in the crash and dead by the time we found them. The third was seriously injured but refused to be taken for treatment."

"What was the matter with him, and what did you do?"

"Compound fracture of his right leg."

"You just left him to bleed out?"

Again, I laugh. "Do you really think we would do that?" I pause a second to let the question sink in. "He has a medical bay with something he calls an auto-doc that we helped him into. He calls his aircraft a shuttle, and it's packed with technology he doesn't want the authorities to get a hold of."

"Is it American?"

"No."

"Then what?"

The question is asked just as we come around the corner and into view of the alien shuttle. Pointing at it, I say, "He claims to come from another world."

Justin is speechless for a second, then laughs. "You've got to be kidding me."

"That's why I wanted you to see it with your own eyes. I didn't believe it until I went into his shuttle."

"And he wants to keep it hidden from the government?"

"For now, yes. He says they aren't ready to receive him yet."

Justin smacks his hands together. "We…," he drags out the word, "are going to make a fortune on this."

IKNOSAN SHUTTLE

We pull up close to the shuttle, where Mac and Alex are waiting for us. As we exchange greetings, I note that the bodies of the two dead aliens are no longer laid out on the ground near the shuttle hatch.

As I point, I ask, "What happened to the two that were over there?"

Alex shakes her head. "They disappeared. There one minute, not the next, and no sign of what happened to them."

"Has Captain To'Kana come out? He should have finished his therapy an hour ago."

"No," Alex replies. "We decided to wait until you got here to check on him."

The words are barely out when we hear the hatch open and see Captain To'Kana standing in the opening.

"Who is this?" he asks, pointing at Justin.

"My business partner and principal investor in our solar farm."

The words seem to puzzle the captain. "That means he is with you, not the authorities."

"That is correct. He's one of us."

"Then come. We have much to discuss and little time."

I motion for Justin to follow, then move to enter the shuttle.

"We'll stay out here and keep watch," Alex offers.

As I step in, I'm once again taken by the technology on display. Behind me, I hear Justin whisper, "Oh my God. This is real."

Captain To'Kana, having little patience, indicates seats then starts, "My people, the Iknosan, came under attack by vicious marauding predators that call themselves the Xeric Dominion. Here is an image of one of the Xeric, with one of our people superimposed at the same scale. As you can see, they are twice our size, four times our weight."

I hear Justin's shocked inhalation as he recoils at the sight of the monstrous creature.

"Their ships are equally impressive and repulsive. Here is the image of one of their dreadnaughts, with my ship and my shuttle superimposed on the same scale."

It's my turn to be shocked. The captain's ship, which I haven't previously seen, is ten times the length of the shuttle we're currently sitting in. The Xeric dreadnaught is maybe seven times larger than the captain's ship.

"The Dominion dreadnaughts are fast, despite their size. In normal space, they can accelerate at rates up to twenty gravities. In faster than light (FTL) they can achieve effective cruising speeds of up to five thousand times light. Our ships are slower in normal space and until recently were slower in FTL. About a year ago, our scientists made a breakthrough that now gives us the advantage in FTL."

"We have nothing like that," I blurt out.

"We know. That's one of the reasons I'm here."

Justin asks, "Can you explain that?"

"In a minute," the captain replies dismissively. "The Dominion dreadnaughts have excellent shielding, enough to deflect a one-hundred megaton antimatter weapon detonated right up against the shield. Until recently, we were nearly toothless against their shields."

The captain's voice catches for a second, then looks at the two of us cautiously.

"About a month ago, the Xeric Dominion attacked and ravaged our world. In the year preceding, they had done the same to our colony worlds. During that year, we developed defensive weapons that gave us a chance to resist. We also obtained a list of worlds they were planning to attack next. You are the eighth on the list, one of only five that might be able to adapt our technology in time to save yourselves."

I raise my hand, drawing the captain's attention.

"When we first met, you said it was too soon to contact our government. It seems they are the ones to whom you should tell your story."

"Few worlds have the natural resources required to use our technology. Probes that have been monitoring your world for the last hundred years have identified locations where such materials might exist in minable quantities. My first job is to verify availability before approaching your government. If I cannot verify timely availability, I am to move on to the next planet on my list."

With the captain having laid out the basic situation, Justin inserts himself. "You think the likely locations are in the American southwest. That's why you learned our language."

"That is correct."

"We can help you," Justin offers. "I control enormous blocks of land in the southwest. I can give you less conspicuous transportation and access to local resources."

"And in exchange?" Captain To'Kana asks.

"I want access to technology I can use for non-military purposes."

"If your help proves valuable, then I'm sure we could reach an agreement."

I cringe at the captain's statement. Justin is a shrewd investor who doesn't even finish listening to pitches that vague. But to my surprise, he smiles, "Then let's start. What do you need?"

"Initially, three things. Help to repair my shuttle. Help to update the portable scanners on my ship. And transportation to the five sites shown on the map."

"What could you give us if we did those things?"

"While I was waiting for you, I scanned your solar concentration system. The materials in your lens limit its efficiency."

Justin glances at me, begging me to confirm or deny. "Lens efficiency at full capacity drops to 85%," I confess.

"I have materials that could run at 98%. With a lens redesign and heat storage increase, we could get two to three times the capacity with the same footprint," To'Kana comes back.

"That might be interesting," Justin replies. "But we don't need to settle it now. Let's get to work on repairing your shuttle. Have you diagnosed the problem? And do you have the parts that would be required to fix it?"

"I have everything I need except the labor," To'Kana replies.

Justin locks me with a stare. "Who should we put on it?"

"Mac and me. There are others we can pull in if necessary."

"Then let's get started," Justin says with a smile, extending his hand to shake with the captain.

To'Kana stares at it a moment, then asks, "Is this not the traditional greeting gesture?"

"It is," Justin replies. "But it is also used to affirm an agreement."

"Ah," To'Kana whispers, as he takes the offered hand. "Our surveillance of your world did not discern that use."

NEAR WELL #8

By some technological miracle, Captain To'Kana got the shuttle to hover long enough for its landing gear to deploy. Now, the damage to the shuttle is clearer. Its belly is scratched, but not seriously dented. Several of the little dimples that line the shuttle's belly are clogged with goo or torn open. And most of the sensor apertures on the shuttle's leading edge are clogged with more goo, dirt, and sand.

Shaking his head, Mac asks, "What did you hit?"

"We don't know," To'Kana replies. "We ran into a field of space junk that took down our shields. They can deflect debris up to fifty kilograms at one thousand meters per second."

"Mach 3," Mac whispers, while clearing an aperture of debris. After a few seconds of work, he yelps. "What the heck? Some fluid squirted out onto my uniform. Oil, by the look of it." Turning to look directly at To'Kana, he adds, "Looks like we have a leak. What do you have up here that might leak?"

To'Kana, who is doing a closer inspection of the ship's belly, comes over to look. "Nothing, no liquid in the bow at all, just metal, sensors, and waveguides."

"Then where did it come from? There's no oil on the ground here."

To'Kana rubs the handful of whiskers protruding from his chin. "It must have been in the space junk."

"I bet I know what it was," Justin offers from the folding chair he'd situated in the shade of one of Well #8's lens support poles. "Old Russian spy satellites were nuclear powered. At the end of their lives in the fifties or sixties, the satellites jettisoned the reactors, then dove into the atmosphere, burning up while leaving the reactors in stable orbits. In the late 2020s, the Russians recovered a few of them. Most are still up there, as is a thin ring of oil that was expelled along with the reactors."

I chuckle, wondering where he came up with that wild idea.

"It was on NPR this morning. One of the old soviet reactors deorbited today. No one knows why. It was tracked plunging into the South Atlantic."

"Your people need to deal with the space junk," To'Kana chides. "If we find the materials I need, you will become a spacefaring civilization within a year. The space junk could be your undoing."

Justin nods. "Unfortunately, we don't have the means yet, but I agree with your point."

Stepping over toward Mac, To'Kana waves his tablet over his soiled uniform. "No sign of radiation." Turning, he looks closely at a drop clinging to the sensor opening, then waves his tablet over it. "Curious. An alkane oil with ten parts per million Bismuth—the one element that can blind the sensors. You've found the problem. Keep up the good work."

I've worked on a lot of weird things in my life. Cleaning out sensor apertures on an alien space shuttle pretty much tops the list. Well, maybe working side by side with an alien tops the list. Either way, I hope Captain To'Kana knows what he's doing, because his shuttle is smack in the middle of fifty very expensive electrical power generating stations, and I only have parts to fix the one he's already broken.

Time passes, then To'Kana emerges from under the shuttle, data pad in hand. "Good news. Most of the field emitters just need to be cleaned out. Seven need to be replaced. It is a precision procedure that requires special equipment and attention to detail. It is also one you should learn."

"Sounds good to me," I reply. "It's always good to pick up a new skill."

"It will take me an hour to replicate the parts, then we can begin."

On hearing the exchange, Justin gets up and comes over.

"You said *replicate*. Can you show me how that's done?"

To'Kana nods and waves for Justin to follow. "I think our replicators are like equipment you have that you call 3D-printers. Although I imagine ours are more advanced. We built every part of this shuttle using a replicator. The one I have in the shuttle can only produce the smaller parts, but the one aboard my ship can replicate them all, including the shuttle's hull plating and superstructure."

IKNOSAN SHUTTLE

It took three hours to finish cleaning the clogged emitters and replacing the broken ones. Now it's time to test them.

"Bringing up main power," the captain reports from one of his couches.

A moment later, perched on another couch, one with no control panel, I feel a vibration pass through the shuttle. It's accompanied by a whining sound that I presume is the electrical system coming up.

Minutes tick by and I can feel Justin, who's sitting next to me, getting fidgety.

Finally, Captain To'Kana announces, "All systems are operational."

The captain turns to Justin. "Kyle and Mac are quite capable. I need to return to my ship now. Have you arranged for a survey tomorrow?"

"Of three sites, yes. I own the property and have aircraft scheduled."

"I would like to take Kyle and Mac up to my ship with me. Is that permissible? I will grant you one of our replicators for your people's time."

"I'm willing to go," Mac volunteers.

Justin eyes me.

"I suspect we work differently than you," I reply to Captain To'Kana. "I will go with you. But any technology you release to us will be released to me. I am the manager of the venture whose property you damaged and whose employees have helped you. Justin is a silent partner whose input I value."

"I meant no offense," To'Kana replies. "Your society differs from ours in ways our surveillance has not revealed to us."

He turns to Justin. "Do you agree with this condition?"

"I do. Kyle and I have equal responsibility for the solar power venture, but we have different roles to which we have agreed. You've seen that in action. He can build things, fix things. I secure resources. We work in equal partnership."

To'Kana bows his head toward us. "Our world has nothing like this. But that does not matter. I am here to help you save your world. So, I will abide by your laws and traditions to the degree we choose to work together."

"Then I'm in," I reply. "When do we leave?"

...

To'Kana instructed us to sit on the central sofa. At first, I didn't see how this could be a viable way to fly. But as I'm learning, everything on this shuttle is virtual. The captain simply needed to reprogram the sofa into two seats with safety restraints. He says it's smart material, able to change shape on demand.

On the shuttle's main view screen, the image of the moon seems to grow larger every minute.

"How fast are we going?" I ask.

"Let me see," To'Kana replies as he works some controls. "If I converted the units properly, approximately one hundred kilometers per second, relative to the center of the Earth."

"And what's our flight time?"

"Approximately six hours: one to accelerate, four at cruising speed, and another hour to decelerate."

"Why didn't I feel much acceleration?"

To'Kana laughs. "The shuttle uses a grav-drive."

I've read enough sci-fi stories to be familiar with the concept of a grav drive, but that doesn't seem to answer the question. So I prod. "I'm not sure I understand."

"Our grav-drive repels the shuttle from the Earth. To protect the interior of the ship, grav-plating inside the shuttle pulls you up almost as hard as the force pushing the ship up. The forces mostly counterbalance. It's like floating in water. The gravity is still pulling you down, but buoyancy is pushing you up."

"How many gravities can your drive generate?"

Again, To'Kana laughs.

"What?"

"Gravity is the force generated by two masses at distance: mass times mass divided by distance squared. On the surface of the Earth, where there is plenty of mass close at hand, the shuttle can generate about three gravities. In interstellar space, where there is no nearby mass, it generates no effective acceleration."

"Then how do you go star-to-star?"

"Using a faster than light, or FTL, drive. We have two kinds. One transitions the ship into another layer of space-time in which the speed of light is much higher, something you can think of as a sub-space. The other uses a mechanism human science does not know about yet that can move you from one place to another in an instant."

"Are you going to give us this technology?"

"If I can."

"What do you mean by that?"

"As I said earlier, I can give you the math and science, the designs... Everything you need to know. But without the right materials, you couldn't do anything. Worse, you might try with inadequate materials and blow yourselves up. Therefore, I will grant you the technology, only if I can find the right materials and show you how to mine and refine them."

During the captain's explanation, I noticed a slight change in the ship's feel. "We're slowing down, aren't we?"

"You are very perceptive, Kyle Wimberly."

IKNOSAN LEGACY SHIP

My first surprise on our trip to the far side of the moon is that the shuttle doesn't have any windows, peepholes, or any other means to see what's outside with our own eyes. Sensors do that for us. Anything visible outside the shuttle can be seen on the shuttle's view screens. The only way to see anything going on outside this shuttle is by looking at one of them. I have no real complaint about that, even though most filtered information I've seen paints a less than truthful picture of what's really going on.

Right now, the image on the shuttle's main view screen is of the ship we are approaching. It still looks small, but like images of the moon we saw earlier, it grows larger every minute.

An image of the moon's surface is on one of the auxiliary screens. We lost sight of the earth ten minutes ago, which is kind of creepy.

Captain To'Kana points to the main view screen. "I'm opening the shuttle bay doors and transferring shuttle control to the ship's automated landing system."

Great. My life is now in the hands of an automated, alien system. Although I suppose it has been since the instant we took off. As I watch, the ship and shuttle bay entrance grow. Then we are in, and one by one the shuttle's systems shut down.

"Come," Captain To'Kana says, then leads us to one of the engineering labs aboard the ship. As we enter, a female voice greets us. "Mackenzie Stone. Kyle Wimberly. Welcome." A moment later, an odd-looking woman takes form in front of us.

"This is our automated lab assistant," Captain To'Kana announces. "She is an artificial intelligence, who has taken the form of a human female and chosen the name Thelma."

I step forward, holding out a hand. "Hi, Thelma."

She looks at me, frozen in position for a moment. Then she steps forward to take my hand.

"Sorry. It took me a second to find relevant data on this custom," Thelma says, then extends her hand, which I take.

I feel her palm against mine, her fingers touching the back of my hand. Then, pow, I'm hit with a surge of energy that makes me feel profoundly alive.

"Thelma," the captain starts. "I need six of the portable sampling units, modified for remote use. Kyle and Mac have the skills to make the customizations. Please coach them through it."

"As you order, Captain."

Again, Thelma seems to freeze. A moment later, she turns to the three of us. "It is taking more bandwidth than I have been allocated to operate this avatar. Allow me to take a simpler form before we continue."

Once the words are out, Thelma simply disappears. A few moments later, she's back, looking like a female version of the captain. "Ah, that is better. While I was away, I issued orders for worker bots to bring the items required."

"Excellent," Captain To'Kana exudes. "I need an hour in the ship's auto-doc to complete my treatment."

"Hmmm... I wasn't expecting to be left on my own aboard an alien ship above the far side of the moon," Mac whispers to me.

"But you are not alone," Thelma assures. "Shall we begin your training?"

"I will leave you to it," the captain says, then exits the room.

A moment later, a pair of floating carts laden with boxy-looking devices enters. It's followed by something that looks like a fork-lift.

"Over here," Thelma says to the new entrants, then turns to me. "As you can see, there are five sets of three different sized boxes on the two carrier bots. There are also some smaller packages that contain the parts we need to install. The largest box in each set is a mining transporter. It weighs about ninety kilograms. The somewhat smaller box is the sample analyzer. It weighs about seventy-five kilograms. The bot that looks like a forklift is basically what it looks like. It can move the boxes for you. Would you like to use the lifting bot? Or would you rather move these around on your own?"

I nod to Mac. "Want to try it?"

We go over to look at the closest box.

"Does it have handles?" Mac asks.

"Just tap the end," Thelma replies.

We do and handles appear on either end. "Where did that come from?" Mac asks.

"It's smart material," Thelma replies.

"OK, if we put this one on the lab bench?" I ask.

She smiles. "Yes. Please do."

I grab a handle; Mac grabs the other. Then one, two, three, and we lift. I groan as we slide it onto the bench.

"Excellent," Thelma says, bubbling with enthusiasm.

"A two-man lift for sure," Mac whispers.

"Let me give you a quick orientation on this unit," she continues. "Step one is to turn the machine on. You do that using a voice command. These units do not have the English language pack installed yet, so I'll turn it on for you."

She makes a guttural sound and the unit powers up.

"Why did this one turn on and the others not?"

Thelma eyes me, then says, "I was talking to this one, not them. Our bots only respond to you if you address them directly or by name."

"Cool," Mac whispers.

"There are two things we need to do on each of these units: install the English language pack and install the remote communications pack."

Thelma wanders over to the second of the two carrier bots, then points, "Come get these. This gray package and this orange one."

I go over to get them and see that the packages are tiny. They can't weigh more than a pound or two each. I stare at the packages for a second, then pick them up.

"You can't lift these, can you?"

She puts her hand out as if to shake again. "I am an AI. I can operate this holoprojection, but it has limits. Take my hand."

I do and feel its warmth.

"Now squeeze. Don't worry, you won't hurt me."

I squeeze and feel the resistance, then squeeze harder and my fist closes.

Thelma laughs. "The look on your face…" She laughs some more. "My holoprojection comes with a force field that can exert up to one kilogram of pressure before it collapses. The warmth you feel comes from the force field."

"Can I try?" Mac asks.

She puts out her hand to Mac. "It's considered rude to collapse an AI's force field. So, you only get to do this once."

"Your hand feels so real," Mac says, then releases it. "I don't need to collapse it."

Thelma turns back to the lab bench. "Come on, let's get this job done. The gray bag contains the English language upgrade. Open the bag, pull out a chip, then touch it to the transporter. A slot will open in the back, into which you'll slide the chip."

I lean over the transporter, touch the chip to it and a slot opens.

"Smart material, right?" I ask as I slide the chip in.

"Right," Thelma replies. "Now repeat the process with a chip from the other bag."

As Mac opens the second bag, I ask, "Thelma? Why are we here? Surely, To'Kana didn't fly us up here just to touch some chips to the side of these boxes."

She looks at me with an unreadable expression, then says, "Of course he didn't. But you are here, and this does need to be done before we move on. So will you upgrade the other boxes for me?"

Once we've installed the remote communications chip, Thelma says, "OK, last step. Let's turn the unit off so we can test it. To do that, touch the unit with your finger, that should make the power button appear. When it does, touch the power button and the unit will shut down."

I do as asked, then Thelma says. "I'm going to disappear for a moment and connect with the unit remotely to confirm that it works. Will be back in a second."

When Thelma disappears, I say to Mac, "Let's hoist the other four transporters up onto the bench while she's running her test."

"I wish it was this easy to configure our equipment," Mac mutters.

A moment later, Thelma is back. "The remote connection works. I'll activate the other four, then you can start doing the upgrades. I'll test them as you finish them."

"Will do."

Thirty minutes later, all five transporters and all five sample analyzers are upgraded for remote operation and work in English.

"OK. Let's turn on the first transporter," Thelma says.

I nod to Mac. "You want the honor?"

Mac smiles. "Sure. What do I need to do?"

"Its name is Sample Transporter One. Ask it to activate."

Mac looks at the transporter then says. "Sample Transporter One, please activate." To our surprise, a three-dimensional control panel appears above the transporter box. It's filled with view screens and controls, all labeled in English. A red alert light flashes in the upper right corner.

"See the alert light flashing?" Thelma asks. "Touch it and it will tell you what the problem is."

I touch it and a message pops up. *Sample container missing.*

"Let me guess... If we touch a sample tray to the unit, an opening will appear."

"You are a fast learner, Kyle Wimberly."

A minute later, the sample tray is installed.

"Now, let me show you how the machine works."

...

Two hours later, I know how to scan for materials, specify the sample I want to take, and initiate the mining process, which, in Star Trek fashion, uses a mini-transporter to transport a tiny sample of the designated material into the sample tray inside the box. Looking at my watch, I see that it's 8:00 PM back at the solar farm.

"Thelma? Is Captain To'Kana OK? He said he would only be an hour."

"Yes. His treatment finished on time. He's been working on the shuttle's shields. He's just about finished."

"What's the plan for tonight?"

"He has one more thing he wants you to install before you leave."

"What's that?" I ask.

"A comm device."

"Wasn't that part of the remote communication package we installed?"

Thelma looks at me with a puzzled expression, then a faraway look. "He will return in a moment to explain. Once that is done, he will transport you home."

...

A *moment* ended up being another hour. While we waited, Thelma taught us how to use the sample analyzer. Finally, the captain entered the lab.

"Gentlemen, Thelma has kept me appraised of your progress. Excellent work. There is one last thing we need to do before I send you home." He looks around, then points at a living room-like set up with a coffee table, between a pair of sofas. "Let's sit over here."

He indicates seats for us on one sofa, then sits on the sofa opposite. Once settled, he pulls out two small packages and places one in front of each of us. "Please open the packages."

I open mine and see a little earpiece in the small package.

"These are comm devices. Once placed in your ear, it will enable you to connect with me or Thelma, or any of the other bots or AIs on the ship or shuttle, no matter where you are. It will also enable me to locate you and use the ship's transporters to transport you from place to place."

"Does that mean we need to wear it all the time?" Mac asks.

"I suppose the answer is yes. But you don't feel it, so you won't notice that it's in your ear. Come on, try it. You will understand once it's in. But fair warning. It tickles when you first put it in."

Mac and I look at each other. "You first," he says.

I look at Captain To'Kana. "What do I do? Just shove it in?"

"Yes. Place it in your ear, push it in with your index finger, and give it a little twist."

I eye my earpiece, then shrug. "Here goes."

I pick it up, push it in, then twist my finger. An explosion of shivers runs through me, which I shake off. "That was weird."

"Can you hear me?" Thelma asks.

I look around, but she's not here.

"In your ear, silly."

"Yes, I hear you."

"Good, I have a clear reading on you as well. Tell Mac it is his turn."

I turn to Mac. "This is the clearest headset I've ever had. Thelma says it's your turn. To me, it sounded like she was right here."

Begrudgingly, Mac picks up his earpiece and twists it in. The motion is followed by the same intense shivering that I experienced. "What the hell," he mutters.

"Excellent," the captain says, then a holoprojection appears between us, showing a map of my solar operation. "Where would you like me to return you? I can return you directly to your home, if you show me where it is?"

"I'm not sure I understand," I reply.

"Now that you are connected to our systems, I can use the ship's transporters to send you anywhere on Earth, or ship, or shuttle, for that matter."

"You're just going to beam us back?" Mac asks.

"Curious expression. But yes. I will beam you back. In the morning, just touch your finger to your ear when you are ready to start the survey. I will send down the equipment and participate remotely."

"Send me here." I touch my finger to the map, pointing out my cabin.

"You can send me to the same place," Mac adds. "I'm just a couple of cabins away."

CHAPTER 2: VERIFICATION

[08.10.2033] OPS CENTER

As Mac and I jog up to the rendezvous point for the morning run, Ty asks, "Sleep in today?"

"We're only five minutes late," Mac grumbles with a head nod towards me. "Would have been on time if not for this lug."

A minute later, Ashton Baird, a retired master-at-arms with the Navy's shore patrol, joins us. "I heard that you two had quite the adventure yesterday."

"Ash, good to see you. Are you feeling better?" I ask.

"Think so. Haven't had a flu that kicked me that hard since COVID."

"Guys. Let's go! I want to get this run in before noon," Ty complains, then jogs away. I turn to follow, Ash coming up alongside.

"Glad to have you back," I add.

"Rumors about what happened yesterday are circulating through the company. Is it true that Alex shot an alien?"

I snort. "Definitely not true."

I can tell Ash isn't buying it, but thankfully Mac comes up on the other side, drawing attention away from the topic.

"You heard from Thelma yet?"

"No. I was going to call her when we finished the run."

"You finally got a girlfriend, Wimberly?" Ash teases.

The words cut deeply. As an ex-service member trained in policing, Ash has been a welcome addition to our team, a good fit with my crew from Afghanistan. But he doesn't have the history, so doesn't know which topics to avoid.

"No," Mac replies for me. "She's someone we're thinking about bringing aboard."

Apparently realizing his gibe wasn't well received, Ash back peddles. "Just as well. I would have stolen her from you anyway."

As I laugh, Mac says, "You're batting oh for two this morning, buddy."

"OK, I get the message," Ash replies. "I'll just have to take my humor some place where it will be better appreciated." He puts on a little more speed, then calls out, "Ty. Wait up."

...

Two miles into our five-mile run, I hear the unmistakable rumble of Justin's Gulfstream 800 (G800).

"Up there." Mac points.

"He's early," I reply. "I need to turn back. It's dangerous letting him roam the office unaccompanied."

Mac laughs. "You two. You're like an old married couple."

As I slow, Mac does as well. "I'll come with you." Then, he yells ahead, "Guys, we need to turn back."

Once Ty waves an acknowledgment, Mac and I head back at a slightly faster pace than we ran out.

"As soon as we are back, I'll ask Thelma to transport the equipment down into my cabin. We can hoist it into the truck, then go meet up with Justin."

OFFICE, HEADQUARTERS

By the time Mac and I got to the runway, Justin's G800 was buttoned up. Ten minutes later, I find him in my office, Jill standing guard in front of the closed door to my glass-walled space.

"Justin's on a call. He should be done before much longer. Want to grab a coffee while we wait?"

My instinct is to say no. I want to get the plane loaded and, in truth, don't want to spend that much time alone with Jill.

She laughs. "Justin said you'd probably want to go load the plane. But he wants to talk with you first. Come on."

Through the glass, I see Justin motioning toward the kitchen. I give him an irritated look, which makes him smile, then turn to follow Jill.

"Kai, got a minute?"

I turn and see Gabe coming my way. Thankful that I'm being rescued, I step toward him. "Sure. What's up?"

"I called RayPrec to see if we could pull the next lens forward. The short answer is that for a ten percent expedite fee, they can have it here in two weeks."

I groan. "Do it."

Gabe gives me a sideways look. "Are you going to have the time, given the other things going on?"

"We'll make the time. I don't want to lose that well."

"You or Justin will need to sign the purchase order."

"You have us for at least another five minutes."

As Gabe runs for his office, Justin walks up. "What was that about?"

"RayPrec Industries, the company that assembles the lenses for us, can get a replacement lens delivered in two weeks for a ten percent expedite fee."

"Good, one less thing to worry about." Justin points back toward my office. "We don't need to leave until 8:30. That gives us a half hour to discuss today's agenda. I had a long talk with To'Kana last night and need to bring you up to speed."

"What? I was up on his ship until nearly 11:00."

Justin laughs. "I gave To'Kana my contact information yesterday. He called me on my Starlink phone while he was having his treatment on his ship."

"How?"

"Don't know. But I learned a lot more about the material requirements."

Now back in the office, Justin taps his finger, then starts in. "The most important thing on To'Kana's list is a mineral called Thortveitite."

"Never heard of it."

"It's composed of Scandium and Yttrium, two of the so-called rare earth metals. The Iknosan use these in their weapons, power generation, and power distribution systems. They are also components in the alloys used in the ships' hulls."

"How much do we need?"

"To'Kana says we need fourteen thousand metric tons of scandium and twenty-one thousand tons of yttrium, to build a fleet capable of repelling the Xeric Dominion. Current global production is nowhere near those numbers."

"This will be our first stop?"

"It will," Justin starts, then a big smile blooms.

"What?"

"The deposit is on land adjacent to land I already own, which is up for sale. I was on the phone with the broker representing its owner. Assuming the sample is good, we can get that property and its mineral rights for less than five million."

"Where is this property?" I ask.

"Sixty miles northeast of Las Vegas, but more on that in a minute. There are four other minerals he needs, and he's found multiple sites for each. But none of these have the same purity. So we may need to test multiple sites to find enough of the underlying materials."

"What are the four other minerals?"

Justin taps his finger on the table, an odd tic that I've noticed before.

"Xenotime, Monazite, Euxenite, and Gadolinite."

"How do you remember all this stuff?"

Justin taps his glasses. "Smart lenses. When I tap with my index finger, it advances to the next page."

"So that's how you do it."

"Everyone on Wall Street has them. You really can't be competitive without."

"Thank God, I live in the desert."

Justin laughs, then shakes his head. "One more thing before we go."

"OK."

"I plan to buy the land with the Thortveitite. I propose we hold it in a separate company whose purpose is to commercialize Iknosan technology."

"Why separate?" I snap back, the response a little too sharp.

Justin shakes his head. "Several reasons. Let's start at the top. Who's going to own and operate the fleet?"

His question takes me off guard. "The government."

"And what role are we going to play?"

"I haven't thought that far ahead."

Justin sighs. "We are going to lead the effort. Captain To'Kana can't and won't. And he is adamant that he wants you leading things."

He motions with his hands in a way that makes me think he wants me to fill in the blanks, but I'm clueless.

"That means we are going to become a major government contractor. The laws governing those companies, even the accounting standards they're required to follow, are different than they are for Full Cycle Solar. In the end, we'll probably need to form three or more companies and a holding company. But that's down the road..."

Justin goes on for a while. I catch most of it. Then his alarm sounds.

"More on that later. Let's get the plane loaded and go exploring."

As we exit, Gabe comes running over. "Kai, I need that signature."

I take the clipboard Gabe's holding out, confirm the vendor, product, and price, then sign.

"Thanks, Gabe. Good work."

I get a big smile. "Thanks boss."

DESERT, AMBER, NEVADA

An hour ago, we loaded all our equipment into the G800 and flew to Las Vegas. There, we transferred the equipment for the day's pulls to a Bell 429 executive helicopter Justin rented for the day.

The pilot's voice comes through the noise suppressing headset. "We're passing over town now. Our destination is fifteen miles ahead on the left, near the foothills. We'll be on the ground in a few minutes."

Despite the spaciousness of the cabin, Mac and I are crammed together in opposing seats on the pilot's side, while Justin is seated comfortably on the passenger side with our equipment stacked in the middle. Jill is up front in the co-pilot's seat.

"Now I get it," I mutter. "This deposit is fourteen thousand feet down. More than twice as far down as the deepest mines in the world. To'Kana's sampling transporter can reach down that far to get a sample without having to dig it up. But how will we get that much out in time?"

"I asked him the same question," Justin replies. "He has an orbital mining transporter. He says he can pull two thousand metric tons per day up to his orbital ore processing facility. There, he can refine it the next day, then transport the waste products back down into the mine and land the finished product on Earth."

Mac, who's been really quiet this morning, lifts his eyes to Justin. "When did you talk with To'Kana?"

"He called me last night and was surprisingly chatty. I think he's realized that he may not be able to deliver his technology to another world without his original crew."

"How did he call you?"

"On my Starlink phone. I gave him my contact info. He said his bots had no trouble hacking it."

Jumping back in, I ask, "Does that mean he's throwing in with us?"

"He hasn't said that yet, but I think that's his plan."

The pilot's voice comes through our headsets. "We are on final approach."

...

It took an hour, but we now have the sample transporter set up and the deposit in our sights.

"It's huge," Justin declares.

Mac points at the color variances in the density scans. "The density is inconsistent."

"But the size," Justin comes back. "The dense section is what? A half mile across? And the depth, it starts about ten thousand feet down and runs to sixteen thousand."

"It's also hot, near the limit of what our sample transporter can handle," I add.

We stare at the three-dimensional holoprojection of the deposit in silence for a minute, then, mind made up, I designate ten locations within the deposit. "I propose to draw samples from these locations."

"Rationale?" Justin asks.

"The samples are spread throughout the deposit, which will allow us to test the deposit's internal consistency. It includes some of the most significant density variations, which will tell us about its internal structure."

"You good with this, Mac?" Justin asks.

"I'd have chosen more or less the same."

"Then let's draw the samples," Justin proposes.

A second later, the sample transporter puts off a vibration, then it displays its *Sample Collected* message. Mass: 97.7 grams. Temperature: 241° C.

A half hour later, ten similar samples pulled, we transfer the sample container to the analyzer, then pack everything into the helicopter and make our way to the next site.

UPPER BURRO CREEK WILDERNESS, ARIZONA

Once in the air, Justin brings us up to speed on our target at the next site.

"The next item on To'Kana's list is a mineral called Monazite. He says their scans show a massive deposit, one that could contain millions of tons."

"What do we need the Monazite for?" I ask.

"Two things. It contains an element called Ytterbium, element 70, symbol Yb, which is not to be confused with Yttrium, one of the two elements we got at the last site. Only fifty metric tons of Ytterbium are produced worldwide each year. The Iknosan believe that the minimum quantity required to build a viable defensive fleet is about five times that number."

With the requirement this small, it strikes me as odd that this would be the next item on the list. "Millions of tons in the deposit, but we only need two hundred fifty. What's the catch?"

"Multiple. Monazite is a family of phosphate-based minerals. Ytterbium makes up about 2.6%..."

"Still, that's more than ten times the requirement."

"As I said, there are multiple catches. Ytterbium has numerous isotopes. They need Ytterbium-174. Until we get a sample, we won't know how much of the deposit is Ytterbium-174. To'Kana says the best case is about 12%."

As the shock of this news passes, I understand for the first time the materials challenge we face. "So best case, the Ytterbium we need would only be 0.3% of the monazite we mine. That means we'll need something like seventy-five thousand tons of monazite to get the Ytterbium we need."

"Bingo," Justin replies.

"Is there any good news?"

"Depends on how you look at it."

I laugh, knowing I'm about to get the next piece of bad news.

"The next biggest item on To'Kana's list is neodymium-142. We are going to need nearly fifty thousand tons. Global production currently runs higher, but it barely meets demand."

"I presume To'Kana has a candidate for that."

Justin nods. "Four percent of the monazite in the Upper Burro Creek deposit is neodymium; 27.2% of that is neodymium-142."

"What else?"

"The monazite deposit is down around six thousand feet."

"And?" I look at Justin, waiting for the hammer to drop.

"The land is managed by the Federal Bureau of Land Management. We got clearance to land there today, but it could take a long time to get a mining permit, so my plan is to just steal it."

"What!" I exclaim.

"No one knows it's there. If it were traditionally mined, we wouldn't even get the first ounce before the United States government fell to the aliens. To'Kana can use his transporter to mine the deposit. So, we steal the monazite, extract the neodymium, then backfill the hole with the filings."

I look at Justin, somewhat aghast. Doing this without the government's approval opens us to so much liability. But To'Kana will be the one doing it and they have no authority over him. We'd be complicit, but that would be an impossible thing to prove unless one of us confessed.

As the helicopter descends for a landing in the mountainous terrain, I steel myself for the next round of sample extractions.

PEACH SPRINGS, ARIZONA

Monazite samples pulled, we make our way toward our third and last target for the day. "What are we after here?"

"Erbium, another one of the so-called rare-earth metals. To'Kana has found a deposit of a mineral called Xenotime in the mountains between Peach Springs and Travertine Canyon Falls, Arizona. It also contains two other materials on his list: dysprosium and terbium. Again, this is a deposit we can take without securing the rights. It's at nine thousand feet, unreachable by existing mining technology."

Once again, I'm struck by Justin's brazenness. "So, we just steal this, too?"

Justin locks me with a stare, one I've only seen once before. And suddenly I see Air Force Captain Justin Wicks about to explain the realities of war the same way he did ten years ago on one of our most deadly missions.

"Kyle. You understand what's happening here, right? A pestilent species, one the Iknosan couldn't turn away, is about to descend on us in what? Eighteen months? Maybe two years? Who's going to protect us? To'Kana? The US government? The Chinese?"

His words sputter out, but the stare does not drop.

"You've been to the far side of the moon and transported back," he continues. "You and Mac are the only ones that understand the reality of what the Iknosan are capable of. But even with all that technology, it wasn't enough to save them."

I'm surprised by Justin's ire, but the helplessness in his voice isn't lost on me.

"Tell me what you're thinking, Justin."

"We need to do something that's at least ten times the magnitude of the Manhattan project. Neither of us can pull that off on our own. Neither can the US government. A joint command international collaboration would have even worse odds."

"Your point?" I ask.

"The value of the minerals we are going to extract and refine are worth tens or hundreds of billions. Overnight, the value of our company will explode, enabling us to compete with the Boeings and the General Dynamics of the world; maybe allowing us to buy one of them."

"They'll do that just because we'll have money?" I ask, incredulous.

"No. They'll do it because To'Kana controls the resources, and he wants you to lead the effort."

I look at Justin wide-eyed. He said something like this earlier in the day, but... "Why me?"

Justin shakes his head. "Because he trusts you to take the technical lead and me to take the political lead. And, in his culture, the technical lead is the one they bet on. So, it's you and me, buddy. We're being given a multi-billion-dollar gift because you saved his life and stood up for your direct interests, and because I can play the political game."

As I take in the news, Thelma's voice sounds in my ear.

"Kyle, the analysis results are in. They're mixed. Two of the ten samples you took are a full twelve percent Ytterbium-174. Captain To'Kana will begin mining in that area today. Based on the mapping data you recorded, he's hoping to pull as much as five percent of our requirement today."

"What about the first site?"

Thelma laughs. "The samples proved what we already suspected. The thortveitite deposit is sufficient for our scandium and yttrium requirements. You have the magic touch, Kyle Wimberly."

OFFICE, HEADQUARTERS

Despite the tolerance I've built up for the August desert heat, three hours of work on the ground, plus four hours in a helicopter, have left me feeling spent. In truth, I'm surprised Justin held up as well as he did. Yes, he had it a little easier—a more comfortable seat and no equipment hauling responsibilities—but he also piloted the G800 to and from Las Vegas. Now we're gathered around a conference room table where a hearty meal is being served while we wait for the results of the day's work, which are due shortly.

"Justin, thanks for the arrangements today. We covered an enormous amount of ground and got a lock on all three of the day's targets."

He nods toward his companion. "Jill helped with the arrangements, including this meal, and did most of the flying today."

"I needed the helicopter hours," she says, diverting attention from herself.

My eyes linger on Jill for a moment, noting for the first time that she looks as worn as the rest of us do. When she notices my gaze, I smile. "Thank you."

She smiles back. "You're welcome, Kai."

I turn back to Justin. "What's the plan for tomorrow?"

He taps his index finger twice, then says, "If today's results are good, then two more sites—the first near Blanding, Utah, the second near Navajo City, New Mexico."

"What will we be looking for?"

"Two minerals: euxenite, which contains niobium, and gadolinite, which contains terbium. According to To'Kana, niobium is the key to the shield collapse weapon."

"Then I hope we find a vast supply, because without it, the war may be lost before it even begins."

My words are barely out when Thelma's voice sounds in my ear. "Kyle Wimberly, Captain To'Kana is ready to transport to your location."

"Thank you, Thelma. Initiate transport at your leisure." I reply, then turn to the others. "Captain To'Kana will be here momentarily."

A moment later, To'Kana appears, and I hear Jill whisper, "Wasn't expecting that."

His eyes go to her immediately. "Who is this?"

"She's with me," Justin says. "Co-pilot of both my plane and my life."

"The two of you have mated?" he asks, to a snort from Mac.

"Yes, the two of us are mated," Justin replies with a hint of embarrassment at the question.

To'Kana continues to stare at Jill for a second, then snaps back into action, placing a tiny cube on the table. A moment later, a holographic projection pops up, showing the list of materials we need.

"I am pleased to announce that we have enough of the first elements to mount a viable defense. We still need to validate niobium and terblum availability. Once that is done, we can commit to full-scale development. But I have enough confidence those supplies will be validated that I've started mining operations on the Ytterbium and prepared a list of next steps for which resources will need to be secured."

The captain looks at Justin, who nods his head. Then he launches into a detailed review of the results of today's scans and samples. In my exhaustion, it goes in one ear and out the other, little sticking in between. Then at last, he says, "Well done. With any luck, your work tomorrow will launch us on our mission to save the Earth. Now, get some rest."

And with that, he transports out.

[8.11.2033] KITCHEN, HEADQUARTERS

Today followed the same pattern as yesterday, starting with a morning flight to a major airport, in this case Santa Fe Regional. Then a transfer to an executive helicopter, today the swanky Bell 525 Relentless—a fast, comfortable ride with sufficient range for the day's three-legged, five hundred mile journey. At our first stop, near Blanding, Utah, we scanned and sampled a huge euxenite deposit that was cleaner than any of the ones yesterday. The second stop, near Navajo City, New Mexico, yielded almost exactly the opposite—a low concentration gadolinite deposit, scattered across a wide area.

Unlike yesterday, Jill, who co-piloted the flight to and from Santa Fe, stayed at the airport while the rest of us were out, apparently ineligible to co-pilot the Bell 525. Justin, who came with us, spent most of his time whispering on the phone in the back of the cabin, only stepping out of the helicopter for a few minutes at the two sites.

Now back at headquarters, my exhausted colleagues and I sit around a conference table waiting for the results, while munching on the Mexican food Jill had secured for us in Santa Fe.

"Justin, you kept to yourself today. What were you working on?"

He looks up at me. "Resources." Then, he takes another bite of his burrito.

"Care to elaborate?"

He washes down the burrito with a pull from his bottle of Dos Equis. "This project has taken most of my attention the last couple of days, leaving me with a few critical issues that I had to deal with on the first leg of the helicopter ride. But I spent most of the trip on the resource aspects of this project."

I motion with my hands for him to keep going.

He gives me a look, then launches in. "I had a call with my incorporation lawyers to set up four new Delaware companies. I put in an offer on the land in Amber, Nevada, and arranged transition financing with Chase in New York. Then, I filed for mining permits on my land near Amber, in the name of the first Delaware company, ExoMaterials Corporation. After that, I contracted for a one-hundred thousand square foot steel building to be built on my property near

Amber, with a bonus for completion of the first section within a week..."

As his voice trails off, I ask, "Is that possible? A building in the middle of nowhere in a week? And why do we need it so soon?"

"Can you construct a hundred-thousand-square-foot-facility in a week? Of course not. Will paying double to have the thousand-square-foot lobby framed get people and material on site tomorrow? There's always someone that will take that deal."

"Why the hurry?"

"To'Kana started mining Monazite at the Burro Creek location. He pulled a thousand tons yesterday. If all goes to plan, he should have over ten tons of refined product by midnight. He can store some of it on his ship, but will need ground-based storage starting in a few days."

"Amazing," I whisper, mostly to myself.

"Unlike anything seen on Earth before," Justin reflects.

A few minutes later, Thelma's voice sounds in my ear. "Kyle Wimberly, Captain To'Kana requests your presence, and that of Justin Wicks, aboard the ship. Please ask him to install this communication device in his ear." A small box appears on the table in front of me. "As soon as it's installed, I will transport you aboard."

"Thank you, Thelma," I say aloud as all eyes turn to me.

"Well?" Justin asks.

I open the box and present it to him. "Captain To'Kana would like to speak with us aboard his ship. Thelma wants you to put this earpiece in so she can transport us aboard. Fair warning. When you put it in, it tickles enough to make you shudder. After that, you never notice it again."

Justin recoils at the suggestion. "I'm not putting alien hardware in my ear. And I'm happy here with my feet firmly on the ground."

Jill laughs at his statement.

"What?"

She shakes her head. "Justin, you can be such a baby. How many flight hours have you logged? Twenty thousand? Not exactly something done with your feet on the ground."

"Not what I meant," he complains.

"The tickling only lasts a couple days," Mac adds, throwing more fuel on the fire.

"Come on, Justin. Let's get this over with," I add.

"Isn't there a pill I can swallow?"

The grumbling goes on a bit until Jill saunters over and grabs the earpiece. "Come on, baby. You usually like it when I tickle you."

As Mac and I howl, Jill finally gets the earpiece into Justin's ear. A moment later… "Thelma?"

IKNOSAN LEGACY SHIP

For all the fuss a few minutes ago, Justin is now laughing. "In the office one second. In a spaceship on the far side of the moon the next."

A moment later, Thelma appears in front of us, and shock replaces Justin's laughter. "Welcome Kyle Wimberly." She extends her hand toward me.

I take the hand gently and feel its warmth. She smiles as I give it a modest shake. "Good to see you again, Thelma."

Thelma smiles at me, then turns to Justin. "Justin Wicks. Welcome. I am Thelma, the ship's lab AI. My holograph makes it easier for me to interact productively with organic beings."

Justin takes the hand offered. "It's a pleasure to make your acquaintance."

She smiles at him and nods toward one of the lab's doorways. "Captain To'Kana will be here in a moment. He is very pleased with your performance today."

"Would you mind giving me a tour of your laboratory space while we wait for the captain?"

Thelma seems to freeze for a second, then motions with a hand. "Please, this way."

I almost laugh as Justin steps up right next to her in full smoodge mode as they make their way across the lab. I've seen this shameless behavior many times and wonder how it will work on an alien AI. Nonetheless, I follow along as she points out various pieces of equipment. A minute later, I realize we are being led toward an enormous machine that looks like a scaled-up version of the replicator on the captain's shuttle, the one he used to replicate the grav-field emitters.

When they are a few steps away from it, Thelma stops and looks at Justin. "You are attempting to ingratiate yourself with me, are you not? Does that work with humans?"

It's my turn to laugh. But Justin the Shameless looks back at her sweetly. "I'm simply trying to be a polite guest. And yes, being polite to other humans frequently results in them being polite in return. A much better way to live. Is it not?"

Thelma stares at him a moment longer. "I suppose it is."

As she turns back toward her goal, Justin winks at me before resuming the smoodge. Seconds later, Captain To'Kana enters the room through a doorway next to the enormous machine.

"Excellent work today," he says to Justin, before turning to me. "Kyle, the deposit mapping you did over the last two days was outstanding. Combined with the samples, we can now say with confidence that we have sufficient availability of the eight rare elements to build a capable fleet. As I agreed with Justin, your payment for that is a replicator like the one I have in the shuttle. However, I want you to have this instead." He points to the enormous machine Thelma had been leading us toward. "It's a small industrial replicator with the ability to replicate larger, more complex items, including prototype versions of equipment your fleet will require. We have already upgraded it with the remote communication package and an English language user interface."

I bow my head in acknowledgment. "Thank you."

Justin, as effusive as ever, steps forward to give To'Kana a two-handed handshake. "Captain, thank you for your generosity."

I note the expression that comes over To'Kana. I've spent enough time with him now to have seen it before. It seems like a mix of wry amusement and anguish. The amusement brought on by the antics of this audacious alien. The anguish at the reminder that he was the lone Iknosan survivor on a world that is not his.

Motioning with his now free hand, To'Kana indicates one of the seating areas sprinkled throughout the lab. "Come, we have much to discuss."

Curiously, Thelma and a couple of their more humanoid looking bots gather around as we sit.

"While you were completing the survey and sample gathering operation over the last two days, I deployed one of our orbital mining and refining robot ships. As mentioned earlier, I started mining Monazite at the Burro Creek location, pulling a thousand tons yesterday. Today I had it refined, yielding over three tons of Ytterbium-174 and ten tons of Neodymium-142. I also got a pleasant surprise—Niobium. Sometimes, these rare transition metals are found in phosphorus-based minerals like monazite, but concentrations are low enough, we rarely screen for it. With this pull, we got a three-hundred-kilogram bonus."

"Excellent news," Justin affirms. "What do we need to do next?"

"Several things." The captain turns to me. "Kyle, we need to begin the prototyping phase. The first thing on that list is power systems. Of all the problems that need to be overcome to become a spacefaring species, power is the most significant. Your government and their space agency will know this, so the first thing they will need to see is a high-density power system."

I nod, but hold my tongue, sensing the captain has more to say.

"Therefore, I want you to build a twenty-megawatt power generating unit and add it to your company's power grid."

"That's incredibly generous, sir."

"More importantly, it's necessary." The captain nods as if affirming his own words. "All the instructions are available to you in the replicator. I think our user interfaces are familiar enough that you can figure it out on your own. But if not, Thelma is available to you 24/7, as you say."

"Understood, sir."

The captain turns to Justin. "I've made no attempt to hide my three orbital mining machines. Hopefully your government will have detected it by now. I would like you to contact them on my behalf to open discussions. We have a basic understanding of your government—three coequal branches, and so on. But in truth, we do not understand how it actually works."

"I'll start working that process right away, sir. How should I describe my role in this?"

"First contact goes smoother when all information flows through a single representative. For now, you are my representative for all things political, Kyle for all things military and technical, if you will serve in that capacity."

I lock eyes with Justin and nod.

He returns the nod before turning back toward To'Kana. "Count us in."

KITCHEN, HEADQUARTERS

Justin and I arrive back to excited chatter on the television. Mac is the first to see us. Pointing at the TV, he says, "Looks like the secret is out."

I stand there frozen, staring at the fuzzy image of a cube-shaped object with latticework covering its sides and a circular lens of some sort emitting a conical glow.

Blather from the soundtrack catches my attention. "...speculate that it is a Borg ship with its deflector pointed down toward earth..."

The words snap me out of my reverie, anger building over the nonsensical drivel.

Mac apparently sees my ire. "It's been going on like this for the last hour. I don't know where they find these guys, but you'd think they could come up with something better than Star Trek bad guys as an explanation."

Justin, who seems to take this in better stride than me, snaps into action, pawing at his Starlink phone as if it was covered in ants.

"Found it!" he announces.

A second later, I hear the line ringing as it connects. He looks at me, then points toward my office and takes off in that direction. Halfway there, I catch up. "Who are you calling?"

"Jace Elliott, Assistant Secretary of Defense, Legislative Affairs. A classmate at Harvard. Long story."

The line connects, and I hear muddled words, which sound like a polite brushoff.

"Jace, I know who the aliens are."

There's silence on the other end of the line.

"I'm going to put my business partner on the line."

I hear another word then, "...do you mean, you know who the aliens are?"

"Jace, the aliens call themselves Iknosan. The cube-like ships they're showing on TV are unmanned robotic ships which pose no threat. They parked their main ship on the far side of the moon, at..." Justin looks at me. "What did he call it?"

"Earth-Moon Lagrange 2."

"How do you know this?"

I beat Justin to an answer. "His shuttle crash landed on our solar farm. He was badly wounded, his crew members killed. My team helped nurse him back to health and repair his shuttle. I've been up to his ship."

There's silence for a few seconds, then an exasperated sigh. "Justin... What am I supposed to do with this?"

"I need to speak with someone in the administration. You're the highest rank person I know well. Will you give me an introduction?"

"Justin..." The exasperated sigh is back. "You know how long it's taken to get to this position."

Justin whispers to me. "Ask Thelma if she'll transport us."

Returning his attention to his friend, Justin asks, "Jace, where are you?"

"Washington."

"I mean, where are you right now? Home? Office?"

"Home. Why?"

"The aliens have transporters. If Kyle and I transported into your living room, would that be sufficient proof to move this forward?"

He laughs. "Sure. 838 New Hampshire Ave. But not the living room. I'll be in my study on the second floor for the next half hour. Back of the house on the right as you look at it from the front. Don't come to the front door."

The last words are said rudely, the line dropping before Justin could reply.

"Did you get that?"

"I got it. Thelma did, too."

"I've found his townhouse." Thelma says in my ear. "Scanning for him now."

I repeat the message to Justin.

A moment later, Thelma says, "Found him. Ready?"

As we position ourselves for transport, I can tell from Justin's attitude and body posture that he plans to really play up this entrance.

STUDY, JACE ELLIOTT'S RESIDENCE

This is my fourth transport, and it still has all the magic of the first. But like the three previous, there is a moment of disorientation on arrival. My senses clear in a fraction of a second, and I see Justin hand outstretched, already on the move.

"Jace. Buddy. Good to see you. Who would ever have thought it would be aliens that finally got me to your place across the street from George Washington University?"

Poor Jace yelps at the shock of two people just appearing out of nowhere in his tiny study.

Several expletives escape before he finally regains control of himself. Then he gives Justin a look that morphs into a huge smile. "Justin Wicks. What the bloody hell? You get yourself into the craziest..." Jace seems to run out of words, then turns serious.

"I'm in Legislative Affairs, one of DOD's deepest backwaters."

"Meaning?" Justin asks.

"Normally, my directorate wouldn't get involved until the administration is ready to brief the legislative branch. In this case, the brass will probably want all the limelight, so we'll just coordinate. I'm guessing it'll be a couple of days before I'm in the thick of the crisis." He pauses, then asks, "Tell me again your role in this."

Justin gives a remarkably concise summary of events, hitting everything important.

"So, you're their spokesperson, and Kyle's the new king of the Earth?"

I'm shocked by the words. Then understanding dawns. Washington is a far more alien place than To'Kana's ship.

"Until the Iknosan change their mind, I am the one they've chosen as the go-between," Justin replies. "And Kyle is the one they've chosen to manage the technology flow. I don't see the latter changing."

Jace shakes his head. "This is going to be a hard sell. The government has little trust in intelligence volunteered by civilians."

"What can you do to help us?" Justin asks. "Time is short. We expect to have our first prototypes sometime next week."

Jace turns to me. "What's the first thing you plan to demonstrate?"

I glance at Justin, who nods.

"A high-density power source."

"Go on," Jace presses impatiently.

"Twenty megawatts, constant load, no fuel, twenty-year life. Power sources like this are the key to interplanetary or interstellar spaceflight."

"How does it work?"

"Think zero-point energy. The Iknosan say that's an imprecise term. But they admit it's the closest idea humans have at this point. I'm still studying the physics of it."

Jace scoffs. "You're going to need a better answer than that to sell this thing."

Justin, clearly offended by Jace's reaction, shakes his head. "In a couple of years, marauding aliens are going to come and pillage the earth. We will have weapons and delivery systems that have a chance of stopping them. Our sole concern should be getting those systems in place, not winning an academic debate about the underlying physics."

Jace puts his hands up. "Sorry, didn't mean to offend. I'm just giving you a heads up about what you're going to run into."

There's silence for a minute, then Jace brightens. "I'm supposed to have fifteen minutes with SECDEF tomorrow. If he agrees, could you transport in? I'll need dossiers on both of you before the meeting."

"What time?" Justin asks.

"11:15."

"It'll be commercial grade—the stuff we put in our securities and regulatory filings. I can also give you both our military ID numbers, so you can tap our service records."

Jace looks at me. "You were in the service."

"Six years in the Army. Two tours in Afghanistan. Honorable Discharge. PhD in Physics from Caltech eight years later. Specialty: Sustainable Energy."

Jace smiles as he nods. "I may be able to get you in the door after all. But it's on you from there."

Justin stands and extends a hand. Moments later, we're back in the kitchen at headquarters.

CHAPTER 3: POWER

[8.12.2033] TRAIL, FULL CYCLE SOLAR

Despite the long hours and physical exertion of the last two days, I wrestle myself out of bed and head out to meet the guys for the morning run. As I approach, I note that we have a big turnout today—sixteen or seventeen, not the normal six or seven.

"Kai, mind if I join today?"

Taking my eyes off the crowd at the starting point, I turn toward the deep voice that reminds me of James Earl Jones.

"Marion, good to see you. You're always welcome to join."

"Thanks," he grunts and pulls up beside me.

Although this gathering is not restricted to ex-military, few civilians ever join us. Today is the first time I've seen Marion Black turn up, which makes sense, I suppose. He lives about an hour away in Quartzsite and works the graveyard shift, so the timing rarely works for him.

"You off today?"

"Yeah. Wife's visiting family in Baltimore for a couple of weeks, so I've taken a cabin here for the week. I'll be joining them next weekend at the shore. Her folks have rented a place in Ocean City. It'll be good to spend some time with the kids."

I glance at the huge African American man next to me, envious of the bond he has with his family, thankful that he agreed to drag them out to rural Quartzsite from LA, where he had served with the LAPD until his job was defunded a couple years ago.

"You going to tell us anything about what's going on while we're out on the trail?"

Looking at the eager faces that are now only a few strides away, I realize Marion has asked the question on all their minds.

"Seems I'm going to have to."

A deep rumbling laugh answers my statement. "You called that one right, boss."

CABIN, FULL CYCLE SOLAR

As I approach my cabin, soaked in sweat, I see Jill sitting on the porch, waiting. She seems more rumpled than I've seen her before, but the smile I get as I approach is as warm as ever.

"Have a good run?"

"Great run," I acknowledge. "Are your accommodations OK?"

"I've survived worse," she teases back, then stands as I stop short of the steps. "Justin tried to call you earlier and left a message. He asked me to check in on you."

"Why?" I ask bewildered.

"Meeting in DC at 11:15?"

"That's three some hours from now."

Jill looks at her watch and shakes her head. "That's thirty-three minutes from now. And you need to be in a suit. Figuring you probably won't get presentable enough on your own, Justin sent me to help." She motions toward the door.

In a flash of insight, I realize that Washington DC is on daylight savings time in the Eastern time zone. I'm in Mountain standard time. The meeting is at 8:15. I leap up onto the porch and race through the door, shedding my running clothes as I go. A moment later, I'm in the shower, water on cold.

I hear Jill laughing out in the main room. She politely closes the bathroom door, saying, "I'll see if I can find appropriate clothes in your closet."

OFFICE, FCS HEADQUARTERS

We arrive at the office by 11:00 Eastern. The few people there quietly snicker as I walk by in the only civilian business suit that I own, wearing one of Justin's yellow power ties, and sporting blown dry hair held in place by some sort of *product*. Jill is beaming with delight at the accomplishment. I'm feeling a bit like a fool.

When Justin sees me, he laughs as he pulls out his wallet. "Didn't think it was possible."

Eyes sparkling with delight, he pulls out a hundred-dollar bill and holds it out. "I bet Jill a hundred bucks she couldn't get you here and presentable by 8:00. Seems she won."

Jill snatches the bill, then saunters towards the door, whispering, "Justin always underestimates me." Based on the body language, I'm thinking she's won more than a hundred bucks, but don't want to speculate. I truly do not understand the relationship between these two.

"Thelma says Jace is waiting in SECDEF's outer office. Others are sitting inside, so this may take a while."

Justin's words pop me back into the moment. "Sorry, I got confused about the timing."

"Not a problem. I hope Jill didn't embarrass you too much."

"I'll survive."

Justin looks up at me more seriously. "You've led a focused life here, Kyle, and nursed something truly important to life. But that's about to change. I'll do what I can to help you succeed, but you need someone like Jill. Since she's come into my life, everything has improved. She loves me as much as I love her. Our goals are aligned. Everything we accomplish, we accomplish together. And we can count on the other to cover things we can't on our own."

"Like this morning," I fill in.

Justin nods his head. "Like this morning."

"I see how that works for you. But how has it worked for her?"

Justin suddenly looks away. "Thelma says the meeting in SECDEF's office is breaking up." As he stands, Justin says, "Jill was in a bad place when we met. I helped rescue her, and that was that. Some years later, I was in an equally bad place. She helped rescue me. A year or two later, we were introduced to each other by a mutual friend, connected the dots, and there was a spark. We're both who we are because of the other."

Justin's words shock me. I'd assumed Jill was just another piece of arm candy, like ones I'd seen him with before.

As he holds out his phone, Justin says, "Jace is in the office."

On the screen, I see the layout of the Secretary of Defense's Office; the large man behind the desk reaching a hand toward the more diminutive person approaching.

Seeing my shock, Justin says, "The Iknosan scanning and imaging systems are amazing, aren't they?"

"Unbelievable," I whisper in awe.

The two sit and are remarkably still for several seconds, then the visitor, presumably Jace, places a couple of documents on the desk. A minute passes, as the man behind the desk examines the documents, then sits back. Another minute passes, then the man leans forward, obviously nodding his head in approval.

I watch as Jace pulls something out of the breast pocket of his jacket, and a few seconds later, Justin's phone sounds.

OFFICE, SECRETARY OF DEFENSE

I've learned to close my eyes as transport begins; it lessens the disorientation on arrival. When the surrounding sounds change, I open my eyes and see the familiar face of Alaster McDaniels, the Secretary of Defense, who seems a little smaller than he does on TV. Greetings are exchanged and seats taken, then he starts in.

"Jace tells me you've been in contact with the aliens. The fact that you transported into my office lends credence to the claim. He also says that they've come to warn us of a pending invasion by other aliens. What evidence do you have to support that claim?"

Justin lifts the right lapel of his suit jacket, then freezes as he starts to reach in. "May I? Our visitors have given me something to show you."

Secretary McDaniels nods. "Proceed."

Justin reaches his left hand in and pulls out a small cube that he places on the table. "This is a holoprojector. It contains images of the aliens in orbit, who call themselves Iknosan, and their enemy, known as the Xeric Dominion. It also contains images of their ships and weapons, as well as video footage from the final battle between the two. I'll play you a clip, if you would like to see it."

"Please."

Justin plays the clip of the final battle in which ten Iknosan ships jump in, then take down the shields and incapacitate five of the Dominion's enormous ships.

"An impressive display," the Secretary says as the clip finishes. "Impressive, but insufficient."

"In what way, sir?" Justin asks.

The Secretary sits back in his chair as he eyes Justin.

"I'm putting words in his mouth, but Jace implied that your alien friends want us to start a Manhattan-like project to build a space defense system of enormous scale that will cost tens of trillions of dollars. I doubt whether such a thing is possible, but I'm certain we'll need more than what you've shown me to even start such a conversation."

In a sudden shift, the secretary turns to me. "Sergeant Wimberly. What's your role in this adventure?"

The use of my old title puts me off a bit. As a non-commissioned officer, now resigned from the Army, I no longer carry a rank.

"I'd prefer to be addressed as Dr. Wimberly. I am no longer part of the military. I'm a physicist with a PhD from Caltech and the President of Full Cycle Solar, one of the very few 24/365 baseline solar power generation companies."

"Noted," the Secretary replies. "Your connection with the aliens?"

"I met the leader of the alien mission, Captain To'Kana, shortly after his shuttle crash landed on the company's land. I helped save his life, repair his shuttle, and modify some of his most critical equipment. I've also mastered the use of his prototyping systems, equipment unlike anything seen on Earth before. To'Kana has designated me as his point of contact for all technology transfer."

"Wouldn't you concede that there are others more qualified for that role than you?" the Secretary asks.

"No, I would not, sir. No one else on earth can even turn on the equipment."

The Secretary exhales with a bit of exasperation. "Technology transfer for military purposes is a complicated business. For all your accomplishments, neither of you have the qualifications or experience. Surely you can see the problems that could arise if this is not handled properly."

I stand. "I've been authorized to present an opportunity for your consideration. If the United States does not wish to participate in this opportunity, then my business here is done. Thelma…"

"Kyle." Justin grabs my wrist, then turns to address the secretary.

"You are welcome to keep the holoprojector and share it with others in the administration. Please do not tamper with it. It will burn up if you do. If you'd like to schedule another meeting, Jace knows how to reach me. If you would like to visit the alien ship, we could arrange that for you. Thank you for your time today."

"What else do you have to demonstrate, besides your transporter and holoprojector?" The secretary's eyes are locked firmly on me.

"Later this week, I will have a twenty-megawatt power cell the size of a suitcase ready to demonstrate."

"Fuel?"

"None as such. In normal use, the unit has a twenty-year life."

"That, I would like to see. What else?"

"Hull plating. Light and impervious to any human tactical weapon."

"After that?"

"Gravity field generator. Configured as a grav-drive it's the Iknosan's preferred propulsion mechanism for inner system use."

"Weapons?"

"Shield killers and terawatt lasers, I haven't decided the order in which we will build prototypes for demonstration."

"You'll be building demonstration systems for each of these?"

"Yes, but some of the demos will be space-based for safety reasons."

"Please contact Jace when you're ready to show us something. Weapons and space technology I can sell. A vague alien threat? Unlikely." The Secretary nods his head as if his words are final. "Thank you for your time."

"I'll contact Jace when we have something to demonstrate," Justin replies. "Thelma, transport us back."

[8.15.2033] OFFICE, FCS HEADQUARTERS

Three days have passed since my first morning run with Marion Black. He's joined us each day since. This morning he asked if I'd be willing to talk with a friend of his back in Baltimore—ex-military police, divorced, kids in Phoenix, looking for a better job. I said yes, as I do for all those that served.

Now in the office, I'm completing the specs for the power generator I plan to replicate later this week. Western Interconnect, the electric grid operator to whom we supply our electricity, has agreed to expedite our petition to supply an additional twenty megawatts of base-line power on our existing 135KV transmission line.

My problem is mapping the Iknosan power sources, which are intrinsically DC, to our AC connection with Western Interconnect's AC transmission system. The good news is that the replicator has an embedded chopper system—one that converts DC to AC—that I can use. The bad news is that none of them maps well into the connection systems I have at my disposal.

Frustrated, I call Thelma to pose the question. After a long silence, she answers. "Kyle Wimberly... It has perplexed me that you have AC transmission and distribution systems. Now that you have prompted me to research this issue, the answer is clear. AC is superior for low power over short distances. For spaceships, where terawatts are required to do anything, DC is superior, even over comparatively short distances. Patterns for those systems are not included in replicators like the one Captain To'Kana has issued to you. If you provide me with the specifications you need, I can forward you a pattern from our master library.

I forward my requirement: fifteen hundred amps at thirteen kilovolts, sixty cycles per second.

Minutes later, my replicator dings. Checking it, I find a new pattern just downloaded, one for fifteen hundred amps at 13.7 kV. The message attached reads, "If Earth survives a Dominion attack, you'll need a serious upgrade to your electrical grid to become a modern, advanced species."

I have little doubt that Thelma has called the grid issue right. But I don't live in her world yet, so am thankful for the specs she has sent. I'll need to tamper with our grid connection to implement the new design. But if there's one thing my painful experiences have taught me, it's how to work the grid connection issues for a compatible AC source.

As I'm completing the replication request, my mobile phone sounds. The 410 area code tips me off that this call is coming from Baltimore.

"Wimberly."

"Dr. Wimberly. My name is Audell Knight. I'm a friend of Marion Black. He said you would take my call."

"Audell, thank you for the call. Marion told me you were ex-military police with kids living in Phoenix, looking for a better job. Fair summary?"

"It is, sir."

"How can I help you, Audell?"

"Please hear me out before you judge."

For the first time in a while, well, since the other day, anyway, my spider senses tell me something is amiss here. "Go on."

"I'm an independent reporter working for WBAL, channel 11, in Baltimore. I've known Marion and Cylia most of my life. I never fully understood what drove them to LA, and really struggled to understand why they moved to Quartzsite. Now that your solar farm has become the epicenter of alien influence on Earth, I get it."

"Is there a point to this call?" I demand, a little pissed that Marion, of all people, has ratted me out. Yeah, we've only run together for four days. But, by then, I usually know who I can trust.

"I'd like to represent you in the media. I can do that today through WBAL, if you'll cooperate. I can do that for you as spokesperson at your headquarters, though WBAL will give me better cover in the short term. But just as you have your special talents, I have mine, which sharply contrast yours. And given my current situation, I believe I can represent your interests better than anyone else you'll find. I'd like to be part of this, and you won't regret hiring me, no matter the short-term affiliation."

As Audell's voice sputters out, I find myself believing him.

"If I flew you out, how would you suggest we begin?"

Though no audible sound comes over the line, I sense a sigh of relief.

"Invite me out. I was a cameraman before I was a reporter and am the master of the one-man crew. Give me a day; view the result. Whatever you approve will go out on WBAL, then everyone will want it. This is the story of the century. Give it to me and we'll both become famous."

"Is that why you're in it? The fame?"

There's silence on the line for a minute. "No, and yes."

I chuckle at the unexpected response. "Explain."

"I believe what Marion has told me and deeply believe that the way the story is released will cement people's opinions for years. If you walk blindly into the media cesspool and just announce it, the way most technologists do, they will crucify you." Audell pauses.

"Go on."

"I can land this in a way that will convince. I can be your defender. And if I do those two things, which is my goal..." He pauses again. "Then I have a shot at earning journalistic credibility. It's not my goal, just fair acknowledgment for accomplishment. No?"

"How soon can you be ready to fly?"

LABORATORY, FCS HEADQUARTERS

The call with Audell, then the subsequent call with Justin, left my head spinning. I could tell from his response that Justin would have turned this opportunity away. Nonetheless, he accepted my decision to invite Audell to Full Cycle Solar with minimal argument and offered to fly him out, increasing the pressure on me to get the prototype power source replicated today.

Satisfied that the specs are complete, I compile the pattern and run it through a simulation. Forty-five minutes into the run, the simulator reports an error—insufficient copper supply to complete the integrated busbar. The irony of this error makes me laugh. My replicator can build a twenty-megawatt, electric power generator the size of a suitcase without a problem. Add the external connector? No can do.

But this gives me pause to think. Where does the raw material for the replicators come from? Surely, it's not being fabricated out of thin air. A moment's research reveals the answer, the replicator needs to be *linked* to source materials, the link being the transport coordinates for containers holding the source material. Examining the link database in my transporter, I see they are all linked back to To'Kana's ship and he doesn't have very much copper.

Refocusing on the replicators control panel, I notice two recommended solutions. The first? Link to a larger copper source. The second? Provide connection specifications for four installable busbars. The humor of a moment ago morphs into shock. I have an inventory of copper busbars optimized for use with the step-up transformers connecting us to the transmission line.

After following the link to the specification instructions, I learn that the best way to provide the specification is to scan a sample. Now on my feet, I run to the supply shed where the busbars are stored.

[8.16.2033] TRANSMISSION SUBSTATION

Connecting to the grid is a multi-step process designed to minimize transmission losses and avoid populated areas. In the desert, the latter isn't really a problem. The former is because of the mountains and intense August heat. Our substation is on the western edge of our property, twenty-some miles from our headquarters building. Half a dozen huge power transformers will eventually live here. Two are currently installed: one that connects our current wells to our branch line, a second that is planned to go into service later this year.

Our branch line runs sixty miles west to another substation that links to Western Interconnect's existing Bouse-Kofa 161-kV line that parallels State Route 95. Everything on our property is ours. We paid to have it installed and are responsible for its maintenance. Everything on the other side of our step-up transformer belongs to Western Interconnect, who built it out on a cost sharing basis and are responsible for its maintenance.

Ahead, I see the substation coming into view, the new utility building Mac and his team built yesterday looking good at this distance. Our new twenty-six-hundred-pound power source is battened down on the deck of the flatbed I'm driving.

Mac, who has probably been watching the dust cloud I've kicked up over the last hour, waves as I approach. I note Marion, with whom I have a bone to pick, standing there with him.

"Missed you on the run this morning," Mac greets.

I point toward the power source. "I was up most of the night wrestling with this beast."

As Mac walks over to the truck to check out our new power source, Marion steps up beside. "Audell called me last night; said you'd invited him out. Thanks for talking with him."

I give Marion a dark look.

"Would you have talked to him if I'd told you what he wanted to ask?"

"Probably not."

"Then you should thank me for making the introduction."

"If there's a next time..." I shake the misgivings away. "Thanks."

A big smile spreads across Marion's face. "Anytime, boss."

With that behind us, I ask, "Are you doubling up on your shifts?"

"Yeah, I'm grabbing some extra spending money while the family is away. I want to give the kids a night out on the boardwalk."

"Look for a thousand-dollar referral bonus in your next paycheck."

Marion looks at me, shocked.

"How much does this thing weigh?" Mac's whining voice breaks the moment.

"A little over a ton and a quarter."

"Is it safe to touch?"

"The mechanical safety is engaged."

Mac kneels to take a better look at the busbar connections. "These look just like our standard connectors."

I smile. "They are. Pressure fit and bolted in place."

"Then this is going to be a piece of cake, once we hoist the *beast*..." he stretches out the word, making fun of my previous reference. "...in place."

"Then let's get after it."

Despite the simplicity of the installation, two hours pass in the August desert heat as we connect the unit to the step-up transformer, button up the utility building that houses the power source, then call Western Interconnect to coordinate the power up process. Another hour later, Western Interconnect gives us the go-ahead to begin supplying power.

As power begins flowing, a sharp vibration passes through the ground, rattling the utility building. Unaccustomed to start up vibration, Marion yelps, drawing laughter from Mac.

I give Mac a look, then smile at Marion. "Sorry, should have warned you. The vibration will pass in a second."

As the vibration settles down, I hear the rumble of Justin's G800 in the distance.

"Got to go. Mac, you've got the truck; I'm taking the jeep."

"Thanks," he says sourly as I run for the jeep.

FCS HEADQUARTER'S RUNWAY

I arrive and see Justin on final approach, landing gear down with another mile or two to go. Relieved that I got here in time, I step out of the jeep. A shiver runs down my spine as a gentle breeze triggers evaporative cooling from my sweat-soaked shirt. A glance back into the jeep reveals fresh, dried mud formed from sweat and dust accumulated during the ride back. What a way to greet a first-time visitor.

The screech of wheels pulls my attention back to the moment. A minute later, the G800 comes to a halt fifty feet away, and the engines shut down. I look up and see Jill wave, but there's no sign of Justin. Seconds pass as I watch Jill, the consummate professional, complete the shutdown procedures, then stand. She catches my gaze and smiles at me. The sound of the plane's hatch opening draws my attention.

Justin starts down the stairs, then catches sight of me and stops.

"What the hell happened to you?"

"We just finished putting the new twenty-megawatt power source on the grid."

A smile breaks out. "It's up? Delivering power?"

"It is."

The words trigger a celebratory, "Yes!" followed a moment later by, "Then you're forgiven."

I snort as Justin turns around and runs back up the steps with no explanation. Puzzled, I wait, wondering what is going on aboard the plane.

"Oh, nice look."

Jill's voice catches my attention. She starts down the steps, pilot travel case in one hand, carry-on in the other, and a bulky leather bag over her shoulder.

"Can I help you with that?"

She gives me a look. "Kai, you're filthy. What have you been doing?"

"I brought up a new power system in the middle of the desert."

"No wonder Justin's so happy. He likes your guest by the way." She turns toward the Jeep and takes one step, then looks at the headquarters building another hundred feet away. "Can you call someone to come help unload? Audell has brought a lot of equipment."

CONFERENCE ROOM, FCS HEADQUARTERS

When I finally realized how dirty I was, I went to get cleaned up while Justin and Jill had an early lunch in the kitchen with Audell.

"Congratulations on bringing the new power generator up," Audell says, opening an unrecorded background interview. "Justin told me it is the first piece of alien technology to be deployed on Earth."

"Did he tell you we made it?"

"You made it?" The surprise in Audell's voice confirms that Justin did not tell him.

"I did. They helped with the design and provided the machine I needed to fabricate it. But yes, I built the new power generator in the basement of this building."

"Excluding the background research, it only took a day."

"And the background research?"

"Less than a day."

"How big is it?"

"The generator itself? It's the size of a large suitcase: thirty-six inches high, forty wide, and thirty deep. The step-up transformers and other equipment needed to connect it to the grid are the same as we use for our solar generators."

"How large are conventional power generators with the same capacity?"

"Much larger. I haven't looked into this in three years. Back then, quality, compact systems a quarter of this capacity were thirty feet long, six feet wide, eight high and needed a dedicated building and gas pipeline hook-up."

I see Audell scribbling out some notes. "What are you thinking?"

He smiles. "When we do this piece, I'll want shots of the equipment you used; the generator you built, including its grid connection; and a state-of-the-art conventional generator. One of the points the piece will make is the aliens are already helping us in important ways."

Justin nods. "I like the way you think."

"Why start this way?" Audell asks.

"Power is the key to space. You need incredible amounts of it and can only burn the fuel you carry with you."

"Like nuclear?"

"Conventional nuclear is sufficient for submarine and aircraft carrier applications, but not for interstellar space flight. For that, you would need fusion or anti-matter, although the Iknosan say no real spacefaring species uses those."

Audell nods. "This was their idea?"

I smile. "It was."

"Why are they helping us?"

Justin pulls out another little cube that he places on the table, then launches into an enhanced version of the pitch he gave Secretary McDaniels the other day.

"The government didn't buy this, did they?"

"How did you know?" Justin asks.

"CGI—Computer Generated Imaging. The movies these days have much better imaging than your recording, which is almost certainly more accurate. But we've all been trained to believe the enhancements are real."

"How do we counter that?"

"Will the aliens agree to an interview?"

I look at Justin, who shrugs. "We're not sure."

Audell shakes his head. "Then we'll need to work on that."

OFFICE, FCS HEADQUARTERS

The first session with Audell went better than I could have imagined. This guy is a real pro.

The realization startles me. Why is a guy like Audell Knight a second-string player in a backwater like Baltimore? It doesn't add up. Sitting down at my computer, I google him and the startling answer to my question pops up. On January 6, 2021, Audell Knight was in Washington D.C., filming the riot. He eventually followed rioters into the building, filming and interviewing many. He was later arrested and held nearly a year before the charges against him were dropped.

The article makes my blood boil. Anyone who's spoken with the man, seen his work, would know Audell was a journalist at heart, not an insurrectionist. But as a young black man from a poor neighborhood whose camera was confiscated and never returned, he didn't have the connections, resources, or evidence to expedite his release.

With renewed purpose, I initiate the call I came back to my office to make. "Thelma?"

"Kyle Wimberly, so good to hear from you. How can I help?"

Despite my focus, a part of me smiles at the way she's picked up on my speech patterns. "Would it be possible for me to speak with Captain To'Kana?"

"Does this have to do with the visitor Justin Wicks flew out to your company today?"

I stare at my phone, wondering how much of what's going on here my alien friends know about. "Ah..."

"Justin called earlier, asking if the captain would speak with your visitor."

"And?"

The line goes silent for a second then, Thelma asks, "And what?"

"Will the captain speak with our visitor?"

"He was hoping you would ask him to transport down."

It's been an odd day, one I've struggled to wrap my mind around. That the captain was waiting for me to ask, pushes me over the edge with laughter coming from a place so deep it is new to me.

"Kyle, are you OK?"

The question triggers another round of laughter, which I struggle to contain. "Please transport the captain to my office as soon as you can."

A few seconds later, Captain To'Kana appears opposite me with a look of concern on his face that sobers me in an instant.

"Would you be willing to speak with our visitor?"

The captain looks at me sternly. "Has that not already been established?"

"Implied," I reply. "But not established, at least not with me."

The way the captain cocks his head reminds me of the crows that would periodically invade my parents' backyard when they found a shiny new object. But he holds his silence.

"Come on. His name is Audell Knight. He's African American, meaning his skin is darker than mine, and..."

"We've studied this planet long enough to know what the expression means. We've also scanned enough of your news to understand his situation and his reasons for wanting to work for you. I would very much like to meet and talk with him."

"This way."

CONFERENCE ROOM, FCS HEADQUARTERS

To'Kana and I enter the room and all conversation stops. At this point, Justin and Jill are familiar enough with the captain that his presence does not startle them. For Audell, the reaction is completely different.

"So, it's true," he whispers.

"Audell, please meet Captain To'Kana of Iknosan Legacy Ship #5."

On seeing Audell frozen in place, I offer the reverse introduction. "Captain, please meet Audell Knight, journalist extraordinaire."

The captain steps forward, hand outstretched. "Audell, good to meet you. You'll notice my hand is cooler than yours."

Audell stands and takes the hand offered. "Captain, thank you for agreeing to meet with me. Has Kyle told you why I am here?"

"I am aware of your purpose and credentials. I am also aware of your motivation for being here. How would you like to begin?"

...

Over the last two hours, the entire story of the captain's mission has spilled out with all the anguish of someone whose home and people have been destroyed. Unlike his opening sessions with us, Audell has recorded the entire thing.

Of the many pieces of information new to me was the captain's first name, Ro'Masa, and that of his wife, Lo'Sada, presumably killed in the invasion.

Also of interest was his insistence that I be the one to lead the technology transfer. When Audell pressed him for a reason, To'Kana replied, *I can perceive things about your people that you cannot. Trust me when I say he is the one. Those who do not trust place themselves in grave danger.*

"You've said your ship is in a stable orbit on the far side of the moon. Can you explain that to our viewers, who know little about orbital mechanics?"

To'Kana gives a quick version of the Lagrange points, noting that his ship is anchored in place by gravity from the earth and moon, whereas the Webb Deep Space Telescope is similarly anchored by the sun and earth.

"What about the ship in stationary orbit over Arizona? The experts I've talked with say it is impossible to do what your ship appears to be doing."

"It is a simple, though large, robot whose mission is to assist Kyle with one of his most important initiatives. As to its orbit... It's simply hovering there as everyone can see, which leads me to question the expertise of your so-called experts."

"Back to the invasion. When do you think it will happen?"

"Worse case? A year and a half? Most likely? About three years. Best case, five."

"Can we build a large enough fleet in time?"

"If we'd had a year and a half, we would have prevailed. The real question is whether the Earth can. There are several limiting factors: materials, power, hull plating, grav drive, jump drive, shield disruption weapon... The list goes on."

"How can we overcome any of these?"

"Justin and Kyle have already proven that the required materials exist in sufficient quantity on Earth. They are procuring enough to support full-scale production."

"What else?"

"Today Kyle brought up a high-density power-source, twenty megawatts in a generator the size of a large suitcase."

"Can you give me an example of what twenty-megawatts means?"

"It's enough to power eight to sixteen thousand homes. Ten of these units packed in a closet could power a nuclear aircraft carrier. A larger unit could power an anti-grav drive sufficient to land a shuttle on the moon within a couple hours of take-off from Earth."

"Is this why you have so much faith in Kyle?"

"As I said, Kyle is uniquely qualified. I've placed my trust in him. He will control the flow of technology to the people of Earth. Those that cooperate with him will prosper. Those that do not?" He shrugs. "I suppose they are not my concern."

"That's a strong endorsement." Audell shifts his attention to me. "What do you think about that, Kyle? Do you believe you are the one?"

All eyes in the room turn toward me, and, in my mind, hundreds of thousands of others do too.

"I don't like the spotlight. Neither do I enjoy the pressure that comes with this endorsement. But, just as in my tours in Afghanistan, they have given me a job—one I can fulfill. So that's what I'm going to do!" The last part comes out with a lot more emotion than intended.

To'Kana nods, and for the first time, I think I get it. I'm like the people on his world who came up with the technologies that could have liberated them.

"Captain To'Kana, you seem to agree," Audell prods.

"You've just seen what I saw from the first day. I'll leave it at that."

Audell's gaze lingers, but To'Kana offers nothing more. He looks at me, then shifts to Justin.

"Justin, you are an accomplished investor, the product of a Wall Street legend. What say you?"

"I served with Kyle in Afghanistan. I've pledged nearly a billion dollars to his stewardship in the years that followed. No one can save the world on their own—not me, not Kyle, not To'Kana. But together? That's a bet I'll take."

Audell looks at his watch. "Almost 3:35. I missed the evening news, not that the network was expecting a report today. But I'd like to put together a teaser for tomorrow. It will get better coverage if I submit by 4:00. Would it be OK to take a break?"

"Could I see this teaser before you release it?" To'Kana asks.

"Normally, in the American system, that is frowned upon. Given that you are new to our system, I will show it to you and allow you to reject it if you disapprove. But that would mean we lose a teaser tonight, which will reduce our coverage tomorrow."

To'Kana bows his head in acknowledgment. "Thank you." Then turns to me. "Shall we retire to your office so Mr. Knight can work in peace?"

OFFICE, FCS HEADQUARTERS

Now seated in my office, To'Kana directs the conversation. "Congratulations on bringing up the power source today. This helps your company, does it not?"

"It does," I reply.

"It also helps you muster resources?" This question is directed at Justin.

"It does. A generator this size will generate over a million dollars a month in free cash flow."

"I do not understand your economic system well enough to know how much that helps. Let me explain my concern."

Justin nods.

"We've discussed the materials issue and your rights concerns. From Audell's questions today, I realize we need to improve our story about the orbital mining platform."

"Go on," Justin prompts.

"I'll need to deploy at least two more mining platforms to extract the required material in time. That will need to be explained. I would like to claim that all this material is coming from land you own."

"I'm good with that. Kyle?"

"I'm good with it as well."

To'Kana redirects his gaze toward Justin. "Our legal AI has been studying your mining and mineral rights laws, as well as other American mining norms. It believes that the deception is at risk of failing if the material cannot be proven to be sourced from your land."

"Go on," Justin prompts.

"Let me cut to the chase, as you Americans say. We proposed to build a massive industrial complex on your land near Amber, Nevada. It will house refined materials. It will also house the full-scale industrial replicators required to produce critical components your government will want to inspect."

"I always assumed most of this would happen in orbit," Justin replies.

"On a more advanced world, it would. There would already be space-based manufacturing complexes. Final assembly of large vessels will ultimately need to be done there. But we cannot wait that long to start building the critical components."

Justin, always two steps ahead of me when it comes to resourcing issues, completes To'Kana's argument for him. "That means I need to expedite the construction of our manufacturing facility in record time, which will require a lot of money. I'll also need to bring in thousands of people to operate the facility and manage the dignitaries that will want to see it all."

To'Kana nods. "What will you need?"

"I'll need to do some research to come up with a sound answer, but first guess... Ten thousand people, a hundred grand each... A billion dollars per year, a little over eighty million a month."

To'Kana redirects his gaze toward me. "Your replicator can produce power sources as large as fifty megawatts. How many of these could you put online?"

"Our contract is for four-hundred megawatts over the next eight years. We've already pulled some of that capacity forward. I'll need to negotiate more with Western Interconnect."

"Let me handle that," Justin volunteers. "I know people there that will bend to a persuasive argument. I'd be surprised if we couldn't bring up at least a hundred meg more within a month."

"But is that enough?" To'Kana asks.

"I can make it work," Justin asserts, drawing a skeptical look from To'Kana. "Trust me. There's more than one way to raise money. With seven million a month in unencumbered free cash flow, it'll be easy to raise ten to twenty times that much."

"Unimaginable on my world," To'Kana replies. "Maybe that's why my world is no more."

CHAPTER 4: GRAVITY

[08.17.2033] OFFICE, FCS HEADQUARTERS

I cut the morning run short today; just wasn't into it, too much on my mind. Audell stayed over last night. We put him up in the cabin next to Marion Black. Alex played tour guide, driving the two around the property, allowing Audell to get additional background footage and some stills.

Now in the office, I see To'Kana followed through on last night's promise, replicator specs for a fifty-megawatt power source showing up in email this morning. Also in email is a link to Audell's teaser. Unable to resist, I click through. The thirty-second clip starts with a sunset shot that I recognize as one from our video library. The camera pans across the horizon, accompanied by an eerie soundtrack until Audell appears—the green screen insertion is flawless.

"Who is behind the mysterious spaceship in synchronous orbit above Arizona? Why is it here? Tune in tonight as NBC reporter Audell Knight presents his exclusive interview with Captain Ro'Masa To'Kana of Iknosan Legacy Ship #5." A silhouette of the captain fades in next to Audell, almost fully resolving as the last of the sunlight flashes away and the screen cuts to the NBC logo.

Part of me is surprised the network ran something this sensational. Another part presumes that Audell had to have released a lot more footage to the network to convince them the story was real. I suppose we'll find out later today. But for now, I have replicator specs I need to confirm, and a power source I need to run.

LABORATORY, FCS HEADQUARTERS

Thankfully, after an hour's work, the fifty-megawatt power source is now being built. As with the twenty-megawatt unit, I needed to change up the busbar configuration, this time with a thicker one available at a distributor in Phoenix. I ordered eight busbars for expedited delivery—the cost of the special carrier exceeding the cost of the eight weighty copper bars.

With that done, I'm now searching for a compelling anti-grav demo. Last night, To'Kana suggested something simple, like a grav cart. There are enough standard cart designs in the replicator's database that it would be easy enough to do. But a cart is too pedestrian—so ordinary that the miracle of the antigravity device will be lost in the cart's boringness. The replicator pattern library has literally thousands of devices—everything from cars and carts to elevators and lifting devices. As I step through the list, Defense Secretary Alaster McDaniels' words pass through my mind. *Weapons and space technology I can sell. A vague alien threat? Unlikely.*

Switching gears, I pull up the weapons directory, looking for a remote-control missile of some sort. Five minutes in, I hit pay dirt—a sleek remotely piloted surveillance device, four and a half feet long, two wide—a flying triangle with thin swept wings. Although it's optimized for high-altitude silent subsonic patrol, it has a maximum speed of Mach 5, enabling fast deployment almost anywhere on earth. "McDaniels will want a thousand of these things as soon as he sees it," I whisper to myself.

I check the replicator status and see that the new power source will not finish until the wee hours tomorrow morning, giving me plenty of time to add the English language pack and a couple of other customizations before queuing up my new flying wonder.

"Wimberly, you have a call on line one."

Our lab is in the basement of the headquarters building. To prevent radio frequency noise from escaping the lab, we built it as a Faraday cage. The design was sound. No radio noise escapes. Similarly, none gets in, therefore our mobile phones won't work down here. I grab the nearest wired phone to answer.

"Wimberly."

"Dr. Wimberly, this is Jace Elliott, DoD Legislative Affairs."

"What can I do for you, Secretary Elliott?"

"Please call me Jay. Um…" There's a moment of silence, as if he's changed his mind about something and is no longer sure what to say. "Let me cut to the chase. Our meeting with Secretary McDaniels didn't go very well last week. I had not prepared him sufficiently for that meeting. Hadn't prepared you well enough, either. That's on me." Again, he pauses.

"Go on."

"I'm calling to ask a favor."

This time, instead of prompting him, I simply wait him out.

"I saw the trailer last night for the special NBC is doing this week, the first part of which will be aired tonight. I assume you are part of this and would like to know what you are intending to disclose."

"Shouldn't you be contacting NBC? They are the ones airing the special."

"I contacted NBC. They were not cooperative. I contacted your partner, Justin Wicks. He told me any comments the company might make on the matter would come from you."

It would have been nice if Justin had told me that, but I've been down in the lab all morning, which to use Jace's words, is on me.

"I spoke with Audell at length, as did Captain To'Kana, my contact with the Iknosan people. We told the same story we shared with the secretary. Audell was more interested, so got a lot more detail. But it was basically the same story."

"Were you critical of the secretary? Or of the administration?"

"I don't remember talking about either. It wasn't the focus of the interview."

"OK," Jace says, sounding a bit defeated.

Taking advantage of the fact I have Jace on the line, I change topics. "Regarding demonstrations... I have two technologies I can demonstrate later this week, if you're interested."

"What might those be?"

"I just put a twenty-megawatt power source on the Western Interconnect grid. It is the size of a large suitcase and uses no fuel. A fifty-megawatt unit will be ready sometime tomorrow, although it may take longer to get that one connected to the grid. We've not received approval to add that much power yet."

"No fuel?" Jace asks. "How is that possible?"

"Any technology sufficiently advanced is indistinguishable from magic," I reply, quoting Clarke's Third Law. "In this case, the technology is called Boundary Particle Sourcing—BPS, for short. At some point, I will release a paper disclosing the underlying physics. For now, I'm just demonstrating working units."

"You said two technologies?"

"I will also have a remote-piloted surveillance device with gravity-drive propulsion and essentially unlimited flight time."

"Please tell me you are not discussing things like this with NBC or any other news outlet."

"Ahh... Why not?"

"Kyle, what do you think the Chinese, Russians, Iranians, North Koreans, or any of our other adversaries will do when they find out what you have? Do you have security sufficient to repel one of their special ops' teams? And even if you do, you'll become a target. You know the mantra. If you can't steal the invention, kidnap the inventor."

For the first time, I realize that inviting Audell here has put me in danger. Not as immediate as it was in Afghanistan, but at much higher risk. "Didn't think about that. Thanks for the warning."

"Back to the demos, we'll need to come to you, right?"

"That's the only way you'll get to see the generator that's now part of the grid. It will also be easier to demonstrate the grav drive. There's no air traffic congestion out here in the desert."

"I'll get something set up for next week," Jace replies. "And be careful what you say to the news outlets. Technology this advanced will attract a lot of attention."

I find Jace's rejoinder ironic. Last week, I pitched this stuff to him and got a yawn. Suddenly, we're on the news and now he's worried everyone will be interested. I suppose that's a statement about the power of the press.

CONFERENCE ROOM, FCS HEADQUARTERS

"There you are," Justin declares with unmasked exasperation. "We couldn't find you anywhere."

"Sorry, just down in the lab. I have two more demos queued up that will take a day and a half to finish."

"Power and anti-grav?" Audell asks.

Justin obviously briefed Audell on our conversation with To'Kana last night.

Not wanting to answer, I ask a question of my own. "What have you all been up to?"

Justin smirks. "You first."

The moment passes, then I respond to Audell. "Yes, but we need to be careful about how this is reported."

"Come again?" he replies, obviously offended.

"What do you think the Chinese will say if we broadcast this to the entire world?"

"Didn't think about that."

The words of déjà vu give me pause. "Neither had I until I got a call from the Department of Defense this morning. They're worried about what you're going to say about them."

"Curious. They saw the teaser last night?"

"They did."

"Seems I'm already helping you out."

Justin inserts himself into the conversation. "What's the plan for today? I've got a lot on my plate for the rest of the week."

Audell takes a deep breath. "I'd like to get an idea about your general plan. The marauding aliens could be here in a year. We basically have no defense at this point. How do you see this playing out?"

Justin looks at me. I nod, letting him take the lead.

"As you've already heard, we have no hope of defending ourselves without technology. Kyle has the lead on that. But technology alone is insufficient, as the Iknosan have proven. It needs to be reduced to practice, then put in the hands of the military force that will provide the defense. Kyle will have the lead on much of the reducing to practice part. I will play whatever role is needed to keep things moving, essentially a project manager."

"Can you give me examples of what some of those things are?"

"Two are very high on my priority list for this week: power and materials. We will have another fifty-megawatt clean energy base-line generator to put on the grid later this week, another the week after. We can't do that without permission from the grid operator. It's currently my highest priority."

"This is part of your reducing to practice effort?"

"It is."

"Tell me about materials."

"The Iknosan technology is dependent on rare materials."

"Such as?" Audell asks.

"Elements like Yttrium, Neodymium, and Bismuth, which may be familiar to some of your viewers. Others like Ytterbium, which is essential to jump drive technology, are also critical. Only fifty metric tons of Ytterbium are produced worldwide today. We'll need at least five times that much to mount a viable defense."

"How are you going to make that happen?" Audell asks.

Justin smiles. "I started collecting land in the desert southwest years ago in the belief that we could put massive solar arrays there to collect solar energy. What I could never have anticipated at the time was that this land would be rich with these materials. One of my properties in Nevada has over five hundred metric tons of Ytterbium. It's too deep in the ground for any known human mining technique. Fortunately, Iknosan mining technology is far more advanced."

"You are going into the mining business?"

"We are." Justin's smile broadens. "We set up a company called ExoMaterials Corporation, which, over the next year, will produce all the rare materials needed to mount a credible defense."

"What is your biggest concern?"

Justin's smile vanishes. "Obviously, Kyle and I cannot fight this war. The governments of the world will need to do that. As of now, no government has signed on."

"You haven't spoken with anyone at the DOD?"

"We have. They are being cautious, as they need to be. But the clock *is* ticking, and if no defense is in place when the Dominion arrive, then it's game over."

"Have you approached any of the major defense contractors to gauge their interest?"

Justin shakes his head. "Not yet. We have a lot on our plate. Once the demos are available, we'll be in a stronger position to pursue manufacturing partners."

An alarm on Audell's phone sounds. He picks it up, then turns off the alarm. "I have to break now. Our first pre-production meeting for tonight's segment on Captain To'Kana starts in a few minutes. The network and WBAL are still negotiating what we can show in Baltimore before the Nightly News airs at 6:00. They also want a second teaser for tonight and the first one for tomorrow night."

"Does this happen often? A local affiliate getting a prime spot on the nightly news?" I ask.

Audell smiles. "Rarely. Compounding the protocol problem is the fact I'm a so-called contributor. I have a piece work contract with WBAL, not an employment contract with NBC. I brought this piece to them; they didn't commission it. So, we're still negotiating compensation." Audell laughs. "I bet someone is getting their butt kicked over that one." He stands. "I've got to go. I'll catch up with you after the show."

SUN DECK, FCS HEADQUARTERS

Most of the staff know of the sequence of events triggered by the failure of Well #8. They also know that Audell is here, and the first installment of his report will be going out tonight. People started gathering in the kitchen to watch the TV there, but by 6:00 it was standing room only. So, despite it being monsoon season in the Arizona desert, we've taken the party outside to the sun deck on the east side of the building and turned on the evaporative coolers. It's a pleasantly cool 85° F, with humidity in the upper thirties. Beer, chips, and a show about aliens... What could be better?

Everyone cheers when the anchor introduces Audell. A moment later, when he introduces Captain To'Kana, there's stunned silence. I'd forgotten that few of the people here have met or even seen the captain. The piece runs three and a half minutes. I'm blown away by the seamlessness with which the story is told. When it's done, the anchor asks, "Has Captain To'Kana contacted any government officials?"

"Not yet. His plan is to work with Full Cycle Solar Chairman Justin Wicks to make introductions and with company president Kyle Wimberly to manage the technology flow. Both have spoken with representatives from the Department of Defense, and Wimberly is preparing technology demos to drive the discussion."

"Does it strike you as odd that the Iknosan have chosen two civilians that head a clean energy firm as his go between? Why hasn't he approached the government directly?"

"I've asked that question. He says first contact works better this way, and Kyle Wimberly is uniquely qualified. He also said we needed to trust him on this point."

"Trust. That's a big ask," the host comments.

"I've spent one day with him and do trust him. Over the next couple of days, I hope to show you why."

"Audell Knight, NBC special correspondent, thank you for this story tonight. Now in other news..."

As the camera pans out and the show goes to break, someone turns off the TV and everyone chants my name.

[08.19.2033] LABORATORY, FCS HEADQUARTERS

I woke this morning slightly hung over, which is rare for me. The second segment of Audell's story played last night. Where To'Kana was the focus on the first night, I was the focus last night. In a fifteen second montage, he covered my background with pictures from high school graduation, my squad in Afghanistan, graduation from Caltech, the first well coming up at FCS, an aerial shot of the current operation, and the last of me standing next to the new twenty-megawatt generator at the substation on the western edge of the property.

As promised, Audell included a thirty-second clip featuring a state-of-the-art, gas fired twenty-megawatt peaking plant in the Phoenix area, which included snapshots of the site, various locations within the plant, and a short clip filmed inside the control room. When Audell commented on how loud the roaring machine was, the operator said it was nothing compared with the power plant floor, where hearing protection was mandatory. His point struck home at the next location where my twenty-megawatt unit couldn't be heard over the morning's gentle breeze.

It was humbling to watch the praise being poured on me and the reaction of those on the sun deck. My new celebrity status really didn't affect my core group—Mac, Alex, and Ty. But some of the newer folks, like Marion Black, seemed more deferential when I talked with them.

Because it was Friday night, we wheeled two kegs of beer out and two dozen pizzas, and I made a point of circulating and talking with everyone present.

Sadly, Justin and Jill weren't here. They'd taken off earlier for meetings with Nevada's Commission on Mineral Resources and with the contractors doing the development on our property in Amber, Nevada.

My first task today is installation of the copper busbars into the new fifty-megawatt power generator. The bars are pressure fit, meaning that my 6.35 mm thick bar needs to go into a slot that is only 6.34 mm wide. To do that, I need to bathe the bars in liquid nitrogen, which will cool them to -195.8° C, causing them to shrink to just less than 6.33 mm thick. It's an interesting trick, and a dangerous one at that. It will require a lot of liquid nitrogen, which comes with the risk of catastrophic injury and asphyxiation.

We have a liquid nitrogen facility in the lab with a separate ventilation system that prevents much nitrogen from escaping into the building. We also have alarms in the lab that detect if oxygen levels drop too low, and oxygen masks good enough to enable an escape if the alarms go off.

But doing the install down here would be too dangerous. So the plan is to take the new generator outside, then take the containers holding the frozen bars outside, then open the containers, let the nitrogen boil off, then install the bars before they warm up too much. From lid off to installation, we've got two minutes.

Mac and I took the generator outside earlier. This one is truly a beast, weighing in at nearly three metric tons. I suppose the good news is that we mastered the skills to do this kind of work as part of the development of Full Cycle Solar. Each well has tons of salt held at over 600° C. It took years to master the process to package, heat, transport, then insert each well into its containment system. For the busbars, the hazard is the cold not the heat.

Now the three of us are in the lab, Alex positioned at the exterior door, Mac locking the cart we'll use in position, me standing at the door to the nitrogen room.

"Oxygen masks on," I order, then wait for the confirmations, which come as a thumbs up.

The lock on the door to the nitrogen isolation room releases as I tap my ID to the key lock entry system, then ease the door open. I count to five, long enough for the nitrogen alarms to go off if there's been a leak.

I prop the door open, then Mac follows me in. Each of the four busbars is in a separate container. We grab the first, then walk it out to the cart. Mac places the safe handling equipment on the cart next to the container as I close and relock the door to the isolation room. A moment later, Alex opens the exterior door for us and we're out.

"Quick confirmation," I say to Mac. "You're going to clean the slots in the generator. On your mark, I'll open the release on the container. When the nitrogen has boiled off, we'll use the grippers to lift off the lid, then grab the bar. Together, we insert it in. We have two minutes max from the time the nitrogen vapor cloud disappears until the bar is in place."

"Roger," Mac replies as if we were talking over the radio.

I nod. "You're up."

Mac opens his case of tools, pulls out one of the cleaning cloths we use for operations like this, pours some alcohol on, then rubs down the slots into which the bar will be inserted. A second later, I hear, "Done."

I put on my thick extreme temperature gloves, then grab one of the long-handled grippers from the cart. Once Mac has his gloves on, I position myself orthogonal to the pressure valve I'm about to open, then use my gripper to pop the pressure valve open. A spray of vapor shoots out two or three feet, forming a frozen cloud of ice crystals. I step back as I feel the cold approaching, holding my oxygen mask tight against my face. By now, the gas is warm enough that it's not really a threat at the edge, but the oxygen levels in the area around that cloud are dangerously low.

As the spray reduces to nothing, I signal Mac. "Two minutes, starting now."

Together we grab opposite ends of the container's lid, then on the count of three, lift it off. More frozen air wafts away, then we step in and clamp our grippers on either end of the bar. A second later, we lift it, then walk it the last three feet, align it with the slot, then slide it in.

"Tight fit," I say, relieved that we got it placed in time.

"Easy-peasy," Mac says, as we release the bar, then step away.

Alex steps over toward us. "One down, three to go. Remember not to touch the container with your hands."

...

Three hours later, as we're coming up on lunch time, the last bar gets installed and we button up the area. The plan is to leave the beast outside under the shelter of the overhang, protecting the area. Although we aren't expecting weather, we cover the unit with a tarp.

"Want to install it tomorrow?"

"Ah," Mac comes back. "Tomorrow's Sunday. I'm planning to drive to Phoenix after lunch, have dinner with Kaylee tonight, then do some shopping tomorrow before coming back."

"Good. I forgot that it's Saturday."

"Kai, you need some time off. When's the last time you took a full day?" Alex asks.

I shrug. "This is my life. And it's just become a lot more complicated."

She shakes her head but holds her peace.

Once the others leave, I head back over to the replicator on the other side of the lab and confirm that the little surveillance drone I'd queued up was completed last night. I touch the holographic button that opens the replicator and see the thin triangular device that I requested. Its controller, a tiny cube, sits next to it. Realizing that I'm going to have a hard time moving the hundred-kilogram surveillance drone on my own, I pick up the cube and carry it over to my desk. Addressing the drone by its name, I say, "Raven One, power up, please."

The drone's holographic control panel pops up in front of me.

"Please play the training videos."

A fraction of a second later, the training library pops up. There are over eighteen hours of training material.

"Open the beginner's tutorial."

The still image of a uniformed male appears opposite me. After a second, it seems to come to life. "My name is Raven One, captain of the robot bearing my name. It is my goal to work with you to accomplish the missions you assign to me. Please address me by name when you are ready to begin."

"Raven One, can I communicate with you using the communicator implanted in my ear?"

"For remote operation, that would be the preferred method. Would you like me to link with your communicator?"

"Please."

A second later, the person in front of me disappears, but his voice sounds in my ear. "This communicator only provides audio communication. I would recommend that you upgrade to one that provides video and data as well. Until that is done, I would recommend that you have me appear in front of you when working together in proximity to my cube."

"Please appear in front of me."

In an instant, he's back. "Shall we begin your training?"

"Please begin."

CABIN

I spent the rest of the afternoon training with Raven One. The interface is so seamless that it takes little time to learn. My last act of the afternoon was to open the lab's exterior door and order Raven One to fly outside and settle on a shelf for the evening.

Now back in my cabin, I catch the news as I eat dinner.

Audell doesn't have a segment tonight, but as I flip through the cable news feeds on my tablet, I see that To'Kana and I are the number one topic; the hosts playing clips from the NBC broadcast and the talking heads making ridiculous speculations over the ten minutes of material broadcast so far.

After a half hour of it, I'm done, and, as I have nothing else to do, call Thelma. "I'd like to upgrade my communicator."

IKNOSAN LEGACY SHIP

"Kyle, we are pleased you want to upgrade your communicator. I've prepared a new one for you," To'Kana says, placing a tiny case on the table, then opening it to reveal its contents.

At his request, I remove the old one, which triggers a shivering fit as intense as it did when I installed it. When the shivering passes, I realize that I now feel somehow empty, incomplete.

On seeing my expression, the captain nods. "The communicator augments your perception to a degree. It's a side effect of its connections with the frontal and temporal lobes of your cerebral cortex."

"Will it come back when I install the new one?" I ask.

"Yes. This one..." He points to the one sitting in the case in front of me. "...makes connections with all four lobes: frontal, occipital, parietal, and temporal. You will feel the difference immediately. Your connection with the world will seem more vivid; your IQ will probably test ten points higher."

"The installation?" I ask with caution.

"More severe. You will also want to be careful about engaging the visual functions while standing or moving, at least until you've learned to balance images coming in from the implant with those coming in through your eyes. It can cause balance or spatial confusion issues."

I nod, then take a deep breath to calm myself.

"I'm ready."

To'Kana lifts the case and presents the communicator to me. A moment later, I twist it in and am overtaken by the tickling. The shuddering lasts a full minute; well, maybe thirty seconds. When I settle, the world around me seems to expand and I feel more alive than I've ever felt before.

"I can see the new implant agrees with you," To'Kana says.

"Incredible."

"Thelma?" To'Kana asks. "Can you connect Raven One to Kyle's new implant?"

"Would you like me to do that for you?" she asks me.

"Please."

"If you open a channel to him and ask him to appear. You will see him in front of you. We will not see him. The image is simply being formed in your mind. Similarly, if you talk with him, we will not hear him, but we will hear you if you speak out loud. Try it here, where it is safe."

"Raven One. Please appear," I say aloud.

An instant later, he's there, right in front of me.

"You can't see him?" I ask.

"No."

"Raven One, please drop the visual feed," I say to myself.

The words are no sooner thought than he's gone.

"You just dismissed him, did you not?" To'Kana asks.

"Did I say it out loud?"

"No. Over time, you will be able to read others, catch the expressions that betray where their attention is. You are easy to read, Kyle Wimberly. You are also a fast learner."

Our business settled, To'Kana stands and shakes hands, then takes his leave. If this was an interaction with another human, his departure would seem unnaturally abrupt. But as I've learned, the Iknosan don't linger the way we do when our business is done. At first, I assumed the Iknosan culture was simply more transactional, less relational. After nearly two weeks, I don't believe it anymore. They simply build relationships differently than we do. Over the coming year, I'll probably learn a lot more about that.

[08.20.2033] TRAIL

The Sunday morning run has always been the least predictable. Some Sundays, no one shows. Others, there are twenty of us. As I exit my cabin, I see that today it's going to be a sizable crowd, which makes me smile. Because today, they will be the first to see something no human other than me has ever seen before.

"Raven One, please activate."

His voice sounds in my ear. "As ordered, sir."

"Can you track my location?"

"Location tracking enabled," he replies. "I have you on sensors."

"Do you detect any air traffic in the area?"

"Several above twenty thousand feet; nothing below one thousand."

"Please take position five hundred feet above me. Maximum stealth."

"Estimated flight time: two minutes, twelve seconds."

"Thank you, Raven One. Please advise when you are on station."

"Acknowledged."

Satisfied that my surprise is en route, I step down off the porch and jog over to the gathering point. None of my inner circle is here this morning. Ty is usually the one to lead things off and keep us on time. That responsibility apparently falls to me today.

After quick greetings, I turn to start, but am stopped when I hear Marion Black's voice. "Audell is planning to join us this morning. Can we give him another minute?"

"I'll start us off if you'd like, boss." The voice belongs to operations manager Gabe Wilson, who rarely joins us, preferring to run in the evening.

"Thanks, Gabe."

"Let's get a move on, troops," Gabe shouts as he moves out onto the trail.

Others slowly follow, the line stretching out a bit. Certain the issue is that I haven't started yet, I catch Marion's eye. "I'll need to go soon."

"Not a problem."

When I'm two steps away, Marion calls out, "There he is."

I look back to see where he's pointing and see that Audell is ahead of us, angling in from I'm not sure where.

Several minutes later, I come up alongside. "Thanks for joining us this morning."

"Sorry, I'm late," Audell replies. "I had to give Meet the Press five minutes at 9:10 this morning, 6:10 here."

"Ouch," I reply. "Good show?"

"It's the hottest thing on TV right now. Technically, I'm still freelance. I could grab ten or more slots a day if I wanted, a couple grand each."

"Why aren't you?"

Audell looks at me before replying.

"Mission first. Fame and fortune second."

The terse reply surprises me. "I have something for you this morning."

"Yeah?"

"A surprise. Up ahead. Too bad you don't have your equipment."

"I always...," he stretches out the word and pats his chest. "...have equipment."

"Really?"

Audell smiles and reaches down into his shirt. A moment later, a lanyard comes out holding something the size of an ID card, but maybe twice as thick. "It's the latest in mobile recording equipment.

Only 4k resolution, but it can record up to an hour of audio-video on a charge, and it's fully charged."

I point ahead. "It'll meet us up there, about a mile ahead, at the turn."

"Can't wait," Audell replies, then steps up his pace. "Meet you there."

As he pulls away, I realize Audell runs lightly on his feet. I have no chance of catching him if he wants to get there first.

"What was that about?" Marion Black asks, pulling up alongside.

"Poor guy was on Meet the Press for five minutes this morning."

"Nothing poor about that," Marion replies.

"Hey, boss." I turn to see Ash Baird, former Navy Shore Patrol, coming up next to me on the left. "Mac told me you wanted to install a piece of equipment today. He felt bad about being away. I can help if you're paying overtime."

"Rescheduled. Maybe next time."

"I'm here. Call if you need me."

Once out of earshot, Marion says, "That guy," while shaking his head. "Always seems to know how to run the wrong way."

It's one of the few words of complaint I've heard about another employee.

Over the next mile, the guys cycle past. Most with a question; some just a greeting. It's not like it was in the service, but I feel the same sense of interdependence among those living here in this harsh place, far from civilization.

As we come around the bend toward the midpoint of our run, I reactivate Raven One. "Please come down and hover ten feet above the large cactus at the crossroad. Max exposure."

"Beginning descent. Expect some noise and dust."

A minute later, someone points. "What the hell is that?"

I'm not sure how he's doing it, but Raven One is making the sound I associate with a plane descending out of control.

"It's going to crash!" someone else shouts.

Everyone slows, looking up at the odd triangular object corkscrewing down toward the trail ahead. I pick up my pace, wanting to get closer. Audell, who's clearly figured out that I'm behind this, has his camera out narrating the pending crash.

Then it just stops and hovers ten feet above the designated cactus.

Shouts and other sounds of dismay fill the air. I wave my arms and shout out, "Everyone gather around! Keep this area here clear."

No one moves fast, most eyes still glued to the strange hovering object.

Using my implant, I send, "Raven One, hover five feet above the ground, ten feet in front of me."

Then, in a loud voice intended for show, I shout, "Raven One! Come to me!"

The object points in my direction then drifts over to me, stopping at chest height, centered ten feet in front of me.

"Everyone! This is our new surveillance drone! It is powered by Iknosan technology, patterned after one of their designs."

"How does it stay afloat?" someone calls out.

"Gravity drive. This is the first human designed device to incorporate a Boundary Particle Sourcing power system and gravitational propulsion. This is one of a dozen demos we are producing as proof of concept for our new Space Defense System capable of turning away the threat posed by the Xeric Dominion. Gather around. Have a close look. But please do not touch it."

After a second, the spell breaks, and people gather around in unmasked awe. Out of the corner of my eye, I catch movement. It's Audell running toward camp. I've just done what they warned me not to do and sometime later today the world will know. What's the matter with me?

OFFICE, FCS HEADQUARTERS

After the morning run, a shower, and a quiet breakfast in my cabin, I return to headquarters. As enthralled as I am with Iknosan technology, I have a pile of Full Cycle Solar reports to wade through. An hour in, my mobile sounds. 703 area code, which my phone identifies as Arlington, Virginia. I don't know anyone in Arlington but know there are a lot of government agencies located there. I'm tempted to let the call roll over into voicemail. Nonetheless, I answer with resignation. "Wimberly."

"Dr. Wimberly, my name is Faith Lee. I'm with DARPA's Tactical Technologies Office. I head one of its 'special projects' teams. Jace Elliott asked me to call you. He said you were planning to demo some technology to the Pentagon brass sometime soon. That's kind of what I do for a living. He thought I might be able to help you prepare."

"Um..." I'm so shocked by the call that I'm not sure how to respond. "Thank you for calling... Ah, Faith?"

"I hope I'm not intruding."

"No. Definitely not intruding," I reply, scrambling for something intelligent to say. "How might you help me?"

"There's a protocol for demonstrations like these. Those new to the process find it irritatingly bureaucratic, which I suppose it is. But there's a method behind the madness."

"Which is?" I prompt.

"Senior officials have broad responsibility. Most are incredibly smart and well versed, but none have your depth in your specialty. So, if you start at the heart of your technology, there's no chance they will understand what you are pitching. Over the years, we've developed a protocol that helps expose the key distinctions, peeling away the layers of complexity so they can see the uniqueness of what you are doing."

"Can you give me an example?"

"Jace told me you have an anti-grav drive you're developing. A twitter alert just flashed-by saying something similar."

"I have anti-grav technology, yes."

There's silence on the line for a moment, then Faith asks, "You mean you have a theory that proves out, right?"

"No. I have a remote piloted surveillance device that uses a grav-drive that I demonstrated for our staff this morning."

"How does it work? Are you using one of the three known methods: electrogravitic, magnetogravitic, or nucleogravitic?"

"A combination," I reply, not really knowing the answer.

"Bismuth or Moscovium?

I don't really know what Faith's asking, but the answer is obvious. "Bismuth."

"Hmmm, wasn't expecting that. How do you power it? Previous attempts have had interesting, but ultimately useless, results for lack of a suitable power source."

Thankfully, the replicator specs are open on the screen in front of me. "A ten-megawatt portable generator."

"Fuel?"

I can hear the pushback in her voice. "None."

"Zero-point energy?" The skepticism of a moment ago is now replaced by something more like awe.

"That's a harder question. We refer to it as Boundary Particle Sourcing—BPS, for short—which may be the same thing."

"And you've made one of these BPS devices?"

"I put a twenty-megawatt unit on the Western Interconnect transmission system yesterday. I've also built a fifty-megawatt generator that I plan to put online as soon as Western Interconnect agrees to take the power."

"If you've reduced this all to practice, why are you seeking government funding?"

"I'm not seeking funding. I am trying to get the government interested in building out a space-based defense system."

"For what purpose?"

The question stops me in my tracks. Is it possible Faith has not seen TV news in the last three days?

"Google me. Then call back if you still have questions." With those words, I drop the line, feeling guilty for having done so. A government official calls on a Sunday afternoon and that's the best I could do?

I wait a few minutes, then call Faith back. I'm really not cut out for this game.

CHAPTER 5: CELEBRITY

[08.21.2033] CABIN

Long ago, I put my phone on *Do Not Disturb* from eleven to six, but it really didn't help last night. The phone didn't ring, didn't vibrate; but, every fifteen minutes, I would startle awake, haunted by a dream that someone had just called.

Now, at 5:30, I'm awake again and finally surrender to my fears. I get up to hit the head and kick my phone out of *Do Not Disturb* mode. Seconds later, my phone buzzes, and I watch as the number of missed calls and voice mails tick up.

Scanning through the missed voicemails, I see three from Jace Elliott and listen to those first. Suffice it to say, he's not happy with me.

I call him back and he picks up on the first ring.

"You just couldn't help yourself, could you?" he accuses. "Clips of your flying wedge are all over TV, YouTube, Twitter... Everywhere, with headlines like *Alien Gravity Drive—Real or Fiction*."

"Jace," I interrupt. "I had to test the unit. There was no way to do that without someone seeing, so I made a show of it for the employees. I forgot that Audell Knight was on site until things were underway."

There's silence on the line for a minute, then Jace snorts out a laugh. "Well, you got the Secretary's attention. He'd like to see your demo, learn more about how it works. He has asked the Head of the Joint Chiefs, Admiral Nelson Sloan, to join him."

"When and where?" I ask, happy this is finally happening.

"They will be at Edwards Air Force Base in California on Thursday. If Justin is coming, I can probably arrange clearance for him to land there."

"I'll check with him."

"The Secretary has also asked me to come inspect your twenty-megawatt generator. Western Interconnect has already agreed to meet me there to verify that your generator is the source of the power now flowing into their system. It would be best if we can do that the day before."

"Wednesday? No problem."

"Cabinet level meetings like this with…" Jace hesitates before continuing. "…unknowns like you are rare."

"Your point?"

"Bring your 'A' game and a plan for the next steps. Faith Lee, from DARPA, is willing to work with you to figure out what that should look like. She's good at her game, very good. Call her."

"We talked last night."

"I heard it didn't go that well."

Mention of the call is more than a bit embarrassing. "We mostly talked past each other."

"Which is exactly what we want to avoid when we get to Edwards."

"I'll call."

"Be sure to tell her about the other technologies in your pipeline. She can help you string that story together in a way that will sell to DOD."

"Understood."

"I have a call with Justin on another matter later this morning. OK if I coordinate with him?"

"Please do."

"Thanks Kyle. I'll get back to you by the end of the day regarding logistics."

LABORATORY, FCS HEADQUARTERS

Despite the time zone differences and my promise to follow up with Faith Lee, I have something else on my mind: weapons. I have five requirements for a weapons demo. First, it must be replicable in one day. Second, it must be portable, so I can take it to Edwards. Third, it must be shocking when demonstrated. Fourth, it must be useful to our long-term goal of turning back the Dominion. And fifth, it can't be so appealing that they want thousands of them tomorrow to shift the balance of power among existing terrestrial adversaries; it needs to be about space.

Flipping through the replicator's database, I quickly rule out laser, projectile, nuclear, and antimatter weapons, the latter because I don't want to demonstrate anything that powerful. Now, forty-five minutes into this venture, I've ruled out more-or-less everything. The most tempting is a small shield generator, which is ironic, because it would be the biggest game changer for the American military. Put shields on our planes or ships and they would be invincible against most existing weapons.

As I ruminate on this reality, an idea comes.

"Raven One, please activate."

Its voice sounds in my ear. "As ordered, sir."

"Do you have shielding?"

"I do, sir, though it is weak."

"How weak?"

"Just over one thousand mega-newtons per square meter, sir."

It's nice to know there's a metric for shield strength, but... "Raven One, can you give me an example of what that would be? Could it take a hit from the M16 I had in Afghanistan?"

"Searching." Silence reigns for nearly ten seconds, then the answer comes. "Approximately fifty times the penetrating power of the standard 556 NATO munition used by the M16 rifle."

"How about a hit from an M1 Abrams' tank?"

"Searching." The silence stretches out thirty seconds this time. "Approximately three times the penetrating power of the 105 mm, M392A1 round at one thousand meters."

"Could you actually withstand a hit like that?"

"No, sir."

"But you said the shield could sustain the hit."

"The impact energy would not cause the shield to collapse. But I am a light vehicle. That much kinetic energy would send me flying, the acceleration breaking my internal components."

"Not damaged on the outside; broken on the inside," I whisper to myself, then in full voice, "But if you were a thousand-ton spaceship, you would be fine."

"Correct, sir."

"Thank you, Raven One."

Unhappy to have just wasted an hour, I decide to change gears. What next, Mac or Faith? I pick up the old land line phone to call Mac.

A moment later, the line connects and Mac's breathless voice answers. "Not joining us on the trail today, Kai?"

I look at the time. 7:15. Argh.

"We need the fifty-megawatt installed by noon on Wednesday."

"You got the go ahead from Western Interconnect to put it online?"

"No. But their representative and someone from the DOD will be here to inspect it sometime Wednesday afternoon."

"This is the one we put the busbars in on Saturday."

"That's the one."

"Marion and I can get the shed in today. You going to join us?"

"Not sure. I have something else I need to do first. Should only take an hour, but don't know."

"Got it," Mac replies. "Marion and I will head out around 9:00. The pad is already in place, so we can probably be ready for installation this afternoon if you're up to it."

"Great. I'll touch base when I'm free."

When the line drops, I get up and head for my office. Better to call Faith from there.

OFFICE, FCS HEADQUARTERS

"Faith Lee."

"Faith, Kyle Wimberly. Sorry about last night. Your call really caught me off guard."

"Kyle, thanks for calling. I spoke with Jace this morning at greater length and realized I misunderstood what he was asking of me. Then, I saw the video of your flying wedge. Very impressive."

"Thank you. They have asked me to demo this technology on Thursday. Jace said you could probably help me plan a successful demo."

"I'd love to. None of this is classified yet, is it?"

"No."

"Good. We can talk freely. Who is the audience for this demonstration?"

"Secretary of Defense McDaniels and Admiral Sloan, Chairman of the Joint Chiefs of Staff."

"Wow," Faith responds, clearly shocked. "This is your first presentation to them?"

"We met briefly with the Secretary a week or two back. It didn't go so well."

"What was the nature of the meeting? Reception, pitch, demo...?"

"A demonstration, I suppose. We transported into his office at Jace's invitation."

"You did what?"

"We have a transporter. You know, like Star Trek. We transported into his office as proof that we have control over a swath of alien technology that they will release to us, so we can prepare a defense against another alien species, who are planning to ravage the earth in the next year or two."

"Are you kidding me?"

"No, I'm dead serious."

"But how do you know it's real?"

I've been asked this question before, but for the first time, it gives me pause to think. Why do I think it's real?

"The technology. Why would they give us technology like this if it wasn't real?"

Faith sighs. "Because they want us to start a war; have the humans do the dirty work of thinning the herd before they attack us? Or because they want us as a client state to engage in war with other worlds. Or because they want to extort vast resources from us under the guise of helping us build a defense..."

"So, you think this is folly? We should just walk away from it?"

There's silence on the line, which I let stretch out. Finally, a reply comes back.

"No. The gift being offered is too valuable. What else are they offering you?"

"Everything required to build a thousand warships capable of turning back the Dominion, including new weapons that have the power to take down the Dominion's shielding systems."

"The Dominion is the name of their enemy?"

"Yes, the Xeric Dominion."

"It sounds like they want us to fight their war for them."

"The Dominion destroyed their worlds. I don't think there's a large enough reproducing population left for the Iknosan species to continue another generation. They call this their legacy and chose ten worlds to receive the gift."

"OK," Faith says, closing the matter. "What the US government does is their decision. My job is to help us acquire the technology being offered. Do you have a technology inventory?"

"Not as such. As regards ships, we have power, propulsion, hull materials, shielding, energy and projectile weapons, scanning and navigating systems, everything."

As the conversation drags on, I share most of what I know. I also grow increasingly suspicious that I'm being pumped for too much information, which is worrisome.

Finally, the questions stop. "Dr. Wimberly, thanks for all the background. I think I know how you should proceed. You need to approach this as a system sell—everything required to build a fleet of space-based warships. Your primary contention in this demo, the first of several, is that power is the largest of the problems we do not have the technology to solve. After that comes propulsion, which is tightly entwined with strong, light hull materials. Those are the things you are demonstrating. Follow so far?"

"I do."

"Good. Your primary power demonstration will be done off-stage, so to speak. Western Interconnect will verify the source of the power, and a DOD representative will confirm there is no fuel connection to that generator. The secondary demonstration will be the flying wedge just hovering there with no noise, no exhaust, defying gravity. I wish I was going to get to see that live."

"I'm sure we'll be able to arrange it someday."

"While it is hovering there, you will pass around a sample of your hull material, focusing on how light it is. You'll have a comparable size piece of aluminum and steel they can handle, which will drive home the weight distinction in a visceral way that they will not forget."

"I would never have thought of that myself," I confess. "Thank you."

"Validation of strength will be done by submitting a piece of your material to the base's Test Management Division, which handles material strength testing. Fair warning, I've worked with those guys. They are superb, but scheduling time with them is nearly impossible. One measure of the success of your demo will be how quick the test gets done."

"Thanks for the warning."

"Next will be the grav-drive. We'll demo this in three ways. First, I will have the unit hover there while introductions are done. Second, we will place a scale underneath the unit, showing increased weight underneath it. Then, we will rocket the wedge up to 100,000 ft in less than a minute. I'll have Jace confirm the tower can make that measurement."

"Which leaves us with the shielding." I add, completing Faith's thought.

"Which leaves us with the shielding," she echoes back. "We can request someone to shoot at it. But they will require that to be done on a proving ground, which would need to be scheduled."

"And I would need to be there," I remind. "Someone needs to operate it, and, at the moment, I am the only one that can."

"The other option is the heat test. Are you confident this will work?"

"It should, but I haven't tried it."

"OK, that's your homework," Faith orders. "Nothing gets demonstrated unless it is tested first, and the test is reproducible. And nothing undemonstrated can be part of the larger sell."

"Got it."

"Then we're done. I'll ask my boss to authorize a trip out. If this moves forward, DARPA will be involved. It would be a special project, so part of my responsibility."

"I hope you can be there," I confess.

When the line drops, I look at the time. Almost 10:00. As good a time as any for me to run the heat test.

WEST SUNDECK, FCS HEADQUARTERS

I step out of the building and take in the beautiful desert view, rimmed by rugged mountains, rutted by washes, and sprinkled with a cacophony of cactus—saguaros, prickly pears, cholla. To the north, mushroom-like wells dot the hills. To the south, our runway sits empty, awaiting its next plane.

A dust cloud in the west catches my eye, confirming that Mac and Marion have gone out to our substation too far away to be seen from here.

After a minute of musing, I summon my attention to the task at hand. "Raven One, activate."

"As ordered, sir."

The now familiar retort comforts me. My so-called *Flying Wedge* is alive and well.

"Please come to my location."

"Coming to your location, sir."

A moment later, I'm startled as my flying marvel silently comes over my head, close enough that I feel the induced weight of the additional gravitational field it generates. It stops five feet in front of me, then turns to point at me. It's scary that it knows how to do that.

"Raven One, are the airways clear enough for you to climb to 100,000 feet without hitting something?"

"The sky is clear, sir."

"At maximum acceleration, how long would it take you to get there?"

"Fifty-five point eight seconds, sir. My speed at arrival would be just over thirty-five hundred feet per second."

"Will traveling that fast heat your hull?"

"No. The shields might glow, but the hull would not heat."

"If I wanted the hull heated to the maximum safe temperature at the point of return, how would you do it?"

"Calculating." There's silence for a second. "I would alter course on the return, stopping ten miles north of here at an altitude of one thousand feet, then flying horizontally through the thickest part of the atmosphere with shields down. When I come to a halt, the hull would be approximately 500° C."

"Please run the following flight path for me. Travel up to 100,000 feet at maximum acceleration, then return with shields on so the hull is cool. Then repeat, this time returning with the hull hot. Execute."

Raven One rotates so that its nose is pointing straight up, then accelerates away. It's out of sight in seconds. At the thirty-second point, I hear the distant sonic boom.

As I watch the flight instrumentation using my inner vision, I see the speed climb, then, just before the sixty-second point, start to slow, ticking back toward zero faster than it had increased earlier. At first, I'm puzzled, then I realize the obvious—gravity, which had resisted the ascent, is now assisting the slow down. At the minute and forty-second point, speed finally hits zero and Raven One flips over, nose pointed down. Then, it accelerates back toward earth.

Within seconds, it's clear the descent will take a lot longer than the ascent. It doesn't take long to figure out why. On the way up, it reached its goal, traveling nearly thirty-four hundred feet per second. On the way back down, it wants to reach its goal at a dead stop.

Minutes later, Raven One comes gliding down to a halt, pointing at me as it did before.

"Raven One, can I touch your hull to confirm that it is cool?"

"Dropping shields, sir. Hull temperature is 30°C, slightly below ambient temperature."

My *flying wedge* creeps closer to me. When it is close enough, I reach out and touch it, noting that it is cooler than the railing on which my other hand rests.

"Raven One. Please repeat this time with the hull coming in hot."

Like before, it rotates until its nose is straight up, then races away. I watch its control panel using my virtual vision, tracking the ascent, then descent. It arrives at one thousand feet altitude ten plus miles north of our headquarters building, where it turns towards me, drops shields, and accelerates to twice the speed of sound. I watch as the hull temperature increases 100°C, 200°C, 300°C. As soon as hull temperature hits 550°C, Raven One decelerates. More seconds tick by, then the sonic boom hits. A moment later, I spot it. The slight glow on its leading edges fading as it races toward me. I step back at the sight of my flying wedge coming toward me at unthinkable speed. Then a wave of heat hits me as Raven One snaps to a stop.

"Raven One, have you experienced any damage?"

"None, sir."

"Ascend to an altitude where you will cool at an optimal rate. Hold position until hull temperature drops below 40°C, then return to your parking spot."

"As ordered, sir."

I watch it soar up into the sky, taking in this marvel of ingenuity that was gifted to me. It's hard to see how this demo could fail to impress. The military will want millions of these things. But that might be the failure of this demo—the military becoming fascinated with these as a means to change the global balance of power, while losing sight of the real objective—a fleet of spaceships sufficient to turn away the Dominion.

My cell phone sounds, bringing me back to the moment.

"Kai, the shed is up. If you can bring the generator, we can install it today. Otherwise, we'll come back in."

"Be there in less than an hour."

"I hope you beat that time," Mac snorts and drops the line.

TRANSMISSION SUBSTATION

To my surprise, Mac had loaded the fifty-megawatt generator onto the truck earlier. All I need to do is drive it out to the substation.

Despite the head start of a preloaded truck, my aspirational one-hour delivery time is blown by twenty miles of potholed gravel road, where the viable speed is more like fifteen miles per hour with the truck's bottomed-out springs doing a number on my back.

"Well... There he is," Mac announces as the truck grinds to a halt. "Thought you might've taken a nap first."

"Cute," I reply, really pissed at the situation. "I think your next job should be grading this road."

Mac puts his hands up. "I don't own this road, you do." The guffawing that follows amps up my anger, which quickly morphs into laughter. I guess that comes with the territory. Brothers-at-arms are tighter than blood; at least that's true for me.

It's curious to see Marion's reaction to the exchange. Then I remember; he's LAPD, or at least he was. From what I've heard, camaraderie there in his last days was far worse than it was in the closing days of Afghanistan. I need to do more to integrate him into the team. Then again, at the end of this week, he's off to family out east. Then when he returns, it's the hour-each-way commute from Quartzsite for the graveyard shift here. Given the expansion we're expecting, maybe we should open a school on site, making it possible for families to live here. Marion's not the only one with a family.

"Earth to Wimberly," Mac shouts, pulling my attention back to the here and now. "Are we unloading this thing or what?"

I pop out of the truck and do the mandatory greetings exchange, then we walk over to inspect the shed that will house this unit.

As we walk through, I see that they have not built the pad and shed to spec.

"Mac, what the hell?"

"You like the improvements?" he asks with enthusiasm.

"Improvements?" I ask in dismay.

"Come on, Kai, surely you can see this. The collapsible walls let us sink the anchoring bolts ahead of time. We lower the generator onto the bolts, crank them down, then pull up the walls. We should do this for everything. By the way, we build the shed to withstand winds up to a hundred miles an hour."

I look at the site where our new power generator will go while taking in Mac's words; then I see it... Division of power work responsibilities. People like Marion can put this infrastructure in place well before installation day. Once it's there, high-voltage certified people like Mac and I can do the truly dangerous work in half the time.

"Clever," I say, truly impressed by this innovation. Maybe it's time to make Mac the operations manager of Full Cycle Solar, so I can focus my attention on the defense initiative.

EAST SUNDECK, FCS HEADQUARTERS

I'm feeling pretty good about today's accomplishments, so decide to kick back and have a beer and some leftover pizza with the crowd that's gathered to watch the third installment of Audell's week-long special. Tonight, the spotlight is back on To'Kana and the legacy technology he has brought to Earth.

"You've said that your people had two technological breakthroughs near the end of the war, which had the potential to turn the tide against the Xeric Dominion. Can you tell us what those were?"

"Yes, I can. Disseminating this information is my principal purpose for visiting Earth. As context, the Dominion ships are large, strong, and immensely powerful. A single direct hit from one of their weapons would destroy one of our ships. In contrast, it required dozens of direct hits on the same spot on one of theirs to breach the hull."

"Did you ever destroy one of their ships?"

"No. We damaged several dozen severely enough during the war that the Dominion destroyed the ships rather than let them fall into our hands."

"Back to the breakthroughs. What did you discover that led you to believe you had a chance?"

"The first was a way to collapse the Dominion's shields. As we proved in the last battle, once the ship's shields were down, we could disable a ship and take it out of the fight."

"How does the weapon work?

"The answer to that question is quite technical. The short version is that it uses a superconducting mesh to short-circuit the gravitomagnetic field from which their shields are formed."

Audell chuckles. "I should have realized I would not understand the answer to that question. But how far beyond human science and technology is this weapon?"

"Humans discovered the relevant physics long ago. I am sure there are human scientists to whom I could explain it. The technology, on the other hand, is a completely different story. That is where the gap is."

"Moving on, how have you overcome the vulnerability of your ships?"

"In a way no one expected," To'Kana opens. "We developed something we call a jump drive. It allows our ships to move between two points in space without passing through all the space in between. If hit, our ships will still be destroyed. The jump drive gives us the ability to pop in close to our target, fire, then jump away before the enemy returns fire."

"Then how did the Dominion defeat you?"

"We only had ten warships with that capability. They could jump in and fire. But those ships had a five-minute recharge time. They successfully disabled the ships they attacked but were destroyed before they could jump out."

"Have you solved that problem?"

To'Kana stares at Audell but doesn't answer immediately. Then he nods. "Kyle Wimberly has solved that problem."

As Audell opens his mouth to respond, every head on the sundeck pivots to look at me. The shock of this statement is so thorough that I can't move, can't react in any way.

"So that's why you chose Kyle to be your technology gatekeeper?"

"That is why I chose Kyle Wimberly."

As the scene on the video screen shifts back to the live feed with Audell in one window and the Evening Report's anchor in another, questions erupt around me.

"When did you make this discovery?"

"How did you do it?"

I sit frozen, watching Audell and the anchor talk to each other, but not hearing a word for the cacophony going on around me.

Then someone shouts, pointing south.

"Looks like we've got company."

I turn and see the dust cloud near the horizon clearly moving in this direction. "What now?" I whisper to myself.

RUNWAY, FCS HEADQUARTERS

We get very few visitors here. Most schedule a visit. Others call and ask for the gate to be opened for them. But the truth of the matter is that our property is over a hundred thousand acres with a border fence that is more about defining the border than protecting it.

But the occasional vandal breaks in and all our ex-military and ex-police are armed. In the distance, we can see a van with some kind of gear on its roof coming our way. It's on the paved road, so not kicking up dust anymore, not much anyway.

The road runs alongside the runway to the small parking lot near the entrance to the headquarters building. Mac and Ty accompany me out the front door, then into the parking lot. I have a handgun holstered on my belt. Mac and Ty have their M16s hanging by their side. On the roof, Alex has her sniper gear set up.

Alex's voice comes in through my ear. "I have them in my sights. It's a news truck. Channel 8 News Now. You might want to make the guns a little less visible."

I nod to Mac, who just got the same message, and my two protectors walk back to chairs set in the shade near the building.

A minute or two later, the truck comes to a halt twenty feet away and the passenger door pops open. A woman gets out and steps toward me with a well-practiced smile, extending a hand toward me.

"Kyle Wimberly, thank you for coming out to greet us. I'm Crystal Reid, with Channel 8 News Now in Las Vegas. I'm a co-host of our local morning news show, Vegas Talking."

Although the name Crystal brings unwanted emotion, I put on a smile and shake the hand offered.

"I was doing some background work on another story in the area this afternoon. I called several times but got no answer. But since we were here, I thought I'd come by. Any chance we could talk for fifteen minutes? Maybe give us a tour?"

"Sure. Fifteen minutes."

"Any chance we could do it up there?" She points to the west sundeck. "Good late-afternoon sun. Splendid view, no doubt."

"Sounds good."

A moment later, I'm introduced to cameraman Max and audio technician Janet, then we head up the steps. Along the way, I catch my reflection in a window and realize how dirty I am from an afternoon out in the desert.

"Crystal, I'm going to duck inside to clean up a little. Mac will help you get the equipment set."

"Not a problem. Take your time."

Why do I think this fifteen-minute talk is about to turn into an hours-long affair? Thankfully, I keep a comb and clean shirt in my office. Ten minutes later, I'm on the west sun deck clean from the waist up.

"Well, don't you clean up nicely," Crystal says, reminding me of someone else with the same name. She points to an area they've set up with two chairs, then waves over Janet, the audio technician. "Set Kyle up with a lapel microphone and minimal makeup."

As Crystal goes to touch up her own appearance, Janet approaches with a friendly smile. "She's a bit chatty at times, but don't let that fool you. She's a real pro. Now just hold still for a second."

A brush comes out, seemingly from nowhere, touching nose and cheek, then in an equally smooth motion an unseen device goes through my hair.

"Just one more thing," she says as she grabs the collar of my shirt, attaches the tiny microphone, then pats everything back in place.

"What did you do?"

"All skin in bright light like this looks glossy in the camera. Same with hair. I have product for both face and hair that kills the gloss and dampens static in the hair. It wipes right off, so try not to touch either until we are done."

I admittedly like Janet's matter-of-fact approach.

"I have a dozen questions I'd like to ask, but I said fifteen minutes, so will only ask three, maybe four. Do you have any ground rules, meaning things I may not ask about or that you are not willing to talk about?"

I'm startled by the change that seems to have come over Crystal. The larger-than-life gadfly of a few minutes ago, now comes across as a professional reporter. I wonder if that's how she works her way into places that she hasn't been invited.

"Probably," I reply, surprised by the question.

"I was hoping for a list."

"It might be easier if you told me what you wanted to ask me."

My words evoke a stern look.

"Sorry, I'm new to this game."

"You live on site here, right?"

I nod.

"Our show is mostly human interest, so I'd like to know about that. I'd also like to know about what it's like to interact with the aliens. What do you really know about them, not things they've told you, but things you've seen with your own eyes? And I'd also like to see your Flying Wedge, touch it with my own hands, experience what it's like."

"Sorry, I can't do the wedge. Maybe at some future date, but not today."

"How about family, childhood home, love interest, time in the military?"

I shake my head no. "Maybe another time."

"What about the tradeoff between your work here and work to save the world?"

"I'm good with that."

Crystal smiles. "See, not that hard. My show is soft news, human interest, mostly targeting stay-at-home parents."

"We ready?" Max, the cameraman, asks.

Crystal casts her questioning eyes at me.

I nod back.

She straightens, then launches into her introductory spiel. I listen, feigning interest, and a minute in, the first question comes.

"Kyle, NBC has been running a special segment on their evening news shows in which you are featured, along with an alien called Ro'Masa To'Kana. Let me start there. Is it true that you are working in collaboration with an alien?"

I nod. "It is true."

"Can you tell us what that's like?"

"We met when his shuttle crash landed on our property. Until I saw him, I was worried about the damage done to our solar farm here in Arizona. When we found him, he was severely injured. Two of his crew were dead."

"That must have been terrible."

"My first reaction was concern for his injury. I saw worse in Afghanistan, which trained me to respond with action first, emotion later. So, my visceral reaction was probably more like an emergency room doctor's than a normal civilian's. I knew it was critical, therefore I had to deal with the injury first."

"Our world is lucky to have people like you."

Although the words strike me as patronizing, I doubt that was the intent.

"Anyway, from the very first moment, I knew To'Kana as a living, breathing, flesh and bone person. True, both flesh and blood were different, which was a novel experience. But I saw him as a person from the very first instant. I empathized with his pain and his predicament."

"What is the name of his people?"

"Iknosan."

"What do you know of the Iknosan people? Not stuff they've told you, but things you've learned through your personal interactions?"

"Well, the only Iknosan I've met is To'Kana. Therefore, he is the only one I have any experience with. Personality-wise, he is a little more reserved than I am. He's very conscious of the influence his presence on Earth could have, so wants to minimize that aspect of his work here. That is why he is adamant that he works through proxies, such as me."

"What about his claim that he is here to help, to bring technology and weapons that will allow us to repel a marauding alien species? I presume you believe it's true or you would not be helping him. But isn't there some lingering doubt that this is something much different? A clever way to entrap or enslave us?"

"As you say, I believe he is who he presents himself to be, and that the world is in significant danger. If at some point I should come to doubt it, then I will disengage. But as of today, I'm totally committed to the plan we've laid out."

"How is that affecting your work here at Full Cycle Solar?"

"Positively, I think."

"How so?"

"I developed the technology we've deployed here. It was the topic of my PhD thesis and the fulfillment of a decade's work. And I've treated it like my baby, wanting to be hands on with everything. Since the day we found To'Kana, I've had to let go a little. And in only two weeks I've seen the teams here rally together to take responsibility that I previously wasn't willing to give up. Couple that with the new Iknosan power systems we've brought online, and the company is becoming more secure operationally and financially."

"Last question," Crystal says. "Your location here is quite remote. I'm told you offer your employees housing here. How does that work? What fraction live on site vs. off? And what's it like living in this remote an area?"

"Let me start with the mechanical part of that question. We have something like one hundred cabins here. They come furnished. All are air conditioned. Any full-time employee can sign up for a cabin."

"How much do you charge for them?"

"We don't. About two-thirds of our employees choose to live here full-time. Some commute, going home every night. Some split. Here ten days, home four. At the moment, we have one commuter with a home in Quartzsite, who is staying with us all week, picking up some overtime while his family is out east. He'll head out on vacation later this week, then go back to commuting when they return from vacation."

"How rustic are the cabins?"

"I suppose that is in the eye of the beholder. I don't think they're all that rustic."

"Doesn't this lead to an imbalanced work/social life?"

"I suppose some would say that. I'm happy here. But I understand the premise of your question. Not everyone is cut out for this life. For most of the people here, it's good, incredibly good. For the average city person who likes to be out and about... They'd probably be miserable here."

"Well, I'm sad to say we are out of time. Kyle Wimberly, thank you so much for speaking with us today."

As the recording light turns off, I note that our fifteen minutes of questions turned into a half hour of prep and twenty-five minutes of on camera interview. In the end, it was fun. But I have to shut down activities like this in the future. I have too much on my plate.

CHAPTER 6: DEMONSTRATIONS

[08.23.3033] LABORATORY, FCS HEADQUARTERS

A lot has gone down over the last thirty-six hours. Dozens have come to our gates, flooding onto the property. Several have made it to the headquarters building. About half have been reporters, trying to score an interview the way Crystal Reid did; the other half curiosity seekers, who left disappointed when they were told there were no alien artifacts on the property.

If the notoriety had come last year, because of the clean energy operation, I might have considered offering a tour and opening a gift shop. Why not pick up the extra buck by educating people about clean energy while pedaling related trinkets? That's clearly not in the cards and soon I'll have to take additional security measures, because the number of intruders has increased almost every hour since Crystal's visit. So today, I'm going to investigate shielding. Is there a design that could prevent unauthorized entry that did not pose a significant health risk to those that tried?

Conveniently, the replicator's pattern library is searchable by topic. I start by narrowing the search to shields, then choose land based. Numerous configuration options pop up, one of which is wall. Following that path, I come to one I like: a shaded wall with doors. The picture attached to the description is a small black box about two inches high, three wide, and one deep. Reading through the description, I learn that these boxes, in tandem with a neighbor box, will form a shield panel. There's a long list of panel properties, including attachment, height, strength, porosity, failure mode, response, and image.

I scan through the property descriptions, which are a lot to take in, then hit pay dirt. There's an AI option. Knowing that's what I want, I queue up a run that will produce ten of these little bricks with an AI controller, then run the replication simulation, which will take about a half hour.

Curious to know more about the response settings, I open the user guide and start reading. After all, I have a half hour to kill. Response comes in two ways. The first is the visible reaction to the hit. Its default setting is a colored circle, where the depth of color and diameter of the circle are proportional to pressure applied to the shield above a threshold. The second part is the physical reaction. Its default is no reaction. But the strike back options include electrical shock and heat, with amplitudes from tickle to terminate. We'll run with the strike back options disabled.

The sound of the simulator chiming brings me back to the moment. It was a success. The replication will take just over two hours. I launch the run, then head back up to my office to deal with company paperwork.

OFFICE, FCS HEADQUARTERS

Just as I'm finishing up my paperwork, there's a knock on my office door. I look up, see it's Audell, and motion for him to come in.

Cursory greetings are exchanged as Audell takes a seat.

"I only have a few minutes before the pre-show production meeting. Tonight, we'll be airing the final segment of our week-long special on the Iknosan Legacy."

"How's the reception been?"

Audell snorts and shakes his head. "Unbelievable. Recently, the network has been number three in the rankings. Last night, we were number one, picking up almost two million additional viewers."

"Congratulations, you deserve it."

"As you might expect, they want more. And unexpectedly, they've offered me a job and a desk on the evening news."

"A desk?"

"A regular slot, covering news related to the Iknosan presence and any build out of Space Force."

"Which will only be meaningful if there is continuing news on that topic," I add.

Audell nods. "In some sense, this is what we were hoping for, right? To bring attention to the Iknosan and build support for a defense initiative. I hoped, but didn't expect, it would be this successful."

"Does that mean you're moving to New York?"

"Could, although I don't think that makes any sense. The people that cover the White House visit New York now and again, but live and work in DC. I think it would be the same for me. The question is how you want to handle it. All the networks will assign someone to you soon. CBS is considering that morning talk show host from Las Vegas."

"My mistake," I confess.

"Don't say that. You made a real time decision that helped you, despite the side effects."

There's silence for a second, then Audell adds, "I'd like to stay here for now. Cover your demo this afternoon, whether or not DOD or Western Interconnect will make a statement. And with your permission, I'll attempt to get press credentials to cover your demonstration at Edwards tomorrow. The front office says they think they can make that happen."

"Is there a point where you'll flip and come inside?"

"I think so, but it's not in either of our interests for me to come inside yet. What you're doing is newsworthy, but it is the network access that's making it news right now."

"Sure. Attempt to get credentials. It'll be nice to have a friendly face there tomorrow."

"Thanks." Audell looks at his watch. "Got to go. I'll be free at 4:00 if your demo hasn't finished yet."

Mac walks by a second after Audell's out the door. I wave him down. "Got a minute?"

"Sure boss. What can I do for you?"

"I want to put shields up around the property."

"Shields?"

"You know, like in the sci-fi movies."

"OK. How are we going to do that?"

"I just replicated ten units. Enough to place nine ten-meter panels."

"Where do you want to put them?"

"At the end of the parking lot, arcing around the building. You know... As a test."

"Would make more sense around the substation."

"Maybe later. If we can get one or two panels installed in the next three hours, both Justin and the DOD will see them."

Mac smiles. "Then we better get hustling."

FCS HEADQUARTERS

The ten little shield generator bricks are heavy for their size, maybe five pounds each. So Mac and I load them onto a cart, along with the small AI cube and some other gear, then wheel it all outside. The exterior door to the lab is on the north side of the building, the parking lot on the south.

Once out the door, we turn right, toward the east, where the helicopter and fuel storage tanks come into view on the opposite side of the runway. As we come around the corner of the building and turn right again, the entirety of the runway stretches out in front of us—two miles of concrete a previous owner had put in for reasons unknown. Maybe it's the mood today, maybe it's just the sheer quantity of concrete while pushing a cart, but the memory of a similar stroll down a runway at Bagram Air Base in Afghanistan flashes through my mind.

Mac apparently notices the shiver that runs through me. "You too?"

"Yeah."

He points at the little bricks. "Too bad we didn't have these over there."

The melancholy holds for the full three minutes we take to get to our destination.

"Where are we putting these things?" Mac asks.

"I was thinking of running them down the west side of the parking lot, then at a right angle to the west until we run out of bricks."

"Humm," Mac grunts, then strides off to the southwest corner of the parking lot. He stomps around a bit, then says, "Here. Let's put the corner piece here."

"Let's measure it off," I reply, holding up the rope. "I've cut this to the optimal spacing distance.

Mac points toward the building. "Then we should probably start over there."

"Deal." I grab four bricks, then walk over to the northwest corner of the parking lot.

Mac beats me there and has picked a spot by the time I arrive. "Two feet from the sidewalk?"

"Let's do it."

I put three of the bricks on the sidewalk, then hold the fourth out to show Mac.

"We can mount these on any flat surface. It doesn't need to be smooth, but the flatter the better. The top is the side with the small holes running along the long side." Holding the brick flat in my hand, I point out the small holes. "This is the top of the brick. The shield will form on the side with the holes, so we'll want these on the parking lot side."

I flip the brick over. "This is the bottom. It has three larger holes along the center line. A field projects out of this anchoring the brick to the ground." I hand the brick to Mac. "Place this one.

He puts it down on his spot, shuffling the brick around in the gravel until it sits flat. "How's that?"

"Looks good to me. Now take this end of the rope and go place the next brick."

Mac grabs an end and paces away as I spool out the rope. It takes almost no time to place the first four bricks.

"There are two more parking spots. Do we stop here, or go way past the end?"

"Let's stop here. You want to take the next one?"

Fifteen minutes later, we've placed the remaining bricks and we're ready to configure our shield fence.

I place the little AI cube on the ground in front of me, then address it.

"Headquarters shield one, activate."

"Activating as ordered," it replies.

A holographic control panel pops up in front of me with a red exclamation point in the upper right corner. I reach out to touch it and a message pops up.

No shield panels associated with this shield.

I touch the button labeled, *Add Panels*, and a screen pops up, showing the nine viable panels formed from the ten emitters.

"Cool display," Mac notes.

I touch the *Select All* button. A second later, a 250-to-1 scale 3D image of the shield appears along with a list of options that we work our way through.

"Height? Ten meters?" I suggest.

"That's tall," Mac replies.

"Strength? A thousand mega-newtons per square meter?"

"What the hell does that mean?" Mac asks.

"It's the default strength of the shield on my flying wedge. In the real world, it means the shield can withstand two simultaneous hits from the main gun in an M1 Abrams."

"That's a big hit."

"Tell me about it..." My eyes narrow as I notice more choices associated with strength. "Check this out. There's a flexibility option. What do you say? Five percent?"

"Why not," Mac replies.

"Next, porosity? Isn't this interesting?" I push an information button associated with this option and more information comes up. "...allow air, water, and other small particles through. The default setting is one micron. I think we should dial it up higher than that, maybe one millimeter?"

"Given the wind and dust storms we get here, that might be a good idea."

"Failure mode? The default is shield collapse."

"Just leave it at that," Mac asserts. "This is just a demo. Anything complicated will require a complicated explanation. You don't want that in a demo unless that's the thing your customer wants the most."

"Agreed. Response? Let's go for a visual response, the shield lighting up when hit."

"Sounds good," Mac replies, then asks, "What about a physical response?"

"For here, on campus? I don't think we want it to hit back."

"Agreed. Next is image."

There are a huge number of options, from transparent to opaque. Instead of trying to create something, I flip through some samples.

"I like that one with the light brown sandy wall the first third of the way up, followed by metal rods to the top," Mac says.

"Let's try it." I select the option, then ask, "Ready to turn it on?"

"No time like the present," Mac replies.

"Headquarters Shield One, save this configuration, then activate the shield."

"Configuration saved, activating shield."

An instant later, the holographic control panel vanishes, and our new security fence appears.

"Damn, that looks real," Mac says.

RUNWAY, FCS HEADQUARTERS

I watch as Justin's G800 touches down. He's nearly a full hour earlier than I was expecting. According to Gabe, our operations manager, a call came in while I was working with Mac. The Western Interconnect representative had to handle an emergency restart down at the massive solar farm near Quartzsite this morning. Justin was already in the air coming out of DC, when word came that the Las Vegas pick up was canceled. I'm sure he's not thrilled about that, but equally sure we need time to discuss our new fence shield.

A minute after, the plane rolls to a stop, the main engines shutting down. Two or three minutes later, the door opens, the stairs fold out, and Justin appears at the top, a briefcase in each hand. As he carefully makes his way down, I see Jill wave; her smile contagious. I wave back, realizing I'm not put off by her the way I used to be. I also note for the first time that she is in the left-hand seat—the pilot's seat—as she has been the last couple times I've seen them land.

"Kai, stop ogling Jill and come give me a hand."

I almost rise to the bait, but push the emotion away.

"I didn't know we were building a new fence. How did you get it done so quickly?"

"Mac and I put it up this morning."

Justin looks at me, obviously wondering what I'm up to.

"Here, take this. It's Jace's briefcase."

I take it and notice that Jace is on the last step, lugging a small wheelie.

"Jace, welcome to Full Cycle Solar," I call out.

"Quick. What's the deal with the fence?" Justin whispers urgently.

"It's a shield, same strength as the one in the surveillance drone that we're demoing tomorrow."

The look of shock on Justin's face almost makes me laugh.

"How strong is it?"

"A shot from an Abrams will just bounce off."

The shock is back, but it quickly morphs into a smile.

As Jace pulls up alongside, I notice the sweat forming on his brow.

We shake, then I point at the building. "Let's get you inside. It's too hot out here for a suit."

CONFERENCE ROOM, FCS HEADQUARTERS

Once inside, Joe, the guy who maintains our cabins, checked Jace in, then showed him to his room, giving Justin and me a chance to catch up.

"I have a lot to bring you up to speed on," Justin starts. "But I need to know about the shield first."

"Let me show you the control panel."

I place the cube on the table, then activate it, then quickly step through the setup: ten emitters, nine panels, strength, flexibility, response, then the image.

"So it's a solid shield with a picture painted on it?" Justin summarizes.

"It's porous with millimeter wide holes in it, but yes, the shield itself is square, ten meters by ten meters. The space between the bars is just a transparent shield."

"We could make a fortune on this," Justin moans, as the door opens, and Jill comes in.

"Another day, another fortune," she teases.

"You saw the new fence, right?" Justin asks.

"Looks kind of like the border wall. Do we really need that here?"

"It's not a fence. It's a gussied-up force field. Kai and Mac built it in two hours."

"It took the replicator two and a half hours to fabricate the pieces; Mac and me two hours to place the emitters and configure it."

"Oh. The military is going to want millions of those things. Isn't that going to be a distraction?" she asks.

"I'm sure they will. But we needed proof of concept for ourselves and we're getting lots of intruders, so I made a sample bit of fencing. The question is whether-or-not we tell Jace."

"We have to," Justin says. "It's part of tomorrow's demo, the weakest part. If Jace sees the real thing here, he can vouch for it. They could come here to see it."

"Or we could build a three-panel shield for them there," I add.

"Let's show Jace the fence and ask for his take on it."

PARKING LOT, FCS HEADQUARTERS

Jace, now in khakis and a short-sleeve shirt, looks at the fence. "This is an alien-tech demo? It looks like the border wall."

I put my hand out and lean against the wall. "Come feel how cool it is."

Jace shrugs. "Sure, I'll play along." He steps over and touches the wall, then a moment later, he cocks his head. "I've touched the border wall before. The metal bars get hot. I don't know what this material is, but it is cool. But you're not pitching improved fencing technology, are you?"

"No," I confirm, then reach down to pick up a hammer I'd asked Mac to put down here for me.

"Try hitting it with this."

Jace's mouth opens, then he hesitates. "Come on Kyle, just tell me what you want me to know. I don't want to go hammering on your wall."

"Then watch. I'll do it." I pivot and slam the hammer against the wall with all the power I can muster.

Jace shouts, "What the hell!"

I notice a ripple emanating away from the impact spot where the wall flashes red.

"What just happened?" Jace asks.

"This isn't a wall," I reply. "It's a shield, painted to look like a wall."

"What?" Jace asks in astonishment.

"Headquarters Shield 1, please deactivate."

At the words, the wall simply disappears.

"Oh, my God," Jace exclaims. "This is unbelievable. Can you put it back up?"

"Headquarters Shield 1, activate shield."

At my words, the wall flashes back into existence.

Jace puts out his hand, asking for the hammer. I give it to him, and he hits the wall several times at different intensities.

"It shows you where it's been hit."

I nod, noticing Justin's smile, but otherwise remain quiet.

"And it's voice activated."

"Not in the way you think."

"How so?"

"It only recognizes my voice, but the controller isn't here. It's in the building somewhere. The Iknosan gave me..." I tap the side of my head. "An implant that lets me speak to the shield controller remotely."

The pursed lips are back, and I can feel a question coming.

"What's the purpose of this demo?"

"Shields are an essential part of any spaceship. Everyone thinks of them as a defense against enemy weapons, which they are at their highest settings. But they also reinforce structural integrity. We'll see that tomorrow when our surveillance drone accelerates up to Mach 5 without its leading edges glowing red."

Jace takes on a serious look. "You realize they're going to want all of this, and they'll go to lengths you may not expect to get it. Are you planning to demo this tomorrow?"

"It would be easy enough to do, but at the moment, no."

"You should add it. We have drones. Yours are probably a lot better. But we have nothing like this. It's a game changer. They'll look at you differently once they've seen it."

Justin points. "Looks like we have company."

"This shield is ten panels. Would a two or three panel demonstration be sufficient?"

"How many panels comprise this part of the wall?"

"Three."

"Three's enough."

"Let me get that started." I say, then turn to Justin and point at the approaching dust cloud. "If she gets here before I get back cover for me."

TRANSMISSION SUBSTATION

Our representative from Western Interconnect is an African American woman named Breechelle Patterson. Her title is Sr. Field Engineer, and her weathered skin gives witness to a life lived outdoors.

"Don't know if you remember, but I did the final inspection on this substation before we brought it online. I can't remember if a company rep was here or not. But your contractor, JJ, did a good job."

"No, I wasn't here. JJ had invited me, but we were having a crisis at one of the wells."

"Was smart of you to have put all four pads in. Most companies don't, which means they need a site inspection every time an additional source comes online. I see you have two new sheds here. One of these has the new unit I'm supposed to be certifying?"

"This one. It has the new twenty-megawatt generator in it."

I get a suspicious look, then another question.

"What's in the other one?"

"A new fifty-megawatt generator that's ready to go online."

From the frown I get, I know I'm in trouble, although it's not clear to me yet why.

She motions toward the smaller shed. "Let's get on with it."

We walk over to the shed, and I unlock the door. I wave Ms. Patterson over, then point to our suitcase-sized generator.

"This is our new twenty-megawatt generator..."

"That's a generator?"

"It is, ma'am."

"Where are the fuel lines?"

"There are no fuel lines. This is a clean energy source that works via Boundary Particle Sourcing, BPS." Getting no response, I wave her over to our step-up transformer. "Standard three-phase step up.

13.7kV, chopped at 60 cycles, synced to the line. Fifteen hundred amps. You should be able to confirm the current flow."

Again, I see the frown. "Is there a problem?" I ask.

"Let me confirm the voltage and current flow first," she replies, before pivoting on a heel and stepping back toward her van.

"What's going on?" Justin whispers.

"I don't know. She seems put off. Maybe it's the new generation technology."

For the next ten minutes, we watch as she enters the substation control room, runs various tests, and records the results—all without a word.

When she finally emerges, she says, "One more test," then returns to the van to get some equipment. A few minutes later, she's back wearing huge rubber gloves and carrying a large clamp like device.

"What's that," Justin asks.

"It measures the current flow. Current flowing through a cable generates a magnetic field. The clamp contains a coil that can measure it."

We watch as she tests each of the three cables coming out of our little shed. When the last one is done, she reconfigures her measuring device and lowers it to the ground like a metal detector, then walks around the shed twice. She stands there for a second, then waves for us to follow as she returns to the van.

The gloves are off, and equipment stowed, by the time we arrive.

"Mr. Elliott, the control systems confirm that twenty megawatts are flowing into the grid from the small shed we inspected. I took the additional precaution of manually measuring the current flow in each of the three lines coming out of the shed. All are performing as expected. Not understanding how that much power can come out of the box in the shed, I did a cautionary scan for underground power lines that might supply the power from another source. That much power should be detectable if that was happening. I could not detect anything. May I ask DOD's interest in this matter?"

"At a high-level, the Department wants portable power systems that use minimal fuel. When we learned of this one, we asked for independent confirmation. Based on your results, we will continue down the path of exploring this option. Thank you."

Breechelle nods, then turns to me.

"Mr. Wimberly, I have several issues with what you've done here. Your petition to increase supply was as early fulfillment on an existing permit for solar energy, which this clearly is not. Compounding the problem is the proximity of the generating system to the step-up transformers. I contend the boxes should be on the other side of the fence. That you have positioned another larger generator in proximity demands further investigation. I will recommend that your permit be suspended, pending further investigation. It is, of course, your right to appeal that recommendation."

I'm stunned, speechless. Thankfully, Justin steps into the exchange.

"Ms. Patterson. I have been in discussions with WAPA's Desert Southwest Regional Manager, who has given us provisional approval for the twenty-megawatt generator under our current contract. I'm also working with your Chief Strategy Office on a new contract for this generation type. We have permission to stage assets for quick expansion after approval. I'm sorry we did not loop you in on this before the visit."

[08.24.2033] HEADQUARTERS, FULL CYCLE SOLAR

The best laid plans... Yeah, ours kind-of went sideways today, but maybe that is for the best. Justin got civilian landing privileges at Edwards. Audell got his press pass, so could fly in with Justin. Jace is DOD, so didn't need permission, just convenient transport. But our demo? Well, it couldn't get into Justin's G800. Strictly speaking, that's not true. Big enough gorillas could have carried it in, if they were small enough to get in through the door. But Justin, Jace, and I were not big enough gorillas, and Raven One didn't have the maneuverability to fly in on its own. So here I sit on the north side of our headquarters building, waiting for the call. When it comes, me and my drone will transport to Justin's coordinates.

In some sense, I'm good with it. An hour in a jet, a couple hours milling around waiting for the brass. Who needs it? Yet here I sit, waiting anyway.

An eternity passes, maybe forty-five minutes, then Thelma's voice sounds in my mind. "Kyle, Justin is ready for you. I have a lock on you and your gear. Are you ready?"

"Ready." I close my eyes as I say the words.

EDWARDS AIRFORCE BASE

A moment later, the sound of a military jet taking off replaces the quiet of the desert breeze. I open my eyes and see America's two highest ranking military officials ten feet in front of me; Jace sitting next to the Secretary of Defense; Justin is next to the Chair of the Joint Chiefs. The latent sergeant within wants to snap to attention; but the Iknosan Emissary responsible for technology transfer squashes the impulse. And off to my far left, I catch a smile from Audell.

"Mr. Secretary, Admiral Sloan. Thank you for meeting with me today."

My greeting is met with gracious words, introducing base commander Brigadier General Walter Umberg, and a handshake from each. The reception is as welcoming as our first meeting was dismissive. Then I realize how much I've benefited from Audell's work.

"I will demonstrate two devices for you today, both critical for any space defense America would choose to mount. As you'll see, both would also apply to our defense against other adversaries. But our alien benefactors have not authorized the use of these technologies for terrestrial defense."

Both men I'm here to pitch remain completely still, seemingly unfazed by the restrictions described. But I know better than that. Neither wants me to read it in their expressions, but neither will ever accept those terms.

"So let me start with the demonstration of our grav-drive, a propulsion system optimized for use within a planetary system, or within the inner planets. It interacts with nearby mass, amplifying or reversing the attractive force of gravity."

I pull the controller cube from my pocket and hold it up. "This cube will project a holographic image of our drone's control panel. I will issue orders, speaking them aloud. You will see its control panel in the image presented. Activating it now."

Over the next hour, I run through the demo practiced earlier, running the drone up to a hundred thousand feet, then diving back down without the hull heating. Then back up and down, this time with shields off for the last leg of the trip, arriving back glowing hot.

"Very impressive display," Admiral Sloan congratulates. "I presume this technology is scalable. How large a spaceship could it support?"

"Iknosan battlecruisers are wedge-shaped, approximately three hundred meters long and sixty meters high; fifty meters wide in the bow, one hundred meters wide in the stern. They use this technology for main propulsion in the inner system."

"That's nearly the size of one of our nuclear-powered aircraft carriers," the Secretary observes. "One hundred-thousand-ton displacement. How do we get that much mass into space?"

"Iknosan battlecruisers have much less mass. The hull plating is only two centimeters thick; the alloy they use is lighter and stronger. So we have much less mass to put in space. And we will do it using Iknosan bulk transporters."

"I struggle to believe that a two-centimeter-thick hull is viable," Admiral Sloan challenges.

"Shielding is an integral part of the hull. As you saw in the demonstration, the shielding allows our little flying wedge to travel at Mach 5 through the atmosphere without burning up."

"Do you have a separate shielding demonstration?" he asks.

"Shielding is the second demonstration I planned for today. It will take five minutes to set up. We could do it on the proving grounds if you'd like to test it."

Admiral Sloan turns to base commander Umberg. "Doable?"

General Umberg looks at me. "How big a hit can it withstand?"

"An M1 Abrams round from a thousand feet."

"Target size?"

"Twenty meters wide, ten high."

He turns back to the admiral. "I don't know that we have anything here of comparable power. Most aerial munitions pack a bigger punch."

The admiral asks Justin to give them a moment of privacy. Then the three men huddle together to discuss.

A minute later, General Umberg says, "Assistant Director Elliott has convinced us we should see the *border-wall* version of your demonstration. Is that something you can do?"

Three minutes later, the wall is up, and our hosts are whacking it with the hammer I brought with me.

As we wrap-up the event, Secretary McDaniels comes over to shake my hand. "Thank you for your time today, Dr. Wimberly. This was one of the most impressive technology demonstrations I've ever seen. Jace will get back to you with our proposed next steps. I look forward to the next time we meet."

CHAPTER 7: CRISIS

[08.29.2033] FCS HEADQUARTERS

It's been five days since the demonstrations at Edwards Air Force Base. I thought it went well and, based on the enthusiastic response we received, expected that we would have heard something by now. Justin has point on the follow up, but he's been completely silent on the matter.

In stark contrast to the government's response, the news has been filled with international outrage triggered by our demo. Russia and China have been the most vocal in their complaints about American access to alien technology. But even allies like Canada and the UK are *looking forward* to meeting with President Powell to discuss a collaborative effort on space defense.

And unlike their government, public curiosity about our work has attracted more and more unwanted visitors. The night we got back, intruders made it all the way to the headquarters building, startling the guards on duty and almost getting themselves shot. In response, I've decided to extend the shield fence all the way around the building. Doing so will create access problems I'll need to fix by the end of the day. Nonetheless, I queued up a replicator run that will produce the seventy shield emitters required to complete the half mile fence.

...

As we finish placing the emitters on the south and west side of the building, Mac says, "Kai, we're halfway there. Shouldn't we test these before we continue?"

In truth, I hadn't thought about a test procedure. How much fencing should you test before going on?

"It's going to be a hell of a lot harder to find a failed emitter once the circuit is complete," Mac chides.

I consider Mac's words, then have a flashback to my youth.

...

"Kyle! Test the strand before starting the next."

The voice belongs to my father. It's Thanksgiving and my younger brother Mark and I are helping him put up the Christmas lights in the winery's tasting room—the lights that won't light if a single bulb has failed.

"Come on Dad. Can't we just get this done?"

He looks at me, shrugs, then says, "Your choice. But the lights need to be up before you go to bed tonight."

...

It was a painful lesson, one that comes flooding back at Mac's words.

"Thanks. Good call." I reply to Mac, before calling out, "Headquarters Shield One, activate user interface."

The control panel for the shield opens in my inner vision.

"Add panels."

The command causes all the unassigned shield emitters in the area to light up in the control window I see with my inner vision.

"Add all," I command.

In the control window, the shield now extends halfway around the building, from the edge of the parking lot on the south-east side to the northwest corner where we placed the last shield emitter.

"Testing!" I call out.

"Clear!" Mac calls back.

Satisfied that it's safe, I order, "Headquarters Shield One, activate shield."

The familiar hum of shields coming alive follows the order. A fraction of a second later, a piercing squeal causes me to shudder.

"Headquarters Shield One, deactivate shield."

The squeal stops before the hum does, but I'm in motion, heading toward the now silenced squeal, before either sound stops resonating in my ear.

"Over here," Mac calls out.

I look in his direction and see him pointing.

"Desert cottontail," he adds.

A few steps later, I stop in my tracks. A desert cottontail, one of the sweet little rabbits that dot the desert floor during the morning dawn and afternoon twilight, lays bisected near one of the shield emitters, head and forearms on one side, feet and cotton tail on the other.

I stand frozen at the sight. I just killed one of the desert's most vulnerable creatures while testing my new shield fence.

"Didn't realize how deadly these things were," Mac says. "It cut the damn thing right in half."

Part of me wants to weep. Why are the innocents always the victims? A deeply cynical part of me answers. *Because they are of no consequence.*

I'm repulsed by my own thought.

"The first half of the shield obviously works," Mac says, apparently pleased with himself. "Let's get the other half of this done."

[08.30.2033] FCS HEADQUARTERS

More intruders came on site last night. Apparently, they went looking for other targets when they couldn't get into headquarters. Two cabins got banged up before security came. The intruders scattered and ran into the shadows as security tended to the damaged cabins and their distressed occupants. This morning, Well #27 failed to fully come up.

"Things are getting totally out of hand here," I complain.

"But is fencing the entire property the solution?" Justin asks from the comfort of whatever city he's camped out in.

I can feel imagined-steam seeping from my ears.

"What are we supposed to do? Two cabins and one well damaged last night! It gets worse every day."

"Kai. You're the one closest to this issue. It's your decision. I will support you no matter the outcome. Maybe To'Kana can give you the sanity check that I cannot."

Justin's words give me pause. Can he possibly think this is not a problem?

"I'll talk with To'Kana. But for the record, something is not right here."

"Kai, I respect your judgment on this matter. If something is wrong, then figure out what it is. This is your domain. I will support you in whatever you do. That said, fencing the entire property will take an enormous amount of replicator time and an equal amount of the material To'Kana is mining and refining for us. Clear any use of this resource with To'Kana before you use it for an off-mission purpose."

Justin's words ring true to me. "Thanks," I whisper. "You're right. I'll discuss this with To'Kana."

"Thank you, Kyle."

A moment of silence later, the line drops.

IKNOSAN LEGACY SHIP

To'Kana locks me with a stare. "Kyle, Thelma told me of your security concerns. As it deals with your people, you are the better judge of appropriate next steps. But I share your worry. Something is amiss, though I can not put my finger on it. If you believe this is the right course of action, then the materials are yours. But let me offer one more gift."

As the words hang, my data pad beeps.

"I've just sent you a replicator pattern. It's a restricted one. I'm only giving you the rights to five replications."

"What does this pattern replicate?"

"A personal firearm, a laser with multiple power settings. On high, it will kill almost any species known. On low, it will cause lower life forms to lose consciousness, disrupting, but not destroying, their sodium channels."

"Do I really need this pattern? Are humans among the lower forms you refer to?"

"Kyle, trust me. Something nefarious is afoot. Devices such as these are a last line of defense against a more powerful enemy."

Uncertain where this conversation has gone, I come back to my original request. "Then I am free to engage the resources I need to secure our facilities?"

"Your choice," To'Kana says, then turns and walks away.

LABORATORY, FCS HEADQUARTERS

For the first time in a long time, I'm frozen by indecision. Do I replicate the personal firearm that To'Kana gave me? We already have powerful weapons. Is this one more powerful? In what situation would it be relevant? Do I really want to spend the resources required to build a sixty-mile fence around the entire property? It would require nearly ten thousand shield emitters. At present, we only use five percent of the land. It would only require a thousand emitters to fence the land we use—headquarters, the cabins, the wells, and the substation. But to do the entire property in little chunks like that would take a hundred times as many.

Frustrated by my indecision, I activate the replicator and launch a simulation for the ten thousand emitter build. Within seconds, the simulation fails. Shuffling through the error messages, I see that the maximum run for these emitters is one hundred units.

Frustrated that I've wasted so much time over nothing, I launch the run for one hundred shield emitters, then sit back in my seat.

What's the matter with me? When did I become this vassal of indecision? And what's up with To'Kana? Why does he think something nefarious is afoot? As sleep comes over me, I rebel. Something is wrong.

As consciousness fades, I grab a pen and stab my leg. An impulse of adrenaline spikes, waking me enough to queue up To'Kana's personal firearms. Then my head nods again. I stand and shake myself, hoping the activity will put some energy back in me. But the world feels wobbly somehow.

"Kyle Wimberly!" Thelma's voice screams in my mind. "You are in extreme danger. You must transport aboard immediately."

I reply, but can't get the words out as my vision narrows. At the edge of my consciousness, I hear Thelma say, "Invoking emergency proto…"

...

I feel a shake on my arm, then ice cold water lapping against my feet. "Hey, buddy. You alright?"

I open my eyes, but the tidal wave of vertigo that washes over me makes me snap them shut.

"Let's get you out of the water."

Hands grab both arms and a moment later, I'm on hard packed sand.

"You still with us, friend?" Another voice asks.

I open my mouth to speak, but struggle to get any words out.

"I think we should call 9-1-1," the first voice says.

"I'll stay with him if you want to run back to the car."

"Be right back."

I open my eyes again. This time the world is stable enough for me to get my bearings and immediately I know where I am—Morro Bay, fifteen miles west of San Luis Obispo, California, the town in which I grew up. Morro Rock, the six-hundred-foot behemoth jutting up from the ocean, is about a quarter mile to the south of me, the familiar sounds of Highway 1 behind.

As I struggle to get up, my voice comes back. "Thanks."

The wet-suited person next to me offers a hand. "I'm Remy. My partner, Jørgen, saw you fall." He points to the man running towards the highway. "We were out surfing. You must be freezing."

A shudder runs through me. "I am."

"We have a blanket in the car. Would you like me to get it?"

I turn. The car is a long walk away. Jørgen hasn't made it there yet.

"I think I can make it on my own." Then as memory comes flooding back, I say, "Please don't call 9-1-1. I can't be seen here."

The words come out with more emotion than intended and Remy, whose been standing close to me, takes a step away. "Are you in some sort of trouble?"

"Not in the sense you're thinking, no. But I cannot be seen here."

Remy jogs toward his partner. "Jørgen!" It takes several strides before his partner hears enough to turn and look. Then he looks at me. Our eyes lock and I can tell he knows who I am.

"Kyle Wimberly?" It's Thelma. "We have an emergency here. I may not act without your instruction."

"Thelma. What happened?"

"I know things I am not permitted to know."

A thousand retorts go through my mind, but I hold my tongue.

"Is Captain To'Kana available?"

"He is non-responsive."

"Was I the only person at Full Cycle Solar to be affected?"

"No. Mac is down as well."

Thelma's words strike me with a fear I haven't felt since Afghanistan.

"Does this have to do with the Dominion?"

"I believe it does. I think one of their scout ships is here."

My mind churns for a moment, then I assert, "They have a weapon that can paralyze the Iknosan mind."

"We believe they have a weapon that can corrupt the function of the ear implants. Essentially, all Iknosan military personnel have these implants."

"Why are you not allowed to know this?"

"The captain has blocked my access to all confidential information related to the Dominion. He was reading a document on this topic in his isolation room when he called out for help. The document was open, seemed relevant. I read it."

"Is Justin affected?"

"No, that's why I transported you away."

"Is Mac still down?"

"He is."

"Are you able to transport him?"

"Not without an order to do so."

"Give me a second."

As I ponder where I can have Thelma transport Mac and me, I notice two pairs of eyes locked on me.

"You are Kyle Wimberly. Something has gone wrong with the aliens. That is why you appeared out of thin air."

I stare at Jørgen for a second. "Gentlemen, thank you for rescuing me, but I have an emergency on my hands."

"Maybe we can help. We've rented a home near here for our holiday. You could get cleaned up there. You could transport your friend Mac there."

I put up my index finger, signaling for quiet.

"Thelma? Is Mac in immediate danger?"

"I don't think so. His vital signs are stable."

Looking at Jørgen, I ask, "How far away?

He points toward Highway 1, where it turns towards the mountains. "Four miles."

"Thelma, I'll get back to you in fifteen minutes." Then to my rescuers, "Let's go."

VACATION RENTAL

On the ride to their place, a charming two-bedroom cottage on a farm overlooking Churro Creek, I get the lowdown on Remy and Jørgen—Danish, gay, married, avid North Sea cold water surfers. Remy's a nurse; Jørgen's an EMT. Both are avid sci-fi fans, blown away that they've actually met me, and deeply apologetic they didn't recognize me sooner.

Now showered and warm, dressed in clothes Jørgen's lent me, Remy and I sit watching over Mac, who's still unconscious on the couch. But it's all I can do to sit still. The Dominion are here. They've found the captain's ship and deployed a weapon against him that's put him in a vegetative state. Equally bad, they've found First Cycle Solar, my home, and used the same weapon against Mac and me.

We have no idea where they are, but I have little doubt that they're gathering tons of data they will use against us.

"As soon as Jørgen's out of the shower, I'll start dinner. You must be famished; you were in fifty-five-degree water for at least fifteen minutes," Remy asserts.

"You were in a lot longer."

Remy laughs. "Nice and toasty in my wet suit, and this water is warm compared to home."

"Thank you for taking us in."

"Can you tell us anything about what's going on?"

Mac stirs on the sofa, saving me from having to reply.

Remy is immediately at Mac's side, whispering, "It's OK. You're safe here."

I get up and stand at his feet. "Mac, wake up."

He stirs more.

"I think he's coming around," Remy says.

"Mac, wake up," I coax.

An eye flicks open, then shuts just as quickly as a shudder rips through him.

"It's vertigo. I went through it a half hour ago. It helps just to listen for a while." I advise Mac.

Mac opens his mouth, but words don't come out.

"It passes pretty quick, once the vertigo eases up."

"Where are we?" Mac grunts out.

"In the mountains along the central California coast. I had Thelma transport you here."

"Who's the other guy?"

"His name's Remy. He and his partner, Jørgen, rescued me when Thelma transported me into the ocean."

"What's happened?"

"We think it's the Dominion. Their scout ships have weapons that screw with the ear implants. They took out To'Kana, you, and me, but not Justin."

"They must not know about him." Mac concludes, opening an eye and keeping it open.

"They may not know about us either."

"Why do you say that?" Mac asks, locking both eyes on me.

I smile, seeing he has both eyes open now. "I was transported out an hour ago and they haven't found me yet. Maybe they only know we have Iknosan tech at FCS."

"If they find Iknosan tech on Earth, I bet they'll come for it post haste. Do we know if they've done anything to the mining platforms?"

"Good question. Thelma?"

"How can I help you, Kyle?"

"Do you know if the Dominion has taken any action against the mining platforms?"

"Checking." The silence drags on for a while. "The mining robots are not responding to my requests for status. Scanners show energy emissions consistent with the ongoing mining operation. Maybe their comms are down.

"I see our guest is awake."

I turn to see Jørgen walking over to shake Mac's hand, then I step away so I can concentrate on Thelma. "Anything else to report?"

"Kyle, can you look at something for me? Best you sit down first."

I step into the dining room, pull out a chair, then sit and close my eyes.

"Let me see it."

A close-up shot of one of the mining robots appears in my mind. I look intently at the box-shaped robot, then notice a transient shimmering.

"Did you see that? Shimmering along the edge, on the right, near the top."

"Does it mean anything to you?" Thelma asks.

"I'm not sure I understand the question," I reply.

"I perceive movement, but it does not correspond to any of the patterns in my databases. Therefore, I can assign no meaning to it."

"Keep watching."

"What's going on Kai?" Mac asks.

"I'm looking at an anomaly on mining platform three. You up to looking at this thing?"

"Still a little dizzy."

"OK, I may be at it for a while."

"Got it."

Though I cannot see Mac, I sense his presence receding. A moment later, I see similar movement, this time see structure to the movement.

"Thelma, can I see this with parallax? Two simultaneous views, one to each eye?"

"Give me a moment. Got it. Ready?"

"Ready."

The view shifts, the images not lining up that well, then the shimmering movement happens again, and I see it, a translucent octopus-like creature flowing around the box-shaped robot. The movement is as mesmerizing as it is terrifying.

"Thelma. Search the human internet for something called an octopus."

I watch in fascination as one tentacle at a time moves across the mining platform.

"Kyle, can I show you something else?"

"Go."

A two-dimensional drawing labeled Dominion Scouting Robot pops into my inner vision. It has a ball-shaped top, eight tube-shaped appendages, and a footnote that reads, "Actual number of appendages unknown. Drawing extrapolated from distant sensor readings of battle wreckage. Believed to be cloaked when in use."

"I think you've nailed it, Thelma. Scan the other robots, see if you can deduce anything from previous sensor recordings."

"As you order, sir."

Thelma's sign-off is almost as shocking as the discovery of the scouting robot. Why is she calling me sir? Is To'Kana still alive?

I go back into the living room to find it empty, then follow the voices I hear into the kitchen, where Remy is tossing a salad.

"Jørgen and Mac are about to start the burgers. What's going on?"

"Thelma spotted a Dominion scouting robot."

"That's not good, right?"

I snort. "No. I think my company might be its next stop."

"Do you have a way of defending yourself?"

Mac strides into the kitchen. "What's this I hear about a scouting robot?"

"We just spotted a Dominion scouting robot examining Mining Platform 3. I'm worried its next stop is the headquarters building."

"Think the shields will hold?"

"No. The shields on the Iknosan battlecruisers were a hundred times stronger. But they dropped on the first hit."

"From one of their big guns," Mac snaps back.

Remy asks his question again. "Do you have a way to defend yourself?"

I look at Mac. "This morning, To'Kana gave me patterns for handheld weapons that he said were powerful enough to kill one of the Dominion warriors."

"He knew they were here?" Mac accuses.

"No, he knew something was wrong, wanted us to have more powerful weapons, just in case. I queued up five of them just before I went down."

"You didn't just run them?"

"I had a hundred shield emitters running."

Mac groans. "So, we have five weapons that will be run when the field emitters are unloaded. We need to go back. And we probably ought to evacuate the campus."

"But won't that just knock you out again?" Remy asks.

I look at Mac. "When did you feel it coming on?"

Mac shrugs. "An hour before?"

I nod. "It spent a long time creeping up on me. But the take down at the end went fast, maybe five minutes."

Thelma interrupts. "Kyle. We have a problem. The scouting ship just decloaked. The robot is crawling toward it."

I lift my eyes to Mac. "I have to go. The scout ship just decloaked. We need those weapons."

"But what if they get you again?"

"Have Thelma watch me. If I go down, you come in, grab me, then transport both of us back out."

"I don't like this," Mac growls.

I close my eyes. "Thelma, transport me back to the lab."

LABORATORY, FCS HEADQUARTERS

When the sound of Mac's protest vanishes, I open my eyes and see the replicator's finished light flashing. I issue the order for the door to open. Three minutes later, the shield emitters are neatly stacked on my lab bench, and the swoon is already setting back in. I touch the close button, then hear it close and lock. A moment later, the control panel status changes to run. Estimated time to completion: forty three minutes.

I stagger as another wave of vertigo washes over me. "Thelma, transport me back."

VACATION RENTAL

I was afraid to close my eyes before this transport, worried that I might go down if I did. The additional vertigo induced by the transport robs me of all balance on arrival, and I swear as I fall over.

Mac and Jørgen come barreling out of the kitchen, which in my punchy state makes me laugh. Two guys, whose first instinct is to run towards trouble, bump into each other as they do.

Mac extends a hand. "That didn't take long."

"You were right, by the way. The replicator had finished the emitters, but the queued-up weapons hadn't started. I barely got the shield emitters cleared out in time."

"You verified the weapons started?" Mac asks.

"I did."

"I've been talking with Thelma. She reminded me we can take our implants out if we need to. We'll be cut off from her, unable to transport without them in. But she thinks we can operate normally if we take them out."

I shake my head, not liking that option very much.

"Then there's the bad news."

I look at Mac, "You serious?"

"Thelma confirms that the scouting robot examined and knocked out comms on all three mining platforms."

"Not good."

"She also found evidence that it crawled the hull of the legacy ship and suspects they're behind a series of failures among the ship's minor systems. Thankfully, the comms and transporter are fully functional."

"That it?"

Mac shakes his head. "The scout ship is dropping from orbit. Its shields are up, but they're following a ballistic reentry orbit."

"That makes no sense. Don't they have a grav drive?"

"Thelma says this is normal,"

"Full Cycle Solar is the target?"

"Their course will take them to the desert southwest."

I exhale loudly. "I wish we'd put up more shields."

As Mac paces, my stomach growls loud enough to be heard.

The noise causes Remy to spring into action. "The burgers are in the warming tray. Sounds like you could use some fuel."

A minute later, we're all gathered around the table on the back porch, chilled by the fog pouring in from the ocean.

"The weather is so amazing here," Remy says. "I read about it before we came, but it's hard to believe until you see it. Sweltering hot in San Luis Obispo. Ice cold on the ocean. Fog pulled in through the valleys every day."

"It's what makes for the superb wines produced in the region." I say, lifting the glass they'd poured for me.

Mac, who's sitting across from me, eyes the glass and scowls. "Bad idea tonight."

Momentarily distracted, I miss as I set the glass down, my hand hitting the tines of my unused fork, causing it to pop up in the air and knock over Remy's glass.

The glass shatters, but thankfully, Remy had finished his wine.

I extend profuse apologies, which are graciously accepted, but Mac says nothing, eyes still locked on my fork.

"What?" I ask.

"Maybe that's our solution."

"To what problem?"

"The scouting ship."

"My fork?"

"Flow with me for a second," Mac says urgently. "Where are they going to land?"

I put my hands out. "Beats me."

"Come on, Kai, be serious for a second. Thelma says it's odd for Dominion scout ships to land. Of the seven planets where scout ships were spotted, they only landed on one. What's drawing them down to the surface on Earth?"

"Iknosan technology?"

"And where on Earth is there Iknosan technology?"

"Our substation and our headquarters building."

"Forgot about the substation," Mac mutters, then more brightly, "I don't care about the substation. They aren't going to get all hot and heavy over a power generator. They're going to want your replicator or flying wedge, and maybe your shield emitters or guns. But it's hard to believe it is anything other than your replicator."

"Go on."

"Thelma says they do hover-landings. Where would they land?"

"The runway? Parking lot? Maybe the gravel directly north or west? Is there a point to this?"

"Suppose there were shield emitters there that were not activated?"

My mouth drops open in shock. "Like that poor cotton tail. We could turn them on and slice the ship right in half."

Mac stands. "We have time if we go now."

I shake hands with our hosts and apologize again for the glass, but am not that worried about it. They both look like they've just had the experience of a lifetime.

LABORATORY, FCS HEADQUARTERS

Mac and I materialize in the laboratory, and I feel the effects of the Dominion weapon immediately. Sticking a finger in my ear, I twist, and the implant pops out. The dizziness wanes more slowly than it came on and I'm momentarily overcome with shivers equivalent to those experienced during the earpiece's installation.

Mac, on the other hand, seems determined to soldier it out.

"Mac, eject the damn thing!"

"Then how will I rescue you?"

I'm so frustrated with Mac that I want to kick him. Instead, I turn to the replicator. The weapons are done, so I open the door, pull out the five weapons and stuff them into my belt, then launch a run for ten more emitters. On the control panel, the replication status pops up reading zero percent complete, four and a half minutes remaining.

Mac is starting to look glazed over. I punch him in the shoulder, "Wake up, God damn it. What's the status of the Dominion scout ship?"

Light momentarily shines in Mac's eyes, then fades.

"Thelma! I know you can hear me through Mac's implants. Transport him out of here."

As Mac collapses, my heart sinks. I can't do this on my own.

Then Mac disappears. I'm encouraged that he's safe now, but as the reality of the situation sinks home... Sorry, not going there. I'm on my own against a vastly superior force. It's not the first time, but... Sorry not completing that thought either.

I race to my lab bench, then load my pockets with shield emitters. Only six fit and, with this much weight, my pants start to slide off. I cinch my belt, then grab an over-the-shoulder carryall. Eight more emitters slide in before I step toward the exterior door.

As I'm about to open the door, I freeze again. I need allies before I walk out into the open. I also need my command cubes, since I no longer have implants to talk with any of my alien devices. Back to the bench, I grab the two AI cubes already programed and four more that I haven't programed yet. Then I shout, "Alex."

The response is immediate. "Wimberly, where are you?"

I'm speechless for a moment. We installed this AI comm assist three years ago, but it's never worked before. "Meet me outside the door to the lab. We have incoming."

"On my way." Her voice is accompanied by sounds of equipment being hastily grabbed, then a door slamming. "Who else is in?"

"Mac is compromised." It's not a complete answer, but it does the trick.

"I see Ash. He's on duty. I'll get him. What's the sitrep?"

"A Dominion spy ship will arrive shortly. We have a shot at killing it, but the timing is tight."

The panting of extreme physical exertion comes over the line, then it goes silent. I assure myself that Alex has switched channels to contact Ash, but fear grips because who can really know?

"Raven One, activate."

"Raven One at your service."

"Dominion inbound. Can you silently get aloft and determine their location?"

"Deploying." The single word reply gives me little comfort and as I come to the exterior door, I wonder whether I should wait for Alex to knock.

A flood of guilt washes over me for the errant thought. No! I'm here for Alex as much as she's here for me!

As the door slides open, I step out into the night. The darkness reminds me I need my night vision goggles and tactical comm system. I dash back inside, grab the gear I need, then step back out.

"Seal laboratory," I order.

I hear the door slide shut, and the magnetic lock engage.

The silence of the night floods my ears as I stand scanning the area, heart pounding, barely breathing. A flash momentarily lights the sky, the silence totally undisturbed. Moments later, a light appears near me, shocking me to the core. Then I realize one of my control cubes has lit up. I fish them all out of the carryall, setting them on Raven One's stand, the lit one's holographic control panel showing my flying wedge's location. It's hovering a thousand feet directly above me.

"Raven One, report." The silence that follows reminds me I've lost my audio connection and need to touch the blinking exclamation point. How does anyone fight a battle like this?

"Wimberly, what the hell?"

Alex's voice cuts through my confusion.

"They're here. The Dominion are here. They just blew up our substation. Mac is offline. Take this."

I pull one of the hand-portable weapons from my belt and hand it to her. "To'Kana says these are more powerful than our weapons."

Alex takes it and sticks it in her belt. "Haven't trained with it…" Her voice trails away.

I nod. "Weapon of last resort. Fair enough."

She nods, and I hand her the carryall. "Lay these down, ten meters apart, forming a giant X at this end of the runway." I pull a unit out of my pocket and put it out for her to see in the dim light of Raven One's holographic control panel. "Place them with the small dots up and aligned the same way as the others in the same line."

"Like this?"

She pulls out one of her units and holds it next to mine in proper alignment.

"You've got it. Where's Ash?"

"A minute behind. I'll connect with him and guide him here."

"Good. I'll take the north and west side of the building."

She looks at me and nods. "Where do we rendezvous?"

"West side. I've put the shields down. If anything is above them when reactivated, it will slice it in half. Stay on the sidewalk if possible."

"Done." Alex turns, then vanishes around the side of the building.

I feel guilty for not having given her a proper sitrep, but we have little time left. Seconds later, I'm a hundred yards north of the building aligned with its east side. I take a calming breath, lock my eyes on the building's northwest corner, then pace off ten of my three-foot strides. Ten, twenty, thirty paces in, the sound of the substation's explosion rumbles the earth. I sprint to complete the first leg of the X, then redirect to the northeast corner of the building to start the other leg.

Ash sprints by without greeting, heading toward the runway and Alex.

Halfway to the crossover point, a pressure wave passes over me. It's the Dominion scout ship. It's huge, two or three times the length of To'Kana's shuttle. We are so screwed—out in the open, the enemy spy ship passing straight overhead, about to land on the runway.

I'm a third of the way to my goal, but stop. This part of the plan is blown. I place an emitter, the third of ten, on this leg, then run for the cover of the building, and more importantly, my AI control cubes.

Seconds later, the new shield controller is up. I've given it the name Runway Shield 1. Alex and Ty laid eight emitters that I've formed into a three-panel broken X.

The Dominion Scout Ship has landed with its stern over the southern half of the X.

Alex's voice comes over the tactical comm channel. "Kai, where are you?"

"Near the lab door. I have the new shield configured. Are you clear?"

"Sidewalk. West side of the building, near the southwest corner."

"Stay out of sight. I'm activating the shield."

"Roger."

"Activating in 3, 2, 1." I touch the activate button. A second later, the vibrating sound of shield activation starts, getting louder and louder. Then, in an instant, the vibration stops and there's a giant crash. The crash is followed by lurching sounds, then the long squealing sound of metal tearing. I cover my ears as the noise gets so loud, I fear for my hearing. Then all sound stops.

"Going in for quick recon," I send, then move to the corner of the building.

Consistent with the sounds I heard, a huge slab of the port side stern has been cleanly cleaved off and is now resting on its side on the ground. The starboard stern was cut cleanly, but wedged between two of the shield panels. The metal in the wedge is what ripped, some of the wedge falling toward the bow, the rest falling toward the stern. This ship will never fly again.

Relaxing some, I step out a little further. That's when I notice movement. One tentacle of the octopus-like robot has flopped out of the cleanly cut port side stern and is crawling toward the ship's bow. Every couple of feet, it stops to tap the shield separating it from the ship. It will be a while until it clears the end of the shield.

On the starboard side, the one closer to the building, another tentacle has detached and is making its way out through the torn metal. It has a relatively clear path toward the bow but needs to slide along the shield some twenty or thirty feet before it's free. The way it writhes, I'm not sure it's going to make it. Unlike the previous shields, this one reacts with heat and electrical shocks.

I step back behind the cover of the building to report my findings.

"The ship is badly damaged. One tentacle from their octopus-like scouting robot has escaped and is crawling toward the ship's bow. It's on the opposite side of the ship, moving slow. Maybe a half hour from the bow. Another tentacle has direct access to the south side of the building, but has to slide along the shield to do it, getting electrical shocks and burnt as it goes. I don't know if it will make it."

A loud boom interrupts. I spin around the corner to see what happened and am shocked by what I see. An exit hatch near the bow has been blown open, smoke from the explosion still rising, and the ugliest creature I've ever seen has slid out onto the ground. I recognize it as Dominion from images To'Kana sent. But what I see, lit only by the building's exterior lights, reminds me of a spider—eight limbs extending from the center line of its ellipsoidal torso. But unlike a spider, four of the limbs look like four-jointed elephant legs, the other four look like octopus tentacles with a single suction cup and opposing thumb at the end.

When it first jumped out, all four of its eight- or nine-foot-long legs were straight, standing tall. One of its five-foot long arms was up, the other three resting along a corresponding leg. And its stationary head, dotted with an array of darting eyes, presumably takes in the scene.

One by one a hundred eyes come to rest on me, the creature's crouch lowering further with each eye that settles. With its torso now only three feet off the ground, it seems to be leaning in my direction, every visible eye pointed straight at me.

I step backward, eyes still locked on what appears to be its dominant eye. Then it springs right at me, one whip like arm flinging out straight at me.

The shield separating us flashes red at the point of impact, maybe sixty feet from where the creature was standing. The red is so bright that I can't see through the shield to see what it threw. But its aim was damn good.

"Into the building," I shout into the tactical comms. "I'm going to put up the shields."

As I round the corner and head for the Lab door, I hear the creature bellow, then the sound of the shield taking another hit.

"Laboratory door open!"

The door slides open, and I vector toward it. With three paces left, I hear another projectile hit the corner of the building. The damn creature has found its way around the shield. The light pouring out of the lab reflects off one of my control cubes sitting there on Raven One's platform. I dart right to scoop up the controllers, then dart left and dive into the building. Behind me, another projectile shatters the platform where the controllers were sitting a second ago.

"Lab door, emergency close!"

The door swooshes, the power of the pneumatic close assuring, but a thwack sounds. The tip of a tentacle has slipped in, preventing complete closure.

"Alex, are you in?"

"We're in."

Thwack, a second tentacle grabs the door.

"Headquarters Shield 1, activate shield."

As the Dominion warrior bellows, the hum of the shields comes alive. The horrendous squealing that follows penetrates my bones. It's the most terrifying sound I've ever heard.

"Raven One, I need imaging of the lab door. Do not approach within a half mile of the building."

Raven One's cube lights up. In its control panel, a window opens, showing the nose camera's view as it swoops in toward the building.

The Dominion warrior lays stretched out in a growing puddle of black blood. Five of its limbs were severed, two still attached to a slab of torso cleaved away. Blood still pulses out of the creature, but all noise has stopped, and each pulse produces less blood.

Relief floods through me. We did it, against all odds, we did it.

A giant explosion rocks the building, the pressure wave causing Raven One's camera to wobble. But what happened is clear. The Dominion ship just self-destructed. Thankfully, the shields seem to have saved the building.

Seconds pass, then there's another explosion. Raven One changes focus and my heart sinks. We just lost the fuel depot and my helicopter.

The lab's interior door at the top of the stairs opens. "Kai, you in here?" It's Alex.

"I am."

"Thank God you made it." Her words tumble out as her steps rattle down the stairs.

I stand up as Alex comes into view and flings herself at me, weeping.

"It's OK, I got it."

"Ash...The other one got Ash. It ran off towards the cabins."

IKNOSAN LEGACY SHIP

Thankfully, with the Dominion scout ship blown up, the weapon messing with our implants has gone offline. To'Kana is still unconscious, but Thelma's earlier idiosyncratic behavior is gone, and she now treats me as the ship's captain. She's tracking the escaped Dominion warrior that killed Ash.

The good news is that it's headed for our substation, not the residential park where the cabins are located. Which gives us a few minutes to gather our forces and prepare before taking up pursuit.

Three former squad members, who are part of the FCS security team, have volunteered to join Alex, Mac, Ty, and me in the hunt—Aaron Smith, Olivia Knox, and Denzel Yang. Each knew Ash and want a piece of the beast that killed him.

Thelma has made earpieces for the three additions. Each installed theirs without squabble in the headquarters conference room, and each has transported up to the ship.

I point to a map that shows the western part of our property. "The plan is simple. The Dominion warrior is running through this dry riverbed. He will arrive at the bend in about a half hour. We will install shields here, a hundred feet into the boxed canyon, and here, a thousand feet in. The walls are steep enough that he'll be trapped once we raise the shields. We will also mount shields at the top of the canyon to give ourselves cover. We'll use our standard night gear and tactical comm, and we'll each carry the weapon of our choosing, plus an Iknosan one. I will also be carrying an Iknosan tag gun, which shoots tags the transporter can lock onto."

I pause. "We'll trap him and kill him. Then we'll put a transporter tag on him and transport his body out into space. The Iknosan weapon I'll be carrying is a transporter-tag gun. If I can get the shot, I will tag him before we kill him and transport him into space alive."

"Maybe you should give the tag gun to Alex," Ty snipes.

"That was the original plan. Now this is the setup. Olivia, Ty, and Mac set the emitters at the canyon entrance, then transport up to the top of the eastern wall. Alex, Aaron, and Denzel will set the emitters mid-canyon, then transport up to the top of the western wall, where I will set up the controllers. Once at the top of the wall, you'll set your own cover shields. Once the emitters are set, stay back from the edge until the shields are up."

"OK, check your equipment. We roll in five minutes."

As everyone does their final check, Alex sidles up alongside. "The plan may be simple, but we have four people who have no experience with the equipment; five that have never even seen this enemy. We need to err on the side of caution and get out if anything goes wrong."

"Alex, we can't let this thing run free. For all we know it has assets here it can trigger when it gets to its target."

"You're the boss, Kai. Withdraw at the first sign of trouble. No one saw what was coming at headquarters."

BOX CANYON

I open my eyes and scan for my team. The canyon wall is steep enough that I need to shuffle closer to the edge than expected to see them. All are present and proceeding with their mission.

I move back, then remote activate my control cubes which are in the lab at headquarters. The controller designated Canyon Shield One comes up and immediately identifies twenty shield emitters, then links with them. The four at the canyon entrance are set in less than a minute.

Mac's voice sounds in my ear. "Emitters laid. Entrance team ready for transport."

Thelma copies me on the acknowledgment. A second later, I look up and see my three colleagues atop the wall on the opposite side.

Switching my view back to the Canyon Shield, I assign the four shield emitters at the canyon entrance to a new panel: Panel 1.

Several more seconds pass as Alex and Denzel seem to have run into a problem. Then Alex's voice comes over the comm. "Kai, can you confirm we have the alignment right? We are having trouble seeing the small holes."

I run a quick test, then report the results. "The second emitter from the east wall is backwards."

We still have plenty of time, but as the seconds stretch out, the first pangs of worry strike.

"How about now?"

"You've got it."

I assign these emitters to a second panel, which I cleverly label Panel 2.

A half minute passes, then I hear people joining me on the western cliff top.

"We've set the top shields on the Eastern cliff and are backing away," Mac reports.

"Copy."

I scramble to set up the eastern cliff shield so I can turn them on or off, individually or collectively.

Alex reports that she, Aaron, and Denzel are ready, then asks if I am. Of course, I'm not. I crawl out to the edge and find a spot about eight feet wide that gives me two good angles—one to the north, the other to the south—then set my emitters.

"Your target is two minutes out," Thelma reports.

I scramble back to my safe spot and finish configuring the Western Shield Panel, then save the configuration. With all my prep done, I sit back and take several deep, calming breaths.

I flip my internal vision to an aerial view and see our target has picked up his pace a bit, using its four powerful legs to bound eighty or a hundred feet per stride. Is it possible that this thing could jump over our ten-meter shield?

It slows a bit as it comes up on the bend in the canyon, then stops completely at the entrance. Has it sensed us? Can it detect the shield emitters?

"Kai, what's happening?" Alex whispers over the tactical comms.

"It stopped at the canyon entrance."

The silence stretches out as our target just stands there, then with a sudden leap onto the western wall, it climbs.

"It's coming up the western wall. Does anyone have a shot?" I broadcast over the tactical network. But there are no immediate replies. We are all out of position, waiting for our shields to come up.

"Kai, you need to get us out of here," Alex pleads.

"I have him in my sights," Mac says. A second later, the shot from his M16 echoes through the valley.

"Damn, it moves fast. It's like he can hear the shot before it arrives."

I hear Alex on the move. "Taking the tag gun," she whispers as she moves further down the canyon wall.

Four more shots ring out from the eastern cliff top, then Mac's voice broadcasts over the line. "Hold fire until my mark. We need to all fire at once, aim off target. Ready, three, two, one, mark."

A salvo rings out, then Olivia shouts, "Winged him!"

"Kai, he's coming over the top in fifteen seconds. You need to go. Now!" It's Mac.

"Thelma, I need transporter lock on the four of us on the western cliff."

Another shot, one that sounds much different, rings out and an instant later Alex says, "Tagged him. Transport the alien to space."

I repeat the order to Thelma, and a second later, she says, "Got it."

But as we all know, it takes a second or two for transporters to get a sufficient grip on their target then pull them away. I watch in horror as the alien comes sailing over the top of the cliff, twisting in the air to plant its landing. As it does, an arm whips around, pointed in my direction. The alien disappears before it lands, but it does so milliseconds too late. The barb it tossed rips into my right side, gutting me. Mind numbing pain radiates throughout my body, as the world seems to slow down. Then intense sadness settles in as I realize it's over. As my vision narrows, I realize that we may have killed the alien. But sadly, it claimed this soldier. I hope my mother forgives me…

CHAPTER 8: AFTERMATH

[09.10.2033] UNIVERSITY MEDICAL CENTER

Voices in the room wake me from a deep sleep. I open my eyes, not recognizing where I am, then see a woman in scrubs. She notices me and a huge smile blooms.

"Welcome back, Dr. Wimberly."

"Where am I?"

"University Medical Center of Southern Nevada in Las Vegas."

"How did I get here?"

"According to your chart, you were brought in at 10:17 last night, non-responsive, suffering severe anemia. You were given a liter of blood and put under observation. Have you suffered from anemia before?"

I stare at my caretaker, uncertain what's going on. The last thing I remember is being killed by a Dominion warrior. Was that just a dream?

I see her impatient look, then shake my head. "Umm, I was hit twice in Afghanistan, once bad enough that they had to give me blood."

She looks at me appraisingly, the way doctors do at times. "Your chart notes the scarring on your legs and abdomen, but it doesn't explain last night's low blood count."

To deflect, I ask, "Do you know how I got to Las Vegas?"

Again, the appraising look. "You don't remember?"

I shake my head no.

"The sold-out appearance?" she prods.

Again, I shake my head no.

"Dr. Kyle Wimberly? American hero? Leads the team that stopped the alien invasion?"

"I'm sorry, but I don't know what you're talking about."

"I'm sorry to hear that. You had a sold-out appearance at the Wynn last night. The TV and radio ads played non-stop for a week. You're a hero, Dr. Wimberly. It's all over the news. I'll schedule a consult with our neurologist. I'm sure he can sort this out. Meanwhile, your business partner, Justin Wicks, is in town and would like to speak with you. Would you like me to contact him?"

"Please."

...

There's a knock on the door.

"Come in."

The door opens, and Alex comes running in. "I didn't think I'd ever see you again." Tears flow as she hugs me.

Jill slips in next, followed by Justin, who closes the door.

Alex yields to Jill, who gives me a hug and a kiss on the cheek, then Justin puts out his hand to shake. "You scared the hell out of me, buddy."

"What happened?"

"No one realized you'd been hit until you arrived on the ship. You were gone at that point, but Thelma put your remains in stasis. She said Iknosan in your condition could be saved. But with To'Kana still down, she couldn't help you, so she put you in stasis, thinking it might keep your body viable for another week."

"The third time in the same day that she saved me," I whisper.

"To'Kana woke up the next day and spent the next three figuring out how to modify his equipment to repair a human. Three days in the tank and it was clear you were going to make it. Then we worried about how we were going to bring you back."

"Wait a minute, how long was I gone?"

"Eleven days. It's Saturday, September 10. You were hit two Wednesdays ago."

"Who knows I was killed?"

"The three of us, Aaron, and Denzel are the only ones that saw it with their own eyes. Mac, Ty, and Olivia have figured it out, but don't know it for sure."

"I told them," Alex confesses. "They know it for sure. We talked about it at great length."

Justin sighs. "It will eventually get out. We've kept it out of the press so far, even staged a big show for you last night at the Wynn to keep speculation down and get you into a proper hospital without blowing the secret."

"They gave me a transfusion."

"That was the one thing To'Kana couldn't make work. Several of us volunteered blood. Jill's Type O, she donated twice. But we tapped out the three people that knew what happened and had compatible blood. To'Kana kept you under until he thought your repairs would pass inspection by human doctors, then brought you here for blood."

I'm impressed by the effort Justin has taken to keep this quiet. But puzzled, why?

"What happened?" I ask with urgency.

Justin smiles and nods his head. "Audell."

"What did he do?"

"He wanted to report on the intruder problems we'd been having. The network wouldn't run it without more evidence, so he went out wandering at sunset, fully geared up for low-light video recording. He caught the scout ship landing, its destruction, which was fantastic by the way, your encounter with the Dominion warrior, and Ash's murder. Some of the footage came from cameras he'd planted on the sundecks. You made an incredible showing for yourself, by the way, and your mother's been ringing my phone off the hook because you haven't been answering yours."

"That's what gave you the cover to bring me here."

"Bingo," Justin replies.

"Has that moved anything on the government front?"

"Oh, trust me, it has, big time. A Congressional Investigation has been launched. I've testified. They're getting irritated about your lack of response and asked me about it. I told them you were off planet at the moment, which shut them up, at least until the evening news cycle. Audell has been politely asking. I think he's worried you're up to something big, and he's going to miss the scoop."

Justin's rant makes me laugh.

"But more seriously, Jace is preparing a legislative brief on steps forward to *counter the alien crisis*, as he puts it. Mac has been helping me put material together, but we're lost without you, Kyle."

"How much time do we have?"

"Jace wants something more real in two weeks, something we can take to committee the first week of October. The committee chair has asked for time on the House floor on November 1st."

"How do I get out of here?"

Justin smiles. "You have no idea how glad I am to hear those words. I'll see what I can do."

[09.11.2033] OFFICE, FCS HEADQUARTERS

True to his word, Justin arranged for me to be fully examined: poked, prodded, CAT scanned, memory tested, and full blood panels drawn. The only problem found was residual anemia, for which I was given medicine—a month's supply and a prescription to take to my local pharmacy. I'm impressed it all happened on a Saturday.

When I got home last night, I took off my shirt to examine the wound. The cosmetic work To'Kana's machine did is quite good; someone with a good eye might spot it, but the damage has been remarkably well hidden. But I can see and feel the difference. No more washboard abs on this body. I have little strength and zero stamina. The road back to my former self will be long and hard. Nonetheless, I'm alive and have a mountain of payback to pile on the next Dominion ship I see.

But how am I going to do that? Maybe it's time for me to reengage this conversation with To'Kana. "Thelma, any chance I could meet with Captain To'Kana today?"

"Kyle Wimberly, it is good to hear your voice again. Captain To'Kana can see you now. May I beam you aboard?"

I think it's funny how much of our lingo Thelma is picking up.

"Please beam me aboard."

IKNOSAN LEGACY SHIP

I open my eyes and find myself in the Lab again. It's curious that this is where they always bring me. I'll have to ask about it someday.

A door swooshing open attracts my attention to the far end of the room, where To'Kana shuffles in, looking much older than he did a few weeks ago.

"Kyle Wimberly, I was afraid we lost you."

"Thank you for putting me back together, sir."

His large, wise eyes focus on me for several seconds, then dart away. "I trust you've determined that you are not the same as you were before."

To'Kana's statement catches me off guard. "I've noticed that my abdominal muscles are much weaker."

The eyes are back, which worries me.

"We don't really have the ability to fabricate human tissue, which forced me to do things you might consider unnatural."

"Do I need to know this?"

To'Kana looks away. "In our society, it is illegal to do what I did for you without consent. From what I've learned of yours, American doctors have more flexibility when saving a life than ours do. I took that liberty, harvesting and transforming enough tissue to create a new kidney to replace the one you lost. Most of that tissue came from muscles, which I subsequently augmented to make up for the tissue harvested."

"Augmented?"

"You feel weaker, the energy draining from you quicker. Correct?"

"I do."

"That will change. I've made you much stronger, vastly improved your cardiovascular system, response time, and mental capacity."

"How?"

"Do you really want to know?"

I ponder the question for a second, then shake my head no. "How long before I feel better?"

"Within a month, you will feel like a new man."

"Then, thank you again. But that's not the reason I wanted to meet with you."

"No?" he says, clearly surprised.

"Recordings of what happened during the Dominion attack were on the news the next day. Public support for building a space fleet has skyrocketed. I don't know if the President has announced her support yet. But we are being pressed to propose a plan. Do you have one, or the outline of one?"

"Not as such. A thousand ships like this one, configured for war not research, with a five second jump recharge would be enough."

"Is that what the material requirements were based on?"

To'Kana looks perplexed for a second. "No."

In my mind, this seems like the oddest flip-flop. He came with a materials plan, but not a fleet plan?

He apparently notices my look. "Don't judge me, Kyle Wimberly. This mission was put together in less than a month. I was scrambling to get this ship ready while others were developing the plans."

"When did you learn of Earth?"

The eyes are back, and, as the silence drags out, I fear something is about to be revealed that I really don't want to know.

"This must stay between you and me."

I swallow.

Left index finger extended, he slowly rubs behind his stubby left ear. "Right here. Right behind the left ear."

He motions with his right hand, putting it out palm up towards me.

"Right here," he repeats, rubbing his left ear again.

As if in a trance, I do the same index-finger-behind-the-left-ear trick. Then my mouth drops open. There's a lump that wasn't there before.

"Don't worry," he says with compassion. "The swelling will go down."

"What did you do to me?"

"Every high-ranking member of our society has implants embedded in their skull. They vastly increase both mental capability and memory capacity. Knowledge packages can be downloaded that allow you to incorporate new skills and new languages overnight." He makes a poor approximation of snapping his fingers as he adds, "Just like that."

Instant learning, yet another miracle.

"Earth, the history we know of and the English language, was downloaded into my mind two weeks before departure. It's as real to me as anything else I know."

"That's how you figured out how to save me."

To'Kana nods. "The exobiological manipulation package."

"And you gave me one of those implants?"

"I did, and someday you will thank me for it."

The events of the last hour shock me to the core. I came up here hoping to get information I could use to mold congressional legislation. Instead, I've been brought up to speed on topics I could never have imagined could exist.

To'Kana puts out his hand and a cylindrical device appears. He stares at it for a moment, then one end glows.

"Here. It's yours if you want it—our alternatives for possible defenses against the Dominion. I didn't have room for it. You do. Transfer is almost instant. For me, integration takes six to twelve hours. For you, it'll probably take a little longer."

I pick up the cylinder, which reminds me of a lipstick tube. "Blue end against the ear?"

To'Kana nods. "Just press. You'll know when it's done."

I close my eyes and take a calming breath, then lift the cylinder up, wondering if this is a good idea. I'm sure the normal rational me would say no. But the me that's just been brought back from the dead can't wait to fill his head with alien wisdom. Positioning the cylinder above my new lump, I press it down.

There's a buzzing sensation that only lasts a second, then stops. I lower the cylinder, see the glow is gone, and hand it back to To'Kana.

"Good luck to you, Kyle Wimberly." With those words, he stands then walks back toward the door he entered from. It zips open for him, then swooshes shut once he's through.

As I sit there, staring at the now closed door, memories of alien spaceships pass through my mind as real as if I'd seen them myself.

I stand and close my eyes. "Thelma, please transport me down to my office."

"As you wish, sir."

OFFICE, FCS HEADQUARTERS

It's only one o'clock, but I'm beat and tempted to go back to bed. Nonetheless, I settle into my desk hoping to pull up knowledge of the various plans the Iknosan prepared.

Surprisingly, this topic feels very familiar, as if I'd been studying it for years. *Earth barely made the legacy list because it has no space capability.* The Iknosan part of me knows this to be true, which irritates the human part of me and makes the Iknosan part laugh. *Solid fuel rockets are a primitive means to gain orbit, but they play no role in modern space exploration.*

So why were we included?

Because we are rich in the rare materials needed.

I wonder if this is what To'Kana meant when he referred to an integration period for the new knowledge downloaded. Right now, I feel like I have two personalities arguing with each other.

With resolve not to argue with myself, I take a calming breath, wondering why the Iknosan think we have a lot of these rare materials.

Rare earth materials are created in two ways: by the s-process in asymptotic giant branch stars, or by supernova nucleosynthesis. They are rare throughout the galaxy. Earth formed during a period of intense supernova activity in its local region and was gifted with an unusually high quantity, most of which are located deep in the crust. Humans are unlikely to extract them in a useful time frame, which opens the door for us to collect them and help a more advanced species.

My mouth drops open in shock. The Iknosan planned to steal our rare materials and send them to someone else!

Only if humans did not mount a defense.

A knock on my office door brings me back to the moment. It's Audell. My mind reels. What is he doing inside the building on a Sunday?

"Welcome back, Kyle. I'm glad to see you are well. Have a minute?"

"Sure, why are you here on a Sunday?"

"I've added a ton of cameras around the building to capture video of intruders. Gabe gave me a keycard, so I could get in after hours to check them. I signed a confidentiality agreement."

Maybe it's the paranoia brought on by the Iknosan knowledge, but a non-employee in the building, unsupervised on the weekend, bothers me.

"Anyway, I was hoping to get an interview with you about the Dominion attack. You actually saw these guys up close. I was a couple thousand feet away and the fixed camera stills are not that clear."

Mention of the Dominion warriors makes me shudder even more than the memory of their scouting robot.

"Do you know what happened to the robot?"

"I know nothing about a robot," Audell replies.

I really don't want to give an interview in my current state, but the recent memory—*if humans do not mount a defense*—floods back and I reluctantly say yes.

Audell smiles. "I set my gear up in the conference room."

CONFERENCE ROOM, FCS HEADQUARTERS

"Kyle, you are one of the few people who have seen someone from the Dominion up close. Can you share your impressions with us?"

"My high-level impression is that they are fearsome warriors. They're huge, agile, and move incredibly fast. They can also throw their weapons fast and accurately. If they were pitching baseballs, every player would strike out."

"An analysis of our recording puts the estimated speed of the spurs they threw at you to be a hundred eighty miles an hour, plus or minus twenty. Does that sound right to you?"

I shrug. "I don't have enough experience with things being thrown at me to give a number, but two hundred sounds right. It blew the little wooden table outside my lab to splinters with a single hit."

"Quite a few experts have studied the images we captured and made numerous speculations. Consensus is that when they stand straight-up, they're ten feet tall; with arms extended above their heads, fifteen feet. What do you think?"

"Rings true to me."

"When squatting down to jump, expert consensus is that they are only four or five feet tall."

"That also makes sense to me. They remind me of spiders the way their legs fold up."

"What can you tell us about their arms?"

"There are four of them, maybe five or six feet long. They are not jointed the way ours are. I suspect they are more like a monkey's tail or an elephant's trunk, because they smoothly bend. They have a suction cup shaped pad and opposing thumb at the end of their arm that serves as a hand, and when they throw, the arm whips around. It's a terrifying thing to see."

"Did you know you could use your shields as a weapon? Or was that something you came up with on the fly?"

"While testing the shields, we accidentally killed a rabbit—a desert cottontail. It hopped through as we turned the shields on. We filed the issue as something our safety procedures would need to address. When we learned the Dominion Scout Ship was inbound, we set up shields where we thought the ship might land. We didn't know if it would work. But it was something."

"Several critics have complained that you attacked and killed these aliens before even speaking with them. How do you answer this concern?"

"This incident was part of a larger attack initiated by the Dominion. They attacked the Iknosan ship in orbit. They attacked three other Iknosan assets in orbit. Then they blew up the electrical substation on my property, taking our solar operation off the grid. We speculated they were going to attack another extremely valuable asset housed in our headquarters building. Knowing we could not stop them once they landed, we laid a trap, which they sprung. The only loss of life occurred when they attacked with lethal force."

"What happened to the one that escaped?"

"We captured it and transported it off Earth."

"Where did you send it?"

"I'm not at liberty to talk about that."

"Do you think we could ever exist in peace with them?"

"The Iknosan say no. I'm an optimistic person who would like the answer to be yes. But we're clearly starting from a dangerous place. They destroyed the Iknosan home world and the vast majority of their people, and on their first visit to Earth, they attacked six of our assets before they were stopped. Their track record has been to destroy every civilization they encounter. So my guess is that someone would need to stop them before they will come to the table."

"Kyle, thank you for your time today."

"My pleasure, Audell."

Once the lights are out, Audell asks, "You were injured, weren't you?"

I shake my head. "Sorry, but I'm not answering that question."

Audell nods. "I hope your recovery goes well. The Earth needs you, Kyle."

[09.16.2033] TRAIL

Sunday's trip up to To'Kana's ship tired me out. The interview with Audell finished the job. Shortly after, I went back to my cabin and fell asleep. I didn't wake until nearly dawn, just in time for the morning run. That was my first day back, and everyone was excited to see me. I'm like a hero now for having used the shielding as a weapon that killed a Dominion ship and a Dominion warrior.

The run started out ok, but, by mile marker one, I was done. Mac walked back with me.

Today, my fifth day back on the trail, I'm feeling strong, really strong. I doubt the stamina's there yet, but I think I'm going to be able to complete the course today.

As I jog out to the trailhead, the ten or so people milling around cheer for me. It's a gratifying reception, but I wonder how that would change if they knew *what* I was now.

"Think you'll make it all the way today?" Mac asks as he comes up alongside.

"Think so."

"How's the work coming?"

Although asked innocently enough, work has become a loaded topic. The Dominion totaled our substation. The new generators were their target, but they blew up everything: generators, step-up transformers, control room, even the first tower in our transmission line. So, even though our wells are all functioning, we are delivering no power and the company is bleeding cash. Worse, with me offline for two weeks, the recovery effort isn't very far along. The rest of the guys are blindly confident that I'll get it fixed. Mac knows all my effort is going into the new fleet design.

"We have business continuity insurance. Their first settlement proposal is due today. I expect to hear from our lawyers this afternoon."

Mac glances at me. "We *are* going to fix it, right?"

"We're going to fix it."

"If you say so, boss."

Yeah, that's the sentiment I'm running into. The people here have largely given up a normal life to come live in the desert. Full Cycle Solar is more than just a job to them. It's their family, their mission in life. But the alien invasion has taken my eye off the ball, and everyone knows it.

OFFICE, FCS HEADQUARTERS

Mac's five-word inquisition reminds me that I have people here on the ground that are at risk. One has already been killed. I survived by being converted into something not wholly human.

As much as I want to rail against the Dominion, I realize my first priority is here. I have people to protect, property to secure, but I can't lose sight of the fact that the Dominion is here, and they represent a threat to all mankind. So, which do I choose? My people here? Or the defense of all humanity?

It's a stupid question. I can't choose one or the other, I need to figure out how to serve both. The insight brings me clarity. I need to serve the people here. Not to the very last detail, but enough that others can drive the work to conclusion. My special gift, the task that only I can fulfill, is the fleet.

With renewed energy, I take to the phones. I need to get the transmission line back up, new step-up transformers installed, and power flowing back into the grid. I'll give it one day, max. Then turn back to the defense of Earth.

I pick-up my phone, and dial Breechelle Patterson's number. We need to get the transmission tower rebuilt. We need new step-up transformers delivered. Top of the line, first class, a new control room too. We'll pay whatever it takes. We need to get back online. Period.

Her response surprises me. "We have everything queued, Kyle. We were just waiting for the word."

Life holds numerous surprises. This is one of them. In our previous encounter, Breechelle was less than supportive. But now, faced with the loss of a significant power source, she's more than happy to help.

I agree to her charges, ask her to coordinate with Mac, then request expedited installation.

To my surprise, she says teams will be here on Tuesday. One day job. Full Cycle Solar is responsible for connecting the power. We do the verbal handshake, then the line drops. Who could ever have believed it would be this easy. Maybe celebrity is worth its cost.

Next on my list is the fleet manifest. As much as I want to get it perfect, I need to get as much down on paper as possible. It won't be exact, but that doesn't matter. Others will ultimately fix it. I'll let them argue about where the commas go.

[09.30.2033] HOUSE OFFICE BUILDING, WASHINGTON, DC

Two weeks have passed since my call with Breechelle, and the mood around the company has totally changed. Our solar operations are completely back online.

The staff is rejoicing, which I'd expected. But there's more to it than just that. It's like new life has been injected into the company. All our existing wells are back online. Two twenty-megawatt generators are online. And we have permission to add eighteen more over the coming year. I've celebrated by giving Mac the lead on it all.

Justin, who's been on a crusade since my injury, has secured hearing times for me with both the House and Senate. He cautions that my appearances are well past the requested dates and recommends that I come clean on my injuries. I'm not planning to volunteer that information. Dr. Jekyll has already had his way with me; I'd prefer to meet Mr. Hyde bearing gifts, not making excuses. The analogy makes him laugh. But he strongly agrees with the principle.

...

I was ushered in a half hour ago and listened patiently to the long meeting introduction with its listing of HB numbers to which this meeting pertains. Then I was sworn in as the meeting's sole witness. The committee chair made several more introductory remarks and imposed a ten-minute max for each member to question me. Thirty-two members, ten minutes each. I'm going to be stuck here for over five hours. Argh.

Finally, he turns the floor over to the member from Arizona to ask the first question.

"Dr. Wimberly, when did you first learn an alien attack on the state of Arizona was imminent?"

"About an hour before they destroyed our substation."

"How did you find this out?"

I start by telling him about the circumstances that led up to being transported into the ocean and the two guys that rescued me. A minute in, he interrupts.

"I only have ten minutes. Can we cut to the chase?"

I cut straight to the part where Thelma asked me about the sensor anomalies and the scout ship decloaking.

"Did you contact anyone in the government to warn them that hostile aliens were about to attack Earth?"

"No sir, I did not. I had no idea who to call, little faith they would believe me, and barely enough time to protect my property."

"So your first thought was to destroy the alien ship?"

"I doubt it was my first thought, but it was the only one I came up with that could be implemented in time."

"Do you think you have the right to destroy an alien spaceship?"

"I think I have the right to defend myself. I also think I did the world a huge favor by stopping these spies from reporting our lack of preparedness for the invasion they are planning."

"Do you think it is appropriate for you to control technology critical to our national security?"

I came prepared for a lot. But this question challenges my loyalty. So many friends died in Afghanistan, the sweet Hawaiian kid that gave me my name... And this bastard dares to question my loyalty!

"I control no technology," I answer with as much humility as I can muster. "It all belongs to a species that knows this enemy. At the end of the day, I don't really know this enemy, only their actions."

I pause to collect my breath. "Is it your assertion that an alien species that takes megawatts of power off the grid is a friend of our world? Is it your assertion that people who kill innocents, like those on my staff, should have priority over those of us trying to make the Earth a habitable place?"

OK, kind of went over the edge there, but might as well continue. "My contention is no. Aliens have no standing. If they want to gift us with technology, then great. But if they want to kill us, maim us, then no. They have no standing."

The representative in question shakes his head. "Sergeant Wimberly..." More head shaking. "What could you possibly know of the priorities of our nation? Are you in any position to make policy?"

I hold my retort, doubting it will help my case. Shaking my head, I answer, "Aliens are on their way. Embrace the defenses we've been given, otherwise accept the destruction that will follow." I bow my head, then sit back, waiting for the retorts that will come. But one thing is clear in my mind. If we are going to win this war, then this clown is totally irrelevant.

After six hours with no breaks, I'm dismissed. Not all the questioners were as nasty as the first. In fact, several were friendly, thanking me for my service in the Army and my efforts to build a clean energy economy. My takeaway from the meeting is that maybe a third of the members consider it possible we may be facing an alien invasion. Half or more are worried about a civilian organization having weapons more advanced than the government. I mostly agree with them and am eager to get our weapons in the hands of the military.

"Kyle," my lawyer says as we are exiting. "Subpoenas were forwarded to me from the Senate Committee for Homeland Security and the House Defense Committee while you were testifying today. You're being called in again next week."

Great, just great.

[10.03.2033] PENTAGON, ARLINGTON, VIRGINIA

I open my eyes and see that Justin and I are surrounded by a tight ring of armed guards, all with their backs to us. Thelma had assured me that a place had been blocked off where we could transport in safely. I was expecting it to be roped off, not enclosed in a human shield.

A moment later, the guards break formation, and Jace enters the circle with us, all smiles. "Word got out you would transport in. The lobby's packed. So…" He points at the guards.

Then, looking directly at me, he says, "Justin has been here several times before. This is your first, right? First official visit anyway."

I nod. "It is."

"Good. We don't have records of a previous visit. I've done all the paperwork ahead of time. Just need you to sign a couple documents, then have a picture taken, then we can go in. This way."

We pass through a scanner and are met by someone who takes me into a small office, where I show my driver's license, put an electronic signature on a handful of documents, and have my picture taken.

"That's it, you're done. Have a productive day, Dr. Wimberly."

Jace escorts us to a conference room where seven others have already gathered. After introductions and a quick review of the day's agenda, Jace turns the meeting over to me.

"I have three key topics I'd like to discuss today: our enemy and their capabilities, the force we'll need to overcome them, and a possible ship design. There are many possibilities for the ship. I've chosen one for a high-level review today."

"Will there be a discussion of alternatives?" team leader Morgan Owen asks.

"As much as you like. The ship I have in this presentation is a superset of Iknosan capability, showing the entire range of options for which they will transfer the technology. Looking at this alternative should open the door to any other you'd like to discuss."

Morgan nods an acknowledgment.

"Let me start with the Dominion." One of the Iknosan holographic projectors appears on the table, then projects a three-dimensional view of the warrior that attacked me. The room's ceiling is too low to show it at scale, so I add an image of myself scaled correspondingly.

Everyone around the table shows some sign of disgust.

"This is our enemy. It is huge, fast, and deadly."

I explain its gross anatomy, then play a simulation of its attack on me at the headquarters building.

"You're lucky to have escaped alive," weapons specialist Max Harris says. "Any idea where the spur it threw at you came from?"

"Not conclusive, but we think they may grow them."

"Evidence?"

I pull up two pictures, before and after images of the hand that threw the first spur, the one that hit the shield.

"Note the fingernail like surfaces on the back of its hand in the before image, and the spot where one is missing in the afterimage."

"Poor picture quality," Max comments. "Not conclusive, but certainly supports the hypothesis. What other evidence do you have to support your speed conclusions?"

I pull up a satellite image of the dry riverbed leading into the box canyon. "I got this from Google Earth. You can see the measurement from the edge of the screen to the entrance to the box canyon is three miles. Now let me play back our satellite imaging of it running down that riverbed."

The playback starts, and a moment later, April McDonald, the team's intelligence analyst, observes, "It's hopping. The bounds are what? A hundred feet?"

"Around there, maybe a little less," I reply.

Team leader Morgan Owen asks, "How long does it take him?"

I jump the recording to the entrance to the box canyon and pause it there. "Four and a half minutes. Forty miles an hour."

"Jesus," Max says. "You can't run a jeep down that wash as fast, can you?"

I shake my head no. "And one last thing."

I put up a picture of the west wall of the box canyon. "The cliff face is nearly a hundred feet high. It has plenty of holds. I'm not a good enough climber to do it, but several of our employees are. I have sensor readings of it climbing that wall. Poor image quality, but it should get the idea across. Watch as it jumps up onto the wall."

I play the last part of the recording. "Look how fast it moves."

Everyone watches, mesmerized.

"At twenty-eight seconds, it comes up over the wall. I know, because I was there."

"It disappears," April notes.

"Just as it came over the top, we got transporter lock and pulled it away."

A shiver passes through me at the memory.

"You must have big ones," Max comments. "It almost got you twice."

I nod. "Almost."

A half hour later, when the discussion of the Dominion and their ships is finished, Morgan declares a five-minute break.

As the room empties, Justin comes over. "I'm surprised you showed the clip of the beast coming up and over the cliff."

"They need to know what they're up against."

"Agreed, but still."

Justin shifts a bit, and I can tell he's about to give me some feedback. "We need to tighten up the discussion of the Dominion ships a bit. You've got pictures and size estimates, anecdotal evidence of their power, but we need something like you showed in the first segment: battle scenes, something. I'm concerned they're going to walk away from this presentation very impressed, but not sold."

"Agreed. I need to do a deep dive into whatever recordings To'Kana has of previous space battles with them."

"We should raise that at the end, so they know we are working on it," Justin concludes.

As fate would have it, the first question asked when the meeting resumes is the one Justin anticipated. I promise to have something for them at the next meeting, then go on to the next topic.

"The Iknosan battle plan for their final conflict with the Dominion assumed they would have thirty of their battlecruisers per Dominion dreadnaught. They could only muster a little over nine hundred versus the Dominion's one hundred and they got slaughtered."

"To be clear," Morgan says, "They needed three thousand ships and only had nine hundred?"

"Correct."

"Does that mean we need three thousand?"

"No. They developed weapons near the end that were only deployed on ten ships. Those ten ships made suicide runs against five dreadnaughts and disabled them. They had plans that would have made those ten ships defensible, but could not upgrade the ships in time."

"The new order of force estimate?" Morgan asks.

"They say five. I say half that."

Morgan lifts an eyebrow. "I'm interested in hearing that story and your justification."

"Then let's begin." I pop up an image of my flying wedge. "You probably recognize this from the demo I gave the Secretary."

Several heads nod.

"It is like their battlecruisers, just miniature. This is the ship they recommend."

A photo quality drawing, rendered from a three-dimensional model, pops up. Technically, the shape is called an isosceles trapezoid. I think of it as being a triangle with its nose sawed off.

"The ship is three hundred meters long. At the bow, it is thirty meters wide and at the stern, fifty. From top to bottom, it is twenty meters. Internally, the sides of the ship, which I think of as its wings, are engineering spaces. They contain the ship's power sources and capacitor banks. The forward half of the center portion of the ship holds the crew spaces, organized as four decks. The aft portion of the ship holds three giant ion drive units."

"Armaments?" Max asks.

"Fore and aft facing railguns on each side. Energy weapons in crawl spaces above and below with a total of forty-six emitters. Defensive weapons include shields and jump drive."

"Earlier you said two innovations. What are they?" assistant team leader, Rebecca Cox asks.

"The first is a new munition for the rail guns that will knock down the Dominion shields. The second is a propulsion system known as a jump drive. It allows you to move instantly from place to place, so that you can pop in, take a shot, then pop out without giving your opponent time to acquire a target."

"How certain are you it works?" Rebecca asks.

"The science is sound and the ship in earth orbit used their jump drive to get here. The ten ships that sacrificed themselves jumped in, deployed their shield killers, then rammed the Dominion ships."

"Why didn't they jump out?"

"They had a five-minute recharge cycle. They couldn't jump out."

Conversation goes on for a while, then Morgan asks what's on everyone's mind. "How do we build these things? What help are the Iknosan offering?"

"Justin and I are forming a company that can supply all the components and critical materials. We can also offer transport services to get things into space at little expense. We propose to work with a defense contractor who will have the prime responsibility for building the hull."

"Have you spoken with anyone yet?" Jace asks, speaking up for the first time in this meeting.

I look at Justin.

"Off the record, yes. But there's no program or request for proposal (RFP) open, so we get interest but no follow up."

Morgan raises his hand, as if to stop the discussion. "That's my team's job. You have the secretary's ear and the president's interest. This team's job is to figure out what the proof-of-concept RFP looks like. You've done a decent job of casting light on the issue." He pauses, head cocked, as if a new thought has just occurred.

"Dr. Wimberly, would it be viable to do something smaller, a scale model, so to speak? Something that proves the concepts without us having to build a space dock first."

My first instinct is to say no, then I remember To'Kana's words the day we met. *The replicators aboard my ship can replicate all the shuttle's components, including its hull plating and superstructure.*

"Maybe. It would only hold a couple of people, not a full crew. We could scale back the weapons. I'm not sure about the jump drive. But maybe. Can I get back to you?"

"Certainly." He turns to Justin. "I think I have what I need in order to frame an RFP. OK, if I send you a draft for comment?"

Justin smiles. "Please."

IKNOSAN LEGACY SHIP

Instead of transporting home after the meeting, I came up to the ship to talk with the captain.

"Build a modified shuttle with jump drive and weapons…" The words just hang there as he gets a faraway look in his eyes. He stays that way for a while, then he says, "I think we can. It would be dangerous, but I think we can."

"What would be dangerous?"

"There's not enough room for both the jump drive and the ion drive. So, if you jumped into deep space, you could end up stranded there because the grav-drive wouldn't be able to generate enough thrust to change course. But you could jump to Jupiter or Saturn and back. I can see how that would be an interesting demo."

A second later, my tablet vibrates.

"I just sent you the pattern. You can view it on your replicator. This is an exciting development."

CHAPTER 9: PROOF OF CONCEPT

[10.04.2033] SENATE OFFICE BUILDING

Today is my second day of testimony. This time it is the Senate Committee on Homeland Security. Thankfully, there are only fourteen members, each of which has been given fifteen minutes today. The initial questioning goes pretty much the same as last week.

Did I alert any authorities? Do I have the right to battle aliens? Do I have the right to develop advanced weaponry except by contract with the government?

And the answers were the same. No, I did not know who to alert. I have the right to defend myself and my property. And I'm not developing weapons; I'm simply delivering prototypes created by aliens that the Department of Defense has asked me to demonstrate.

They give me some push back on the last one. "Do you have evidence that you were asked?"

"No, I have no official requests."

"Nothing on forms..." he lists a series of acronyms, none of which I've ever heard of.

"No, sir. Verbal requests only."

Now, coming up on the third hour of interrogation, the senator from Virginia hands me a question I didn't expect.

"Dr. Wimberly, you stand to make a lot of money if we decide to build out this fleet of spaceships you are proposing. What are you giving to the Iknosan in exchange?"

I wonder how this senator knows that I have proposed a fleet and why that's even a valid question for this committee to ask. He's from Virginia, where the Pentagon is, and the biggest defense contractors are headquartered. This question feels like a gotcha question. Is he trying to trip me up because I'd be competing with contractors in his state?

"Dr. Wimberly?"

"Apologies, sir. The Iknosan have come bearing gifts. They've asked for nothing. The short answer is that I am giving them nothing other than my attention at the moment. Nothing more than that has been asked or given."

He looks at me intensely, then asks, "Do you expect us to believe that?"

I shrug. "I don't presume to guess what you will or will not believe. I'm simply answering the question asked as accurately as I can."

"I yield my time," he announces.

IKNOSAN LEGACY SHIP

These days, with all the trips to Washington, I travel by transporter. Commercial plane travel would put me in the DC area all week. Even private couldn't get me back and forth fast enough to merit consideration. Thelma, on the other hand, will get me from here to there in minutes. So, as soon after the meeting as I can find a private spot, I transport. Today, it was the men's room, a stall with the door locked. Not proud of it, but sometimes you need to do what you need to do.

I open my eyes and see the captain waiting for me. "I watched the hearing today."

The words surprise me.

"You know our sensors can defeat any human security protocol," he says, hands outstretched in a very human expression.

He apparently notices my surprise and a somber expression replaces the previously welcoming one.

"It's hard, you know."

"I'm not sure I do?"

To'Kana stares at me, his large empathetic eyes showing what I presume to be disappointment.

"Kyle, my people were slaughtered. My presence here is their dying gift—a gift of hope to a galaxy being taken over by non-humanoids, as you would call them. You and I are more alike than different, the product of one of three master species that seeded the galaxy. Only two lines remain. Humanoids like you and me, and arachnoids like the Xeric."

"You've used the word Xeric before, but I don't know what it means."

"The Xeric are an arachnoid species. Unlike humanoids, the arachnoids have collaborated, formed a union that they call the Dominion. If our peoples cannot form a similar union, then they will soon become extinct in our galaxy."

To'Kana's words stun me. I've been fighting the stigma of working with aliens for two months now. Two of the longest months of my life.

"The senator from Virginia questioned our collaboration today…"

To'Kana lets the words hang, and I wait for the bombshell that is about to be dropped.

"I wonder how much arachnoid blood runs through his veins."

As I think my brain is about to explode, To'Kana continues. "The Dominion has developed viruses that thin the humanoid stock. We have developed something similar, a poison that kills those that carry arachnoid genes. A tiny amount of it is in our air handling system. If a Dominion warrior came aboard, it would die within an hour. You are free of arachnoid genes. I tested you on the first day. But if a human with a significant concentration of arachnoid genes came aboard, they would suffer a slow and painful death."

I struggle to breathe.

"I see my words offend you. My apologies. Let us forget this conversation."

More than once in Afghanistan, I'd developed relationships with locals, who sometimes offered reprehensible options to current problems. With all the other crap that happened over there, I grew somewhat immune. But it's been eleven years now, and the immunity seems to have waned.

"I was hoping to speak with you about a different matter."

"What was it you wanted to discuss?"

"I need more on the Dominion's strengths and weaknesses. How is it they rolled over you so easily?"

"I have very few reports on the imbalance. Few who met the Dominion survived to deliver their data."

"What about the final encounter? Was any of that data streamed to you?"

"All of it. There has been no one to analyze it, but I have it all. I can send it to you if you'd like."

"Please."

"Thelma will send you everything we have, although it could take some time to translate into English."

"Send me video and instrumentation data first. I'll filter through it and prioritize encounters for translation."

To'Kana nods. "It will be as you ask."

There's silence for a moment, then To'Kana brightens.

"Thelma has prepared the first tranche of video and instrumentation data. Would you prefer to view it here or at one of your facilities?"

"Back at headquarters."

"It is done. One thing you should know before you view this data. It is the complete record of the final battle, the one in which we tested the legacy technology. The recording is over twelve hours long and nearly a thousand channels wide. Each channel shows the bridge camera and the contents of its display panels. They are all synchronized. Your projector can only play ten channels at a time. It also has audio translation and captioning. You can choose what you want to view and what you want to hear."

With that, To'Kana stands. I follow suit, then I ask Thelma to transport me home.

[10.05.2033] LAB, FCS HEADQUARTERS

I've assembled my crew—Mac, Alex, and Ty—in the lab, because it's the largest room we have on site, sufficient for displaying ten channels simultaneously. After about fifteen minutes of experimenting with the projector, I decide to start by viewing the flagship. Five minutes later, I fast forward until a Dominion ship drops from FTL, then rewind so we can see it drop and the crews' reaction.

With playback paused, I walk over to the holoprojection and touch the person who appears to be in charge. The projector says, "Admiral Ashok Keren."

"That's cool," Ty says. "It's interactive."

"Projector. Play."

The image comes back to life, and I take in the admiral's intensity as Dominion ships drop from FTL one after another.

The first ship changes course, heading straight for the admiral. When the tenth ship drops and changes course to follow the others, the admiral stands. "Prepare to engage."

As more ships drop, Alex says, "Look at him. He already knows there are too many. But he's still holding his formation."

I step closer to the holoprojection of the main tactical display and note the conical formation in which the admiral has arrayed his fleet. By all appearances, the cone is wide enough to intercept the entire Dominion armada. Numbers at the base of the display indicate that the captain will intercept the Dominion fifty million kilometers from the Iknosan home world.

"Impressive," Mac says with awe. "There must be a thousand ships in that formation."

Alex points to a number on the display. "Nine hundred twenty."

"I thought To'Kana said they had nearly a thousand ships," Ty says.

Alex points to some stragglers approaching the formation from the side. "More are arriving."

"He told me that a dozen or so did not get there before the fleet was decimated."

"Comms." The admiral orders, drawing our attention back to the holoprojection. "Get me Captain Soman."

"Connecting Captain Soman," the communications officer acknowledges.

Another holoprojection window opens next to the first. The bridge camera shows Soman sitting in the captain's chair, his eyes locked onto the incoming Dominion fleet.

The tactical map in the instrumentation panel shows his ten-ship task force positioned one-hundred million kilometers above the system's orbital plane.

"He has an unobstructed view of the inbound enemy," Ty notes.

"These are the experimental ships, the ones with the jump drives and shield killing weapons. If they'd had a hundred of these, they might have prevailed," I add.

"Admiral, I have Captain Soman on the comm," the communications officer announces.

"Put him on the main viewscreen."

A moment later, Soman's image appears on the admiral's view screen.

"I presume you share my assessment of our situation," the admiral says without preamble.

"I count over fifty enemy ships inbound. That makes testing the new technology our top priority. If it works, Operation Legacy may yet succeed," the captain replies.

The admiral nods in agreement. "You may proceed."

Captain Soman stands and puts a fist to his chest. "To the end, we serve."

"To the end," Admiral Keren replies, returning the salute.

Mac, who's standing next to me, mutters, "This is like one of the old World War II movies, only this is real."

I'm moved by the exchange and the sacrifice these people are about to make. Even more moved when I remember we are the beneficiaries of their sacrifice.

Several minutes pass as the task force maneuvers into jump position.

"They're about to go," Alex says, informed no doubt by her assassin instincts. "A hundred million kilometers in an instant," she muses. "My bullets usually take a full second."

"Engage jump on my mark," Soman says.

Alex points. "There's his timer. Three, two, one..."

"Mark!" Soman orders.

On the admiral's screen, the task force disappears.

"The ships have jumped," his tactical officer announces.

The image on Captain Soman's main view screen dissolves into noise for an instant, then a Dominion ship appears directly in his path.

"Fire the shield killing weapon!" he orders.

Again, Alex points. "Ten seconds to impact. They're going to ram the Dominion ship!"

"Enemy shields are down!" the tactical officer exclaims.

"Fire lasers," Soman orders.

"There." Alex points.

A small red glow appears on the hull of the Dominion ship directly in front of us. A second later, a hole appears as liquid metal sprays out of the enemy ship. Then I watch in horror as we seem to plunge into the hole and the holoprojection frame disappears.

"Oh, my God," Ty yells.

Looking back at Admiral Keren's frame, I see five of the Dominion ships shudder under the impact of the collisions, remnants of two Iknosan ships poking out the side of each. Atmosphere venting from the ships adds to the large debris field spreading through the front of the Dominion formation.

The sound of fist hitting chair arm draws my attention to the admiral. "Not a single ship killed!"

The female captain of the ship puts her hand over the Admiral's. "Those ships will never fly again. Evacuation is already beginning. The Dominion will destroy these ships once the evacuations are complete. It is their way."

The admiral nods, then looks toward the comms officer. "Order the departure of the Legacy fleet."

I pause playback, shaken by what I've just witnessed. "Let's debrief on what we just saw."

KITCHEN, HEADQUARTERS BUILDING

To further break the tension, we reconvene upstairs around the table in the kitchen, the familiar surrounding a pleasant distraction from the drama of the last few minutes.

The first round of comments is all about the courage and dedication of the Iknosan crews who sacrificed themselves. Ty is the first to make a tactical observation.

"The task force ships showed up ten seconds before impact. A second later, they launched their shield killing weapon. The shield fell on the fifth second. An instant later, the lasers fired, then impact. Ten seconds, total."

"Your point?" I ask.

"Remember that time in the mess tent up in Kandahar? Sirens sounding? Then the Gatling guns in the anti-missile defense system rattling?" Ty pauses. "Within five seconds of the inbound ordinance showing up on radar, the defense system engaged."

"It wasn't five seconds," Alex snipes. "And we were expecting an attack."

"You saying the Dominion weren't expecting someone to shoot at them?" Ty complains. "My point is the Dominion's reaction time isn't that great."

Alex opens her mouth, but I put up a hand. "Just looking for observations, not conclusions."

Mac whispers something to Alex, who goes next. "Mac and I both noted the laser impact. According to the display, their laser output is something like a thousand terawatts. I presume that's pulsed, but numbers that high tend to just punch through things, the momentum of the photons so high that they erode away material faster than it can heat."

I see Ty nod his head.

"My takeaway," Alex continues, "Is that the hull must be thick and have huge thermal conductivity to have created a visible heat ring."

Mac finishes the thought for her. "That softened the hull enough for the Iknosan ships to penetrate as far as they did."

"Interesting observation. I'll ask To'Kana about it. What else?"

"Back to the attack," Ty pipes up again. "It consisted of three things: jump, shield collapse, weakening the hull, and impact."

"That's four things," Alex corrects.

"Your point?" I ask.

"They did not need the ship for any of those."

"Explain."

"It was all ballistic." Ty motions with his hands, as if conjuring up an image via his machinations. "Imagine an inertial bomb, three tons of spent uranium, with a jump drive and a nose projectile. A ship carrying the bomb lines it up on the target." More hand motions. "Then it releases the bomb." He makes a whooshing sound. "Once free, the bomb jumps, arrives, ejects its shield killer, fires its single shot laser, then hits. Same result, probably better because of the bomb's shape. The bomb gets destroyed, but the ship that dropped it doesn't."

"Good observation. Once the ship was lined up, everything that happened was ballistic."

"Maybe," Mac comes back. "We don't know what goes on inside the jump drive."

"Something else to ask To'Kana. Anyone have anything else?"

When no one offers anything, I make sure the notes I'd tapped out are saved. Then we head back for the next round of viewing.

LAB, FCS HEADQUARTERS

With eleven more hours of data on a thousand channels, we go with a divide-and-conquer strategy. I claim Admiral Keren. Ty claims task force leader Asmok Norval, Mac task force leader Anil Batakor, Alex Captain Banasai.

Over the next hour, the Dominion takes apart the Iknosan fleet, which outnumbers them ten to one. Three hours in, when the die is inextricably cast, I call a break.

"Observations?"

Ty shakes his head. "A slaughter, the Iknosan were totally outclassed."

Mac weighs in with the same conclusion.

"Alex?"

She eyes me. "A slaughter, but maybe not."

"Say more."

"Give me control?"

I look at Alex, wondering what's up with her, and get the strangest vibe. "Sure."

I pass her control and a moment later, playback is reset to 1:57:12, exactly.

"Watch this."

Captain Bonasai appears on the screen. "Deploy all shuttles!"

This comes as a surprise to me. To'Kana has a shuttle that I've become very familiar with. None of the ships we've been tracking have deployed one. Is it because Bonasai has more of them than the others? Or is it because he's doing something different?

One-by-one the shuttles depart, each on a different vector, stopping maybe a hundred kilometers from their mother ship, then assuming a parallel course.

I look at Alex. There's the slightest smile, then I catch the excitement in her eye. Seconds later, the Dominion ship, the one Captain Bonasai was tracking, fires multiple shots. One hits, but does not disable Bonasai's ship. Another hits one of his shuttles, disabling it with a grazing shot.

The rest of the shuttles dart out on seemingly random courses.

A moment later, I get it. The shuttles' movements were orthogonal to their previous trajectories.

As I watch, each shuttle turns toward their enemy and fires its comparatively weak laser. The precision of the shots is stunning. All hit in a tight circle. A full fifteen seconds later, the Dominion returns fire, the energy beam originating from within the tight circle still being pounded by the shuttles. The energy beam hits one of the shuttles, destroying it.

Alex freezes playback.

"What?" I ask, shocked that the tension of the moment is being disrupted.

She points to the source of the Dominion energy-beam. The surrounding area is glowing red. "They apparently need to drop their shields to fire their weapons. Other spots on the ship still seem to have their shields up." She points to a spot where the laser from another ship is being repelled by the shields. "That may have something to do with their slow response times. Watch what happens next." She points to the bridge cam window, then resumes playback.

"Fire!" Captain Bonasai orders.

The ship's laser reaches out, hitting the spot on the Dominion ship where its energy beam originated.

"We're getting feedback!" the tactical officer shouts.

A moment later, an enormous explosion carves a deep hole in the Dominion ship. A second after, the feed from Captain Bonasai's bridge cam whites out, then the line drops.

"Bonasai damaged the Dominion ship, but lost his own," Alex concludes. "I'm also guessing word of this did not get out to the fleet.

Ten ships playing this game could take down a Dominion ship, assuming they each had six shuttles."

"Interesting," Ty pipes up. "But how does that help us? We have shield killers."

"Point taken," Alex admits. "But that still leaves us with a couple of other observations."

Not sure which observations she's referring to, I say, "Go on."

"The Dominion took two shots at Bonasai's ship. Both hit, the second one killed him. They had six shuttles to shoot at. In total, they took eleven shots at the shuttles. Two of them hit, one grazing a shuttle, the other killing its target."

Mac nods his head. "Their targeting isn't that good. The Iknosan nailed that energy weapon from a distance at which the Dominion's hit rate was really low."

"And their weapons must have a long recharge cycle. They only got off thirteen shots in an hour," Ty adds.

As the words and comments go back and forth, I envision a battle in which numerous small ships swarm around the giant Dominion ships, jumping in near the limit of the Dominion's targeting range, landing a shot, then jumping out. Maybe multiple ships, jumping in formation, landing hull-heating shots before the kill shot.

"Good work, Alex. Let's see what else we can find."

...

After another three-hour stretch, I call a break to debrief. Ty is the first to offer an observation. "I used a different strategy this round, focusing more on the movement of battle than individual ship engagements. What surprised me is how good a job the Dominion did of keeping the battle in front of them. I've not seen a single Iknosan ship get around behind one of the Dominion ships. It makes me wonder if the Dominion ships have a vulnerability from behind that we don't know about."

"I noticed the same thing," Mac adds.

Alex shifts her attention to me. "I saw something related, six Dominion ships arranged back-to-back like a jack. I've also think I've counted all the energy weapon emitters, twenty five in total."

She holds up a hand-drawn image of the bullet shaped ship, as viewed from the starboard side.

"There's one here on the ship's bow." She traces her finger along the ship's centerline. "Another here about halfway around the ship's nose. Another here where the side straightens out, then two more here and here along the flat part. This rank of four emitters repeats every sixty degrees, six ranks of four total. It gives them good forward coverage and decent side coverage. I've seen them fire two in rapid succession, but not more than that, which lends support to the idea that they have a long recharge cycle."

"Which would imply they could be overwhelmed if attacked from all sides," I conclude.

"Jumping a ship in between two of the Dominion ships might trigger a friendly fire incident," Ty speculates.

I nod. "Let's keep our eyes open for any evidence that contradicts this set of observations. If we can't find any, this could give us a tactical advantage the Iknosan didn't have."

Heads nod, but no one offers another observation.

"Another round?"

Groans answer my suggestion, then Ty walks up to the battle map shown frozen on Admiral Keren's main view screen. "I want the view from this ship." He points to one far out to the side and near the back of the Dominion formation. "It should have line of sight to the stern of one of these Dominion ships."

...

Ninety minutes into this viewing period, I realize that I'm past the point of diminishing returns. Looking at the others, they appear more glazed over than I feel. Without pausing the recording, I ask, "Anyone seeing anything new?"

When there's no response, I pause playback. "Anything to report?"

I see Ty shake his head as if shivering. "Totally zoned out," he volunteers, then holds up his electronic tablet. "But I noticed something at 7:12:24 in the recording, if you want to rewind to look."

Dutifully, I rewind as we all cluster around the frames Ty was watching.

"Right here." Ty points. "The entire stern is visible on this ship. Note how busy it is. Nine banks of ion emitters, surrounding what looks like a Star-Trek-style deflector dish. That may be what they are protecting. I see nothing that looks like their energy weapon emitters. Then there's all this stuff." He motions toward the stern's perimeter-plating at the perfect circle of spike-like projections. "What the hell is that?"

"Does To'Kana have diagrams of the Dominion ships?" Alex asks. "I would assume they have imaging and analysis that could be useful."

"Good point. He has volunteered nothing."

Mac, who has walked into the holoprojection to get a closer view, calls out. "No sign of energy weapon or shield emitters back here. And these ion emitters look fragile. I think we may have found the Achilles Heel on these bad boys."

OFFICE, FCS HEADQUARTERS

It's been a long day, and I'm admittedly tired, but I need some alone time to think about today's learnings. So here I sit, drifting off.

Snapping awake, I go back to the day's issues with renewed urgency.

"Thelma?"

"What can I do for you, Kyle?"

"Do you have drawings of the Dominion ships or intelligence reports on them?"

"Let me check…"

For whatever reason, the way Thelma stops mid-sentence when she searches the databases strikes me as funny.

My tablet sounds. I pick it up and see a drawing and an intelligence report on the Dominion ships.

Thelma's voice is back. "Just sent you several drawings and our most comprehensive intelligence report. It's thinner and less complete than you are probably expecting. Very few ships that got close enough to a Dominion ship to gather intelligence survived the effort."

"We theorize that the ships have a weak spot along the stern. Is there speculation on this in the intelligence report?"

"One second…"

This time I chuckle as her voice just cuts out.

"Kyle, I can find no references to the ship's stern. No drawings of it either. Would you like me to ask Captain To'Kana if he has secured any information on this topic?"

"If he is available, I'll ask him myself."

A moment passes, then Thelma says, "Connecting you to Captain To'Kana."

"Kyle, Thelma tells me you have a theory about a potential weakness in the Dominion ships."

"We do." I give the captain a quick rundown on the work we did today, our conclusions, and our speculation about the weakness of the stern.

"Curious. We finally captured imaging of the stern of one of their ships. We might have had a different result if we'd discovered that earlier. Could you write up a summary of your findings, including relevant imagery? No one has studied those recordings as thoroughly as you have. I can send it to the other legacy ships. Maybe they can test your theory before the Dominion get here."

"Will do, sir. Expect it sometime early in the day tomorrow."

As the line drops, I realize for the first time just how vulnerable we are. A thousand ships, larger than the ones we plan to build, failed to turn back the Dominion. In fact, they were slaughtered. And now I understand how little the Iknosan even know about their enemy. Their technology and limited intelligence give us a chance, for which I am grateful, but it's a vanishingly small one. Nonetheless, it's all on us—mostly on me—to prepare the world for the onslaught that is only months away.

Returning to the task at hand, I look up the channel and time stamp data for the images I want, then quickly gather them into a file. After a few minutes of cleaning up my notes, I append them and close up the shop. It's far from complete, but it will only take an hour to finish in the morning.

[10.06.2033] LAB, FCS HEADQUARTERS

First thing after this morning's run, I finished the report I promised To'Kana. Shortly after sending it to Thelma, To'Kana called.

"Kyle, your report is a breakthrough for every humanoid species, not surrendering to the Dominion threat. It is going out to all the Legacy ships now. With nine other partner species studying this information, new breakthroughs will come."

"Thank you, sir. Our team, and the human experts with whom we share this, will draw more from it in the days ahead."

"Use caution, Kyle. Arachnoid genes run thick in human veins."

"Sir?"

He shakes his head. "Sorry. I've already said more about this topic than I should have. But as you surely know, not all humans share the same degree of goodwill toward each other. Beware of those that don't." He puts up his hands, ending discussion on the topic, but I suspect there is a lot here that I need to know but don't.

To'Kana brightens. "I've found several more jump-capable shuttles for you. They all share the same superstructure, so I have started its replication. My bots will complete it in a couple of days. Thelma has sent the specs to your replicator. She has highlighted the next decisions we need to make. If you answer them in the next two days, then we can proceed from there. If not, we will wait for your reply."

With that, he terminates the connection, leaving me staring at my now blank video comm monitor. In every conversation, I learn something new, something that seems totally orthogonal to what I need to know or do.

To'Kana clearly thinks the human genome has been corrupted, which makes us questionable allies. I allegedly am not, which is why he's willing to work with me. Nonetheless, I fear he may choose to purify us at some point. He hasn't yet and apparently doesn't plan to in the short term. So, we must have a better chance of stopping the Dominion than I thought.

Shaking away the bigger concerns, I redirect my attention to the task at hand, studying the new specifications to see if I can come up with something better.

It doesn't take long to find the first trade off. The Iknosan have four drive technologies that can be installed in the shuttle: gravity, ion, subspace FTL, and jump. Only three can fit in any given shuttle version. Grav-drive is required for any shuttle that requires surface takeoff or landing. Jump is required for our demo. That means we need to choose between the ion drive and the subspace drive. In interstellar space, ion drive is required for maneuvering.

As I ponder the trade-offs, a thought occurs. I have Morgan Owen's contact info, the head of DOD's proof-of-concept team.

"Owen here."

"Morgan, Kyle Wimberly. I have an update on our proof-of-concept ship. Do you have a minute?"

"Kyle, would love to hear what you've got."

I quickly get him up to speed on our combat shuttle variants: thirty meters long, ten meters wide, seven meters high, supports three of four propulsion systems.

"We need the gravity- and jump-drives. The ability to visit another star will be a POC requirement."

It takes me a second to interpret the government-speak, POC being the acronym for proof of concept.

"Given the contention that it's not safe to do interstellar travel without an ion drive, I'd say the third slot needs to go to it."

"Ion drive it is," I reply. "There are a couple more trade-offs I haven't thought through yet. I'd like to get this done today. OK, if I call later?"

"Sure, let me give you my cell number. This is the top item on my list. What kind of time frame are we talking about?"

"I'm not sure yet, but it shouldn't take long. The shuttle is small enough that we can build it in the Iknosan's existing space facilities. The superstructure will get finished sometime this weekend."

"Are you serious?"

"I am. We will produce a safe and functioning shuttle by the end of the month."

"I'm not sure we will have the RFP approved by the end of the month."

"Then it sounds like we both have some work to do."

Morgan chuckles. "Call me as soon as you have the next set of trade-offs. My cell will be on until 11:00 p.m. Eastern."

As we sign off, I feel as though I have won my first friend in Washington, a funny thought given that he's in Arlington.

Six hours later, my review is done. Of the trade-offs remaining, I agree with the options To'Kana has selected, which specify minimal weaponry, shielding with integrated stealth, maximum human scaled crew accommodations, and a sophisticated AI pilot.

I dump a text-based version of the specs to a file I can email to Morgan, send it and text him so he knows it's there. Then I send the replicator spec file to Thelma, asking her to give me a production time estimate.

That done, I pack up for the evening. Time for dinner, then the mental preparation needed to endure another day of Congressional testimony tomorrow.

[10.07.2033] HOUSE OFFICE BUILDING, WASHINGTON, DC

Before transporting out this morning, I got word from Thelma that the replication specs compiled, and they could fabricate all the parts as soon as next Saturday. Final assembly would probably run several more days, but an AI pilot could run a preliminary test flight as soon as two weeks from today. The news has put me in a better mood than expected as I walk into the meeting room for the House Armed Services Committee.

It quickly vanishes as the chair announces that all fifty-nine members are in attendance today and each will get seven minutes. I'm told that most meetings just make the quorum. Today, they're all here, their time allocations reduced, but we're still talking eight plus hours, if they all behave, which would be a first in my experience. I have a world to defend, but this is what I'm sentenced to for volunteering to save it.

I kind-of zone out as the first three members use their seven minutes to lecture me, never asking a question.

"Dr. Wimberly?

I look up.

"I asked you a question."

"Sorry, ma'am. Could you please repeat the question?"

"What qualifications do you have to represent the aliens in this matter?"

I think I know the answer to that question. I was in the right place at the right time and carry no arachnoid genes. But if there is one thing I cannot say, well, that would be it.

"They chose me."

"Nothing is that simple, soldier."

"I'm sorry. Did you serve ma'am?"

"I did."

"Thank you for your service, ma'am. But I think it is that simple. I was in the right place at the right time and helped save a gravely wounded person."

I get a wry smile. "As I would have," she says. "But explain to me how anything could be that simple."

We lock eyes and I realize that I have an ally, although I don't know how to answer her question. Then I realize the truth is the only option. "Triage, ma'am. There was only one person I could help. He was mortally wounded. Yeah, he didn't look like me, but then again, during my service, most didn't. He needed help, so I gave it. You've experienced that, right?"

Her eyes soften. Or at least it seems that way to me.

"From what I saw on TV, our alien guests don't look very human. Everyone I helped while in the service did," she asserts.

"And that makes a difference?"

She shakes her head and I feel the sword come out. "You did the same for Afghans, even the Taliban?"

"For ones not on the list, yes! Those were my orders."

"And you became best friends with them. Helped them broker weapons deals?"

The wry smile that comes with her words makes me wonder how much arachnoid blood runs in her veins. I shake my head, mostly to clear the aberrant thought.

"I don't remember a Taliban offering me anything that would save the world, or even his people. There is a difference between good and evil."

Several members smirk at that remark. I am a fish out of water, a sacrifice on the altar of the self-interested. Does no one here care about saving the world?

The chairman bangs her gavel. "The member's time is up. I'm calling a fifteen-minute break. The committee will reconvene at 11:55."

As people stand, the representative whose name I am blanking on signals me.

My lawyer whispers in my ear, "Watch this one. She has ambitions."

I stand frozen as my lawyer abandons me and this woman walks my way, hand outstretched.

"Dr. Wimberly?"

"Ma'am."

"Please," she says empathetically, "Natalie. May I call you Kai?"

The words take me by surprise. "Ma'am?"

"You don't remember?"

I hear disappointment in her voice.

"Sorry, didn't mean it that way. I was wounded in Kandahar. You and your squad saved me."

In an instant, I remember the face—younger, badly damaged, but the same face.

"I know who you are, Kai. Your friend, Keone, the Hawaiian boy, held my hand the whole way back to Bagram, until they loaded me on the plane to Germany."

Tears well up at the memory. It was a high-risk mission that we carried off with no injuries.

She smiles. "You remember."

"I don't get it."

"Kai. You are a good man. I take you at your word." She waves an arm. "Few here will. As the first to question you, I asked the questions the worst of them wanted to and went a lot easier on you than they would have. They will still ask, and they will frame their questions more absurdly. When they do, say the following. *The question has already been asked and answered. I have nothing more to say about the matter.* Don't allow them to draw you into their agenda. If anything comes of this meeting, I will vote in your favor."

"Thank you, ma'am."

"Thank you, Kai. And get better representation. You were underprepared today."

With that, she whisks away, hand outstretched, on to the next person whom she presumably wants to influence. I am truly a fish out of water.

Two hours later, a question finally comes that I am prepared to answer.

"Dr. Wimberly, sources at the Department of Defense tell me you have taken part in a scoping meeting regarding defenses the United States might prepare for alien invasion."

No question was asked, yet he waits for an answer.

"Yes, sir. I have participated in several meetings with the Department of Defense."

"Is it true that you want to build a fleet of a thousand battlecruisers?"

"No, sir. That is not true."

"I will remind you that you are under oath."

I nod. "When the Iknosan were invaded, they attempted to raise a fleet of one thousand ships. They came close but did not have enough time."

"Does that mean you want more?"

"No, sir. They made many advances in the final days that they could not implement in time. Integrating those advances and some innovations of our own, I think we can do it with only two-hundred-fifty."

"And how much will that cost us?"

"Too early to know, sir, but as I found out a couple of weeks ago, everything will be lost if we do not take this opportunity."

Several more questions came through the course of the interview. Everyone was painfully skeptical. But there's been a shift. Something like eighty percent of the population has seen Audell's reports. They are being played on every news outlet and talk show—broadcast, cable, and social media. And most of America wants some sort of preparation. There's opposition, but it's the clear minority.

Setting the skepticism and insults aside, I think this was my first good day on Capitol Hill.

[10.22.2033] WATERGATE HOTEL, WASHINGTON, D.C.

Today is my birthday. It's also one of the most exciting days of my life. Our new proof-of-concept shuttle is going for its first test flight. The only two aboard will be Thelma and the AI pilot. To'Kana has given her a bandwidth boost, which is allowing her to take a human form.

Justin put the word out to his various contacts, asking if they would like to view the proof-of-concept test flight. He got enough positive responses that he rented one of the conference rooms at the Watergate for the viewing. To my taste, it's a bit overdone—servers with canapes, a bar offering mimosas and Bloody Marys, and a harpist playing quietly. But most eyes are on the large 3D holoprojection that fills the far end of the room.

Scanning the name tags as I came in, I saw three committee members whose names I recognize: Representative Natalie Wright from Southern California, Representative Logan Williamson from Massachusetts, and Senator Hope Shaffer from New York. Jace is here, of course, as is the RFP team from the Pentagon. From our side, it's Justin, Jill, Mac, and me.

In the holoprojection we see the stern of To'Kana's ship.

"The shuttle bay doors will open momentarily." I announce, hoping to draw the last of the participants away from the bar. I'm surprised how heavily some guests are hitting it, given that it's 10:00 AM on a Saturday morning.

Representative Wright comes up alongside me. "Good morning, Kai. Thank you for inviting me today."

That she steps in this close and uses my team name makes me want to inch away. But against every ingrained reaction, I hold my position.

She motions toward the holoprojection, leaning in a bit as she does. "Where is the camera recording this event?"

The brief contact of her shoulder against my arm sets off my *touch-itis*, as an elementary school teacher of mine described it.

"It's the nose camera view from another shuttle. The Iknosan have agreed to let us record this much of their ship. We won't get a view of the shuttle recording the event."

As the words come out, the shuttle bay doors open. It's not as exciting as the view I got from the shuttle on my first trip up. Not because the viewing mechanism is any different, but because before we were on approach, the Legacy Ship growing in our view as the door opened. But this is still pretty good.

"Excellent 3D imaging," she says, leaning into me again. "The depth really comes through."

"Remarkable, isn't it?" I reply with little feeling.

"The problem, of course, is that modern CGI movies are almost as good. So, this really doesn't constitute a proof of concept. But to your credit, this is much better than any of the pitch material I've seen from Boeing or any of the others."

"This flight is for our internal proof of concept. I will not show you something before I've tested it. This is our test. If it works, we'll repeat this flight, leaving from the surface and carrying people the government chooses. That will be our proof of concept for you."

As we were talking, the shuttle bay doors finished opening, and two more windows appeared in the holoprojection. One contains the bridge camera view, including a uniformed Thelma. The other contains the bridge instrumentation, presented in English.

"Good morning. My name is Thelma, and I am your captain today. In a moment, we will depart for our journey to Barnard's Star, a red dwarf, approximately six light years from Earth. Once departed, it will take us a little more than an hour to line up for jump. On arrival, we will use the star's gravity to loop around, then jump back toward the solar system. We will drop-from-jump outside Neptune's orbit, change course, then jump back in to within an hour of Earth."

Natalie touches me again. "She's not human, is she? She resembles the Velma character from Scooby Doo. You see it, right?"

It's been a long time since I've received this much touch from a woman. I get it. My mom is the same way. But she's my mom.

"I see it. She's an Iknosan AI. She's tried to put on a human face for us. The captain finally gave her enough computational power to do it."

As impressed as I am with Thelma's performance, Representative Wright pulls away and turns to me. "She was previously being denied the resources required to express herself?"

I look at Representative Wright wide eyed.

She chuckles in return. "Kai, you're an easy target. We need to train you up if you are going to be a successful spokesperson for your company."

I shake my head. "I suppose that's true. But I am a technologist first, a business manager second. Spokesperson is way down there on the list."

"So much potential," she muses. "I'm going to get myself a mimosa. Would you like anything?"

"No, I'm good, thank you."

I watch as she steps toward the bar. I know from our encounter in Afghanistan that she's three or four years older than I am. But she doesn't look it. About halfway to the bar, she diverts. "Jace?"

As I turn my attention back to the holoprojection, I see the shuttle lift a foot or so off the floor, then rotate so it points out. It hovers there for a second, then Thelma says, "Departing for our journey to Barnard's Star."

The shuttle eases its way out of the shuttle bay, then slowly inches away.

"Thelma, why the slow departure?"

"Good morning, Kyle Wimberly. We are using the grav drive to move, initially pushing against the ship. Once we are a suitable distance away, we will refocus on the moon, which we can safely push away from with much more force."

Morgan Owen of the RFP team comes over. "Impressive display. It would be cool to watch football this way."

"Someday," I reply, amused by the thought.

He nods toward Thelma. "That was an interesting bit of information. The grav-drive focuses on a gravitation source, then pushes against it. I would have thought that it pulled."

"It goes both ways. It can attract or repel with up to a 3x multiplier. I'm not that sure how they do it, but it works."

"Are they planning to switch to ion drive at some point?"

"I think the answer is yes. Let's ask... Thelma?" I call out.

"Yes, Kyle?"

"Are you going to use the ion drive on this flight?"

"We will. In another minute, it will be safe to go to full throttle on the grav-drive. We'll use that to get us on the right trajectory, then switch to the ion-drive to get us up to our target cruising speed. In fifty-five minutes, we'll jump."

"Thank you, Thelma."

Morgan nods toward Thelma. "Justin told me she's an AI, fully sentient, passes the Turing test. Is that true? It looks that way to me."

"She is as real as any person I know. Her hands are even warm," I reply.

"She's organic?"

"No. She's a holoprojection enclosed in a weak force field, enough to let her touch people lightly."

I can tell Morgan is thinking about something, the thought apparently agitating him. "What's on your mind?"

"Is that really safe? A sentient AI? The government has been worried about it for years. Several of the social media companies have lost server farms to machine learning systems run amok."

"I think Thelma is safe. Every piece of equipment I've seen comes with an AI controller. None are as intelligent as Thelma. But all think, answer questions, do analysis. The Iknosan have a lot of technology that we don't. It wouldn't be a surprise to me if they've found a solution to problems we have not."

Morgan shrugs. "Point taken, and not today's worry. Regarding the POC, I'm sure your shuttle is going to do what you claim it will, which leaves me in a bit of a pickle. I can't issue an RFP for a POC that's already been proven. As Representative Wright has already pointed out to me, today's viewing cannot be considered a proof of concept. Which begs the question, what should we ask for in a proof of concept?"

Questions like this befuddle me.

"Do we need a proof of concept?"

Morgan eyes me suspiciously. "Say more."

"I've been thinking that this shuttle proves the most unknown things. If it works today, then we can take some people up for a flight, run the Secretary out to Alpha Centauri or something. Then launch a program to build out the space fleet."

"How will you get paid for this work?"

"Don't know. Don't really care. I've stared a Dominion warrior in the face, twice. If we are not prepared when they come in force, there will be nothing left. Period."

"Assuming it works, could we just buy this unit from you?"

"The flight controls in this unit do not have a viable human interface. That's something we could work on together."

Our conversation is interrupted as Thelma announces, "Transitioning to ion drive."

On looking back at the holoprojection, I see a long glowing tail form behind the shuttle.

"What's your propellant source?" Morgan asks.

I know the answer to this question. I can feel it. But it's not coming to me. Deploying a trick I learned long ago, I think of something related. What ions do I know? The answer comes immediately. "Salt."

"Salt? Like sodium chloride?" Morgan exclaims.

"Yes. At high temperature, it disassociates. It's easy to separate the ions, then expel them at about half the speed of light."

"How much propellant do you carry?" he asks, laughing.

"One hundred kilograms, which is a lot of acceleration."

"I'm not sure what to make of that number," Morgan admits.

"In space, you only pay for acceleration. Acceleration at 0.1g for one second costs about ten grams of salt."

"Ten thousand seconds of 0.1g thrust per tank full," Morgan concludes. "Sounds like a lot. I'm sure it's not as much as it seems."

"Thelma? How long is the ion drive going to burn?"

"Twenty minutes, Kyle."

"That's like twelve percent of your tank," Morgan says. "You'll need that much again on the return to slow down, right?"

I nod. "Right, we will also need a little more for the U-turn at Barnard's Star. The star's gravity will supply most of the turnaround energy, and the grav-drive will supply most of the rest."

Morgan snorts. "To another star and back for thirty kilograms of salt."

"That's the power of the jump drive. It takes you where you want to go instantly. You only need acceleration to escape the local gravity well and for tactical maneuvering."

"I really like this. Let me go chew it over with the team. I want to hit the ground running on Monday."

"We will be engaging the jump drive in two minutes." Thelma announces. "The camera ship following us is not jump capable. You will see the jump. After that, we will switch to our sensors so you can see Barnard's Star from our point of view."

I stand watching on my own for a while, then Jace comes over.

"Good job today," he says. "The presentation is credible, which always helps. But Justin and Natalie are really working the floor, and Morgan is sold."

"He says our demo today undermines the POC RFP process," I reply.

"Pfft, don't listen to that. It may obsolete some of his text, but DOD and Congress like projects like this a lot more than POCs. They're lower risk. I have good relationships with the secretary, the speaker, and the Senate majority leader. They can take it to the president. She'll make the call, and DOD will take it from there, working the appropriations process as necessary. We'll have a deal by Thanksgiving."

Jace says this as though it's a new international speed record, but Thanksgiving is still a full month away.

"Transition to jump in 3, 2, 1..." Thelma says. Then the shuttle seems to stretch to the horizon. There's a flash, then it's gone.

"What just happened?" Jace asks, as the window that previously displayed the ship now shows a glowing red ball.

In the top frame, Thelma says, "We have successfully jumped into the system containing Barnard's star, approximately two million miles away from it. We will spend the next hour curving around it before jumping back home."

"Did the ship really stretch like that?"

"No, it's an optical illusion caused by the disruption a jump creates in the space-time continuum."

Jace eyes me. "Where did you learn all this?"

I shrug off the question. "I'm a fast learner. The Iknosan are excellent teachers."

Thankfully, Jace does not pursue it, extending a hand instead. "Congratulations on a successful jump."

I shake the hand offered. Then he's away, targeting Senator Shaffer from the look of it.

Mac comes up to me next, extending a hand toward the holoprojection. "What's going on out there is possibly the most thrilling event of a lifetime. But no one here is watching it."

"I think they've seen what they needed to see."

"Probably right," Mac agrees. "Representative Wright seems keenly interested in you. Talks glowingly. I didn't remember her from the rescue, did you?"

"Not at first. She was covered in blood when I picked her up and carried her to the helicopter. I wasn't sure she was going to make it. But she's done well for herself since. No visible scars."

Mac snorts. "If she were the president, this deal would be funded by now."

"Then it's too bad she's not the president."

As the day drags on, I start to understand the mind-numbing monotony of spaceflight. There is little to do, the scenery crawling by at a microscopic rate. Finally, four hours in, we drop from jump within sight of earth and the moon. Our beautiful blue jewel is still distant and small, but at least it's visible again.

"Kyle?" The voice of Natalie Wright startles me. "Excellent event today. I'm extremely impressed by what you've done here. I asked a couple of friends of mine to stop by. You should meet them, if you haven't already. Justin has been talking their ear off."

"I haven't? Who are they?"

"Nick Bennett and Angela Cook. Nick is president of Boeing's new Orbital Services unit. They have some amazing new stuff for automated assembly in space. Angela is with SpaceX, heading their new Orbital Shipyard Division. We are working with them on what I hope will become our first space-based shipyard. If you partnered with the two of them, you might get two-hundred fifty ships built in time."

She touches my arm, then in a low voice says, "Go talk to them. Everything interesting is done here."

That said, she's away, on to her next event.

I look over to Justin and see him beckoning me. I guess it's time to go meet our prospective business partners.

[11.01.2033] TRAIL

The trips out to DC have caused me to miss multiple morning runs. The prep since then for the upcoming manned proof-of-concept flight has stolen away even more. But today I have no choice, because, this afternoon, Mac will supervise the installation of our next twenty-megawatt power generator out at the substation.

I arrive early and am greeted by Ty. "Well, look who got out of bed on time today."

"In my dreams," I shoot back.

Ty gets a funny look on his face, obviously confused. Then, I see it snap. "You pulled another all-nighter?"

"Bingo."

"Kai, you're burning it on both ends, brother. You need to get back on some kind of schedule. No one can skip that many nights in such a short time."

"My next meeting isn't until one. That will give me four plus hours."

As Ty shakes his head, Mac walks up. "You've been hard to get ahold of recently."

"Sorry. My plate seems to be on permanent overflow. Can you give me an update as we run?"

"Sure. Let's go. The others will pass us before we get too far along."

Mac takes off, then after five paces, slows enough for me to catch up. "Wimberly, you are so out of shape."

"Tell me about the substation," I answer back.

"Western Interconnect has approved our request to add a twenty-megawatt unit every month for twenty months. The first one went in about a month ago. Rather than add these piecemeal, I put together a site plan that expands the substation."

"I saw it. Good work."

"Would have moved things along a little quicker if you had sent an approval," Mac chides.

"Sorry, I was in DC. I didn't get to look at the plans until after I got your message saying you were taking my silence as an approval. But I like what you've planned—ten rows of two, foundations laid at the same time, and each foundation wired through a breaker to the step-ups, so we only need to go off-line once. Where are we with it? And what's the plan for today?"

"All twenty pads are in. Infrastructure for the remaining circuit breakers is in. The station will go offline at ten. One team will install the generator. A second team will complete the breakers. Breechelle Patterson from Western Interconnect will be here at four to inspect and authorize us to go back online by six."

"When is the next one going in?"

"The Tuesday after Thanksgiving. That one will bring us up to seventy megawatts."

I smile. "Then ninety megawatts by Christmas. That will be my Christmas present." I muse on the thought for a second, then ask, "Who's your second on this?"

"Enzo Bertolino, the new power engineer we brought on board two months ago. Great guy. Italian. Knows his stuff. Good cook too. He's the one that put out the meatball bake at the last potluck."

"Good. The next two years are going to be astoundingly busy. Do what you can to get him ready to cover for you as soon as possible." With those words, I slow.

Mac does the same. "You OK, boss?"

"Yeah, I'm going to head back. I need some sleep."

CHAPTER 10: SURVIVORS

[11.17.2033] EDWARDS AIR FORCE BASE

Our internal proof-of-concept flight on my birthday, coupled with the continual drip-drip-drip of alien news being put out by Audell Knight, has turned the tide with both the public and the government. Even though this was not an election year, politicians of every stripe have been giving speeches in favor of building out a space fleet, Natalie Wright, the most vociferous.

And here we are, back at Edwards, to do an actual proof-of-concept flight. Dozens of VIPs have shown up, including the slimy Representative Emmett Dodson of Arizona, who challenged my loyalty.

I'm told that the safe return of this mission is the last condition President Powell has put on the program. A fair condition, which increases my appreciation for her.

But here we are with seats for ten, but only six volunteers. For two weeks, the media was all caught up in who we would choose, listing outspoken celebrities and government officials, even Vice President Norwell.

But what a joke. Fewer than ten people applied: me, Mac, Natalie Wright, Morgan Owen, Jill, and Jace—who aren't exactly coming willingly.

Justin threatens to kill me if we don't come back. Sadly, he doesn't have the means. Execution seems like a much better option than being stranded out there, in the void or around another star.

Jill, on the other hand, is buoyant. We agreed to train her how to pilot. Yeah, she's the copilot, a backup for the AI that knows how to fly this ship. But she seems very confident coming out of two weeks' training on To'Kana's ship—another sore spot for Justin.

To'Kana has come to like Jill at this point. Secretly, he's told me she, too, is free of arachnoid genes. So, he's given her an in-ear comm device, allowing her to transport up to the ship and be part of the team flying it down to Edwards.

The three of us—Jill, Mac, and I—transported up earlier and are now on final approach. When we settle, I am to get out, give a speech, then invite the others aboard.

...

Speeches made, farewells given, hatches battened, the countdown begins. Jill, in the co-pilot's seat, seems effervescent. Me? Hopeful.

Natalie, in the seat next to me, grasps my hand. "Please tell me this is going to work."

Her words totally befuddle me. Is this actually a request for reassurance?

"Don't worry," I reply. "I'm betting my life too."

She smiles, a little of the tension draining away. But at the end of the day, I truly do not understand this woman. Then I realize she was blown up in Afghanistan. I wasn't. I rescued her. There is a bond there I cannot walk away from, nor can I take it for granted.

[11.18.2033] WYNN, LAS VEGAS, NEVADA

Needless to say, yesterday's proof-of-concept flight returned home safely and was a success on multiple fronts. Morgan and his team, who ended up issuing a single-source POC contract for the flight, declared the contract successfully fulfilled. So, when we are all back from Thanksgiving break, we'll have the go ahead to start on the fleet design portion of the project, and Morgan will process the paperwork enabling our ten-million-dollar fee to be paid.

On a personal front, the mission was also a success. Spending five hours seated next to Natalie with nothing much to do, we talked a lot. Enough that I feel as though I've come to understand her. Fifteen years ago, I gave her a fresh shot at life. By pushing my agenda and taking a seat on the proof-of-concept flight, she's courageously done the same for me. We both know it's helped her career, but it's helped mine more. But beyond that, there's new trust, new mutual respect, and it is about to be put into action.

Today, the three of us—Justin, Natalie, and I—are meeting with executives from Boeing and SpaceX to hammer out a joint venture agreement. Justin has been working this since the day of the test flight at the Watergate when Natalie introduced them. She has been working the government side of the problem, lobbying for an orbital space dock and shipyard. With the president days away from endorsing the proposal, we are hoping to complete a Letter of Intent today.

We're the first of the principals to arrive. Three pairs of lawyers already have the room set up. A minute later, Angela Cook and her colleague Logan Watts from SpaceX arrive. As introductions are made and greetings are exchanged, one of the lawyers gets up and exits the room. From the look of it, a call must have come in. A moment later, he's back, walking to the front of the room. "Excuse me everyone. My clients will be a few minutes late. Issues at the airport. They are on their way now."

"Dr. Wimberly?"

I turn toward the voice.

"Logan Watts," he says, his voice jittery.

"Logan, a pleasure to meet you."

"I saw the raw footage of your encounter with the Dominion."

"How did you get a hold of that?"

"Mr. Wicks sent it to us. He said it was important for us to know more about our enemy than what was released to the press."

"I didn't know."

He swallows. "I think the ferocity of the enemy, combined with the incredible cunning of our potential partner, is what convinced us to get involved. We usually shy away from joint ventures in opportunities like this, because our tool set is unbelievably good, so good it gives us significant competitive advantage and attracts the best people. I'm surrounded by geniuses every day."

"Your point?"

"We have nothing like your technology. To the extent you share it with us, we will do miraculous things with it. This has the potential to be an extraordinary partnership."

"Your role in it?"

"I work directly with Angela as her technical lead. If we close this deal, then I hope to spend a lot of time working with you."

I nod, appreciating Logan's candor, but not fully on board with it yet.

"While we wait, would you mind if I asked you a few questions?" he asks.

"Go ahead."

"Your jump drive... How does it work? Are you creating an artificial worm hole?"

"No, it's too hard to defeat the radiation issue. We use something called Asymmetric Space-time Disruption (ASD) instead. In laymen's terms, we pop the ship out of space-time on a four-dimensional vector that lands it at a different place in space and time."

"Does that imply you could use it for time travel, too?"

"The Iknosan outlawed that use long ago. Our ability to control the jump lands us within a fraction of a second of departure."

"That would go terribly wrong, too deep in a gravity well, wouldn't it?" Logan speculates.

I nod. "Our controllers lock us out when the space-time curvature is too deep or unstable."

"I've heard you have a weapon that defeats the Dominion's shielding. How does it do that?"

Before I answer, the sound of footsteps entering the room catches our attention. The third party is here.

Ten more minutes tick by as greetings and introductions are made, and I'm a little surprised at how deferential the other executives are to me. I suppose it makes sense; they watched the unfiltered version of me taking down a vastly superior opponent. They also know I am the keeper of the technology driving this deal. But *they* are captains of industry, and I'm just me.

Finally, our lawyer calls the meeting to order and proposes a process and agenda to fulfill the day's objectives. He points out that Representative Wright is here as a representative of the government, willing to offer input and non-binding recommendations on issues relevant to the government. What he doesn't say is what everyone knows. Natalie is the driver behind the program on which our new company will bid.

The lawyers walk us through the opening of the Letter of Intent they have drafted: the parties, their mutual intention to build an orbital shipyard and a fleet of battle ships, and the definitions of keywords—a half hour of mind-bendingly boring material.

Next comes the parties' ownership: forty percent to our holding company, The Wicks-Wimberly Corporation, thirty percent each to the other two companies. On signing of this letter of intent, each party will contribute one hundred million dollars cash to the new company, US Orbital Shipyards, Inc. In addition, ExoMaterials Corp., our mining operation, will contribute a ten percent stake to each of our partners' parent company.

I was wondering what Justin gave up in order to receive a larger share of this one.

After about three hours, we come to the breakup agreement. If at any point one party unilaterally leaves the partnership, then they forfeit their interest in it. Wow, that's harsh.

If we fail to win the contract, then the remaining cash is distributed back equally, the contributed shares in ExoMaterials Corp. are voided, and each party returns all intellectual property to the party from which it came.

Finally, at the four-and-a-half-hour point, we shake hands and are promised draft documents will be ready for review and signature a week from Monday.

...

The bar at the Wynn is beautiful. I say that as if there is only one, but I've lost track of which one this is. We are all staying the night. Natalie didn't want to red-eye home on a Friday night. Justin and Jill are planning to fly back Sunday morning. I had planned to transport back once we had debriefed following the meeting. But a delightful meal with friends after a successful pair of days? Who can say no to that?

"Justin tells me you are going home to visit your parents for Thanksgiving," Natalie says, as if asking me a question.

"Yeah, first time in a couple of years."

"Why so long? Or do the in-laws have their hooks in that deep?" Natalie asks as if it's a joke.

"No. Single never married. The truth is I had a falling out with my brother, that's... Suffice it to say... We don't talk. What about you? Parents? In-laws?"

"Sorry to hear about your brother. I had Thanksgiving with my in-laws every year. Well, until the divorce anyway."

There's a sadness in her voice that I presume is about the failed marriage.

"I only got one more Thanksgiving with my parents before COVID took them. I gave all the ones that they deserved to a guy I should never have married." Then in a brighter voice. "This year, I'll be joining five of my unattached colleagues at the 1789 Restaurant in Georgetown. It's a quaint colonial place, which seems appropriate for the day."

"We're going to be at Justin's father's place out on Long Island," Jill adds. "He does a big event every year. It's a lot of fun."

From the look on Justin's face, I'm not that sure he thinks it's all that fun.

Natalie lifts her champagne glass. "To a successful day. May it be the first of many."

As she puts it down, I see it's empty.

I lift the bottle as I ask, "More?" Then realize it is empty. "Ah... Empty, but we can get more."

She shakes her head. "No, time for me to head up. You?"

I look at Justin, who says, "We're done. Go ahead up while I get the check."

"OK, enjoy the rest of your evening." As I stand, I notice the sparkle in Jill's eye and wonder what that's about.

"Enjoy the rest of your evening," Natalie echoes, then motions toward the elevators. "Lead the way."

As we step into the elevator lobby, the far elevator dings and a handful of people step out. I grab the door and hold it for Natalie, then follow her in. "Sixteen," she says. I hit the button, then touch the button for my floor. A second later, the elevator moves.

"Do you like Cognac?" she asks.

"We tried making it once. What a disaster."

"Someone gave me a bottle of Hine VSOP, made in France. Care to have a taste with me? They say it's very smooth."

The way I look at her makes her laugh.

"Kai, I'm not propositioning you. I have a suite with a living room and a fabulous view out over the city. Come join me. It's not that late. I think we deserve a private toast given our excursion yesterday."

"Sure. Sounds nice."

We get off at sixteen, then head to her corner suite. As the door opens, she goes straight in. I hesitate. Then, I realize this truly is a living room. I'm not convinced it's a good idea, but step in anyway, closing the door behind me. I hear glasses being placed on the counter and come into view as the cork pops.

"Why don't you pour? One finger for me. I'm going to change into something more comfortable."

With those words, she's into the bedroom. The door shut behind her.

"What am I doing here?" I whisper to myself.

I pour a quarter inch of the pungent caramel-colored liquid into each snifter, then recork the bottle, continuing to stare at it as if it were a lifeline to sanity. When I hear the bedroom door open, I swallow, then lift the two glasses and turn to offer one to Natalie. What I see freezes me in place—hair down, make up off, blue jeans, a white V-neck top with red and blue stripes that loosely resembles a flag—she looks twenty years younger.

"What, you didn't think I could be a real person?" Then pointing at the glasses. "I'm not particularly fond of men with skinny fingers."

Her comment takes me totally off guard, then I get it—I didn't pour enough cognac in the glasses. The burst of laughter that follows breaks the tension.

"Here. Let me take those before you break them."

A second later, the glasses are back down on the bar, another glug going into each. She hands me mine, then points to the sofa in front of the window looking out over town.

As I step that way, she goes for the light switch. "Dimming the lights enough to see the spectacle outside."

A minute later, she plops down next to me. "Beautiful, isn't it?"

"It is. So are you, by the way."

"You get it right? The heavy makeup, puffy hair, padded bra… Dressing up to look twenty years older. People take you more seriously. It also keeps the grabbers at bay, some of them anyway."

"I had no idea."

"Most men don't. That's also why I come on so strong. Most men don't like it, which makes it easier to separate the ones I want to work with from the rest."

"I don't think I've ever met anyone as motivated. Or as intimidating," I add.

She chuckles. "You do a pretty good job of it, too. The tall, tanned alien-slayer, who has all the answers, but doesn't say much. I saw the way Logan Watts reacted to you. That guy is as arrogant as he is smart, another Elon in the making, yet he trembles in your presence."

She takes another sip, then leans over against me, which makes me tighten up.

"Oh, Kai. Get over it. Treat me like your sister. We both need allies in this world. People we can trust. The morons in Washington are going to do nothing unless we force their hand. I'm on your side. Be on mine."

We sit in silence for a bit, then she takes her last sip and gets up. "Come on, time to go."

I get up and follow her over to the door. She puts out her arms to give me a hug. I return it, but somewhere along the way lips meet and my male parts act in a way they haven't in a long time.

"You can stay, if you would like," she whispers.

[11.23.2033] WIMBERLY RESIDENCE, SAN LUIS OBISPO, CA

Despite everything else going on, I've caved to pressure from my mother to come home for Thanksgiving. I suppose I owe her that, given the run in with the Dominion two months ago. When I first raised it with Justin, I thought I'd get pushback. The discussion at the bar the other night makes me realize how much he thinks I need this. His only demand was that I fly private, directly from headquarters to San Luis Obispo County Regional Airport and back. He thinks it exposes me too much to transport home, given my family really doesn't know what's going on. And I'm apparently too valuable to risk driving that far. He insisted on arranging it, then booked me out on Wednesday and back Saturday—three nights at my parents' home. Mom must have had something to do with that, too.

True to form, Dad picked me up at the airport, exuberant that I was home for the first time in three years.

"Late harvest this year, the last of it coming in just before Halloween. The pinot looks to be the best in years..."

As I grew up around a working winery, I know most of what there is to know about making wine, and it's what I'd assumed I would do when I grew up. Per family tradition, the eldest son would finish high school, go into the military, then come home and prepare to take over. I did the first part—six years in the Army, including two tours in Afghanistan. But the army changed me in a way it didn't the three previous generations. My father served in a time of relative peace, my grandfather during Vietnam, my great grandfather in the Pacific during WWII. They came home to the prospect of peace and wanted to settle down, work the land, and build a family. I came home to the prospect of renewed terrorism, Russian aggression, and a pending war over Taiwan; not to mention a younger brother whose talent for wine far exceeded mine.

"Kyle?" Thelma's voice sounds in my ear, breaking my musing. "Captain To'Kana would like to speak with you. Justin told him you are taking part in a family holiday today. The captain respects such commitments and would like to know if there is a time you can meet that will not infringe on your family."

"I'm free for the next hour."

"Would it be OK for me to transport you aboard?"

"Give me a minute." I get up to lock the door to my room; it wouldn't be good for someone to come in and find me missing. Then I close my eyes.

"Thelma, please initiate transport."

IKNOSAN LEGACY SHIP

"Kyle, thank you for taking an hour from your family holiday."

"Not a problem, sir."

"I just received an unexpected contact."

"From?" I prompt.

"Another one of the Legacy ships."

"You said there were ten, right?"

The captain nods. "Our instructions were not to contact each other. If none of us knew where the others were, the Dominion could not pry the information from us if we were captured."

I nod. "We had a similar protocol during the war—information on tactical mission deployments was on a need-to-know basis."

To'Kana eyes me, the slight movement of his head indicating his respect. "Most of our fleet got home in time to make a stand against the Dominion. None were expected to escape. But the battle was apparently lost by the time the last of our cruisers arrived. Five cruisers found one of our legacy ships, who were working with a people much more advanced than yours. Together, they developed a new weapon."

"Did they send you the specifications?"

"A clue, but back to that in a minute. They engaged the Dominion today..."

The way the captain lets the statement hang comes across as if it is a test of my tactical reasoning ability.

"And were not defeated?" I venture.

"Each side lost five ships, then the Dominion withdrew..."

"...the attrition rate dropping from thirty-to-one, to one-to-one." I speculate.

The captain nods. "The people we helped have space technology much more advanced than yours. But the new jointly developed weapon system turned the tide."

"You said they gave you a clue."

To'Kana smiles, then points to a holographic projection that pops up at the end of the table. "They did."

I watch as one of the giant Dominion dreadnoughts drops from FTL relatively close to an odd-looking ship.

"It's a decoy," To'Kana notes. "A balloon with a metallic coating that emits the same subspace signature as one of our ally's ships."

"So, they bait the Dominion to a known location," I speculate.

The captain smiles as he points back at the holoprojection. "Watch what happens next."

As I would expect, the Dominion fire an energy weapon and its target explodes, which in my mind is anti-climactic. The attacking Dominion ship drifts forward, then a second later, there's a blur and the Dominion's shields drop. A couple of seconds after that, there are more blurs, and holes appear across the ship, which dramatically depressurizes, then explodes.

"What happened?"

"The Dominion's tactics were used against them. They drop from subspace at a consistent distance from their targets. Knowing the decoy's exact location and the bearing it reports when the dreadnaught appears allows us to estimate its location. When the decoy is struck, dozens of weapons flood the target area, jumping in three phases—shield killers first, then piercing weapons, then explosives."

"The innovation is the weapon systems with a jump drive, right?" I ask.

The captain nods. "Our allies also have larger, more stable antimatter bombs and a better method for recovering weapons that miss their targets."

I think about that for a second, then speculate. "It has to do with the jump drive, right? In normal space, the weapons don't need to be moving that fast—it's the jump that's delivering them."

"You have good tactical reasoning, Kyle."

"Why not jump the weapon into the ship?"

The captain's eyes bulge. "We'll need to try that." He nods, the reflective look in his eyes suggesting he has more to say. "You should be able to build a prototype of the mini-jump-drive using your industrial replicator. Then once we've proven the functionality, we can propose it to your government."

WIMBERLY RESIDENCE

"There you are," Dad gushes as I come down the stairs. "Was worried I might need to come and wake you up."

"Nothing to worry about, Dad. I'm here."

"Great. Mind decanting the 2019 Lot 120 family reserve? I pulled two magnums earlier this week and put them on the table in the cellar."

"Are you sure you don't want Mark to do that?"

"You're just as capable as your brother, but he's off somewhere with Crystal at the moment."

The mention of Crystal's name makes my blood pressure spike. We met in high school, but didn't connect until I met her again at Cal Tech. We were a thing for four years, but it all unraveled during the first year of my PhD program. She complained I was more devoted to renewable energy than I was to her. I argued it would only be for a couple of years. Then one day I came home, and she was gone. Three years later, when it became clear that Mark would be taking over the winery, she asked him out. I obviously haven't gotten over it yet.

FAMILY CELLAR

Decanting magnums of old wine is a delicate procedure. In most wine this age, some crystallization will have taken place and essentially all sediment will have settled, most forming a plaque on the wall of the bottle, the rest as an ultra-fine sludge. The goal is to get the wine out while leaving all the crystals, plaque, and sludge behind. Any movement of the bottle will stir up some of the sludge. Sudden jolts will stir up some of the rest.

My great grandfather jury-rigged some tools we use to get a clean pour. About halfway through the second bottle, I hear feet on the steps. "Kyle, you down there?"

It's my sister Laura, who I haven't seen in three years. "Halfway through decanting a 2019, Lot 120," I call back.

There's silence for a second, then several pairs of feet come shuffling down.

"Mind if we watch?"

This time it's the voice of Chris Burns, Laura's husband.

"Sure. Who all is coming down?"

"Just Chris and his sister, Sophie," Laura answers back.

"Well, hurry up. I'm just about done."

As they gather around, Laura cautions the others to stay back, then points out the decanter, the cradle the bottle is resting in, and the hydraulic dampening system that controls the pour while isolating the bottle from any sudden movement.

Seconds later, the last drop gives way, and I right the bottle.

Finally able to look up, I'm shocked to see Laura with an unmistakable baby bump. "You're pregnant," I blurt out.

"I know," she sasses back, then continues. "Nice tan. The desert seems to agree with you."

"It has its moments." The staccato back and forth has been a hallmark of my relationship with my sister, who's only eleven months younger than I am. It's been three years since I've seen her, but the exchange feels comfortable and familiar in less than three minutes.

"Kyle, this is Sophie. She's just moved to the area. Her background is a lot like yours. Straight into the army after high school, Afghanistan, out after six years, then off to college, and, in her case, medical school."

I lift a hand to shake hers and look directly at her for the first time. Captivating blue-gray eyes filled with sparkles, short-blond hair, long, lean, fit... She looks like a sports model, but with a soldier's metal. She reminds me of Alex.

"Sophie, pleasure to meet you."

She smiles at me, then shakes my hand with a firm grip.

"Nice to meet you. Laura talks about you all the time."

The moment seems to stretch, as if time has slowed down. Then the bubble breaks, and she releases my hand. I turn to Chris and ask, "Shall we take these up?"

I see his smile and realize that Sophie and I have just been set up by our conniving siblings. But for the first time in a long time, it doesn't bother me.

"Laura, do you know why Dad asked me to do the decanting? That's been Mark's job forever."

She cocks her head. "You don't know?"

"Apparently not." I shoot back.

"Mark will not be here for dinner. Crystal's parents invited him to their place for Thanksgiving. I think he's getting ready to pop the question." She looks at me anew. "You didn't know?"

The repeated question gives me a moment's pause. Did everyone know that the real reason I didn't come on the holidays was because Crystal was with Mark?

Laura shakes her head. "Kyle, it's been pretty obvious."

"Sorry...." I sputter, realizing that I've just been outed.

She nods her head towards the stairs. "Come on. Let's go."

[11.27.2033] OFFICE, FCS HEADQUARTERS

For years now, I've worked a seven-day week—some days longer than others, but rarely a day off. Now, on my first day back after three days mostly off, I'm alone in the office on the Sunday after Thanksgiving, totally disinterested in company paperwork. And, despite the quantity stacked up in front of me, here I sit daydreaming about Sophie.

Snapping out of it, I ask aloud, "Thelma?"

"Kyle Wimberly. What can I do for you?"

"Hi, Thelma. Can you release to me any information you might have about scaling down the jump drive?"

The prolonged silence on the line implies that this question has a complex answer. Some minutes later, she comes back to me. "Kyle Wimberly, there is a great deal of information on this matter. Can you narrow your request?"

"Thelma, when it's just you and me talking, please call me Kai."

"Will do, Kai. Now, can you narrow your request about scaled-down jump drives?"

"I want to prototype a miniature jump drive like the ones Captain To'Kana described to me the last time I was aboard."

"Checking."

After a brief silence, Thelma comes back to me.

"Kai, I am not privy to your conversation with the captain. He has marked that conversation private and isolated all information about it."

Thelma's words shock me. Why would Captain To'Kana keep this information secret from Thelma? Realizing this call will not yield anything, I sign off, then pull up the list of data I already have. To'Kana must think I have what I need.

An hour later, I hit gold in the form of a replicator template for small scale jump drives. After another hour playing with it, I see why this is tricky. A jump drive uses an intense burst of energy to break an object free from space-time. The profile of the burst determines whether or not the object will return, and where it will return, if it does.

For example, to jump ahead a light year, the energy burst would need to start at the bow of the ship and ripple uniformly to the stern, hitting the transition threshold in the bow first, then ultimately in the stern. This unzipping from space-time pushes the ship away from the last point of connection.

Instant field-collapse keeps you in the present. Chaotic field-collapse permanently unhinges you from space-time. Phased field-collapse will move you forward or backward in time. I don't understand what phased collapse means exactly.

But back to my point, it takes a lot of power, delivered in an instant, with precision-controlled propagation. Or said differently, a large power source, larger capacitors, massive computing power, thousands of field emitters, and miles of conduit.

The smallest unit I can find weighs four-hundred kilograms and supports a payload of a quarter of a cubic meter. Which raises the next question. Why is the payload measured by volume? Searching through the databases, I find the answer. The energy of transition is proportional to volume, not mass, as it is for other propulsion systems. Who would have thought?

Then the next insight strikes. Jump bombs can be much smaller than the smallest jump ship, because the bomb doesn't need additional propulsion. Just like a regular bomb, the ship will deliver it into the theater of operation and set it on its course. This is exactly what Ty observed when we reviewed Captain Soman's attack on the Dominion dreadnaughts. I wonder what it will take to build Ty's inertial bomb.

Now, with the thought planted, I take the task on with urgency. I need a single-shot shield killing weapon, a high-power laser, and a shaped mass of lead, or even better, spent uranium.

[11.29.2033] LAB, FCS HEADQUARTERS

I've had my head in replicator specifications for nearly thirty-six hours at this point and think I finally have it. I haven't gone two nights without sleep since the final days of my thesis project.

Justin called yesterday morning, saying our meetings scheduled for Monday were pushed back until Wednesday—a conflict on Morgan Owen's calendar or something like that. He recommended I take the time to tighten up our fleet proposal. But knee deep in bomb design at that point, diverting to another task wasn't an option I would entertain.

Yesterday, I told To'Kana what I was doing. He was delighted. What I wanted to know was whether he had access to enough tungsten that I could include a thousand kilograms in my design. He groaned, then asked when I needed it. I said this week. He said he'd get back to me.

Now, here I sit, bomb design done. It's 2:00 AM, and I'm about to send it up to Thelma for simulation.

My bomb is eight meters long, tubular, with a rounded nose, and weighs about two metric tons. It has a jump drive capable of transiting one light year in an instant, a one-shot railgun that's seven meters long, a ten-gigawatt laser that I can pulse ten times a second, a six-meter-long tungsten needle, FTL comms, and an AI controller.

Because it is a onetime use weapon, the railgun and laser are overpowered and under-engineered. For the railgun, that means it will burn out its coils when it fires its preloaded shell containing the shield killing weapon. It should give the shell a thousand kilometer per second delta-V, buying us thirty seconds of laser fire. Similarly, the laser will burn up after about forty-seconds of pulsed fire at a rate of ten times per second.

"Thelma, I am transmitting now."

"Thanks, Kai. Are you going to sleep now?"

"I am."

"Then I'll send you the simulation results without disturbing you."

"And remember to override any material shortage errors," I remind.

"I won't forget, Kai."

"Night, Thelma."

As I get up, the room spins and the walk to my cabin no longer seems viable. So, I flop down on the couch instead.

...

Shaking wakes me from deep sleep, the words, "Kai wake up," barely penetrating my consciousness. I gather the energy to open my eyes and see Justin, in a business suit, standing over me.

"What the hell, Kai. We have a meeting at the Pentagon starting in ten minutes."

"What?" The word barely escapes my mouth as I feel myself falling back down the rabbit's hole.

More shaking. "Thelma said she couldn't wake you, so she beamed me down."

I groan. "Can you do this one without me?"

"Thelma told me to tell you that your bomb simulated out."

I look up at Justin, finally awake.

"I thought that might do it. Come on," he pulls me up. "Once you're in the shower, I'll go. Follow along as quick as you can."

"Thelma, transport us both to Kyle's cabin."

A minute later, I'm in the shower and Justin is gone. I'm never going to get this time zone thing right, not that I remembered to set an alarm.

PENTAGON

Nearly an hour later, I'm escorted into the Conference Room. Morgan wouldn't allow me to transport in directly. "Everyone comes in through the front door."

It's an ironic statement given the number of *front doors*. Anyway, that's where I've spent the last twenty minutes of my time. Worse, things could have happened.

"Oh, someone looks a little worse for the wear." April McDonald, the team's intelligence analyst, greets as I enter. "A little too much Thanksgiving cheer, maybe?"

"Back-to-back all-nighters. Well, close anyway. I finally fell over at 2:00 AM."

"What were you working on?" Morgan asks, apparently more interested in my activity than in my tardiness.

"Have you seen the video of the first Iknosan attack against the Dominion invasion?"

"No."

"Want to see it?

"This is related to our job today, right?"

"I think that would be a fair statement."

He eyes me, as if weighing the decision, then says, "Sure."

I pull out my holoprojection cube, which is now also connected to my implant, and ask it to play from Captain Soman's jump, pausing to make the salient points with as few words as possible. When the ships hit the Dominion dreadnaught, I pause playback, leaving the still image of two hulks sticking out the side of the larger one.

"We owe them a debt of gratitude. This is the sacrifice they made for us. But that's not my point."

Morgan nods and motions for me to continue.

"Once they jumped, what was the purpose of the ship?"

"To fire and die," April says callously.

Morgan eyes me again. It's as if he's trying to read my mind. "You obviously have a subtle answer. I'm curious what it is."

"After the jump, their flight was completely ballistic. At that point, the ship was simply a weapon delivery system that could be replaced by this."

I silently command the projector to show a rotating 3D image of my bomb. "This is a jump-capable bomb. The ship lines up to take the shot, acquiring the vector and the speed, then it jumps the bomb, not the ship."

I silently command the projector to play a simulation I built yesterday. It uses the same background footage showing the Iknosan cruiser and Dominion dreadnaught, but in this version the bomb is released, then jumped, and when it hits the ship, it penetrates and disappears inside.

"That was your all-nighter, the concept piece?" Morgan asks.

"An hour of it. The other thirty-five were spent creating the specifications for it. Our first test unit will be available in two days."

"What?" Morgan asks in disbelief. "How?"

"Suffice it to say, the Iknosan have excellent design tools and fast prototyping systems."

As Morgan broods over my words, Max, the weapons specialist, asks, "But how are you going to test it?"

"I'm still working on that."

Max shakes his head. "I understand why you would want to do this. We could build ten thousand of those things in less time than one hundred ships, which, if it works, increases the odds of us being prepared in time. But until we have proof that it works, we can't back off on the ships."

"Agreed, but..."

Morgan puts up his hand. "We need to focus on the ships, but if you have the prototyping capacity to make a few, I think we will want them."

"How much does it weigh?" Justin asks.

"About five thousand pounds, a thousand of which is the tungsten penetrator. There's maybe ten pounds of the expensive rare earths in the shell, jump system, and conduits. The rest is commodity metals," I reply.

"So, we can probably make these with only a million dollars' worth of materials. We'd be happy to front a couple of them, right?"

I nod.

"We'll work up a price..." Justin pauses, then looks at me. "How much of the fabrication time is the tungsten penetrator?"

"It is the single longest step, maybe forty percent of the total fab time," I reply.

"Then if this proves out, we can probably leverage the domestic industry to increase our production rate, then transport the parts up."

"I like the way you're thinking about this, Justin," Morgan says.

Justin points at me. "He's the genius. I'm just the accountant."

One of the curious things I've noted over the last couple of months is the change in Justin. I've never seen him as engaged in the details of a project, or as committed to it as he is to this one. And he's even put on some humility. Is it Jill's influence? Maybe To'Kana's? Or is it the project itself, something more important to him than money?

"So can we get on with discussion of the fleet?" Morgan asks.

"My concept of the fleet has changed little since the last time we met. We're still targeting two-hundred-fifty of our thousand-foot-long ships. But we're adding a fifth deck, with a shuttle bay and additional propellant and weapons storage. I'll need to double check the propulsion scaling, but the conceptual design is done."

Discussion drags on a bit, but no one challenges the basic concept and I agree to present preliminary plans the first week of January.

CHAPTER 11: DECEPTION

[12.22.2033] TAWNY OWL ESTATE, EDNA VALLEY, CA

As the limo pulls up, I eye the twelve-bedroom estate that Justin has rented for the holidays. It's nestled into the mountainside at the east end of Edna Valley.

Justin elbows me and nods toward the mansion. "Not so bad, aye?"

"Not exactly Aspen," Jill teases from the seat opposite.

"But only an hour by helicopter from Big Bear," Justin comes back.

The banter between the two of them makes me smile. Neither really wants to spend Christmas here, but both have become increasingly protective of me. When my mother insisted that I come home for the holidays, this was the compromise. It's silly when you think about it. I survived two tours in Afghanistan, still work out with my squad every day—well, almost every day. Yet somehow, I'm safer with these two. At least I won't have Mark and Crystal in my face the next two weeks.

We exit the limo and I stop to take in the panorama. Spread across the nearby hillsides and valley floor below is the well-known Tawny Owl Vineyard, purchased and renamed in 2026 by a British friend of Justin's. In the spring, when the grapes are flowering, this must be beautiful.

At the opposite end of the property sits the owner's new mansion. The one we're staying at is the old one, a rental. Justin and Jill will have dinner with them tonight. Me? I'll be having dinner with my sister and her husband's family.

"Let's go inside," Justin prods. "I'm eager to see the cellar."

...

To my surprise, Justin has staffed the house—two butlers, a maid, and a chef. I guess this is the way Justin lives when he's not bunked out in a cabin on site in the desert.

My butler took my bag up, asked where I wanted things, then shooed me out, saying fresh clothes would be ironed and laid out for me before dinner.

Justin and Jill took a little longer. But now, less than an hour after arrival, we're taking the elevator down into the cellar.

"I'm told the cellar is cavernous, stretching back a hundred or more yards into the mountain," Justin pronounces.

"You mean there's a wine cellar down here?" I ask.

"Was. I think it's empty now. Michael put in a vast system when he expanded the winery."

As the elevator dings, the door opens, and I'm shocked by what I see—a hallway with an arched ceiling twenty or more feet tall, lights flicking on one after the other, click, click, click for fifteen seconds.

"First class climate control," Justin says. "No dust, no mold smell. It's perfect."

"You thinking about cellaring wine?" I ask, now confused about why we are here.

Justin snorts. "No...," stretching out the word as if it is obvious. "Come on, I think I see side tunnels."

Sure enough. Thirty feet down, shorter tunnels with lower ceilings branch out on both sides, two dozen of them in total. At the end of the main tunnel, there's a rotunda of sorts with an office-like set up and a phone line.

"This is perfect!" Justin blurts out.

"For what?" I ask, now frustrated that Justin has cut me out of the loop on whatever this is.

"Storing our refined materials." Justin's tone suggests that it has been obvious since the outset. "I'll need to do the math and have one of To'Kana's bots verify the environmental controls, but I think the side tunnels will house most of our stuff. And the main hallway..." He stretches his arms wide. "Room for ten of the Iknosan large industrial replicators. We can't manufacture the hulls here. That will need to be done in space. But we can fabricate most of the ship's components here, then transport them up."

Suddenly, the genius of the plan sinks in. We can manufacture all the critical components for our war effort here, where no prying eyes will ever see them. "You plan to buy this place?"

"Lease. $45,000 a month, twelve months, first two in advance. Includes use of the cellar and a bottle a month of a current release Tawny Owl Vineyards wine." Justin gloats at the cleverness of his plan. "It's a steal. Michael has framed this as a vacation home rental. He gets $3,000 a night, but only rents it a hundred nights a year and doesn't like the constant coming and going. I frame it as a twenty-six thousand square foot manufacturing operation with another two or three thousand square feet of office space. Yeah, Michael can't learn about any of that, but he never will. You good with this?"

"Genius," I affirm. "But what about the warehouse you're building near Amber, Nevada?"

"It's still there and looks busy enough to make it look like what we say it is. But it has attracted too much attention and a couple of break-ins. Going forward, everything of consequence will be done here in complete secrecy. The rest can be done there to maintain the cover."

"Good idea."

"Great. I'll close the deal over dinner tonight."

LE CHATEAU, SAN LUIS OBISPO, CA

The limo pulls up in front of San Luis Obispo's newest French restaurant right on time. It's at the edge of town, built in an old home, rebuilt to look like a French chateau with perfectly carved stone walls and cobblestone driveway.

Laura has wanted to eat here since it opened but hasn't been able to get a reservation. Justin fixed that problem for me two weeks ago. I step up the three wide half-steps and the door is opened for me.

"Good evening, Dr. Wimberly. Welcome to Le Chateau."

I step into the building's beautiful lobby, taking in the African mahogany paneled walls, carved wainscoting, and crown molding. Three red velvet curtains separate the lobby from the dining rooms, a Christmas tree between each entrance.

The host motions toward the curtain on the far side of the room. "This way, please. Your party has already been seated in Dining Room Three."

The scene around me is surreal, like something out of one of those movies about the run up to World War II. What was a place like this doing in SLO, as the locals call our town?

Stepping through the curtain, I see Laura's radiant face. The pregnancy seems to agree with her. A smile spreads when she recognizes me. "Kyle, you're here."

Her husband Chris is on his feet in an instant, stepping over to shake my hand. "Kyle. Welcome home. Thanks for arranging this." He motions toward the fourth seat at the table. "You remember my sister, Sophie?"

Sophie stands to give me a hug. "Merry Christmas, Dr. Wimberly."

I accept the hug and, to my surprise, get a kiss on the cheek as well.

"Good to see you again, Dr. Burns."

Sophie laughs. "I'm only Dr. Burns to my patients."

Once again, our siblings have conspired to set the two of us up.

"I hear you're staying at the Tawny Owl Estate. What's it like?" Sophie asks as the server comes over to pour me some water.

"My business partner, Justin, set up this trip, and…" I put my hands up in confession. "…arranged for dinner here tonight."

"Your company must be doing well."

"It is…"

I'm cut off by Laura. "No business talk! This is a holiday celebration for the four of us."

As if contradicting his wife, Chris asks, "Is it true that you're being selected as the prime contractor for the government's new Space Force build out?"

I glance at Laura, who seems to listen, not complaining. "That's the way many are describing it. But strictly speaking, the joint venture we formed with Boeing and SpaceX is the prime contractor. We are the primary technology providers, so will control about 60% of the budget."

Chris's jaw drops open. "That's like half a trillion dollars, right?"

Again, I put my hands up. "Guys, it's a holiday celebration."

"Kyle, will your company really be taking in that much?" This time, the question comes from Laura.

I sigh, then shrug. "I don't know the number. It'll be a lot. But that's not what our company is about. We are putting protections in place that will hopefully be enough to save our world. And if we can't do that, then it doesn't matter. Does it?"

"Sorry," Chris says. "Didn't mean for the conversation to go that way. You deserve this win, Kyle. You've earned it."

After a long moment of silence, our server comes back. "Do we know what we'd like to have for dinner tonight?"

…

As we stand to leave, Sophie nudges me, then glances toward the bar. "Have a minute?"

The sadness in her eyes compels me to say yes. As we divert toward it, Laura gives me the slightest smile and a hopeful look. Then they are away.

Two or three steps later, we're intercepted by the smiling host. "Dr. Wimberly, Ms. Burns, if you would prefer a more private setting…"

That I'm the one referred to as the doctor really irritates me.

Sophie seems to sense my ire but takes my arm as she smiles at the host. "That would be nice."

The host leads us up a flight of stairs to an empty dining room, then out onto a heated balcony. "What can I get for you?" he asks. "Perhaps a bottle of the Laetitia 2027 Cuvée M Méthode Champenoise Sparkling? Locally produced. 94-point rating. These are hard to find, but I have one for you."

I don't know what the right answer is. Sophie, who had a glass of Chardonnay earlier, answers, "That would be nice."

As the host exits, Sophie turns her eyes toward me. "When we met at Thanksgiving... Well, I thought there was something there. When I didn't hear from you, I was really disappointed."

As I start to reply, she holds up a hand. "I didn't know that you were who you are. In truth, I don't think Laura did either."

The sound of a bottle of champagne popping open disrupts the conversation. Then, two glasses appear and a moment later are filled with effervescent liquid. "Laetitia, Cuvée M. Please enjoy."

As quickly as our server came, he's gone.

I lift my glass. "Merry Christmas."

Sophie smiles. "Merry Christmas."

We clink and sip, two professional adults sharing an awkward moment.

"Do you think Mark and Crystal will go through with it?"

The question knocks me off balance.

"She told me the two of you were a thing for several years and you proposed to her once. My sense of it was that she regretted moving on."

"She broke my heart, then took up with my brother when he became heir apparent—drove me away from my family. No love lost there. What about you? Anyone break your heart that way?"

"Not that way, no. None of the guys I dated dumped me for my brother."

Her statement is so preposterous that my sip of champagne catches in my throat. The coughing fit that follows turns into tear-filled laughter, which is apparently contagious. Eventually, we regain control of ourselves.

I look up at her, and once again am captured by her eyes. "Thank you. I needed a good laugh."

"Me, too."

We sit silently for a few minutes, sipping our wine, me gazing into her beguiling eyes.

"Any plans for tomorrow?" she asks.

The question puts me back into business mode, which thankfully I contain. "Christmas shopping. I haven't gotten anything for anybody. You?"

"Same."

"Want to go shopping together?"

Sophie smiles. "Sure."

[12.23.2033] TAWNY OWL ESTATE

I wake to pounding on my bedroom door. "Kai, get the hell up! We have things to discuss before Jill and I head out to Big Bear."

I scramble out of bed, slightly hung over. Between the wine with dinner and the bubbly with Sophie, I think I drank a full bottle.

"Coming!"

Fifteen minutes later, I arrive downstairs to the smell of cinnamon and strong coffee. That's when I realize the sun isn't up yet.

"Pleasant evening?" Justin asks.

"Very," I answer back.

"Sophie didn't come back with you?"

"What!"

My response is firm enough that Justin raises his hand in surrender. "Sorry, no offense. Laura led me to believe she was hooking you up with her sister-in-law."

Justin's statement is wrong on so many levels that it's offensive.

"Sorry, it didn't work out," he piles on.

I shake my head. "Why am I up at 6:30 AM while on holiday?"

"Your evening may have been a failure, but mine wasn't. Michael signed the lease. The place is ours starting January 1. We're welcome to stay until then. We need to coordinate with To'Kana to start the material transfer and manufacturing setup. He's offered twenty bots that we can keep here for the duration."

"We?"

"Yes, we. I set it up. You do it. That's what makes us *we*."

Justin must have had a good time last night. He's never this audacious on a normal morning.

Jill, who came in during the last exchange, points at me. "I see you've received the '*we*' speech, too."

Our conversation is interrupted by an alarm sounding on Justin's mobile phone. I note his puzzled look as he says, "excuse me," then steps out of the room.

"Do you know what that's about?" I ask Jill.

"Maybe. Quite a few people on his contact list have unique ring tones. He uses ones like that for government people, but I don't recognize it."

We wait in silence, then Jill breaks it. "Justin told me about your brother's engagement. You knew this was coming, didn't you?"

Anger wells up at the mention of Mark and Crystal, but quickly morphs into grief.

"Why do you hang on to her?" Jill asks.

"I loved her; was planning to marry her."

"Did you ask her to marry you?"

"I did. She wanted to wait."

"Let it go, Kai. It's not fair to you or your family to cling to something that wasn't meant to be."

The anger is back. This time, it morphs into defeat.

"Kai, give it up. There are lots of women who are interested in you. You may not, but I see the way Alex looks at you. Justin says your brother-in-law's sister, Sophie, is very disappointed not to have heard from you. You're one of the most eligible bachelors in the world. Crystal was never good enough for you. Go find someone who will be."

As the door opens, I give Jill the slightest smile.

"We need to go see Jace," Justin says without preamble. "Thelma is ready to transport us."

"How long will you be?" Jill asks.

"I'm hoping an hour, but don't know. Sorry to leave you stranded."

"And here I was expecting to go skiing today," Jill complains.

"And I promised to take Sophie Christmas shopping."

"Give me her number. I'll take her," Jill offers. "The two of us can probably have a lot of fun with Justin's American Express."

Justin smiles and gives her a kiss. "Thanks, babe."

I find myself jealous of their relationship.

"Let's go," Justin prods.

I stand and close my eyes. "Thelma, please initiate transport."

JACE ELLIOTT'S RESIDENCE

Before my eyes are even open, I hear Jace. "Gentlemen, thanks for joining me on short notice." Looking around, I see we are in his living room, not in his den.

He turns to Justin. "Did you clue Dr. Wimberly in on the situation?"

"No. I assumed you'd want to do that when we arrived."

Jace nods and turns to me. "First, everything we will discuss here today is off the record, never happened. Are we agreed?"

I glance at Justin, who nods.

"Agreed," I reply.

"A friend of mine—a fellow called Jasper Branch—works at the FBI's Terrorist Screening Center. His team was just looped in on an initiative at the National Counterterrorism Center, which is tracking increased terrorist chatter regarding alien technology."

Inwardly, I groan at the third-hand information I'm about to be handed.

"They think the Iranians, possibly in concert with Russia or North Korea, might plan a raid on sites confirmed to be adapting alien technology."

"Certainty?" I ask.

Jace smirks. "There's never certainty. But that they're picking up message traffic means we need a plan to keep you and your technology safe."

"I agree with Jace," Justin adds, cutting off the complaint I was about to make.

"Jasper called me early this morning. He's giving a talk over at George Washington. I can't imagine who signed up for a counterterrorism talk on the Saturday morning before Christmas. I told him you were here and asked if he'd like to stop by to say hi. He's on his way over."

"The purpose of the visit?" I ask.

"He's FBI, which handles the domestic side of terrorism. Their primary mission is stopping attacks before they can be carried out. Jasper is part of their prevention team. He teaches a course at George Washington on hardening facilities, undermining the effectiveness of terrorist attacks."

Jace offers us seats, and, within minutes, he and Justin are going on about a colleague from Harvard. Bored, I open my data pad and start playing with specs I've been working on for a jump version of my flying wedge.

...

The sound of a doorbell breaks my attention. A moment later, a tall guy, British-white with an ink-black beard, walks in. He reminds me of the British guy who played Dr. Strange in the movies that came out about ten years ago. Introductions are exchanged and I'm the last to shake Jasper's hand.

"I saw the NBC special about you a couple of months back."

"It gathered a lot more attention than I expected."

Jasper nods his head. "Off the record, that's why I called Jace. There are no credible threats directed at you that I know of. But over the last month, your name has popped up in messages among people known to be affiliated with Iranian-backed terrorist groups."

The words confuse me. If he is worried about my safety, why call Jace?

As if reading my mind, Jasper adds, "Given my role, I'm not allowed to meet with you publicly. It would spark speculation."

Jace intervenes. "Why don't we all take seats?" Then, turning to Jasper. "You have some recommendations for Kyle, right?"

"I do." He pauses. "I ran a quick tracking report on you, Kyle. Over the last three months, you've been spotted in only a handful of locations: your facility at Full Cycle Solar; in the Las Vegas area; at the Santa Fe, and San Luis Obispo airports; and at your parent's home and various other locations in the San Luis Obispo area. No terrorist could make that list in the hour it took me. But it really doesn't matter. Everyone knows of Full Cycle Solar now."

"Your point?" I ask.

"You have two options. The first is probably the easiest. Relocate and keep the location secret."

"You mean go into hiding?"

"I suppose you could frame it that way. The second option is to create a lot of doubt about where you are."

"Say more about that."

"Have three, four, maybe five spots where you are seen regularly. Create uncertainty about where you are or have been recently."

"But how would I get any work done?"

Justin, who has been quiet, inserts himself.

"Kyle, you might not want to admit this, but Full Cycle Solar is at a place where it can run itself. The addition of the twenty-megawatt generators has assured its short-term financial performance. If we continue feeding Mac with another one every month as planned, we will blow away all of our original projections."

I nod, thinking I know where this is going.

"The point I'm making is that you've been tied to FCS Headquarters for the last three years. That's no longer necessary. We can name a new general manager for FCS operations and make a big deal about you taking over one of our other companies. With enough pictures and press, we could raise your visibility while obfuscating your location."

As Justin finishes, I see the way he is looking at Jasper and, in an instant, know that something is wrong. Now more apprehensive, I ask, "How certain are you that this is real, if there is no specific plot you can point to?"

He launches into a data driven argument about types of attacks and how they correlate with chatter. That normal people have an infinitesimally small probability of being a victim of foreign terrorism if they have not been associated with one category of chatter or another. And he knows of at least two categories that I am associated with... blah, blah, blah.

Then the question comes, "So, where are you staying now? How many people know that is where you are? And does anyone know where or when you will move on to the next place?"

I notice Justin's subtle head shake and his index finger motioning toward the door.

I nod. "Jasper. Thanks for the heads up. I agree with your assessment of the situation. We'll make this a top priority. If you get specific information, you'd like to share off-the-record, we are in regular touch with Jace."

He stands. "Thanks for listening. It's been a pleasure meeting you both."

A minute later, Jasper's out the door. As soon as it is closed, Jace says, "That was abrupt."

Although the comment is directed at me, Justin says, "Sorry about that. We've been discussing a contingency plan. The conversation was enough to push us into action, and as Jasper suggested, the less he knows about what we are doing, the safer we will all be."

Jace looks at Justin, clearly dissatisfied with the exchange. But a moment later, his smile is back, and he nods his head. "Then let's wrap this up for now."

DINING ROOM, TAWNY OWL ESTATE

"What was that about?" I ask as soon as we materialize.

Jill, who's still sitting at the dining room table, asks, "What happened?"

Justin puts a hand up, quieting Jill, then gives me a concerned look. "I don't trust Jasper. And I'm not sure I trust Jace anymore, either."

"Why not?"

"Kai, he ran a tracking report on you. He didn't say how, but it was almost certainly by tracking your cell phone, and he cited every place you've been since the first day we met with Jace."

"OK," I reply cautiously, sensing that Justin hasn't delivered the punchline yet.

"The terrorist chatter started about a month ago. Our trips to Vegas and Santa Fe were over four months ago. The Privacy Rights Act of 2028 prohibits telephone companies from disclosing phone numbers or location information over three months old without a court order."

Justin's words astonish me. "Are you saying they got a court order to track my location?"

"Or cheated and got them illegally, or maybe they started tracking you after Audell's piece came out, or maybe when you first met Jace. Doesn't build a lot of trust, does it?"

"In all likelihood, they're tracking us too," Jill speculates.

Justin looks at Jill. "True."

He turns back to me. "I didn't get it until he suggested multiple locations and I suggested you didn't need to be tied down at FCS anymore. The look on Jasper's face was the giveaway. He clearly wanted to know all about our locations and operations."

"So, what do we do?"

"I need to think about this more, but two things pop to the top of my mind. First, you need to decide where you want your official presence to be. I'm thinking it should be here. Michael already has a lot of security; we could add more. But that's the only place you can turn your cell phone on unless you're going someplace you want to be tracked. Second, all movement that you don't want tracked needs to be via transporter. They can't track that. Similarly, all phone calls at other locations must be single use phones."

"Maybe after Christmas. I'm not ready to say goodbye to FCS."

"You don't need to say goodbye. You could go there every day. Just transport from the cellar to the lab, leaving your cell phone turned on here, having a prepaid phone, or a phone in someone else's name you leave turned on there."

I notice Jill looking at her watch. A moment later, Justin's eyes follow mine.

"We can still make it to the airport in time," she says.

"Then let's go."

As he looks back at me, Justin adds. "I like this plan. Let's let it rest, revisit it tomorrow. Why don't you invite your girlfriend over for dinner tonight?"

"Maybe I will."

DOWNTOWN SAN LUIS OBISPO

When I called Sophie this morning, she suggested we meet at SLO Provisioning Company at 11:00 AM. "It has the best chicken salad in town."

Now seated there, I'm once again lost in those eyes.

"Who are you shopping for today?" she asks.

"Mom, Dad, and Laura, you?"

"My mom, Chris, Laura, my sister Lisa, and my nephew, Teddy."

"Do you know what you want to get them?"

"Craft olive oil for mom. Some cool toy, yet to be discovered, for Teddy, goofy knit socks for Chris, a last trimester BumpBox subscription for Laura..."

"A what?"

"Gift boxes for pregnant women. I always thought things like this were hokey, but one of my patients raved about it. So why not? What about you?"

"I've heard there's a new non-alcoholic wine that is worthy of drinking. They're tasting it today at..." I snap my fingers a couple of times, trying to remember the name of the store. "The place near the library."

"I know the one you mean," Sophie assures.

"If it's any good, I'll get it for Laura. Beyond that, I don't know."

"Your mother needs a new easel. Her's is getting a bit wobbly."

"You know Mom paints?" I ask, surprised Sophie would have a suggestion.

"I've spent more time at your parent's place in the last two months than you have in the last three years."

"Really?"

"Did you know she's giving art lessons again?"

"No, I didn't."

"I'm one of her students."

"Ah, should have guessed. Do you know what she wants?

Sophie smiles. "The tall Mont Marte Signature Box Floor Easel in Cherry. They have it over at Artists Central. It's expensive, over five hundred bucks. That's why she still has her wobbly one."

"Then that's what we'll get for her."

From the smile I get back, I think Sophie is excited to see the easel in mom's studio.

"And one of your father's favorite tools broke a couple of weeks back. What was it called? Something to do with biscuits..."

"His biscuit joiner? Oh..." I groan, "That's got to be killing him."

As we laugh, our meal comes: rotisserie chicken salad for Sophie, rosemary potato soup for me.

A couple bites in, Sophie says, "Your mother complained that Mark and Crystal were going to her parents for Christmas dinner."

I look up and see her looking at me and am once again captured by her eyes.

"Thanks."

"Someday, you're going to have to make this right," she whispers.

My impulse is to say, *when hell freezes over*. But Sophie seems to bring out the best in me. "Someday."

"So, where are we going to go first?" she asks, all bright and perky again.

"The art store? You can be my guide."

TED'S TOYS

It has been a surprisingly fun day. I got mom a new easel and a ton of supplies. I got dad two new biscuit joiners: a large one like the one he had, and a small one optimized for picture frames. The dealcoholized wine was passable, so I got two for Laura. The store was also tasting a bourbon I'd never heard of before. Apparently, it's one Chris has been wanting to try, so I got one for him. Sophie found the olive oil she wanted; she also found the craziest pair of knit socks I've ever seen.

We're now at our last stop and I'm blown away by the number and quality of toys and games this place has. The display of spaceships and games in the sci-fi section on the second floor has captured my inner child.

"Kai, come look at this."

I walk over and see the toy rocket she's holding. "Did you ever have one of these?"

"Water propelled, right?"

She nods.

"Yeah, but not as nice as this one. Mine was a tiny thing, maybe eight inches long, hard translucent plastic, red, hand pump..." I try to remember the details.

"How old were you?"

"Seventh grade. I played with it a lot, loved seeing how high I could get it to go." I chuckle. "Completely forgot about that toy until just now. This one is much nicer. Thinner plastic, larger reservoir, better launch platform... Mine was just hand-held."

"Should I get you one?" she teases.

As we laugh, my eye catches a space battle scene painted on the wall. In the middle is a wedge-shaped ship that looks remarkably similar to our shuttle but has a second deck for drone and weapon deployment. Something like that, an AI piloted shuttle able to carry AI-guided weapons and drones, would be a huge force multiplier.

"Kai?" Sophie asks, bringing me back to the moment. "You OK?"

I point at the painting. "Seems these guys were way ahead of me."

She shakes her head. "You've convinced me. Teddy is only eight, but his father will love this. Ready to check out?"

As we step outside, I realize our Christmas shopping date is over. "Can I give you a lift home?"

She laughs. "I think my apartment is closer than your car." Then, after the slightest pause, she adds, "Today was fun."

"Any interest in joining us for dinner tonight, over at the estate?"

"Who else will be there?"

"My business partner, Justin, and his significant other, Jill."

When there's no immediate reply, I coax. "It will probably be a good meal. The chef Justin hired is fantastic." No reply. "I'll send a car to pick you up, so you don't have to drive."

She laughs. "No, I'd rather drive myself."

"Is that a yes?"

"What time?"

"Six-thirty?"

"I'll text you the gate code."

She gives me a hug. "See you tonight."

I watch as she walks in the opposite direction of my car, then turn to go. I have one more stop I want to make.

ESTATE HOUSE

It was around three when I got back. My first item of business was to get a gate code for Sophie. That done, I follow my nose to the kitchen where I am greeted by our chef, who is delighted to hear we will be having a fourth for dinner.

Now in the den, I quickly scan my data pad for any new messages. There's one from Mac.

> *Merry Christmas, boss. Your Christmas present went online this afternoon at 1:00 PM mountain time. We are now pumping out ninety megawatts.*
>
> *Enzo took the lead today. Tonight, he's making a lasagna for the few of us working through the holiday here. Alex sends her best Christmas wishes. Enjoy your week away. Mac.*

As much as I'm enjoying my time away, I miss my team and feel guilty for leaving them during the holidays.

I shake off the melancholy and turn my attention back to my surveillance drone. How much would I need to scale it up to add a weapon with meaningful teeth?

...

A light knock on the door frame draws my attention.

"Excuse me, sir. Master Justin just called. He and Ms. Jill will not be returning until tomorrow. It's snowing in the mountains; the helicopter is grounded." He pauses. "Dinner for two... In the dining room...? Maybe in here."

I look at my cell phone. 6:15. It's too late to warn Sophie. "In here, please. What are tonight's wine options?"

"I'll bring you the menu, sir."

I don't like what's happened here. I invited Sophie over for dinner with Justin and Jill. Now, it's just the two of us. I'm not a predator; not a womanizer. Best I meet her outside. I don't want her coming in through the front door until she knows what's happened.

I shutdown my tablet and put it on the desk. Then get up.

"Master Kyle," my butler says. "Your guest just passed through security."

The way he's looking at me reminds me I'm not dressed appropriately for dinner. "I'm a mess? Aren't I?"

"Come. I've set a change of clothes in the preparation room."

I follow as he dashes off. What in the world is a preparation room?

Down the hall, a turn left, then in through the door on the right. I hear the tongues click as I come in.

"Lady Jill's attendants," he says, then exits.

My head spins as three women approach. "Clothes off. We can make you presentable in three minutes." The disdain in the matron's voice is unmistakable. But three minutes later, I'm running toward the front door a new man. I open it as headlights come around the circle. The car parks, its headlights go out, then Sophie emerges, her sundress belying the cool of the evening.

"Kyle?"

With a smile, I walk down the steps to greet her. "Welcome."

She gives me a hug, then asks, "What's the matter?"

I'm obviously broadcasting my discomfort. "Justin and Jill got stuck in a snowstorm on Bear Mountain. I swear it's true. The chef has made us a wonderful meal..."

My words sputter out, then I take in a deep breath. "It's just you and me. I wanted you to know that before you came in."

She takes my hand. "How sweet. Shall we?"

Once in through the front door, she takes in the grand foyer and its imposing staircase. "Is this the way you live now?"

How is it that the women in my life always ask the questions I'm least able to answer? "I don't know. I spent the last three years in a sparse cabin in the desert, where my biggest worry was the scorpions and rattlesnakes that lurked there. This place is Justin, and..."

I don't want to lie about the lease, so I just shut up.

"Laura told me that Justin rented this place for the Holidays. It's iconic in the area, so I'd love to see it. You only have it for a couple of days, right?"

"Ah..."

"You have to be out tomorrow?"

"No." Motioning towards the main sitting room, I ask. "Would you like to come in and see?"

She smiles. "I would."

I give Sophie a tour of the first floor: the sitting room, the living room, and the dining room.

There, we are intercepted by one of the kitchen staff. "Dinner is ready. The table in the den is set. We have two bottles of wine for your consideration."

Once settled, a bottle of Chardonnay selected and glasses poured, the appetizer comes out, shrimp ceviche. Bon appetite.

"Is this the way you live?"

"No," I say a little too emphatically. "I live in the desert, dodging scorpions and rattlesnakes."

Sophie laughs. "When's the last time you saw a scorpion or a rattlesnake?"

"Valid point. There were a lot the first year. Not so many recently."

Sophie reaches across the table, placing her hand on mine. "This place isn't you."

"No, but..."

"But?" she asks.

"This place is Justin. He's planning to rent it for the next year, and I think I will spend most of my time here."

"Why?" she asks.

"Because this place is perfect for what we need."

"And what do you need?" she asks, as the appetizers are cleared.

Another bottle of wine and three courses later, the chef places two snifters of Cognac in front of us. "That's all for tonight's service. We'll be back in the morning for breakfast. Have a pleasant evening."

As they retreat, Sophie says, "I think that was as good as last night." She looks down at her snifter. "But I'm not so sure about this."

Minutes later, we are in the kitchen where the staff is finally eating dinner.

"Master Kyle?" The head server asks.

"You wouldn't have any bubbly, would you?"

"Only the best. Shall we serve it up on the overlook?"

I feel bad about tearing my butler away from his dinner, but the next thing I know, Sophie and I are sitting on the third floor balcony, overlooking the valley floor and lit, on this moonless night, by the stars above.

"Do people really live like this?" Sophie asks. "It seems indulgent."

"Justin seems to. This is a first for me. You've seen my parents' place. You've seen Afghanistan. My home in the desert is more like Afghanistan than my parents' place. And I've found peace in my work there. But it's all about to be stolen from us. So why not live in the moment?"

211

We sit there in silence for a while, then Sophie takes my hand. "I don't want to drive home at this hour."

"Only two of twelve bedrooms are in use. You have the pick of the house."

"Can I share your room?"

CHAPTER 12: CHRISTMAS

[12.24.2033] CELLAR, ESTATE HOUSE

Sophie cleared out early this morning, so she could run a few errands before heading over to the hospital for a twelve-hour shift starting at eleven. Justin called to let me know they were planning to take advantage of the fresh snow this morning, but planned to be back at the estate by sunset this evening. He also told me that To'Kana was ready to send material and equipment down to the cellar if I had time today to supervise.

So here I am. Five bots have already transported down. One is standing with its back to the north wall of the main tunnel. Four others have precisely measured out where the footings for the first replicator need to go.

"Kai, we are ready to transport. Signal me when you are ready."

"We're ready, Thelma."

A three-centimeter square, two-meter-long metal tube appears on the floor. Then, in rapid succession three more appear, lining up end to end. Once joined, these four pieces will form the southern footing for replicator one.

A moment later, a U-shaped piece of metal about half a meter long appears near the first junction point. In short order, two more appear, one at each of the two other junction points.

"Kai, please confirm that this is where you want the first footing to go. If it is, ask the bots to join the pieces."

I walk over and see that the pieces line up exactly with the markings we made. Then, using my implant, I order the lead robot to join the pieces.

The two bots at either end of the south footing hold their position. The other three scurry over and place the U-shaped pieces over the three points that need to be joined. The bots at either end confirm the alignment of the pieces, then each of the three bots deploys a tool that they pass over their U-shaped piece. Amazingly, it seems to melt into place, perfectly smooth, as if the pieces had never been separate.

Again, the bots on the end confirm alignment, then all five return to their original positions.

A second footing is formed, parallel to the first in the same way about a foot apart. An hour later, ten parallel bars, each eight meters long, rest on the floor.

Next comes what looks like plates of sheet metal. One by one, they are transported down and attached until we have an eight-meter long, four-meter-wide platform that appears to my eye to be completely flat.

"Thelma, how flat is the platform?"

"About twenty-five microns. Nowhere near flat enough. The bots have only done a rough alignment. The next step will reduce the maximum variance to ten microns and modify the floor beneath to sit completely flat."

Several more devices appear that float above the surface of our platform. They move back and forth as they vibrate. Activity slows to the point where I'm wondering whether-or-not they are done. That's when I notice the dust accumulating on the floor.

"Thelma, what's causing the dust on the floor?"

"Erosion of the material below the foundation. We are nearly finished. The bots will clean it up when they are done."

Looking at my watch, I see that I've been down here for three hours now and will need to go soon.

Thelma calls me, "Kai. This platform is done. I have five more bots ready to transport down. Would you like me to do that now?"

"Yes, please."

Seconds later, five more bots appear at the end of the hall.

"Kai, given your other obligations today, would it be OK if the bots put foundations in for the other nine replicators? I think we can get it done and cleaned up overnight without supervision."

"That would be perfect."

As I turn to go, the thought occurs. I did nothing today other than watch the bots work. I wonder if that was the purpose—to prove I wasn't necessary. As the alarm on my watch goes off, I pick up my pace. I'm due at my parents in fifteen minutes.

WINERY, WIMBERLY VINEYARDS

Mom and dad have hosted Christmas morning at the winery every year since they took it over. Everyone in the family—aunts, uncles, cousins, both sides—are invited, and most years some come, fewer than in the old days because of the migration east. But it's open to everyone, winery employees as well. Everyone needs to bring at least one unlabeled gift.

As you can probably guess, it takes a lot of work to pull this off, so I've volunteered to help. It also serves an ulterior motive—to deliver the large presents I bought that would be awkward to bring on Christmas morning.

The last time I was here was my senior year in high school. This will be Mark's first year to miss it. Mom, of course, wants both her sons here, but that's not likely to happen in the foreseeable future.

Leaving my stuff in the car, I go in to see who's inside. I'm immediately greeted by Dad. "Kyle, how I've looked forward to this day!"

Funny thing, when Mom says that, as she has a couple times now, I feel like she's laying this big guilt trip on me. Dad, on the other hand, is just happy, which at the end of the day is who he is.

Behind him are two guys: a young guy who I've never seen before, and one of the old vineyard hands, a huge guy who must be in his seventies by now, named Larry, I think. I haven't seen him in ages.

Dad points at him. "You remember Larry, right?"

I put out my hand to shake, but am enveloped in a giant bear hug.

"Kyle, my boy. I was afraid I'd never see you again." He grabs me by the shoulders and holds me at arm's length the way my grandmother used to. "Look at you... Fighting aliens. Building spaceships. I'm so proud of you."

His smile droops a bit as he motions to the other guy, who in truth doesn't look that friendly.

"Kyle, meet Jeremy..."

I put out my hand to shake. Jeremy takes it.

"...he's one of Mark's best friends, who's come to help since Mark is away."

The cursory shake is done by the time Dad spills the beans, but my buoyant smile vanishes as the word *"Pleasure"* comes out of my mouth.

"Well," Dad says exuberantly. "You said you wanted two tents set up. There are several set up already, but they're claimed. There's ten more in storage, including some of the fancy ones. Help yourself."

"Could I also have a crate?"

Dad smiles. "You brought a large community gift?"

I nod.

He chuckles and slaps his leg. "Oh, what a great Christmas this one will be! Jeremy is responsible for the crates. You two have at it."

The lingo of a Wimberly Christmas is a bit unique. The core activity is gift exchange. It's also a party of sorts with food and drink. Everyone that comes is required to bring at least one community gift. You can bring one for immediate family, two others for extended family. Most gifts are deposited on the platform holding the Christmas trees. Bulky gifts can be placed in a crate. Originally, we had old sea chests. For those bringing large gifts, like the easels I bought, you can reserve a tent, not a very descriptive name, but it is the one that stuck. Most of the tents consist of a metal frame three feet by three feet with an opaque shower curtain hanging from it. You can set up your gift any way you want, close the shower curtain, and put the gift tag on the outside.

There's an informal competition of sorts to put together the cleverest large gifts. These tend to be expensive. Most years, five or ten are given in the family section. From the look of it, we may have that many in the community section this year.

The community gifts are given out at random, Santa Clauses—yeah, we have more than one—drawing names from a bag. They are opened one by one. Swapping is encouraged. But unlike some other gift exchange games, stealing is not allowed.

Jeremy helps me carry in the community gift I bought, then helps me choose a crate and to load the gift in it. At first, I was put off because he was Mark's close friend and didn't look all that friendly. But, after a half hour of working with him, I conclude that he's a genuinely nice guy. Mark is lucky to have a friend like Jeremy. Anybody would be.

We shake, then part ways; me to select my tents, Jeremy to get another crate off the truck parked at the freight entrance.

A minute later, Thelma's voice comes through my ear. "Kyle, we have a problem that requires your immediate attention. May I transport you out?"

I shake my head, "Thelma, I can't..." But the transporter has me in its grip and the next thing I know, I'm falling over from vertigo in some dark place.

CELLAR, ESTATE HOUSE

I pick myself up off the floor, wondering why in the hell I've been transported into the cellar. Then I see it, a portion of the floor has collapsed. I walk over to the edge and look down. The cellar has another level, this one more primitive. I see a reflection below, then realize the hole I'm looking down through is a perfect rectangle. The reflection I'm seeing is coming up off the foundation that fell through. On seeing additional movement, I realize a couple of our bots fell in as well. What a mess.

"Thelma, what's the status of our bots?"

"Kai, sorry for the abrupt transport. We are dealing with multiple crises, and I needed to get you to someplace safe."

"What's going on Thelma? Why wasn't I safe at the winery?"

There's silence on the line for a second.

"We should have scanned the floor of the cellar tunnel before we started installing the replicator..."

"Thelma! Answer the question?"

"Did you not ask about the status of our bots?"

"That can wait. Why wasn't I safe at the winery?"

"I don't know. Why weren't you safe?"

"You said you were dealing with multiple crises and transported me abruptly because you needed to get me someplace safe."

"When did this happen?"

"A minute ago."

"Kai, I have no record of having transported you today."

"Can you tell if your records have been modified?"

As the seconds tick by with no reply, my anxiety builds.

"Kyle." The voice belongs to To'Kana.

As panic starts to overtake me, he asks, "Would you consent to coming aboard the ship?

"What happened to my parents?"

"Your parents are fine, but I need your help here for something very urgent."

IKNOSAN LEGACY SHIP

I open my eyes and find myself in a section of the ship I've never seen before.

"Kyle, thank you for coming aboard," To'Kana says. "I think I know what happened. But I need your confirmation and guidance. Before I tell you my theory, I want to show you five people who we are holding in stasis. Two are wounded; one seriously. The three others are in good health."

"Where did these people come from?"

"Let me show you first."

The wall next to me opens, revealing dozens of cylindrical glass tanks, five of which are occupied. Scanning them quickly, I see the first four appear to hold people of middle eastern origin. The last of the four has knife wounds on his legs. But, the fifth person was stabbed dozens of times. The sight of it repulses me, then I see the face. Jeremy!

"Oh my God," I whisper. "Terrorists. They were looking for me, but got Jeremy instead."

"That was my theory, as well. I presume you would like me to repair your friend. I only ask because of my people's traditions."

"His chances?"

"He is at little risk. Which brings us to the other four. What would you have me do with them?"

A hundred thoughts go through my mind, most of which involve the painful death of these men. But To'Kana's intense concentration on me suggests that this is another test.

"We need to find out who sent them. Do you have the means to help with that?"

"I have already extracted their memories. The only name they know is the man that recruited them, Hamid Najafi in Los Angeles. I have a picture of him."

A two-dimensional image of the man appears in a holoprojection, but what I see surprises me: white, wide face, high cheeks, deep round eye sockets... "He looks Russian to me."

"His real name is Pyotr Kovrov."

"How do you know that?"

"Human computing systems with their binary encoding are intrinsically insecure. We have copies of every ID card issued by every government since they began keeping digital records. And we have excellent image-based search engines we can search with images recovered from neural scans. It took less than five minutes to extract the name they knew and a suitable image from these relatively weak minds. Another minute, to find his real name."

"We need to bring him to justice, preferably through our justice system." I assert.

To'Kana's eyes are on me again, their probing stare forming some sort of judgment. "He has instigated an attack on someone under Iknosan protection. In time of war, I have the power and responsibility to execute him. What benefit would it bring to hand him over to your authorities? I will allow him no mercy greater than that which I would offer to a Dominion warrior."

"He is not the leader of this operation. Someone else gave the order."

"Excellent point. I will research the issue." To'Kana pauses as he rubs the handful of whiskers on his chin in thought, then points at the tank holding Jeremy. "Your friend lost enough blood that he will need a transfusion. His injuries will be repaired in a few hours. Shall we attempt a stealth return? At this point, he is simply missing. No one witnessed the attack."

"Two questions."

To'Kana lifts an eyebrow.

"Can you transport my car back to the estate without anyone seeing it?"

"I can."

"Can you make him lose the last couple minutes of his memory, such that he does not remember the attack?"

"Easily."

"Can you put a little alcohol in his stomach?"

"Of course, though I might point out, you asked three questions. Does that mean you have a plan?"

I quickly lay out my plan.

"Clever. Now to our last crisis, your cellar. We have a choice to make. Repair. Or expand. It is easy enough to repair, though it will set us back three days with no benefit to show for the time lost. Alternatively, we could add a second level large enough to support ten more replicators. This would take two weeks, but it would double your production capacity."

"I like the expansion idea, but I would prefer this decision to be taken by Justin."

To'Kana looks at me with what I perceive to be a sense of wonder. "My world has no sense of power sharing like the one you and Justin share. I give this decision to you. You give it to Justin. If my world had anything like this, then maybe it would still live." He pauses, apparently lost in reflection. A moment later, he snaps back. "Then expansion it is."

ESTATE HOUSE

I'm back in the den tonight by myself. Justin and Jill are late again. They escaped Big Bear but had to exit to the east and are now back in

Las Vegas, stranded because nothing is available on Christmas Eve to get them back to San Luis Obispo.

To'Kana says Jeremy's wounds are healed, allowing us to return him to human care. Our plan is for him to be transported just as emergency medical arrives to pick him up. I've called 9-1-1 twice now. They say we are in the queue but recommend that I drive him in myself.

But how could that possibly work? Justin has the place crawling with staff, all of whom are getting testy, because I am the only one here. My cover has been completely blown.

"Kai, we think we have a solution." It's Thelma. "Your father is beside himself. The two of you missing—Jeremy's truck still at the winery, your car gone. He's been calling you non-stop. If you call back and apologize for being late for dinner, he will tell you about Jeremy. We'll direct you to the place where you will find him unconscious. The two of you can discover him and drive him to emergency in your father's truck. No alcohol, just anemia."

"I think I can make that work."

"Step one," Thelma says. "Call your father and apologize for being late. Think carefully about your excuse. Go."

With trepidation, I lift my phone, then click on the most recent of his calls.

"Kyle, thank God. Where are you?"

"At the estate. I had to cut out early because of issues here. Sorry I'm late for dinner."

Dad sighs a breath of relief, then turns somber. "Jeremy has gone missing, his truck still here. Please tell me he's with you."

The litany goes on a bit, then I cut in. "Dad. On my way. Maybe together we can find him."

"Please hurry."

...

I arrive at the winery and pull up to the main entrance. Mom and dad are out before I come to a stop.

In my ear, Thelma says, "Kyle, we scanned through the security camera recordings at the winery and have deleted the Iranians and the attack on Jeremy. We also found a place where no one has been all day—the outhouse in the woods behind the barn. We can add him to the security camera records entering the woods shortly after you leave. Say he wasn't feeling well. That's the best we can do."

As I get out, Dad does his stream-of-consciousness recounting of the events of the day, Mom adding details here and there.

"You know..." I start. "As I was leaving, Jeremy said he wasn't feeling well, needed some privacy."

Dad looks at me askance, but says nothing.

"Has anyone checked the old outhouse?"

"Kyle," mom starts. "It's in terrible condition. No one has used it in years."

"Adding evidence," Thelma whispers in my ear. "We'll transport him down when you are ten seconds away."

"Where else haven't you looked?" I ask innocently.

Now mom is eyeing me. But a second later, they're off, me playing catch up. As we approach, I see what they were talking about. The dilapidated outhouse is a ruin, the door off its hinges, laying on the ground. Then, I notice the body, on top of the door.

Fifteen minutes later, Jeremy is sprawled out on an old mattress in the bed of dad's truck, the tailgate down to fit the mattress. I'm tied down, as is the mattress, so we don't slide out the back. I'm holding onto Jeremy, so he doesn't slide or bounce out as we race for the emergency room at French Hospital Medical Center in the fading light of Christmas Eve dusk.

WIMBERLY RESIDENCE

We got back from the hospital an hour ago. Dad helped me get my presents prepared, then he invited me in for a glass of wine.

"I don't understand what happened today. One minute you were working with Jeremy, the next you were both gone. I thought I was going to lose my mind."

"Sorry, I should have said goodbye before clearing out. But an emergency popped up, and I acted without thinking."

"I suppose your time in Afghanistan taught you to focus on what's urgent."

I snort. "Maybe, but the Army isn't to blame for my performance today. It's all on me, and I'm sorry."

"What was the emergency? Anything I can help with?"

"Have I told you we are extending the lease on the old Tawny Owl estate?"

"No." There's a pause as he takes it in, then a shocked reply. "Why would you do that? How could anyone possibly afford it?"

"I really can't tell you about the work we'll be doing there. It's confidential. But I'll be spending most of my time here over the coming year. The emergency had to do with a piece of equipment we were installing. It was damaged. I think we found a work around."

By the way Dad looks at me, head cocked, his normal smile missing, I can tell he doesn't believe me. But after a second's pause, the smile returns. "I respect your privacy. And very glad you called me when your problem was resolved."

He puts out his hand to shake, closing the subject. Then, with an even bigger smile adds, "I hope this has something to do with Chris's sister. You two make an attractive couple."

TAWNY OWL ESTATE

It's nearly 9:00 by the time I get back to the guard shack at the entrance to the property. In the distance, I see that the estate house is all lit up, so I assume Justin and Jill are back. But at the gate, there are two guards who check my ID before letting me in.

As I approach the house, I see four security vehicles, but only one guard, who is pacing around on the front porch. I park, but before the headlights are even off, I'm startled by a knock on my window.

"Good evening, Dr. Wimberly. My name is Wilber. I'm head of the security detail this evening." He motions toward the front door. "Lestor will let you in. Welcome home, sir."

A moment later, as I come up the steps, I'm greeted again, but the greeting is interrupted when the front door opens, and Justin comes out.

"Thank you, Lestor," Justin says, dismissing him, then putting an arm around my shoulder.

Once the door is closed, the arm drops. "You scared the hell out of me today, Kai."

"Me? I didn't do anything."

"Still, you were the target. How is Jeremy?"

"He was unconscious when we took him in. We aren't family, so they wouldn't tell us anything. To'Kana was optimistic he would be out tomorrow."

Justin nods. "That's what they told me. I'm really disappointed with Jace. A hit was this far along, and they didn't know?"

"To'Kana has a lot of protection in place for me."

"He says we were lucky and the blow back will start soon. That's why I upped the security. Thankfully, Michael flew back to London yesterday. He isn't going to like all the added security."

I hear footsteps, then Jill's voice. "Is anyone going to join me for dinner?"

Justin motions toward the den. "Come on. We have a lot to discuss. If you haven't eaten, there's plenty of food."

Once seated, Justin starts in. "The cellar expansion is underway. When it's done, it will be one of the biggest and most secure cellars in the world. And sometime mid-January, we will have eighteen industrial replicators cranking out parts."

"The lower level is not as large?"

"It will be. We're adding two industrial transporters. To'Kana says point-to-point transfer from here to low orbit from his ship puts too much stress on his transporter."

"I'm surprised he's doing that," Jill says.

"Why?"

"We are dependent on him right now. The less dependent we become, the less control he has over us."

"Should have thought of that," Justin mutters, then in full voice. "This was a very fortunate turn for us. It doesn't offset today's assassination attempt, but still."

"To'Kana said he was going to look for the people that ordered the hit. Do you know if he found them?" I ask.

"I know. He snatched the Russian guy with the Iranian alias," Justin replies.

"About tomorrow…" I pause.

Justin cuts me off. "I've already made the arrangements."

"You know about my parents' Christmas party?"

"We're sponsoring it this year," Jill says. "Did you notice the truck out front?"

"No," I reply.

She laughs. "You're going to love this, Kai. It has twenty community crates and five very fancy community tents."

I am astounded that Justin and Jill know about our family Christmas tradition, even our vocabulary, but the quantity bugs me a little. "Why so much?"

"Your father didn't tell you?" Justin asks.

I shake my head no.

"Nearly two hundred guests have registered."

"What?"

"Your mother listed you as a host on the invite. And everyone wants to meet the Alien Slayer."

[12.25.2033] WINERY, WIMBERLY VINEYARDS

I open my eyes and see that I'm surrounded by a wall of crates.

"Thank you, Thelma."

"Anything for you, Kai."

Thelma sounds more and more human every day—a credit to her learning algorithms.

A moment later, I hear the door to the trailer open, then the ramp pulled out. Steps come pounding up the ramp, then a guy dressed in a Santa suit exactly like mine steps into view. We shake, then he says, "Wasn't sure that was going to work. Your father announced you, then I stepped out of the limo wearing these sunglasses. But there are so many people, I thought someone would figure out I wasn't you."

He takes the sunglasses off, then hands them to me. "Put them on. Go down the ramp. Your father and the girl who won the first gift will be waiting to your left. Take the glasses off at the bottom of the ramp, say hi, then present the gift to the girl. Her name is Ginny."

I put the glasses on, then straighten myself, and grab the dolly that's been preloaded with the first gift. A moment later, I appear at the top of the steps, pushing the dolly, and the crowd roars.

Halfway down the ramp, I stop and remove the sunglasses while I'm still high enough off the ground that everyone can see me. "Merry Christmas."

I start back down the ramp, then move toward Dad and the middle schooler standing next to him. "Merry Christmas, Ginny. I've brought you a very special gift. I think you will like it. But if you don't, you can trade. Why don't you show me to your table, and I'll take this there for you."

"Thank you, Santa," she says, then marches toward the entrance to the winery.

I follow young Ginny as Dad instructs people to part the way, then follow the lucky recipient inside. The whole thing is so corny that I feel like I'm part of a Hallmark Christmas movie. But it's our tradition.

As we enter the building, I see Sophie helping mom and several other volunteers set out the food. She looks up at the commotion and catches my eye, triggering a longing I've not felt in years.

...

The party is over. With over six hundred gifts given and opened, then a lot of them swapped, this party went hours longer than any previous. For me, the day went by in bits and snatches, brief scenes like the handicapped boy getting the electric wheelchair Justin bought; Mom opening her tent to find a fancy new easel inside; the eighteen-year-old whose father bought him a used pickup. But almost every crate brought with it the memory of seeing Jeremy's lifeless body being rebuilt in To'Kana's auto-doc.

If the Dominion come, everyone's life will change. Mine already has. I just pray that Sophie survives it and will still be there for me, if I survive it, too.

[01.01.2034] DEN, ESTATE HOUSE

When New Year's Day falls on a Sunday, as it does this year, the holiday lands on Monday, making this one of the laziest days of the year. It also makes today the first day of official residence in our newly leased facility.

Justin stands and lifts his glass of champagne. "May 2034 mark the most productive and profitable year of our lives."

I return with a toast of my own. "May the equipment we build here this year be sufficient for the defense we will ultimately need."

My toast is received with less enthusiasm than Justin's, but we all take a sip of our champagne, anyway.

"Thank you for raising the topic, Kyle. I didn't want to be the one that did. We have some decisions we need to make today. Jill and I need to return to New York tomorrow, which will leave you here alone."

His statement lands a little awkwardly, given that Sophie has been here two out of the last three nights.

"I would like to propose the following." He looks directly at me. "Item one. We promote Gabe to Chief Operating Officer of Full Cycle Solar, Inc., which will give you the flexibility to be stationed here full time, Kai."

Not getting a reply, he continues, "Point Two. We transfer Mac, Ty, and Alex to this facility. It will increase our security and provide additional capacity to service our operations here."

"Anything else?"

"That's all I have for now."

As if to punctuate Justin's words, his mobile sounds. He looks at it, then asks, "Does this place have a TV and does anyone know how to operate it?"

"I do," Jill replies. "What do we need it for?"

"I've just been alerted that there is breaking news we need to see."

In an instant, I know I don't want Sophie to see it, but it's too late. I look at her, and she asks, "What's the matter?"

I want to weep; I want to run from the room; because at this point, denying our complicity in what she's about to see would be the flimsiest lie ever told.

"This isn't what it appears to be," is my lame response.

What have I done?

The television reporter says, "Fair warning. The images we are about to present may be offensive to some."

The image on the screen switches to a reporter, whose name goes in one ear and out the other.

"Four men were found dead in Los Angeles today, in front of the mosque at which they worshiped."

The scene shifts, and as the reporter drones on, the image of four men, laying on the ground, their heads next to them, forms on the screen. Justin, Sophie, and I have seen decapitations like this many times. It's a first for Jill, who screeches at the sight.

"Numerous mysteries surround the death of these men. All four were decapitated. Each of the men was found with a signed confession nailed to their skull. One claims responsibility for having killed a young man in cold blood. The other three claim to have assisted in the murder."

The reporter shakes his head. "But the inhumanity of their murder only starts there. According to the medical examiner, the bodies had been completely drained of blood before the men were beheaded. He added that the decapitations were done with surgical precision. The bodies were all completely devoid of hair, the epilation done by a process known as electrolysis. A name matching the signature was etched on each man's head. And another name, Pyotr Kovrov, was etched on each man's chest."

The scene shifts to the earlier announcement, where a spokesperson is providing an update. Much of what we just heard is repeated. Then he says, "...and we have confirmed that the names etched on the victims' foreheads are indeed their names." He pauses as he shakes his head. "Ladies and gentlemen, I've been with the LAPD for over thirty years, and this is the strangest murder case I've ever seen."

A reporter shouts out, "Have you been able to determine when or where the murders took place?"

Again, he shakes his head. "This is another of the mysteries surrounding this case. Family members report seeing them as recently as three weeks ago. The medical examiner says the scarring on their foreheads and chests is a type of scar known as a hypertrophic scar. Mature hypertrophic scars like these take two to three months to form. We are seeking additional medical analysis of the scars and any information we can gather on the last sightings of the victims."

The conference goes on, but after a couple more minutes, Sophie asks Justin. "Why did you need to see this?"

Justin looks at her for several seconds, then says, "We were asked not to discuss this with anyone. But seeing that you are here, you deserve to know."

He pauses. It's a pattern I've seen many times before, where he chooses his words carefully to shade their meaning.

"Kyle and I were contacted by a friend of mine at the Department of Defense on Christmas Eve. A friend of his, at the FBI, wanted us to know that Kyle's name was mentioned as a potential target in some terrorist chatter they intercepted. The name of one of these men was connected to that conversation. We don't know if these men were after Kyle, we don't even know if they were terrorists. But one thing is clear. At least one of these men had some involvement with terrorism, and all four were taken down by it."

"Why would they be after Kyle?"

"Because of the technology he controls."

Sophie looks at me. "You knew this, but you didn't tell me?"

"I've known I was a potential target since Christmas Eve. But it was such a distant threat, it didn't seem real. Justin upped the security surrounding this place, but it still didn't seem real."

She shakes her head as she diverts her eyes, but she doesn't say anything.

Justin fills the silence. "Get Mac, Ty, and Alex out here as quick as you can."

"I will."

CHAPTER 13: PRODUCTION

[01.02.2034] DEN, ESTATE HOUSE

Today is New Year's Day—the national holiday, not the day after the ball drops. But for me, the holiday is over.

Justin and Jill took off this morning to return to New York, eager to start the new year, totally invigorated by the long list of meetings and goals for the week.

Sophie took off abruptly last night, saying she had a busy week ahead—twelve-hour shifts the next five days, on call over the weekend, then another week of five twelves. Her point was clear enough. I shouldn't count on seeing her for the next couple weeks. It was like the softest dump ever. No yelling or hysteria, no accusations, just the implication that she's too busy to make time for me.

In truth, I think the terrorist situation has scared her away. And when she sees the news this morning about Pyotr Kovrov's decapitated body being found in front of the Russian Embassy in Washington, and that of Tomas Yesaulov in Red Square in Moscow, I suspect she will never be back.

But maybe it's for the best. We are both committed to our work, and who knows if either of us will even be alive next year?

Nonetheless, here I sit, alone in the den with post-holiday malaise, waiting for the chef to bring me my breakfast.

But the truth of the matter is that I'm not alone. There are six security guards outside 24/7. And someone in the kitchen from 7:00 AM to 7:00 PM every day, mostly for the security team, but for me as well. The cost of this operation still worries me a bit. Not from a business perspective, because the two-level cellar makes this place a bargain. But no one outside our team can know about the cellar, making me look like a spoiled rich kid working from a home he rents for half a million bucks a year.

"Your breakfast, sir."

"Thanks, Albert."

As I eat, it occurs to me that I need to be more like Justin—having a list and taking pleasure from ticking things off it. My list for this hour? Reassign Mac, Alex, and Ty to the estate house and ask them to get here ASAP. Then, promote Gabe to Vice President and Chief Operating Officer, giving him operational control of Full Cycle Solar. Tasks defined, I finish my breakfast, then call FCS.

CELLAR, ESTATE HOUSE

Thelma and the bots have made tremendous strides in the cellar-expansion and development. They have cut a new shaft into the wall that houses a grav elevator, which can safely transport ten tons between the two levels. When the elevator platform is on the lower level, as it is now, there is no trace of the shaft being there.

They patched the hole in the floor and extended the support structure underneath to the entire length of the lower level, preventing another collapse in the future.

To'Kana sent us ten more bots—larger and better suited for heavy construction than the original ones. Those are now working on the lower level. The ten original bots are back on level one, their work today split between the first replicator and the upper-level transporter. Unless there is another incident, the replicator should finish in another hour or two, at which point it will start producing parts needed to support the expansion. Thelma assures me that everything is going to plan, the expansion will be done on Saturday, and I should focus on getting the specs in place for production starting next week.

"Back to work," I whisper to myself, as I turn to walk down the long main tunnel toward the office in the rotunda at the end.

My first task today is to review all the input that came in from Morgan Owen's team over the long holiday week. My first surprise is the draft RFP. It calls for a shipyard to be constructed in a near earth orbit with at least one bay functioning within six months, and the production of two hundred, three-hundred-meter-long, jump capable spaceships within the next eighteen months. It will be curious to hear why the number of ships got cut from two hundred fifty to two hundred. There's also an addendum of related IDIQ programs for shuttles, kinetic bombs, shield killing weapons… The list goes on.

Not understanding what an IDIQ program is, I open the government-acronyms app that Morgan told me to download onto my phone and enter IDIQ. *Indefinite Delivery Indefinite Quantity, a type of contract that provides for an indefinite quantity of supplies or services over a fixed period of time.* Reading further, I see that this commits the government to essentially nothing other than a spending limit while requiring the contractor to make the product available for a fixed time, the alleged benefit to both parties being a pre-established purchasing mechanism.

I purposely tamp down my skepticism because, to me, this seems like a bureaucrat's dream. But as someone commented on a related blog, anyone in the government with money can spend it on an item covered by the contract without negotiating a separate deal. A supplier can simply take orders and fill them, supply the paperwork to the contract office, and presto, get paid after ninety days. I'm glad I'm not the one dealing with this.

In a separate personal note, Morgan says the ships need to come in at less than two and a half billion each for this to get approved. He also suggests that I get in touch with Logan Watts at SpaceX, so we can get our stories straight at the meeting next week. Not remembering that we had one scheduled, I check my calendar. Sure enough, *Monday, January 9, 2034, 10:00 AM, The Hay-Adams hotel. Wimberly to present the preliminary ship design.*

How did I miss that? Time to get cracking. Thankfully, To'Kana gave me access to one of his design AIs. I connect and get an immediate response.

"Kyle Wimberly. How. Can. I. Serve. You?"

The voice of this AI is as monotone and devoid of emotion as the robot that used to say, "Danger, Will Robinson."

I quickly lay out the dimensions, propulsion, weapons, and defense specifications, then share my preliminary designs.

"This. Will. Be. A. Piece. Of. Work," it replies

I'm kind-of shocked by the response. All of To'Kana's AIs with whom I've interacted had some diplomacy in them. This one seems to be a zero.

"Estimated. Time. To. Completion. Twenty-six hours. Twelve minutes. Four seconds. Shall I engage?"

It's a curiosity to me that, unlike the others, the last sentence comes as a complete sentence, not three words. "Engage," I order.

"Engaged."

Can an AI so devoid of personality really get this job done? A second later, the counter-thought comes. Could a chatty AI get the job done in this time frame?

I shake my head to clear it of such nonsense. I can't get this job done in the time frame in question, so I can't complain about the AI that allegedly can. If I'm going to succeed in this portion of the mission, I need to trust in the resources I have been assigned. If it fails, then I fail. Better that I spend my time on the things at the margin I think will make a difference. So back to my war shuttle concept. I wonder if To'Kana has time to talk.

LAB, LEGACY SHIP

I open my eyes to take in the surroundings, then hear the familiar sound of the lab's forward door swooshing closed. Casting my eyes toward it, I watch as To'Kana shuffles toward me with a curved posture and supporting cane. Seeing him in this condition is distressing.

He notices me and smiles, straightening a little as he does. "Please take a seat. I'll get there momentarily."

I step toward him and get the evaluative eye.

"Are you OK, sir?"

He snorts as he changes course toward the sofa. "As a people, we are so similar, yet so different."

"Is it inappropriate for me to ask about your health?"

Again, the evaluative eye. "No. Thank you for your concern."

Now I'm genuinely confused.

"Despite our more-reserved, less-sentimental natures, we live in more intimate communities than you do. Maybe it is a product of our DNA, or maybe the necessities of our world forced evolution to make us this way. But be it as it may, we age much more quickly when separated from our intimates. It has only been half a year and look at me. Now separated, those of us that remain will all be gone in another couple of years. But enough of that. What is on your mind today, Kyle Wimberly?"

I feel deep sadness for To'Kana's plight. "Two things." The words are quiet, the emotion somber.

"Which are?" he prods.

"I doubt we can build enough ships in time to save ourselves if they have to be built by human labor. Can I have, or will you give me the right to replicate, bots capable of doing assembly in open space?"

To'Kana nods his head. "I'm surprised you waited this long to ask. Let me ask a question first. Why do you ask this today?"

"I just found out that our government is on the verge of green-lighting the project this week."

To'Kana breaks out laughing.

"What?"

After a second, he gets himself under control. "Sorry." Another snicker escapes. "On our world, the expression *green-lighting* means something very different. It's the first time I've heard you use it, and, in this context, it's hilarious." He laughs some more.

"Are you going to tell me what it means?"

"I think not. Excuse the interruption. You were saying…"

At this point, I have to remind myself what the question was. "Ahh, why am I asking today? I just found out our project is about to be approved. The budget limit for the ships is two point five billion each. With inexperienced human labor working in open space, I'm worried we won't be able to do it."

"Reasonable concern," To'Kana replies, but says no more.

"Will you give us bots? Or preferably, let us make our own?"

"At any other time in our history, the answer would be no. In fact, my standing orders do not allow what I have given you already."

He stops there, but his pensive expression gives me cause to remain silent.

"The short answer is yes. I will give you bots, but you need to prove you will use them appropriately. Work with the design AI I've given you access to. He knows how to provide the proof. Your second *thing*."

The way he emphasizes the word thing reminds me that this is one of the few English words the Iknosan aren't comfortable with. According to Thelma, there is no word in the Iknosan language with an equivalent lack of specificity.

"Considering the analysis we did of your final battle against the Dominion, I've convinced myself that swarms of smaller jump-capable ships—war shuttles, you might call them—will be an incredible force multiplier."

"Have you proposed this to your defense department?"

"Only the inertial bomb idea, which they dismissed as unproven and untestable."

"Yet you want to pursue it, although none of the individual weapons on smaller ships will be as powerful as the big weapons on the big ships."

"Your military proved the Dominion ships have vulnerabilities. They also proved that precision weapons were more effective than powerful ones, if we can land enough shots. My assertion is that ten small ships with AI-controlled close-in surveillance systems and jump-weapons can land more shots that matter than one larger ship. Period."

To'Kana smiles. "An impassioned argument. Long on belief, short on evidence, but heartfelt enough to be worthy of some research. What do you propose to do?"

"I want to build a shuttle, or modify one of our existing ones, to have a second deck, which can carry jump-capable inertial bombs and surveillance drones. I'll need to do it on the side, the government won't support it. Maybe a dozen of them we can send to the next Dominion encounter and test. What I want from you is assistance building them. Assistance like that you gave us for our proof-of-concept shuttle."

To'Kana locks me with his most evaluative stare, and I realize I am being judged. I hold his eyes, waiting for the verdict.

To'Kana breaks eye contact for a moment, then looks back, his now compassionate eyes pouring over me. "I trust your character, Kyle. But what you ask is so far from what I am allowed to do that I don't know how to help you. You are asking me to build a powerful weapon and give it to you, not your government. My charter allows me to give technology to your government. It allows me to choose our representatives. It even allows me, in special situations, to give manufacturing technology, like the replicators. But the one thing I am expressly forbidden to do is give you or your government weapons—a rule I have already stretched."

"Then don't give them to us. Build them. Keep them. Then at the time of the next battle, conscript me and let me use them against the Dominion!"

The wry smile is back. "Create the specifications. Use our design AI to drive to a complete design. Then send it to me and I will consider building it."

"Thank you, sir."

"Thank you, Kyle."

With that, To'Kana stands and hobbles back toward the door. I watch him go, then run to catch up. "Is there anything we can do to help you find the company you need?"

"Sadly, no. I wish you could. I'm starting to like it here. Kind of you to ask."

With that, he resumes his shuffle toward the door to the forward parts of the ship. I stand there watching until the door swooshes shut, deeply saddened that this person who has come to save us will die here alone.

"Kai, would you like me to transport you down?"

"Thelma, what does the expression green-lighting mean when literally translated into Iknosan?"

"It regards the cleaning process one uses after defecation or certain sexual activities."

It takes a second to sink in, then I get it... The government is close to green-lighting (cleaning the products of defecation from) our project. I break out laughing so hard that tears flow.

"Kai, are you OK?"

"Please transport me back to the cellar, Thelma."

"Transporting."

DEN, ESTATE HOUSE

On return from the ship, I spent an hour in the cellar blocking out my plans for a war shuttle. The idea was simple—keep everything the same, just make the shuttle fifty percent taller. I ran that plan through an estimator that's part of the design tools and found that the increased size of the power and propulsion systems would take twenty-two percent of the additional space. That result, along with the chill of the cellars' cold air, was a wake-up call. The only way I would get this done would be to think through the systems we needed to add, then estimate their weight and volume. With that in hand, I'd be able to iterate my way to an optimal design. And to do any of that, I needed to get to a warmer place.

Now settled down in one of the leather armchairs by the fireplace, tablet in my hands, I start the list of requirements. The current shuttle is for day use. Re-outfitted as a transport shuttle, we could probably squeeze in forty people. The war shuttle needs to support a crew of up to ten people on a ten-day mission. That means we need crew quarters, full sanitation systems, expanded life support, and additional storage for food and water.

We would also need room for our new weapon systems—eight of our inertial bombs, eight flying wedges, both of which need better names if I have any hope of selling these things to anybody.

"Excuse me, Master Kyle. Your colleagues from First Cycle Solar have arrived at the airport and are on their way here. Would you like dinner in here tonight, or in the dining room?"

"In here, please."

Maybe my team can help me with the new weapon ideas tonight.

ESTATE HOUSE

I'm waiting on the mansion's expansive porte-cochere in the late afternoon light, the sun about to drop below the mountains to the west as the limousine pulls up. It stops and the trunk pops open as my team pours out.

"Kai, what the hell?" Ty asks.

"Bro, you finally hit pay dirt?" Mac tacks on.

"Looks like Falcon Crest," Alex says, drawing everyone else's attention.

"Falcon Crest?" Ty asks.

"The old 1980s TV show my grandmother made me watch with her on her old Apple TV setup," Alex answers.

A second later, my squad pours up the steps with handshakes, backslaps, and manly tears barely suppressed. We carry on for a second as the security team unloads bags, then waves the limo away.

Lester taps my shoulder. "Wouldn't it be better to continue this inside, Dr. Wimberly?"

"Guys. Inside." I turn and everyone follows me in.

The staff scatters at the sound of four military people entering. None of them officially know that I was the target of a terrorist attack, but most have heard the rumors. So, knowing they are listening, I layout the agenda. "Security will bring your stuff inside. Most are ex-military, so will respect the integrity of your cases, if for no other reason than they know what will happen to them if they don't."

My words are met with appropriate guffawing, which breaks the tension.

"We have this place for the rest of the year. This will nominally be my base of operation. So, I want to start by giving you a tour of the mansion and letting you choose your rooms. Then before dinner, I want to give you a special treat—a tour of the wine cellar."

There's a moan and complaints about beer.

"Then we will come up to the den and sit by the fireplace. The bar will be opened, dinner will be served, and we can talk about why we are here."

CELLAR, ESTATE HOUSE

The tour went well. Mac and Ty chose rooms on the opposite side of the building from mine. Alex chose the one next to mine—the one with the adjoining door—something that worries me. But from the day we met, she was the better marksman, the one that was always two steps ahead, my protector as much as I was the one that had the muscle to protect her when that was the issue.

Now in the cellar, the discussion has changed.

"Kai, you're a genius."

"No, Justin is the genius."

"We can produce all the Iknosan magic down here?"

"Most of it, which is why this place is the ultimate secret, the one that cannot be leaked; the one I need you to swear to protect. The fate of humanity rests in this space."

"And we are here to protect it…"

I sense the… I don't know what the right word is… In Ty's implied question.

"At this point, we, the four of us, plus Justin and Jill, are the protectors of humanity. The human ones, anyway. Alien benefactors, who themselves were wiped out, gifted it to us. It's on us to use it to save our world, because our benefactors come offering little more than technology."

"I'm in," Mac says.

"I've seen them," Alex says.

Ty eyes me. "I've seen them too. This is impressive as hell, Kai. But is it enough?"

As much as I hate the doubt, I love the quest to expunge any weakness from the plan.

"Don't know. Hope so. But that's what we have to figure out. The plan is for the three of you to split your time backing up security, helping down here, and being my sounding board. For better or worse, the Iknosan have bet on me. We all know I'm nothing on my own."

"Bullshit," Mac whispers. Alex smacks him for the comment.

I repeat, "I'm nothing without the three of you. So, are you with me?"

I'm surprised by the roaring three people can make.

DEN, ESTATE HOUSE

With the bar open, fire crackling, dinner served, doors locked, the discussion moves to our purpose here.

"Some ground rules," I start. "We treat the staff as friends, security as allies. We need and are grateful for their services, are concerned for them and their families. And it will all unravel the day we forget that."

Mac loops his finger as if saying, *get on with it*.

"I'm serious about this. They aren't stupid. We are going to spend hours down below and they will know it. I will disappear for days at a time. And they will know it. All transport in or out will take place from the cellar, where no one but us can see it."

"Good thinking," Ty replies. "I assume we will want to discourage the staff from hanging out near the elevator, so they never really know how long any of us are down there.

"Agreed," I reply. "But we need to do it subtly, because we don't want anyone to think something odd is going on down there."

"Right," Mac chides.

"Do you disagree?" I ask with pointed criticism in my voice. At least, that's how it sounds in my ears.

"Sorry, boss. It's just a tall order."

"I know. It's the privacy of this place that will allow us to succeed. Justin tells me that security is the problem. House staff that sign up for jobs in a house like this get paid four times what they can get anywhere else. Even the accusation of a leak, and they're blackballed for life. Only the youngest of them sell out. And there are no young ones here. Security, on the other hand..."

"I can handle that," Ty says.

I nod, then chuckle. Ty did time as a boot camp instructor. He has the voice, the one that makes anyone who has ever served shudder. Security here is one hundred percent ex-military. "Then I trust it to you."

With the discussion of house rules over, conversation turns to fleet design and my belief that we need a war shuttle, thousands of them that can work in tandem with the handful of battlecruisers the Pentagon is likely to order.

[01.06.2034] DEN, ESTATE HOUSE

With my team here, everything has worked better this week. Security loves having one of these three in the rotation each day. They wear their fatigues, carry their ARs, and whoever's on rotation usually does a tactical brief or simulation every shift. They are also using Raven 1, our surveillance drone, using their implants.

Even the chef is happier. He has more people to cook for and his assistant is back.

But we made two major accomplishments this week, both of which could recapture our world's future. The first is the design of our battlecruiser, which has passed all five simulations: ship function, device function, ship construction, part replication, and bot suitability. Although we have printable plans to share this week, they are not in a DOD recognized format. And our digital versions are not compatible with any known human system.

On the war shuttle front, we've settled on two new weapons systems, which also simulate successfully. The first is our so-called inertial bomb, now renamed the Barracuda Inertial Torpedo, or Cuda, for short. The second is the Space Hawk Tactical Drone, whose primary purpose is surveillance. It has an option slot where we can add an optional feature. But it's the shielding weapon and transporter relay station features I'm most excited about.

With those concepts nailed down, we completed the War Shuttle design. It is slightly larger than the proof-of-concept shuttle, coming in at forty meters long, twelve meters wide and ten meters high. But it will still fit inside the shuttle bay of one of our battlecruisers, which makes replenishment, and crew rotations easier. To'Kana is still weighing the decision to build these. Using his ship as the space dock, he can build one every nine days; two or more in the same period if he's willing to dedicate the resources.

DINING ROOM, ESTATE HOUSE

It's Friday night and I've invited my parents over for dinner.

"This place is beautiful," Mom says. "More than once, I've wondered how the previous owners could afford this place."

"I don't think it's that complicated," Dad replies. "They had four times the land, a better product, and a better price-point for most of that time. Mark has changed that now. But with their economies of scale, I think they were making six times as much as we were. Still, I'm surprised this place is in such good condition. It's no spring chicken."

"The new owner put a lot into it, before giving up and building the mansion he wanted on the other side of the vineyard," I say.

"Well, I'm glad to have you this close. You've been gone nearly twenty years."

"Seventeen, Mom."

Servers coming in from the kitchen, save me from having more guilt piled on.

Plates are set in front of each of us, as the Chef announces the dish. "Lamb shanks, with potatoes fondant and garlic roasted brussel sprouts."

Then, as they lift the covers off the plates, "Bon appétit."

A second later, the server is back to top off the wine.

"Oh, this looks wonderful," Mom says. "Sophie told me it was as good as the new place you went. Le Chateau, right?"

"It's very nice. In truth, I'm becoming spoiled."

There's an uncomfortable, fidgety silence for a second. One I've seen a thousand times before. Mom and Dad are both itching to say something the other has instructed them not to talk about. It's so obvious, I almost laugh. But the dam is going to break in a second. Given Dad's concentration on his food, I bet it will be him.

"Kyle, I still don't understand what you're doing here. I asked around. It's no secret that you've cut a deal and are paying forty-five grand a month for this place. And the security... Someone at the barber shop said your security team is costing you over a hundred grand a month. How? Why? Please tell me you're not doing something illegal."

I see Dad's hands shaking and see the fear in his eyes. Mom looks afraid as well.

"Dad, I'm not running drugs, not human smuggling, not doing anything you would consider immoral or illegal. I'm adapting alien technology to make our world a better place." As I pick up my glass to take a sip, I add. "There is a lot going on here. You just can't see it."

With mouth occupied, I send to Thelma. *I need a prop. Can you transport something that looks like a Raven being assembled by a bot or a holoprojection? It needs to look real but doesn't need to work.*

"Give me a second Kai."

Signal me when you are ready, then wait for my signal.

I've slowly swished the wine through my mouth as I talked to Thelma. Now, I swallow and look at Dad. "Thanks for bringing this over. It is truly excellent."

Then with a sigh, I say, "As much as I wish my word on this was sufficient, I know it's not enough. I had two big fears about moving here. The first was that people would think I've become a spoiled rich kid who's moved home to flaunt his wealth. The second is that people would assume I'm involved in some sort of organized crime activity. I can't explain to you why this property was the perfect place. But I can show you what we are doing."

Without waiting for a reply, I say out loud, "Raven One. Turn your nose camera light on, then descend and lightly tap your nose against the dining-room window."

I stand and put up a finger. "Give me a second. I need to grab something."

I'm no sooner out the door than the bickering begins. But hopefully I can finally put this to rest.

I return thirty seconds later and place Raven One's controller on the dining room table. The room went silent as I entered. Now Dad's asking what the little cube is.

"It's the controller for a security drone on patrol over the estate. Let me show you what it is seeing." The holoprojection pops up in front of the window. In it we can see the estate house, the image zooming in at a distressing rate. As the dining-room window comes into view, we can see ourselves.

"Oh my God. It's going to crash right into us," Mom cries out.

Raven One slows to a crawl, the nose camera light shines into the room, then it taps lightly on the window.

"I'm not selling this product to DOD yet, and I probably never will. But if I offered it to them right now, they would buy a billion dollars' worth tomorrow."

"Why aren't you going to sell it to them?" Dad asks. "It would have changed everything for you in Afghanistan, wouldn't it?"

"Kai," Thelma's voice sounds in my ear. "I'm ready."

Wait for my mark.

I refocus on Dad. "Is it OK if I let my surveillance robot go back to work?

"Yeah," Dad replies, his voice quiet.

"Raven One, resume patrol. Turn your light off once you're at one hundred feet."

It turns, then once clear of the porch, it zooms away. When the light goes out, I turn the holoprojection off, then look back at Dad. "This was an experiment. A very successful one, but I have a much better version, almost ready to go into production. It's better suited to their current need. I'll be spending the week in Washington next week working on the specifications for the systems it will be part of."

"I didn't know," Dad confesses.

"Kyle, maybe you should eat before your meal gets cold."

I guess the good news is that Mom is back to being Mom. I smile at her. "One more thing first. As I said, there is more going on here than you can see. I want to show you what that looks like."

Walking over to the far side of the room, I send to Thelma, *Almost ready. Can you add one of my one-hundred-twenty-volt power cubes to the prop?*

"Added."

When I say the word 'now' transport the package down.

"Acknowledged."

"There is work going on in this room as we speak. It is hidden from sight and sound. In fact, while it's hidden you can walk right through it."

I walk across the room, then back. Then I turn toward the area I just walked through and put my hand out. "But there is work going on right here, right now."

To Thelma's credit. A workbench appears. On it rests a Raven One, being tended to by an alien, who startles when he sees us, then gets up and walks out, disappearing as he exits the dining room.

Mom and Dad are looking afraid again and I worry that I've over played my hand. I pick up the power cube, then say, "I suppose I should let them get back to work." Then privately send to Thelma, *Transport the prop back up.*

I return to the table and place the power cube next to Dad. "A gift for you."

"That's going on here all the time?" Mom asks.

"No. It's the first time I've let them in the dining room while people were here. But yes, work is going on here twenty-four hours a day, every day of the year.

"No wonder Sophie won't come back…" Mom mutters.

"Martha!" Dad scolds, startling her.

"You've been talking with Sophie?" I ask

"What?"

"You said, 'No wonder Sophie won't come back.'"

"I did?"

I bite my tongue. Mom is a wise and wonderful woman, but she is off her game tonight.

"You should talk to her, Kyle. She loves you, but you've scared her away. Don't let her walk away the way you let Crystal."

Offended, I stand. "I think I've had enough for one night. I'm trying to save the world from a monster that I've met face-to-face twice. Millions of them are coming. The Iknosan have given me the key to stopping them. And that's what I'm going to do, with or without the people I love. Everyone has a decision to make. You can choose whether you're in. Or you can choose whether you're out. But it's one or the other; you're in or you're out. There is no in-between."

As I turn to leave, Dad calls out, running over to hug me. "I'm in Kyle. I'm sorry I didn't believe you. Please, be kind to your mother."

"Thanks, Dad. But I can't deal with that right now. Enjoy your dinner. The dessert they're making is wonderful."

BEDROOM, ESTATE HOUSE

Thankfully, I brought my tablet and other gear up to my room earlier this afternoon. I still have several hours of work to crank through before Sunday's trip to DC, so I kick my shoes off, plop down on the bed, then open my tablet to get after it.

A few seconds later, there's a knock on the adjoining door. "OK, if I come in?"

It's Alex. The door opens, and she walks in, wearing nothing but her sports bra and briefs, then plops down on the bed. "I heard the *you're-either-in-or-out-speech* as I came in from my run. You want to talk about it? I'm in, by the way."

I glance at Alex and wonder if my problem has been that I chase the wrong women. "Kind of under dressed for the weather, don't you think?"

"Five miles, too many layers. I've got to cool off before I take my shower. I'm surprised you can't smell the sweat."

On looking at her more carefully, I notice the glistening on her skin. Then a drop of sweat breaks loose and rolls down her chest, which my eyes follow longer than they should.

"So... You like my outfit now."

"Alex, what are you doing here?"

"I'm sorry it didn't go well for you tonight."

"Understatement."

"Kai, they really haven't known you since you were a teenager. In their heads, they know you're rich and famous; but in their hearts, you're still their eighteen-year-old son. It's an enormous gap to close. You need to give them the time and space."

"Well, I'm gone all next week, so problem solved for the next eight days."

"Maybe you are still eighteen."

If I had a towel, I would swat her. But I don't.

"Sorry to hear about Sophie. You two were good together."

"Yeah."

"Don't get mad at me, but your mother almost had it right."

"Meaning?"

"Have you told her about your injuries?"

"No."

"Does she know about your new hardware?"

"No."

"Back to your in-or-out speech... I'm betting she would come in, if you would let her in."

"What?"

"Look at it from her point of view. She's fallen for this guy way too fast, and she knows it. And at every turn, something strange happens that you explain away or confess to having known about but didn't tell her. It erodes the trust. Then the terrorist thing..."

"That's not fair," I snap back. "I just learned about the terrorist thing and didn't actually believe it."

"Maybe you're only sixteen," Alex snaps back.

"You going to explain that?"

"You knew with certainty about the terrorists the night before Christmas. And you hadn't told her by New Year's Day?"

"You're right. I owe her an apology."

"Then go do it! She gets off duty at eleven."

"Will you come with me?"

"Not dressed like this."

"I'm not allowed off site without escort."

Alex shakes her head. "No woman gets excited about a man who won't bend an artificial rule for her."

"Please?"

She puts a hand over her face, then gets up. "Kai, you are so God-damn stupid." A moment later, the door to the adjoining room slams and locks.

I'm totally confused by what just happened, but Alex is right. I need to go apologize to Sophie.

Twenty minutes later, Mac drops me at the hospital's front door, then goes to look for a parking spot. It's surprisingly quiet inside. The receptionist greets me and asks why I'm there.

"I'd like to speak with Dr. Sophie Burns. She works in the emergency room."

"Sorry, I can't page ER doctors. Let me check with the desk over there."

There's chatter back and forth for a second, then the receptionist says, "Oh. Thank you for your help."

She looks up at me. "I'm sorry, but Dr. Burns is not on duty tonight. She worked four twelves this week and is off for the weekend. I can't give you her contact information, but she will be back on Monday."

The words are like a stake to the heart. I whisper a thank you, then turn to leave. Mac and I meet at the door.

"That was quick," he jokes, then catching my expression, "What's the matter?"

"Sophie wasn't scheduled to work today, and she's not on call this weekend."

[01.07.2034] HAY ADAMS HOTEL

Justin called last night while I was out on the apology fiasco. Change of plans. He needed me here on Saturday by 2:00 PM Eastern, 11:00 AM Pacific. He wanted me to bring everything I'd need for the week, if it was possible. The arrangement was simple. Transport into his room between 8:00 and 11:00 AM Pacific time, the earlier the better, then if there was time, to check into my room and move my stuff there. We had an appointment at 2:30 Eastern.

The flip-flopped time zones made me crazy, but the technique apparently worked because my alarms went off at the right times this morning.

It's now 1:45 PM Eastern. I'm dressed in khakis, a white shirt, a yellow tie, and a blue blazer, ready to joust with the bureaucrats. I text Justin and he says Jill will be there momentarily. Please tell me she's not coming down to get me dressed before we leave.

A few minutes later, Jill arrives, all bundled up in an overcoat, looking as grumpy as I've ever seen her. She looks me up and down, then says, "That'll do. Grab your coat and let's go."

"I don't have a coat."

Jill looks at me. "Kai, this is getting really old. I signed on to be Justin's nursemaid, not yours. You need to either grow up or get your own." She stamps her foot, then shakes her head. "Come on. We've got a limo. You won't be outside long."

"Am I allowed to know where I'm being taken?"

The question seems to set her off even more. "He didn't even tell you?"

"Sorry, no."

She opens her mouth to say something, but no words come out. Just a quiver in the corner of her frown and a single tear she shakes away. Then with renewed determination, "Let's go, we're going to be late."

We get to the entrance, where the limo driver is arguing with a doorman. "That's us," Jill says, pointing at the limo. "Let's go, he's being chased away."

She runs out. "Sorry we're late. Someone forgot their coat."

The limo driver leaps toward the back door to get there before Jill does. The door man has an umbrella out, trying to protect me from the wind and driving rain. It's funny how Jill's presence changes things.

A second later, the door is closed, and I realize I'm on the floor, confused about what happened, one of Jill's legs against my face.

"L'agneau Gâché?" the driver asks.

"Please," Jill replies, then looks at me. "Are we done down there?"

I'm coming to hate Washington DC. Six years in the service cemented my loyalty to my country. Two years in Afghanistan made me wonder about the capital. At this point, I know I don't belong here.

"For God's sake, Kai. Get up off the floor. Are you a twelve-year-old?"

I wrestle myself up off the floor, then go to the opposite corner of the limo's passenger section. "Where are we going, Jill? And why am I being subjected to this?"

The tears are back. "Today is my birthday I turned forty today. I gifted myself with a makeover. A good one, not exactly a prudent one. I tell Justin and he says, 'That's exactly what Kyle needs.' An hour later, he says, 'I booked Kyle at L'agneau Gâché. Get him there.' Do you have any idea how much that costs? It's booked years in advance. And it's at the same time as mine."

Now the tears flow in earnest. "Why today?"

I tentatively make my way back and wrap my arms around her. "Let's go to yours instead. It means something to you. La-whatever-the-hell means nothing to me."

"Sweet of you Kai. But I think this is part of today's lesson. 'Greatness requires sacrifice.' And this is what's being asked of me today."

I release a string of expletives, then order the driver to take us to... then realize Jill never told me the name of her place.

A few minutes later, the limo pulls up to the curb. We get out and enter the building. It is next door to one of the big-name department stores. Saks, maybe? I didn't quite catch it.

Jill opens the door. I walk in, which is totally backwards and a bit irritating—I'm the chivalrous one, she's the damsel in distress.

"Dr. Wimberly..." the overtly gay receptionist greets. "Welcome, my name is Claude. Your companion is Mrs. Wimberly?"

I stare at him, perplexed.

"A niece perhaps."

"Ms. Erhart," Jill replies for me.

I look at Jill, realizing that this is the first time I've heard her family name.

"A descendant of the great aviator, no doubt," Claude prattles.

"No. Different spelling."

"No matter," Claude says. "A booking for two was made with an astounding limit. Every service is available to you, though three suits and an overcoat are required for you, Dr. Wimberly. I assume we are doing this as a treatment for two."

"Yeah, a treatment for two," Jill says. "Couples massage, couples saltwater bath. I know the clothes he needs. Maybe we can view them from the hot tub. I know the private services I would like."

"This way," Claude motions toward the wider of the hallways emanating from reception. "Let's get you out of these clothes and into something more intimate."

What hell have I been dropped into?

Minutes later, I enter the spa for two, just as Jill is dropping her bath robe and descending into the bubbly water. All but one part of me wilts at her beauty. Then it's my turn. I stand there paralyzed, then my robe is pulled away and the door to the room closes.

Jill puts a hand over her eyes. "Come on in, Kai. It's safe. I don't bite or touch. Please respect the same boundaries."

"Why is Justin doing this?"

She looks at me with a cocked head. "Kai, whether you like it or not, you are a national figure now. You need to dress and behave like one or your mission will fail. I grew up in this context, taught Justin most of what he knows. You have failed to learn on your own, so he wants me to do for you what I did for him. We did it in an environment remarkably like this. He thinks I can do that for you. So, on the day I gave myself a twenty-five-hundred-dollar gift package, he gives us a forty-thousand-dollar one. So, let's try on some clothes. I know what you need, I'll help you pick. Then, I'll do mine privately. You've seen a bit more of me today than is healthy. And I'll use every penny that you don't. Ready?"

ROOM, HAY-ADAMS HOTEL

We got back to the hotel a little after six. It took four bellmen's carts to bring all the stuff up. One for me, three for Jill. Although it was difficult spending over an hour in a hot tub, naked with my partner's girlfriend, I learned a lot. Jill is genuinely sweet. She's an heiress of one of the richest men in America during the mid-to-late eighteen hundreds. Her parents and grandparents were New York aristocrats and raised her that way. Unfortunately for Jill, her parents were killed in a plane crash eight years ago. That's when she found out the money was nearly gone and her inheritance was an annuity, three grand a month, inflation-adjusted, for life. She tried and had some success as a model, then met Justin. She taught him how to play the game—how to present himself, how to draw attention without appearing to be, how to persuade. He taught her how to live.

"Kai?" It's Thelma. "Captain To'Kana would like to meet with you. Could you do that now?"

"Yes, but it needs to be quick. I only have a half hour."

"Transporting now."

LEGACY SHIP

I open my eyes and see To'Kana seated on the sofa in the lab.

"Welcome, Kyle Wimberly. Please." He indicates a seat.

"It is good to see you, sir. You look better."

"Thank you for noticing. There are treatments I can take to fight the aging effect. I took one. I have a couple dozen more, but want to stretch them out as long as possible. You were in Washington DC?"

"Yes, sir. I will be for the entire week. Design meetings with the government and our partners, then testimony before the House Armed Services Committee on Friday."

"Well, I have some good news for you."

"My request for bots has been granted?"

"Let me tell you what's happened first."

"Please."

"More of our people survived than we thought."

"The Dominion did not slaughter the entire planet?"

He shakes his head. "Our home world now crawls with arachnoids. There are no signs of any survivors. But many more civilian ships escaped than we thought possible. Enough that we may have a sustainable population after all."

I think I know what that implies, but don't want to guess, so remain quiet.

"The upshot is that we have formed a new government. Legacy ship captains have half the seats on the central council. The civilian half knows we need allies. The worlds my colleagues and I are working with are the logical candidates. As an inducement, we can offer almost anything we have as long as the Council of Captains unanimously agrees."

To'Kana pauses, then locks me with a stare. "The Council of Captains has authorized me to release patterns for several categories of bots to you. The ones the design AI specified are all approved."

"What about the War Shuttle?"

To'Kana smiles. "As an experiment, they approve. I got the deal you suggested. We will build some, and hold them in reserve until an experiment can be done."

"Thank you, sir."

"That's all I had. Best you go tend to your business."

As I call Thelma's name, To'Kana raises his hand.

"A word of advice before you go."

I nod.

"War is coming. It is almost upon us. Take comfort when the situation allows, because there is no guarantee of a tomorrow."

He nods, then Thelma is in my ear. "Transporting."

THE LAFAYETTE

Jill designated one of the five suits I got today as casual, for business dinners, or business meetings in casual places, country clubs and the like. It's the one she told me to wear to dinner tonight.

I come down a little early and, to my surprise, see Justin and Jill seated in the bar with another woman, whose rich long hair blocks the view of the rest of her. As Justin waves me over, the waiter watching the table lifts the champagne bottle, and the woman turns to look. It's

Natalie Wright. I make no attempt to suppress the smile I feel growing on my face. It is rewarded by a little peck of a kiss when I arrive. As the waiter stands there holding the glass of champagne, Natalie says, "Looking pretty good there, Kai." Then to Jill, "You did this, didn't you?"

Jill nods. "We went for a little makeover today."

Natalie looks back at me. "I hear there's a new woman in your life."

I roll my eyes. "Dumped me at the end of the first week. At least my brother isn't likely to take up with this one."

Natalie looks at me with concern. "Come again?"

I quickly give her my version of Mark & Crystal and last night's excursion to the hospital.

"Sorry to hear that."

"On the brighter side, it set the stage for a productive week. I have a complete design for our battlecruiser that simulates out. If we had a space platform in place today, our first ship would roll off the line in thirty days."

Justin interrupts. "Does that mean To'Kana approved the bots?"

I smile. "I just got back from talking with him. Long story. The short answer is yes. There are a few strings attached, but we are approved to use all the bots called for in the construction plan."

"Do I understand correctly?" Natalie starts. "Alien robots are going to build our ships?"

"The ships yes, the finishes no."

"Let me say this differently. The number one issue for my colleagues is how many jobs this legislation will put in their districts. You'll be asked about that on Friday, by the way."

"Because of the time constraints, I've worked to make this an essentially labor-free operation until life support on the ship is functional."

"What fraction of the budget will that be?" Natalie presses.

"We haven't discussed that yet," Justin answers for me.

The restaurant's maître d' comes over to announce our table is ready.

...

As the appetizers are being cleared, Natalie asks Justin, "Has Morgan told you about the president's decision to include NATO and the G20 in the space fleet buildout?"

"No. I asked if he thought the allies would be brought in at some point. He said he thought they would, but it wasn't something I needed to worry about. Do you know when this is going to happen?"

"Off the record contacts started shortly after the proof of concept. The United Kingdom, China, and Australia have assembled delegations already. Morgan met with the leader of the Australian team Friday morning. The Chinese team was supposed to have arrived this week, but I've not received confirmation. They've been kicking up a fuss about not having access to Kai, but have been told he's off-limits for now. As I understand it, Morgan is trying to protect both of you since you're not officially part of the government. He wants you working the problem, not the foreign affairs."

"Good," Justin replies. "I've been worried about the legal problems we might face if we were approached by a foreign power."

Discussion moves to food as our meals come out.

...

Dinner is done and as discussion lags, I excuse myself to go to the restroom. As I step into the bar area where the entrance to the restroom lobby is located, Natalie pulls up next to me. "I'm hoping you're planning to invite me up tonight."

"If you'll come."

"Trust me, I'd like to, but really can't. I have obligations starting at 7:30 tomorrow morning, for which I need to be in full costume."

"Sorry to hear that."

"If you'd like to come over to my place and don't mind the alarm going off at 6:00..." She lets the statement hang.

"Deal."

"My car will be outside at 10:00. Be there on time and you can come."

I get back to the table first.

"Care for dessert or an after-dinner drink?" Justin asks.

I look at my watch and see it's 9:43. "No, I think I'll head up as soon as Natalie gets back. Didn't sleep much last night."

"Sorry about Sophie," Jill says.

"My fault. I lost track of how strange my world has become and didn't want to get her all bogged down in the crap, meaning I shut her out of most of my life. Sophie deserved better."

"Natalie's back," Justin points.

I stand and extend a hand.

"You have to leave?" she asks.

I'm kind of shocked at how good an actress she is. "Didn't sleep much last night."

"Suppose not." She takes my hand, giving me a business-like shake. "See you next week." Then she sits and gets right back at it with Justin on another topic. I exit, wondering whether I want to meet her out front at 10:00. Any other day, I'd say no. But I feel particularly in need of comfort tonight.

CHAPTER 14: ACCELERATION

[01.09.2034] CONFERENCE ROOM, HAY-ADAMS HOTEL

We have a large group today. Morgan Owen, head of the contracting team for this initiative, is here with his team: Rebecca Cox, Max Harris, Jackie Beard, Harry Ryan, April McDonald, and Joel Harrison.

Jace Elliott, Assistant Secretary of Defense for Legislative Affairs, has brought two associates, whom he has not introduced. They are presumably underlings here to take notes.

Both our partners in US Orbital Shipyards, Inc. are also here, with Nicholas Bennett heading the Boeing delegation and Angela Cook heading the one from SpaceX. With Nicholas are Emma Hudson and a new guy whose name I missed. With Angela are Logan Watts, the tech lead, and another new guy whose name I missed. Anyway, there are nineteen of us seated around a U-shaped table, everyone facing in toward the center of the U.

Morgan, who is the meeting's official host today, strides up to the open end of the U and welcomes everyone, then states the meeting's objectives. As head of US Orbital Shipyards, Justin agrees to the agenda, and the ball gets passed to me.

"When we last met, I was tasked with preparing a rough design. I am pleased to say that we've surpassed that goal, and I'd like to start by showing you the final product."

A 3D image of our ship pops up in the holoprojection, filling the center of the U. I get an 'Ah' of surprise from the group. I doubt any have seen such a compelling display.

"This may or may not be the ship we want to build. But our tools are good enough that we now know every part we would need to complete this ship, how that part is made, where and when it is installed."

"What do you mean by complete?" Morgan asks.

"I was just about to answer that question, because I know this is a particularly important one. When I say complete, I mean the design of the machine itself—hull, superstructure, propulsion, weapons, navigation, communications, shields, life support, everything the ship needs to travel from here out into the galaxy and back. What's not in that scope is the trim. For example, toilet plumbing is in scope, but not the toilet, the kitchen infrastructure, but not the stove or other kitchen equipment. Crew quarters, but no beds, dressers, closets, carpet, wallpaper. I think you get the idea."

"Why define it that way?" Morgan asks.

"Because given a space platform, I can build this ship in thirty days with no human labor, meaning we, collectively, can use normal labor without space-walk certification to complete the interior."

"Say more about that," Morgan says.

"Working in space is dangerous. It's also slow. The money we spend needs to be spread somewhat proportionally across the country if this is going to get through Congress. I've already been told I'll need to testify on that topic at the House Armed Services Committee on Friday. My thought is to get the core ship hardware up and operational quickly, with little timeline risk and no mortality risk. Then spread the work that needs to be done by humans around the country."

Angela raises her hand.

"Ms. Cook?" Morgan acknowledges.

"In anticipation of an award, we have been investing ahead of the curve as Wicks-Wimberly has. Part of that investment has been hiring and training of staff to work in space. We have a hundred now and hope to have a thousand by the end of the year."

Morgan looks at me. "Dr. Wimberly?"

"We want and need a space-qualified, skilled-labor force. For the next year, that will be a very limited quantity. It should be used for things that only a human can do, such as external inspections, emitter replacements, etc. Assembly is best left to the machines."

"I agree with Dr. Wimberly," Morgan adds. "I'm very grateful that you are investing ahead of the curve to get the human resources we will need."

As the questions settle down, I step through the various ship systems, showing where they are and how they're distributed. Then I run a four-minute time-lapse of a thirty-day build.

I can tell all the tech people are blown away by the design tools on display.

Finally, Logan Watts speaks up for the first time today.

"Your tools are impressive. I thought ours were unrivaled, but I fear you may have us beat. I assume it is proprietary. Will any of us get access to this system? And how can we get copies of the proposed designs to evaluate them? Can you dump your data to any of the standard formats? Thank you."

"It is proprietary Iknosan technology. Access is limited; four of us now have access. The bigger problem is that there is no direct data dump mechanism at this point in time. My team doesn't have the background to take that on right now. It's an area where we could use some help."

"Your equipment. It's telepathically controlled, isn't it?" Logan asks. "But humans don't have telepathy. In that one interview the alien gave to Audell Knight, he said that you were special in ways we could not measure. Are you telepathic?"

All eyes turn to me, waiting for an answer I don't want to give.

As the silence stretches out, Justin says, "I don't think that's an appropriate question for this setting."

Logan opens his mouth to say something, but Angela, his boss, puts a hand on his. "We'd be happy to provide some help. Our team has interfaces to all the standard exchange formats. Who would you like us to contact?"

I raise my hand.

"You are a busy man, Dr. Wimberly."

"I am, ma'am."

Morgan reasserts control over the meeting. "I think we've found our next milestone. By all appearances, we have a viable design and path forward, but we need copies we can study before approving, and copies of the final plan we can post. Dr. Wimberly has the lead on getting a file transfer format implemented."

The way he nods his head and locks eyes with the three main stakeholders has the same feel as a judge banging his gavel.

"Next on the docket is a report from Ms. Cook on the status of their shipyard design. But before we go there, let's take a break."

...

As soon as the meeting breaks, Logan comes over to see me, hand outstretched. "Sorry about my last question. You are such an enigma..."

I interrupt, saying, "Now that's the pot calling the kettle black."

We both chuckle.

"Anyway, I've been trying to figure you out and think I finally have. Whether it's telepathy or the willingness to accept implants, it doesn't really matter. I think there may be an easier solution to the file exchange problem. The AI that produced those drawings in only six weeks probably has access to the internet. If it looks up any of the modern .DWG file formats, it'll be able to build a converter in an hour. I'll text the variants that will be easiest for us. Thanks for your patience this morning. I didn't get it until Justin called me on it."

We shake, then he is away.

Justin comes over. "What was that about?"

"An apology and a possible solution for the file transfer problem."

"A simple solution?" Justin asks.

My phone buzzes. It's the promised text.

"Yeah. He says our AI can look up these file formats and build a converter in no time." I hold up my phone, showing the list of formats. "Any of these will do."

"Send them to Thelma," Justin orders.

"Will do."

"You know, Angela is brilliant."

"How so?" I ask.

"Our ship is about the size of an aircraft carrier. Everyone knows you can't build one of those in a year, couldn't build it in ten if you had to be in a spacesuit the entire time. Her implication that our bot solution has some impact on her company's forward investment is ludicrous. However, it puts her on the record as investing ahead of the curve, something that people like Morgan love to hear." He chuckles. "And as forward investment goes, you blew it out of the park with this one. During his time with the DOD, Morgan has paid hundreds of millions for what you just gave him for free, which puts you in great favor."

"I'm not here to curry favor."

Justin looks at me. "I know you aren't. That's what makes you different and, in some sense, makes you a threat to the others around the table. They are here for the right reasons, just as we are. But they play the game to gain favor. You are given respect because you deliver results better than anyone else."

There's silence for a second, then Justin says, "Time for me to play my game." A second later, his hand is out, shaking Morgan's.

I look around and am amazed at how diligently everyone here works the floor. Not really wanting to take part, I sit, pretend to place a call, then hold my phone up to my ear.

"Thelma, I need some help."

"How can I help you, Kai?"

"Can you read the text that's open on my phone?"

"Read it. Does it mean anything?"

"These are the names of a series of file formats. Data about them is available on the internet. Could you look these up, then work with our design AI to see if we can convert the battlecruiser design into this format?"

"I will. Would you like me to contact you when I am done, or just send the file?"

"Both."

An hour later, as the shipyard presentation drags on, Thelma is back in my ear. "We have a first pass conversion of the battlecruiser design. The file is large and some of our internal detail gets lost in the translation. Sending it to your tablet now.

"Thank you, Thelma."

...

I glance at my watch as Nicholas Bennett gets to the conclusion slide in his presentation. 6:12 PM, and it's already dark outside.

Of the three presentations today, his was the emptiest. It makes sense, his company's work on this initiative is as back-loaded as ours is front-loaded. That's given him more time to plan, and he has well thought out plans. I just wish he hadn't spread it out over two hours.

He surrenders the floor to Morgan, who looks as relieved as I feel.

"Is there anything else we need to discuss before we break up for the day?"

I lift my hand.

"Dr. Wimberly?"

"Thanks to a thirty second consult with Dr. Logan Watts, the data transfer problem is solved, or at least I hope it is solved."

I lift my data pad. "I have the entire file. One point two gigabytes. I placed a copy on our shared server. I don't have the means to validate the file. Hopefully, someone else can tonight."

A flurry of activity at the other end of the table ends with the words, "Oh, this is beautiful." Logan nods to me and says, "Thank you."

"If there's nothing else…" Morgan pauses, but no answer comes. "Then that's a wrap for today. We'll be back here same time tomorrow morning with Dr. Wimberly leading a discussion on weapons. US Orbital Shipyards will host a reception in the private dining room, starting at 6:30. I hope to see you there."

PRIVATE DINING ROOM, HAY-ADAMS HOTEL

As I follow Justin down to the reception, my mind churns through the events of the day. My biggest take away is that we cannot mount a defense in time if we follow the path we're pursuing. The plan for the shipyard will bring it up six or seven months from now, best case. And it won't have enough room to run ten production lines in parallel, meaning we have no path to two hundred ships in the next eighteen months. I think I might have a solution and want to go up to To'Kana's ship to pursue it. Justin just shakes his head.

"You have to be at the reception, Kyle. No one expects you to hold court, or to be a social butterfly, but you are the man of the hour, and it would cost us the goodwill you've created, not to make a meaningful appearance tonight."

The room is mostly set. Justin has gone over to one of the serving tables to review the last-minute details with the hotel's event manager. I plop down in one of the chairs and pull my phone out, once again fake dialing.

"Thelma."

"How can I help you, Kai?"

"Thanks for getting the files converted for me."

"My pleasure, Kai."

"I have another research task for you, if you have the time."

"Which would be?"

"The space platform our partners are making is going to be too small and take too long to complete. I need alternatives. Could we build it on the ground and transport it up? What are the limits on transport size?"

"In terms of surface area, our main transporter is limited to panels slightly larger than the ones used in the foundation for your large replicators. In terms of volume, they are limited to a little more than the replicator in your lab at FCS headquarters. The mining transporters can move much larger volumes. Would you like me to see what its limits are?"

"Please."

"Consider it done, Kai."

Thankfully, I've noticed that I am being watched, so turn off my phone before putting it back in my pocket. As I do, April McDonald steps forward, hand outstretched.

"Good presentation today."

"Thank you."

"A member of our support team confirmed they could open the specifications file. They haven't had time to review contents, obviously. But they're impressed by what they've seen so far."

I repeat myself, saying thank you a second time.

"This was mostly computer generated—the design, I mean," April says.

"As I said, the design tools are extremely powerful, and the sample libraries are extensive. I specified what I wanted, then the tools rendered it."

She nods, but the way she fidgets makes me worry that this was not her purpose in coming to talk with me. She looks around, then puts her hand on my shoulder, pointing the other toward the far wall, then puts her finger to her lips and whispers, "We're not going to make it, are we? The platform size and timeline, the number of production lines we can manage. There's no chance of producing even one hundred ships in eighteen months."

"I share your concerns," I whisper back. "And I'm looking for options."

"Morgan knows. He's under pressure to get this started. The government needs something to show before the mid-terms, so the legislation will get approved. But it is very difficult to change things once a program is underway. It happens all the time, but the schedule consequences are disastrous. Thought you should know."

"There you are." Morgan's voice comes through a moment before he steps up next to me.

"Just talking about the timeline issue," April says.

"Good thing to talk about," he replies, his smooth bass voice washing away the tension of a moment ago. Then he looks directly at me. "The higher ups want this program started ASAP. Heck, yesterday would barely be soon enough." He chuckles at his own joke. "But more seriously..." His voice drops to a whisper. "We'll get away with a little spit balling over the next week or two, but once President Powell signs the bill, we need to move at warp speed to get the first ship up and tested. I like what I've seen so far, but we need a ship to test long before the damn platform is up. I'll leave you to chew on that."

He pats me on the shoulder, then takes off.

"What does spit-balling mean in this context?" I ask April.

"The legislature doesn't need all the details they will ask for. They ask, so they can say they asked. None of them will understand the details. Well, maybe the bitch. What's her name? Ah, Representative Wright, Orange County. She may understand. My point is that the detail that goes to Congress doesn't need to be exact. But the program schedule needs to be perfect by the day President Powell signs the legislation into law." Looking up suddenly, she says, "I need to go."

The last couple minutes fully paint the picture of why I hate working in DC. Nothing needs to be what you say it is. Nothing you deliver needs to be what you promised, just something good enough that no one cares. And this group doesn't think all that kindly of my sometimes consort.

Noise near the entrance draws my attention. Three hotel staff members wheel in a cart with six gold-colored theater stanchions and corresponding red velvet ropes. A few minutes later, they rope off an eight-foot by twelve-foot area in the center of the room. As the hotel staff leave, a 3D image of our new battlecruiser pops up in the roped off area drawing everyone's attention. I've got to hand it to Justin. This was genius.

"Dr. Kyle Wimberly?"

I turn toward the voice, which sounds Australian, to my ear. "Yes?"

He puts his hand out. "Colonel Jaiden Brock, Special Operations Command, Australian Royal Air Force."

"Colonel Brock, a pleasure to meet you. What is your role here this evening?"

"Our governments are in exploratory discussions regarding joint space operations. Morgan Owen is part of that effort. He suggested I come by this evening to get a glimpse of your work." He points toward the holoprojection. "Damned impressive."

"Thank you. I hope your talks are successful. This opportunity came to the United States by chance and the Iknosan have handed us the lead. But this is something the world should unite around, not something we pursue alone."

The colonel pulls out a business card, then locks eyes with me. "My team is exceedingly resourceful. If you're ever in a bind that muscle can solve, call me."

"Thank you."

He nods, then points toward Morgan. "Time for me to check in with my host."

I watch as Colonel Brock strides away, impressed by the raw power he radiates, and puzzled by his offer.

One by one, the other team members show up. Most give me a cursory greeting, then move directly toward the holoprojection.

A group of five men in crisp black suits come in through the entrance, accompanied by Rebecca Cox, Morgan's number two. She spots me, then smiles. A moment later, the group turns and moves in my direction. That's when I see they are all Chinese.

As they approach, I note the way the leader of the Chinese team discreetly eyes me, while the others ogle the holoprojection of the ship, taking in every curve without inhibition.

Rebecca steps up to introduce her companion. "Kyle, please meet General Zeng Shun, a special attaché from the Ministry of National Defense of the People's Republic of China."

The general offers his hand. "Dr. Wimberly, it is a pleasure to meet you, sir."

"The pleasure is mine, General Zeng. I see that your colleagues have taken interest in our first draft design of the battlecruiser we hope to build in the defense of Earth."

"In the defense of Earth, maybe. But I question the assertion America designed this. It looks more like it is something the aliens have given you."

"Iknosan Als did assist me, if that is your question, sir."

"To'Kana, the alien who spoke on television said you were his single point of contact for technology transfer. Yet I am unaware of any contacts you have made with world powers other than the United States. I hope that situation reverses itself soon."

I have no idea how to respond to the general's comments. Thankfully, Rebecca comes to my rescue. "Which is why we have invited you to participate in our program, General. If you participate, you will have access to everything that we have."

He smiles. "And that is why I am here."

He turns back to me. "When the day comes, you will be a welcome guest in the People's Republic, Dr. Wimberly. I look forward to that day."

"Thank you, sir."

As Rebecca leads the General away, Justin steps up alongside. "More guests are coming in. I need you up front with me."

Now, back at the entrance, we greet the guests as they flow in. When Angela Cook arrives, she greets Justin and me, then turns the conversation directly to the ship. "As you were presenting the build sequence today, I noticed panels attached to the hulls interior that I assumed to be insulation. But a keyword search on insulation came up empty. So, I started flipping through the construction steps. I saw one called *installing interior jump plating*. Since the holoprojection is here, could you show me what that means?"

Justin looks at me, then says, "I can handle things here."

I smile at Angela. "My pleasure. Let's start mid-ship." I motion toward the holoprojection and step that way. "The jump system is composed of three major subsystems: the jump-field generator, the jump-field distribution system, and the jump-field emitter array. It's easiest to see the emitters mid-ship."

The crowd parts as we stroll up to the red velvet rope.

I lean into the holoprojection and, using thumbs and index fingers, frame a two-inch square section of the side wall of the hull. "I'm going to expand this section of the ship."

As I send the relevant instructions via my implant, I pull back, expanding the square by pulling my hands until they are four feet apart. Like in textbooks and other technical literature, a square cone grows from the ship, showing a magnified view of the little two-inch section.

There are oohs and ah's at the spectacle, accompanied by lots of whispering.

Now hands free again, I point, "Notice the consistent array of dots. The small ones are the jump-drive field emitters, the large ones are the shield/stealth emitters. There are approximately four billion of each on the ship."

"What are the emitters made of?"

"The portion of the jump emitter exposed to space is made of a niobium-titanium alloy."

She nods. "Like the nozzle on our Merlin Vacuum engines used in our old Falcon 9 rockets... But how does that tie back to the question?"

"To jump, all four billion emitters need to fire in a specific sequence calculated for that jump. And they need to do it with nano-second level precision."

"Ah," Angela says, as if startled. "This would only be possible if the wave guides channeling power to the emitters are exactly the right length. Therefore, you build them as panels that snap into place."

"Bingo," I reply.

Clapping near the room's entrance draws my attention. Justin is the culprit; the camera crew that just filmed my little demonstration is the surprise. No wonder I needed to come!

As I take in the camera crew, I get my second surprise of the evening. Audell Knight is leading the news team, which implies that Justin has turned this into a news event. Then, I see who he is interviewing, Natalie Wright.

I watch for a second as they wrap up. Natalie's eyes connect with mine, and in an instant, she turns away. I watch as she moves deeper into the growing crowd and wonder what's up with her.

Then Audell is in my face asking questions.

...

The party has largely broken up by the time I decide to bail. Sadly, I didn't get a word in with Natalie. Probably for the best, tomorrow is a complicated day.

As I exit, one of the hotel staff approaches. "Dr. Wimberly. Someone left this for you." He holds out a small envelope.

I take it and see my name, but there's no sign who sent it.

"Who gave this to you?"

"The front desk. Someone left it with them."

Burning with curiosity, but not wanting to open it in public, I reach into my pocket for a tip. All I have are some coins and a five-dollar bill. I give him the five, and a curt thank you, then head for my room.

Now, with the door shut, I open the note.

Kai,

Our paths will cross several times this week, but it is imperative that we are not seen together. No greetings. No shaking hands. No eye contact. Just walk past if you see me.

You are being tailed by one of the intelligence agencies. Don't come to my place on Friday evening. I'll contact you if I can find a way to meet.

Otherwise, until next time.

N

[01.10.2034] CONFERENCE ROOM, HAY-ADAMS HOTEL

Today's meeting is with the same team in the same room, but the atmosphere is completely different. A teaser from yesterday's reception made it onto the NBC Nightly News last night. Then Audell's coverage, sourced from NBC, made it onto all the evening cable shows and late-night news and talk shows. This morning, President Powell said it was the most exciting development in our nation's history and she looked forward to signing legislation authorizing the new space fleet into law. But the buzz in the room this morning puts an exclamation point on our concerns related to the timeline.

Morgan calls the meeting to order. "As you all know by now, the pressure is on. President Powell wants a bill to sign sometime next week, and the House and Senate seem to have the resolve to give her one. Our biggest problem is the timeline. We have a ship that, in principle, we can build in thirty days. We need one hundred ships in eighteen months. With six production lines available tomorrow and not a single glitch, it could be done. But we have no production line, and the platform on which we will build them is six months away best case."

Morgan lets his word sink in, then asks, "Does anyone disagree with this assessment?"

Angela raises her hand. When Morgan nods, she says, "We will get it done in six months or less."

"You have an excellent track record," Morgan concedes. "But we need more than that."

Justin eyes me, then nods toward Morgan, who sees the motion.

"Dr. Wimberly, do you have a suggestion?"

"I have two ideas—one along the lines we have been pursuing, the other from a different perspective. But I need to raise one issue first."

"Go on," Morgan replies.

"You said, one hundred ships. Has our target been cut? Or is this a new intermediate target?"

Morgan's face darkens as he holds my gaze. Then after a moment, he clears his throat. "The administration will announce this as being our commitment without commenting on what follows. I think their plan is to tout the success of reaching one hundred, then hit up the allies to fund additional builds. Of course, none of that will happen if we don't have that first batch in eighteen months. So back to the question, what ideas do you have to speed things up?"

"One idea is to construct a temporary platform from building blocks fabricated on Earth and transported into space. I've put some resources into researching this option, but don't have anything tangible to report yet."

"When might we see something?" Morgan asks.

"The idea I'm playing with will either take form next week or it will wash out."

"Then I look forward to hearing from you next week. Your other idea?"

"An updated conception of the fleet. Loosely speaking, the ship we have proposed is the size of an aircraft carrier. The fleet, as we are framing it, is like a fleet of aircraft carriers. No navy on Earth does that. Instead, each aircraft carrier has numerous support ships."

"Do we really have time to design another ship, even if it is smaller and presumably cheaper to build?" Morgan asks.

"I already have a design. It is fully simulated at the component, ship, and production line level. Each war shuttle will take seven days to build on a production line that is less than a third the size of the one needed for our ships. Therefore, with the same platform area, we could have three war shuttle production lines, each producing four shuttles a month. Think about that for a second. We are targeting ten production lines, producing ten battlecruisers a month. Suppose instead, we used eight to build eight battlecruisers, and two to build thirty-two war shuttles a month. Instead of ten battlecruisers a month, we would get eight battle groups comprising a cruiser and four shuttles. That would be a massive increase in our capacity to build war machines."

Morgan looks around the table. "Comments?"

Logan Watts is the first to speak up. "Can you show us your war shuttle?"

I put on the same dog-and-pony show I did yesterday, once again winning my colleague's respect for our design tools.

"I like your theory about force multiplication," Max Harris, the weapons specialist on Morgan's team, says. "But this leaves us with fewer big guns in a war where we are allegedly out gunned."

"Fewer big guns, true. But many more guns, able to operate at closer range with greater precision."

"That's the theory, anyway," Max snaps back.

"Dr. Wimberly, what do you propose as the next step on this?" Morgan asks.

"My first choice would be that we commit to the design and work up an optimal mix—maybe eighty-twenty, maybe something else."

"Your second choice?"

"The Iknosan like this idea enough that they have agreed to build some prototypes that we could test in their next encounter with the Dominion."

"I doubt the department would agree to a joint operation in deep space with unknown alien allies," Jace says. "And we are far enough down the road on legislation authorizing a fleet of battlecruisers that we risk significant delays if we change the plan. My recommendation would be to go all in on the temporary platform idea."

Inwardly, I groan. Without the temporary platform, we will fail. With it we'll probably fail as well, because with one hundred battlecruisers, we would need a better than one-to-one kill ratio against the Dominion, which seems unlikely.

After a little more discussion, we move on to the next topic—the battlecruiser design. The various committee members put in a lot more time studying the plans last night than I would have thought possible. The questions are good, as are most of the suggested changes. But I'm relieved when Morgan wraps it up. I'm tired, discouraged, and in need of comfort, something I won't be getting anytime soon.

[01.13.2034] HOUSE OFFICE BUILDING, WASHINGTON, DC

Like the last time, when I sat before the House Armed Services Committee alone, all fifty-nine members are in attendance, and each will get seven minutes. Unlike the last time, Justin will testify alongside me today, taking on some of the burden. Assuming the committee members show the same discipline as before, they will trap us here until six o'clock this evening.

The chair opens the meeting with a statement of the committee's goals for the session, the ground rules for the discussion, a few words of introduction about Justin and me, and the swearing in.

The first question goes to a member from one of the San Francisco Bay Area districts.

"There is strong public and political support for a war preparation bill that rivals the Manhattan project. Much of that support comes from the news coverage of your encounter with two Dominion warriors, Dr. Wimberly."

He glances up from his notes to catch my eye.

"Both the CDC and the CIA laboratory at Area 51 confirm that the remains of the alien you killed near FCS headquarters did not match any known species on Earth. In previous testimony, you said the Dominion was coming in a year or two. Do you have an update on their expected arrival time?"

Not having a suitable answer for this question, I ping Thelma.

"We are watching, Kai." She comes back. "The captain says most likely twenty months, but it could be as little as fourteen months, or as long as three or more years."

I repeat the answer to the representative.

"If we thought they were coming in fourteen months, what would you do?"

Our lawyer touches my arm and whispers, "This is hypothetical. Only tell him you have contingencies. If you give him specifics, he'll start prying them apart."

"I don't think it will be fourteen months."

"But if you did?"

"Sir, that is hypothetical. I don't think it will be fourteen months."

"And if you found out tomorrow that it would be fourteen months?"

"Then I would start searching for options to get us prepared in that time frame."

He continues to stare at me for a second, then diverts his gaze toward Justin. "Mr. Wicks. You are a financial investor. Prior to that, you served in the Air Force and were honorably discharged in 2021."

Justin nods in acknowledgment but says nothing.

"In previous testimony, you have spoken with authority about technical matters. As I was reading through your dossier last night, I wondered where you obtained this technical expertise."

The representative lets the statement hang, but Justin is good enough at this game not to comment unless asked to.

After a second, he asks, "Please explain?"

Justin sits up straight, then points toward me. "At the feet of a master."

His comment evokes a laugh from a spectator in the room. One which spreads through the room, causing more commotion. Then the gavel pounds.

"The witness will take this proceeding seriously."

Now responding with fire, Justin says, "I object to that comment, sir. The gentleman asked where I learned. I gave a complete and accurate answer. I learned by sitting across from Dr. Kyle Wimberly, the only human who knows—truly knows—about the technology in question."

Justin does not flinch, as the chairperson holds his stare, then the timer dings. "The gentlemen's time has expired. The chair yields the floor to Representative Wright from California.

Natalie starts by addressing the room. "As everyone here knows, I have been an advocate for this program since the beginning, which for me was when I saw the recording of the Dominion warrior attacking Dr. Wimberly. I have worked with the assistant secretary of defense to help craft a defensive plan for us to consider. I bet my life traveling in the proof-of-concept ship that took the first humans to another star system."

She pauses there, letting three of her precious seconds tick by.

"My concern is not about whether we should authorize this program. I know we should. It's also not about the plan. I know it is sound. My concern is about cost."

A murmur passes through the room.

"By that, I mean we need to spend what we need to spend. But unlike previous programs, the normal rules do not apply here."

More murmuring.

"The principles still apply. I'm not challenging that. It is the metrics that do not."

Now turning directly to Justin, she asks, "Mr. Wicks, as we will hear in testimony later today, you are proposing to have robots build the ships in space; robots that were given to you by the Iknosan. As a cost-plus supplier to the federal government, how would you measure the cost of that assembly work?"

"One correction, if I may. The Iknosan are giving us the designs for these bots. We will build them and incur cost in doing so."

"Thank you for that correction. But the question stands."

"I don't know, ma'am. To protect workers from being exposed to open space, we propose to have bots assemble the ships. They will also reduce total construction time to something like thirty days per ship per production line. We will build essentially all the components in the ship using other automated processes. Everything, well, almost everything, that goes into the ship itself, except the interior finish, will be built up from raw materials mined by one of my corporate affiliates or bought on the open market. That said, we can't afford to do this on a couple percent markup on the raw materials."

"Thank you, Mr. Wicks, for making my point clear to my colleagues." She looks around at the other committee members around the table. "That puts the onus on us to craft a bill that allows appropriate compensation for those who have risked their lives to bring us to this point. I reserve the remainder of my time."

...

As the day drags on, I have to credit Natalie for her leadership. I'd had the sense at the outset that our design and credentials would be challenged all day.

The last questioner today is the representative from Louisiana. "Dr. Wimberly. A friend of mine invited me over to his place to watch the raw, unfiltered version of your encounter with the Dominion. I've got to hand it to you, son. It's hard to see how anyone could defeat a creature like that. What assurances can you give us about our chances in this fight?"

"We have thousands of hours of recordings of battle with the Dominion. They won essentially every battle. My team has watched a lot of those hours, not all of it, but enough to have identified dozens of weaknesses in their ships and in their tactics. Another world the Iknosan is working with, a world with much more advanced technology than we have, was able to use one of those weaknesses to turn the Dominion away. If we have the twenty months we think we do, I'm confident we'll be able to do better, because we already have ideas on how to exploit more of the weaknesses. I've prototyped two new weapons that I hope to test against the Dominion before they arrive in our system. I doubt those will be the last."

"Thank you, Dr. Wimberly." Then to the chair, "I yield the remainder of my time."

As the chair calls the meeting to a close, my lawyer whispers, "She got the note."

I glance at Natalie, whose eyes I've been avoiding all day, and see her open the envelope and peer inside. A moment later, there's a smile and I'm hopeful for the evening.

FOUR SEASONS HOTEL, WASHINGTON, DC

The note from Natalie on Monday night hit me hard. When sleep didn't come, I went down to the gift shop and bought a blank greeting card. On it, I handwrote a note saying I could transport from my room to her place completely unseen, just like this note had been transported to her kitchen table. And if I left my cell phone on and in my room at the Hay-Adams, the FBI would not be looking for me anywhere else.

Wednesday, I got a note back saying somewhere else, maybe the Four Seasons. Wednesday night, Jill reluctantly booked a suite there in her own name. Earlier today, she checked in, then came back and dropped the key in my room at the Hay-Adams.

Once Justin and I got back from the committee meeting, I begged off on dinner and went to my room, then Thelma transported me here.

The note my lawyer had delivered to Natalie today confirmed the date and gave her the suite number. Now I wait with a bottle of champagne on ice and anticipation in my loins.

A discreet knock on the door announces her arrival. I open it and she marches in straight and stiff like it's just another business meeting. But as soon as the door closes, she spins around to hug and just melts into me. After a slow, longing kiss, she whispers, "You're so clever. Transporting that note onto my table was genius."

"Desperate times call for desperate measures."

As the embrace lingers, I just want this moment to last.

"Shall we order some dinner?" she asks.

We talk business for a while as we sip champagne and wait for our meal. Then Natalie hides in the bedroom when room service comes to deliver Ms. Erhart's dinner for two.

As we eat, Natalie asks, "Kai, are you going to get back together with your girlfriend in California?"

I'm shocked by the question, tongue tied, unable to get an intelligible word out.

She smiles a rueful smile. "You're so sweet. I really like you, Kai, but don't fall in love with me."

The shock of her words, and the dread of loss that accompanies them, floods through me like fire. "What?"

She puts her hand on mine. "It's OK," she whispers, much like my mother did when I'd panic over something gone wrong. "It's OK. I love your company and will take as much of it as you'll give me. But your life is out there, mine is here, and that will not change."

"What? What are you telling me?"

"Kai. Think straight for a second. This is an affair. A lovely one, but still an affair. You're young enough to find someone to truly love, to marry, to bear your children. I want that for you."

"You're not that much older than I am."

Again, the rueful smile. "Twelve years. I'm twelve years older than you are."

When I do not respond, she asks, "Did you ever find out what happened to me in Afghanistan?"

I'm not sure the relevance of the question but confess that I never followed up.

"I talk about my time in Afghanistan as if I was in the military. But in truth, I had a civilian role, working with State to scout out safe, or at least safer, locations for the media. We were in the wrong place at the wrong time. A mortar round landed in the square we were about to enter. I was in front, the only one in our party that got hit. A piece of shrapnel cut my forehead. That's where all the blood came from…" she pulls back her hair to show the scar. "Another piece hit my side." She points to an area just below her right breast. "I'll show it to you later. And the consequential one, just a tiny sliver, hit me in the lower abdomen well below my navel."

A tear forms, which she shakes away.

"That little sliver embedded itself into my uterus, which ultimately had to be removed. Shortly thereafter, my husband left me when he realized I could never give him a child."

"I'm sorry to hear that."

"The whole situation ultimately brought me here, where I've found that affairs, especially tender ones like this, are better suited to who I am and the way I want to live my life."

"Where does that leave us?"

"With me wanting every minute I can have with you. Now, back to your girlfriend. Promise me you will at least attempt to get back together with her."

"Sure."

"Oh, that was convincing," she teases.

"I'm not ready to give you up."

"I'm not yours to give up. Neither are you mine to hold on to." She stands and glances toward the bedroom. "Let me show you my scars."

[01.14.2034] FOUR SEASONS HOTEL, WASHINGTON, DC

I wake as Natalie gets up. The light of dawn falls on her as she stands. I reach out and touch her, bringing a smile to her face. The sight of her fills me with desire.

"My-oh-my, aren't you the energetic one?"

"More?"

"I've had enough for now, thank you. I can't have you using me all up."

As she steps toward the bathroom, I ask, "Free tonight?"

Her eyes fill with sadness. "Sorry, I have something else planned."

"After?" I prod.

She shakes her head, a tear forming. "Let it go, Kai."

"Why?"

"Another of my intimate friends is flying into town today. He booked this weekend a long time ago."

What is it with me? Why does every woman I fall for run away? I lumber out of bed and urgently search for my clothes. I've got to get out of here.

As I'm slapping them on, the door to the bathroom opens and Natalie steps out, still in the raw. She sees me but doesn't step closer. "I'm sorry, Kai. Go find your girlfriend and win her back. You need more than I can offer. Goodbye, Kai."

I stare at her, feeling the tears welling up.

"Thelma, please transport me out of here."

LAB, IKNOSAN LEGACY SHIP

I open my eyes, expecting to see my room at the Hay-Adams. Instead, I see To'Kana waiting for me.

"Kyle, sorry to interrupt like this, but I just received some concerning news." He indicates one of the side rooms. I follow as he enters.

Once in the room, To'Kana engages the isolation filter, then indicates a seat.

"Yesterday, the Dominion arrived in the second system on their target list. The people there, known as the Pelglik, were more technologically advanced than yours when Legacy Ship #2 arrived. Unfortunately, they never found anyone like you, or Justin, for that matter, willing to take on the mantle of leadership."

"This story doesn't end well, does it?"

To'Kana shakes his head no. "They made a lot of progress, built over one-hundred ships, mounted a defense. But the Dominion rolled right over them. The Pelglik were not warriors. They had no fight in them, were inept with the decoys..." To'Kana's voice trails away.

"Were there any survivors?"

"Seventeen ships ran. Dominion ships gave chase. To the best of our knowledge, the Pelglik do not know about Earth, so hopefully the Dominion are not being led here."

Realizing that To'Kana has not cut to the chase, I ask. "What does that mean for us?"

"Our forecast systems predict the Dominion will arrive here two months earlier than previously expected."

Two months! The words resonate in my mind. How can we possibly pull our plan forward two months?

To'Kana nods. "I see you understand the problem. We're going to need some sort of innovation if we are to prevail."

"What about the war shuttle?"

To'Kana eyes me. "We will build them, as promised. But until your government changes its mind and incorporates the war shuttles into your defense plan, I can only build so many for you."

"What about the space platform? The one our government is building won't be ready in time. Can we modify the transporters to handle larger pieces, so that we assemble more on the ground?"

"You're framing this too narrowly, Kyle Wimberly."

"What do you mean by that?"

"There is an obvious solution. But it is not one I can give you. It is one you need to find on your own."

"Why?"

"Because that is the way it must be."

There is silence for a moment as To'Kana and I stare at each other, then To'Kana stands.

"I have said all I can say on the matter. It is time for you to do some research."

ROOM, HAY-ADAMS HOTEL

I open my eyes and see the depressing sight that is my otherwise empty room. I pick up my phone, which I left here to keep the FBI distracted, and see that it's only 7:55 AM. A text sent ten minutes ago asks if I'm still on for breakfast at eight. I reply with a yes, then realize I can't go down looking like this. A second text promises I'll be down in fifteen. A five-minute shower, ten more for clothes and personal grooming, and I'm on my way.

RESTAURANT, HAY-ADAMS HOTEL

I walk in and see Justin and Jill in deep discussion.

"Hope I'm not interrupting."

Justin looks up. "Jill just told me she arranged for you to hook up with someone last night over at the Four Seasons. Who? And, why?"

"An old friend from Afghanistan. Why there? The FBI put a tail on me. She needed privacy. I could transport there, leaving my phone here. No one's the wiser."

I can tell Justin doesn't believe me, so I change the subject. "I just got back from To'Kana's ship."

"Thought you spent the night with an old friend."

"I did. She's an early riser. When I asked Thelma to transport me back, she transported me up instead. To'Kana had some bad news to share."

"Which was?" Justin prods.

I quickly run down what I know.

"Two months," Justin groans. "I wish this would have come before yesterday's hearing. We need to amend our testimony, or we'll be at risk of perjury charges."

"The lawyers can handle it, right?"

"Yeah," Justin says. "Which leaves us with the problem of the platform. To'Kana says there's an obvious solution, but he cannot tell you what it is. My guess is that it's in the replicator library, but it doesn't involve the transporter..."

"Why do you say that?"

"He said you were looking at the problem wrong. I interpret that to mean building the platform on the surface and transporting it up is the wrong idea. My guess is that the replicator library has something relevant for building platforms in space."

"Good thinking. I'll head back after breakfast."

CELLAR, ESTATE HOUSE

The cellar floor cave-in happened three weeks ago on Christmas Eve. The expansion was well along when I left town last Saturday. Today, the place is humming.

"Thelma?"

"What can I do for you, Kai?"

"I've lost track of what we are building today. The replicators are all busy. What are they making?"

"Parts for the war shuttles."

"Good news, thank you, Thelma."

"You're welcome, Kai."

As I walk down the long corridor, I pass nine of the eight-meter-long replicators. What a miracle these machines are. Then I stop at the large transporter pad, which sits where the tenth replicator on this level was originally planned to go. This machine is an even greater miracle. There are human built machines that do some functions the replicators do; but there is no human machine that does any part of what this one does. What a gift we've been given.

On realizing that I'm wasting time, I hasten my pace, entering the little rotunda at the end a minute later. Cabinets line one wall. I shuffle through them one-by-one looking for the advanced controllers I had replicated before I left. I hit pay dirt in the fifth cabinet.

Now seated at the desk, I light up the controller to do something I should have done a week ago—configure it to interface with the replicators, the pattern library, and the pattern editor. If I'd done this last week, I could have been in the pattern library while in DC. Maybe that would have saved me from Natalie.

I snort aloud. Not a chance of that. What a fool I am. Just a boy toy and too stupid to figure it out on my own.

Configuration finished, it's time to get out of the cold.

OFFICE, ESTATE HOUSE

Now settled in at my desk, with the fireplace lit, I browse through the pattern library. The keyword *platform* yields thousands of patterns. But five minutes of browsing clarifies that this keyword isn't specific enough. The qualifier *space* barely narrows the results. The qualifier *open space* narrows the result to a handful of small platforms that can be transported up fully built.

I try similar searches for keywords: *space dock* and *orbital shipyard* and get similar results, too many hits, lots of parts, nothing that indicates how to start.

On realizing that I know nothing about shipbuilding, I open my tablet and google *stages of building a ship*. To my surprise, an article pops up, *The Ten Stages of Building Cruise Ships*.

I click through and bingo—first get the order, second cut the steel, third lay the keel... The list goes on, but the word keel speaks to me.

Emboldened, I switch back to the pattern library and search on the keyword *keel*. To my surprise, I get hundreds of results. Stepping through them, I finally hit pay-dirt—*keel for rectangular space platforms greater than one hundred square meters*.

I laugh at the size specification. It doesn't say one hundred; I rounded to that. It's a twelve-digit number around a hundred converted to metric from the Iknosan measurement system.

This pattern is actually a template with lots of options, supported by explanatory text. The first option is location. The choices are interstellar space, stellar orbit, planetary orbit. Reading through the trade-offs, the easiest location is star-planet Lagrange two because it has little direct solar radiation, reduced solar wind, and minimal gravitational shear.

Over the next four hours, I build a complete specification for a platform four hundred meters long, one hundred meters wide with a recommended depth of seven meters, positioned at sun-earth Lagrange two, grav-drive for orbital station keeping, garage space for fourteen hundred bots, material storage for nearly two hundred thousand cubic meters of materials and systems, dual transport platforms... It's beautiful, absolutely beautiful, and supported by a construction protocol that requires zero initial infrastructure other than four special open-space bots.

I compile the template, then send the package to To'Kana's design AI for fine tuning and validation.

"You're back."

The voice belongs to Alex. Its tone; a little less friendly than usual.

I look up at her, standing just outside the open doorway, covered in sweat.

"I'm back from DC. You just finished your afternoon run?"

"Yep. Sorry about last week."

"Same. It was an awful night for everyone, I think. Friends?"

She smiles. "Friends. What are you working on?"

"A new design for an orbital platform."

"Isn't SpaceX working that?"

"They are building a nice permanent platform in low earth orbit. It will be a tremendous asset when it's done. Mine is a short-term solution optimized for unmanned use."

"Sounds like a good place for women to hang out."

I laugh at the joke. But as I do, I realize the comment was more visceral than comedic.

"Have you seen any of the news coverage this week?" Alex asks.

I shake my head no.

"I'm going up to shower. Will be back down in a half hour for a snack. Will you join me? There's something I think you need to see."

"In the shower?"

She laughs. "In your dreams, Wimberly." Then she points at me. "Half hour, den. Don't be late, or you're paying for the drinks."

"Deal."

As she takes off down the hall, I worry there's more going on with her than meets the eye. Nonetheless, I'm glad the banter is back.

DEN, ESTATE HOUSE

I arrive twenty minutes later and see things got changed up over the last week. A kegerator sits at the far end of the room. It's loaded with Central Coast Brewing's Monterey Street, Pale Ale. I grab a glass and fill, then notice the little bags of pretzels on the counter. I grab one of those too, then settle in as I wait for Alex.

It's kind of surreal to be back here, where it's comfortable and quiet, devoid of all the DC pretense. Just thinking about last week makes me shudder. What spell did Natalie Wright cast over me?

"Seems like you found the beer."

I look up and see Alex, hair down and still wet, tight form-fitting jeans, and the same flag-like red and blue top that Natalie wore. Only it looks a lot better on Alex. All of it. I guess that's the difference twelve years makes.

"Why are you looking at me like that?" Alex asks.

Her voice brings me back to the moment. "Sorry, I umm... You look great tonight."

"Oh... Now you notice me."

"Can I get you a beer?" I ask, attempting to break the awkward moment.

"No thanks. I've got better technique. Want a little more?"

Acquiescence seeming the better option, I say, "Sure."

She takes my glass as she walks past and I watch as she fills hers, then tops mine. As my gaze lingers, I try not to look at her the way I'm looking at her.

She catches me, nonetheless.

"What's up with you, Kai? Completely disinterested in women for years, then suddenly Sophie, and maybe a little more."

"What are you talking about?"

"Men are so stupid," she complains, shaking her head. "Give me a second, then watch this."

She lights up a holoprojection cube, then a still appears. It's from last Monday's reception. It's me and April McDonald.

"Remember this?"

"Of course I do. She's complaining about something I've already figured out."

"What about this?"

The scene shifts almost a hundred eighty degrees. Reporters are streaming into the room, followed by Audell Knight and Natalie Wright. His eyes scan the room, presumably looking for people to interview. Her eyes lock on one subject. The contrast between Audell's darting eyes and Natalie's fixed gaze, coupled with the upward twist of her mouth, paint the entire picture.

The image twists again, the back of Natalie's head in the foreground, me in the background.

"It gets better," Alex says.

The image switches again, me facing the camera in the foreground, Natalie staring right at me in the background. Then the still image comes to life, Natalie veering my way, eyes and mouth smiling.

Alex freezes the playback. "Look at her, undressing you with her eyes. It's kind of shameless."

When I don't answer, Alex sighs. "Please tell me she didn't seduce you."

When no answer comes, Alex's head drops. "All the women lined up for you here, and you went with HER!"

I put my head down, fingers running through my hair. "Where did you get this?"

"Sophie. She's a C-SPAN subscriber. She doesn't trust anything from the other news sources. Raw coverage for that girl."

"It's not what it looks like. She seduced me. Wearing the same shirt you are, by the way."

"I've had this top for years, Kai, and the first time you notice it is on HER?"

My head droops, and as it hits the table, Alex says, "And now she's dumped you?" There's a pause, then Alex starts frantically looking for something. When the tapping on her data pad stops, she says, "Please tell me it's not this guy. Flew in today from Los Angeles, greeted at the airport by Natalie Wright."

I look up and see the familiar face of the seventy-something year old man Natalie sent me away for. I collapse on the table, head down in shame.

"Sophie's already seen this. She meant to give you a time-out, not a get out of jail free card. If you want her, you need to go see her now."

"Did that last Saturday. Didn't exactly work out."

Alex stands. "It's on you now, Kai. Deal with it or don't. But I've done all I can do."

SOPHIE'S APARTMENT, SAN LUIS OBISPO

I'm not exactly proud of it, but I asked Thelma if she could confirm that Sophie was home and not with someone else. Once confirmed, I jumped into my car and drove over to her apartment.

I've been sitting here now for five minutes trying to screw up enough courage to go knock on her door, then decide that I must. She's my brother-in-law's sister. I'm already estranged from my brother and on iffy footing with my mother. So, I need to clear the air with Sophie, if for no other reason than to prevent my tenuous connection with my family from coming completely apart.

I knock on the door but get no answer. After a minute, I ring the doorbell. The porch light comes on and there's motion behind the peephole. Then I wait, counting off the seconds. At twenty, she releases the deadbolt. A few more and the door cracks open.

I count off another five seconds, then plunge in. "I'm sorry. You were right. I've held back too much, trying to protect you from things I didn't think you needed to know."

"Like that congresswoman?" she accuses.

"Like the terrorists; like the congresswoman; like why we are at the estate. We all have baggage. I would expect most of it to come out, eventually. But it's not the stuff you lead with."

"You've slept with her?"

"She seduced me back in November."

"And last week?"

"I accepted her invitation, yes. You had dumped me and lied to me about your work schedule. She scooped me up on the rebound. But it's not a serious relationship, and now that I know who she is, it won't happen again."

"I can't believe you slept with her."

"I have slept with three women: Crystal, every night for four years. You, a handful of times over two weeks. And a very manipulative older woman, three times. That's it. How many men have you been with?"

The door opens. "Probably better that we have this discussion in private."

I look at the open door, wondering whether I really want to go in. At the moment, a celibate life seems the better option.

"Sorry I misled you about my work schedule," Sophie whispers. "The terrorist thing terrified me. Please come in."

As I step in, I realize this is the first time I've been inside her apartment. It's tiny—a galley kitchen and a great room, which is sectioned off into dining and living areas with doors to a bedroom and bathroom at the far end.

"It's not like the estate house," she says as she closes the door and motions toward the sofa. I take the offered seat. Sophie takes the rocker.

"So where to from here?" she asks.

"I came over here to see if there was something to salvage. But as I sat out front trying to screw up enough courage to knock, I realized you are part of my family now, whether you're part of me or not. That means I can't run away. I need to make things right between us, even if we part company."

"Your mother told me about your in-or-out speech last Saturday."

"I suppose I'm never going to live that down."

"Probably not, but she regrets her role in driving you to make it. She's one of your true believers, Kai. She's also worried about you and about what people are saying."

"What about you?" I ask.

"The thing with the congresswoman really set me off." She puts a hand up, cutting off a reply. "I felt betrayed. Felt stupid thinking I could catch someone like you, stupid for having jumped into bed with you so soon. Felt embarrassed about lying to you."

"Willing to start over? Take it a little slower?"

She smiles. "I'd like that."

"Dinner tomorrow night?"

She sighs and shakes her head. "It's Sunday. I'm on duty."

"Through Thursday?"

"Yeah. Medical school was expensive."

It takes a second to connect the dots. She's working sixty-hour weeks to pay off her student loan debt, which also explains the apartment. "Friday then?"

"Friday," she confirms, then stands and takes a step toward the door.

I follow along, then accept a hug at the door. Maybe this will work out after all.

CHAPTER 15: PLATFORM

[01.15.2034] OFFICE, ESTATE HOUSE

I joined my team for the run this morning, the first in over a week. It's remarkable how quickly the edge slips away when you go eight days without. Needless to say, I fell way behind the pack. Mac usually hangs back with me when that happens. Today, it was Alex.

She asked if I'd connected with Sophie. I told her I had, and we planned to go out Friday night. She asked if I planned to bring Sophie home with me and I said no, things moved too fast last time. Then, after a long silence, she told me she was going to change rooms. She didn't want to hear me *carrying on* with Sophie when she eventually came home with me.

After more prying, it came out that she wanted that room, so it would be easier to hide it from the others if I had ever invited her over. For a while now, I've sensed that Alex might have an interest in me. It might have been an easier path. I've lived in proximity to her half of my adult life, so much so that I think of her as more like a sister than a prospective love interest.

I truly hope this isn't a diverging of paths, because I count Alex as one of my closest friends.

Now showered and at my desk, I open my tablet to see what's happened over the last twelve hours. There's a note from To'Kana's design AI that there were some minor issues with the template I used, which triggered simulation errors. It fixed them for me, and the revised plans simulate out. To'Kana has also reviewed the plans and will unlock the patterns for the special bots we need if I decide to go with this solution.

With excitement, I pop the platform up in the holoprojection, go over every surface, then tour the interior, first the bot garages, then the component storage areas. In the footnotes, the build time for the platform is seventeen days. Curious to see how they built platforms like these, I trigger a one hundred times fast forward of the build process.

Six bots appear, all tethered together. They propel apart, then square metal tubes start appearing near the individual bots. They look remarkably similar to the ones used in the replicator foundation, though I suspect they are of greater girth. The bots slowly position, then join the tubes, then the process repeats a dozen times until the frame for a three-dimensional box is formed. I recognize this as the basic building block of the platform.

After increasing the playback speed, I watch as a dozen of these things are made, joined, and surfaced. The bots disappear into the frame of this mini platform, making me rotate the image to see what they are doing. Components I don't recognize get added and are attached underneath, then the bots fly out and land on the flat surface. There they disconnect the tethers and start rolling on their treads. That's when I get it. They just added the power sources for the grav plating—the bots are now held down on the flat surface by the gravity it generates.

A warning pops up on the display and the bots seem to hunker down. An overlay shows the platform has already drifted a hundred plus miles from the Lagrange point and grav-drive station-keeping kicks in, flying the platform back to where it belongs. At this point, the build seems to go into overdrive with additional bots and material transporting on to the platform. Now assisted by gravity, the new bots move fast; the piles of material are quickly aligned and joined.

I speed up the simulation more and watch as the platform grows to full size. Then the bottom of the platform is surfaced with grav plating and it's done—a four-hundred-meter-long, one-hundred-meter-wide, seven-meter-high platform built at sun-earth Lagrange two. Both the top and bottom surfaces are covered in grav plating, allowing a production line to run on both sides. Truly amazing.

Although I want to push the proverbial go button and have this thing built for real, there's one more test I want to run. I want the design AI to simulate a simultaneous build of two of our new battlecruisers, one on each side of the platform.

[01.16.2034] OFFICE, ESTATE HOUSE

Today started the same as yesterday. Thankfully, I kept close enough to the pack during the morning-run that no one needed to hang back with me, though Mac did for most of the run. He reminded me that the next twenty-megawatt generator would be installed the day after tomorrow. Said he planned to spend the day back at First

Cycle Solar to help Enzo, who would manage the installation and the Western Interconnect inspection team. I'm glad Mac is on top of this. I'd completely lost track of it. It's hard to believe that we're soon going to be at one-hundred-ten megawatts with revenue over seven-million dollars a month.

Now at my desk, I play the simulation To'Kana's design AI ran. Over the next hour, I watch the 500x simulation of the ship builds. It takes thirty-two days, not the thirty previously verified, to build the ships. They fly away in different directions when the simulation is complete.

I send the files to Justin, then call him.

"Hey, buddy. Wondered what happened to you. Did you find a solution?"

"I did. The platform needs to be out at Lagrange two, not in low earth orbit. It will take seventeen days to build the platform, another thirty-two to build the first two ships. We'll probably need a day to prepare, but that means two ships could be ready to be crewed fifty days from now."

Justin is quiet for a moment, then says, "OK. We need to loop Morgan in on this, then Representative Wright. I don't think Morgan can move on it until the legislation is passed. I don't know if you saw the news, but Natalie seems to have taken her eye off the ball."

"What news?"

"The film producer... What's his name? They announced their engagement last night."

"Oh, my God," I whisper.

"Come again?" Justin asks.

I shake my head as more pieces snap together. What a fool I was to believe she cared. But I guess that's the point. She didn't care. I was just her most recent boy toy. Used, enjoyed, discarded when no longer convenient. And she thought it was sweet that I cared.

"Kai, are you still there?"

"Um, yeah, yeah."

"If I can get Morgan tomorrow, can you come out tonight? Maybe we can get Wright on Tuesday? Our JV partners on Wednesday? I have other meetings with them on Friday. We can get them then, if not earlier."

The thought of another week in DC, another meeting with Natalie Wright, is completely revolting.

"Kai?"

"No. I'm not spending another week in DC. Why not just start the platform?"

Justin seems as repulsed by my assertion as I am to his. "It's going to take millions of dollars' worth of our materials to build it. If we do it ahead of time, we won't get paid. We're spending heavily right now and need some revenue. If you come here, we are more likely to get it."

His words trigger a memory of something he told me a couple years back. "Can't we just build the platform and production lines on our own, then charge the joint venture a rental fee for using it? We need to get those two months back. And they will still need our platform once the SpaceX platform is complete, because theirs isn't big enough."

"Good idea. We'd still need approval from Morgan, Wright, and our partners. But this plan would get ships into production well before the mid-term elections, which they all want. Let me see if I can work that angle."

When Justin signs off, I realize that the important things on my plate are all in someone else's hands. For the first time since I met To'Kana, I'm caught up. Every time I've come close before, some fresh disaster struck before I finished.

"Thelma?"

"How can I help you, Kai?"

"What's the status of the war-shuttle build-out?"

"This is day two of our ten-week production plan. Most of your replicators on the lower level are making parts. Later today, we will lay the keel for our first war shuttle. It is all on time and on schedule."

"Do you know if or how that will change if we start the platform build?"

"We have the capacity to do both simultaneously."

"Thank you, Thelma."

"You are welcome, Kai."

Again, I smile at how human Thelma has become.

My phone rings. The caller ID says Gabriel Wilson. I wonder what's up at Full Cycle Solar.

"Kai, something unusual is happening out at the substation. We have a team out there now. Would it be possible for you to join them?"

"Sure. Let them know I'll be there in a minute. It'll be a pleasant diversion."

I put my phone down on the desk, then root through the drawer that contains the burner phones. A second later, the one labeled FCS is in my pocket.

SUBSTATION, FIRST CYCLE SOLAR

I open my eyes and see that Thelma put me down at the far edge of the substation's parking lot, maybe a hundred feet from where the team is standing, pointing at something.

"Thelma, why did you land me here?"

"I can't see the substation very well today. Something is blocking my view. It's clear where you are."

I look around and see no signs of anything unusual. It's a clear January morning in the desert, no clouds, little breeze, no dust in the air. As I step closer, one of the guys jumps, then backs away from whatever the other guys are looking at. When a second guy jumps, then steps back, cold fear creeps up my spine. Even though the thought isn't fully formed, I think I know what I'm about to find.

The first guy, who I now recognize as Marion Black, jumps again, and I catch his words. "Damn, those things move fast."

"Oh, my God, no." I whisper, going into full sprint mode. "Guys, get out of there!"

Marion turns toward me and suddenly seems to connect the dots, jumping again and backing away from me as a small black object flies in front of him. A second later, all the guys are running toward the far exit in the fence surrounding the substation. As they retreat, a dozen other little black things hop along behind, bouncing maybe three feet in the air.

The old truck I used to use is twenty feet ahead. I divert toward it, hoping the handheld energy weapon To'Kana gave me is still in the glove box.

An eight-legged spider-like creature bounds toward me, confirming my fears. It lands ten feet in front of the drivers-side door.

I leap up onto the truck bed, landing in a crouched position and sliding to a stop when my side hits the cab's back window. Pain explodes in my left hip, but I don't let it stop me as I propel myself around and through the open passenger-side window. I open the glove box and see the weapon.

As I pull it out, the eight-legged Dominion hatchling hops up onto the hood, landing on the steeply curved driver's-side edge, before sliding off back to the ground. In an instant, I'm back out the window, making the precarious step back onto the truck bed. As I hear one of the guys scream, my hip gives out and I flop down on the deck, smacking my head so hard I see stars. As the world spins, I hear another failed hop onto the hood. Then a moment later, a second one, which seems to stick. Adrenaline floods through me. I pop up and spin around, as I see the six-inch version of a Dominion warrior throw a spur at me. It strikes the windshield, bouncing away harmlessly, triggering the hatchling to wind up and try again.

    I find the weapon's safety, click it off, then fire through the cabin's rear window and windshield. Clean holes appear in each, before the beam hits the creature, blowing it up. Now standing, I see five more coming and pick them off one at a time.

    With no more in sight, I take a running leap off the back of the truck, away from the substation. As suspected, several of the little creatures are under the truck at this point. But thankfully I can outrun them. Five. Seven. Ten strides, then I spin and fire. Ping, ping, ping. Got 'em all.

    Panting, heart pounding, I look for the other guys. Three are straddling the top of the twelve-foot fence, out of range of the dozen creatures trying to hop up on them. One of them, Aaron Smith, I think, is bleeding profusely. Marion Black is nowhere to be seen.

    I run into the substation and start shooting at the ones on the ground. A minute or two later, they're all down.

    "Didn't know you could shoot so well, boss."

    My head swivels around and I see Marion emerging from the control room, first aid kit in hand. We help the guys down, then carry Aaron to the truck, where the other two tend to the wound on his arm.

    Marion guides me back to where it started, an odd-shaped hole in the ground. Looking closer, I see a fibrous sack that has split open, its frayed top at ground level, everything else below.

    "I stepped on it, felt the ground give, so stopped to see what it was," Marion says. "A minute later, the sack tore open and these giant, odd-shaped spiders came out. At first, they seemed uncoordinated, disoriented. We called it in, sent some pictures, hoping we could find out what it was."

    "They're Dominion. They grow up to be ten feet tall."

    "Hatchlings?" Marion asks.

    "That's my bet."

    As I take in my surroundings, I see Marion is wearing a GoPro.

Pointing at it, I ask, "Was that recording?"

"Still is."

"I want a copy. We need to search this area. I'm worried that's not the only egg sack."

I wipe my brow, surprised that I'm this sweaty given it's only sixty degrees out. My hand comes back with blood on it. "Am I bleeding?"

Marion looks at me. "A little, but your face is really messed up. It looks like you did a face plant on the truck bed."

"I did."

"That will not feel good in the morning."

A shout comes from the direction of the truck. "Time for us to go."

Marion steps that way, as an idea comes.

"Wait just a second?"

"Thelma?"

"How can I help you, Kai?"

"Has the view cleared up?"

"Yes, it has."

"Are there any other spots near here where the view is obstructed?"

"Two others, yes."

"Direct me to them."

As Thelma gives me directions, I ask Marion. "Is there another one of these in the other truck?"

"Should be. Gabe made it standard equipment."

"Get it. We may have a lock on two more egg sacks."

As Marion runs for the truck, I follow Thelma's instructions to a spot near one of the step-up transformers. Sure enough, there's another distinct bulge.

A minute later, Marion is back. We take positions ninety degrees apart from each other. Then open fire. The sack bursts open immediately, and there's a lot of squealing. A few jump out but aren't a threat. Eventually, the sack catches fire and burns shockingly hot, thick black smoke billowing up into the sky.

Fifteen minutes later, we clear the second egg-sack.

I do a quick check in with Thelma to assure these are cleared and there are no more, then send the guys off.

ESTATE HOUSE

When the sound of replicators busily at work replaces that of the desert breeze, I know I'm back in the cellar. I open my eyes but am disoriented despite my precaution. The adrenaline that powered me through the last couple of hours is gone, and I hurt all over. Knowing I need to tend to my injuries, I limp towards the elevator, get in, then push the button to go up. A moment later the door opens, and I step out, the doors closing before I realize I'm in the grand foyer, not the upstairs hallway.

Light feet, coming quickly down the main staircase, draw my attention as I slump to the floor. Then Alex's voice penetrates the buzzing in my ears. "Kai, what happened to you?"

I shake my head, unable to muster the power to think.

"Come on." She lifts my right arm up over her shoulder, then spins into me and lifts, taking the weight off my throbbing hip. Up the elevator, down the hall, then into my room. She sits me down on my bed, then goes into my bathroom saying, "We need to get you into the bath."

A moment later, she's back out. "Your room doesn't have a bathtub?"

I shake my head no.

She goes to the adjoining door and unlocks it. Then she's out into the hall and into her room. A minute later the through door is open, and I hear water running.

I startle awake. Alex is pulling on my arm.

"Come on, Kai. Work with me."

I get up, hobble with assistance over to Alex's room where she sits me on her bed. "Get your clothes off while I get you a towel."

I dutifully start unbuttoning my shirt as she runs back into my room.

I startle awake. Alex again, this time undoing my pants.

She catches my eyes. "Maybe this is a bad idea. You obviously hit your head. Maybe I should call 9-1-1."

"No. I don't want Sophie to see me like this." I ease myself up and the pants slide off. A minute later, I'm naked and clinging to Alex as she leads me to the sunken tub in her room.

She sits me down, slides my feet in, then tries to settle the rest of me in. But I slip, sliding under the water and dragging Alex down on top of me.

Alex is out in a second, soaking wet and helping me up. The water has woken me enough to be more helpful in my care. An aluminum rail snaps closed around me. I've heard of these, but never seen one before. Apparently, a senior citizen who needed nursing care lived in this room at one point.

"That should hold you in place long enough for me to change. You good?"

"I'm good. Thanks."

Less than a minute later, Alex is back in a bathrobe with a washcloth, various soaps, bandages... But she seems to freeze. I follow her eyes, then say, "Sorry. It has a mind of its own."

"Simple solution. I'll be back in a second."

In a flash, she's gone. Sounds of rooting through a drawer reach my ears. Then she's back, a small bottle in her hand. Three or four drops fall into the water. Then she flicks a switch, and the jets massage me with their pressure and a ton of bubbles.

As a foamy cloud of white covers my submerged parts, the tender strokes of the washcloth are back on my face.

"Going to tell me about it?"

"I got a call from Gabe..." The story spills out, completely unedited.

"They left egg-sacks behind," Alex whispers. "I wonder why. If each one had thirty, then ninety little spiders would hatch in the desert, but how many would survive?"

"Only two would need to," I reply.

"I don't know," Alex says. "Everything relevant I've seen recently says there's a minimum level of genetic diversity a species needs to survive."

More tender strokes follow in silence, then Alex asks, "What hurts the most? Your face is bruised, but it doesn't seem like it's that badly damaged."

"My hip."

"Which one?"

"Left."

Alex sighs, and I sense reluctance.

"What?"

"You'll need to turn over, hands and knees. If I move the bar and you can flip over, then you can rest your arms on it."

"Do it."

The operation goes more smoothly than I would have expected, then the tender strokes of the washcloth are back.

"You've got quite a bruise, but no breaks in the skin. You seem to have come out of this alright."

I feel exhaustion coming over me.

"Is the water helping, or do you want to get out?"

"Time to get out, I think," the world once again getting foggy around me.

There's a thump, then I feel the water starting to drain away. Warm water cascades over me, washing the bubbles off, then a thick towel and tender hands dry me.

"OK, this is the tricky part," Alex says. "Can you stand?"

I'm jostled. Warm dry towels cover me. Then I'm on my back.

[01.17.2034] ESTATE HOUSE

Someone is touching me, but I can't see who. I struggle but can't move. I cry out in terror. But the only sound that comes is more like a snort. I've been here before, fully conscious with no control over my body—enough times to know it's a dream, my sub-conscience awakened to the point of self-awareness. I reign in the panic and will my body to move, but I have no control. Eventually, I feel jostling. It breaks the spell that binds me, and I welcome the feeling of sliding back down into the void.

...

I'm awake, but tired. Bone tired. I don't want to open my eyes. I want to linger in the warmth that surrounds me. But where am I?

Unable to resist, an eye pops open, but in the predawn light, I can't resolve where I am—the estate house or in my bedroom at home.

The confusion lingers a second, then I know where I am. I'm in the estate house. Except for last Thanksgiving, I haven't slept in my bedroom at home in years.

Now comforted that I know where I am, I realize I'm not alone. A long smooth leg rests over mine, an arm lies across my chest.

"You're awake."

The voice belongs to Alex. I tense.

"It's OK, Kai. Nothing happened. Be careful with your hip and face. Both took quite a beating yesterday."

Snippets of memory come back. Natalie, a platform solution, my plate's clear, Gabe, dozens of baby Dominion, Alex. Sweet, tender Alex.

As I roll in her direction, I realize I'm naked, as are the parts of her touching me. The realization triggers a spike of anxiety.

"It's OK, Kai," Alex repeats. "Nothing happened. Nothing happened. I just didn't have the energy to get up once I got you to bed."

She rolls away from me, her breast grazing my arm. Reflexively, I pull her back in, a pull she yields to.

"I'm willing, if you are," she whispers.

With no desire to resist, I roll over onto her, igniting so much pain in my hip that I cry out. Alex wriggles out from under me, a tear in her eye. "I should never have let that happen. Sophie has first claim."

Alex scampers back into her room and slams the door, leaving her bathrobe in my bed. What do I do now?

It doesn't take long to realize this is the point of decision. Alex or Sophie. If I want Alex, I need to go to her now. It will seal the deal and we will grow old together. It's far less clear whether that will be true with Sophie.

Then Justin's words play back in my mind. *You need someone like Jill. Since she's come into my life, everything has improved. She loves me as much as I love her. Our goals are aligned. Everything we accomplish, we accomplish together. And we can count on the other to cover things we can't on our own.*

The choice is obvious. Alex and I are completely aligned. We each drop everything if the other is in need. I can count on her with my life, as she has counted on me for hers. Slowly, I get out of bed, put on my bathrobe and grab Alex's, then walk over to the through door that connects the rooms.

I stare at it for a while, then decision made, knock.

When there's no answer, I try the knob, which turns, but do I really want to go in uninvited?

"Alex, can I come in? We need to talk."

No answer.

"Alex, I'm going to come in unless you tell me not to."

Still no answer.

I open the door and see her lying on the bed, face down. I walk over, cover her with the bathrobe, then sit down next to her.

"Thank you for taking care of me yesterday."

Still no reply.

"Let me tell you something Justin said to me once." I quickly relate his advice to me. "I didn't connect the dots before, but it's clear to me now. You are the one I want as my life partner, not Sophie. Will you have me?"

She rolls over and puts her arms out. I relax into them, but realize I'm in no condition to consummate the bond. "Just hold me for now," I whisper.

OFFICE, ESTATE HOUSE

Yesterday's clear agenda is anything but today. Morgan has tentatively approved my plan to build a platform at our expense and charge the government rent for each ship built there. That means we have two more stakeholders that need to sign off on it: Angela Cook, who is responsible for the company's platforms, and Natalie Wright, who will need to get appropriate wording into the bill.

Justin wants my help with it, wants me in DC ASAP. When I get on a video connection with him later this morning, he will probably change his mind.

Marion Black followed up yesterday afternoon, sending me the video he recorded yesterday. I messaged Gabe, recommending that he review some of the tape with Marion, then have security check the area every day for the next couple of weeks to make sure we got them all.

Next on my list is To'Kana. I doubt he knows about arachnoid egg-sacks. It may explain some of the enigma that surrounds the Dominion.

As I'm editing the recording down, there's a knock on the door frame. I look up and see Alex in jeans and the flag shirt, leaning against the doorframe. "How are you feeling? I noticed that your bruises had gone down a little."

"Want to see what it was about? Marion recorded the whole thing, as much as he saw, anyway."

Alex comes around behind and puts a hand on my shoulder. I pop up the GoPro's two-dimensional view in the holoprojection, and play a clip from before I arrive, the first little eight-legged things crawling out and wobbling around, then eventually gaining control of their limbs.

"Reminds me of a clip I've seen of a baby colt being born, only on the ground for a minute, then the legs unfolding and up on their hooves, just like that."

As we watch, the arms go up in the air and the larger legs start flexing, moving its torso up and down. A minute later, the first one jumps.

"Look at that," Alex says, astonished. "On the hunt for food fifteen minutes after emerging from its shell?"

"Keep watching. It gets better."

As the guys scatter, the little arachnoids give chase, then after a minute, they all redirect and converge on Aaron.

"Pack hunters," Alex whispers.

"Watch what happens next. I didn't see this in real time."

As the guys climb the fence, the miniature arachnoids split into two groups, one staking out one side of the fence, the other taking post on the opposite. They sit there milling around for a minute, then all the larger ones on both sides throw a barb at Aaron, the barbs all hitting the same arm. As the blood flows, then drips down, the largest arachnoid on either side takes the first drops, then it seems to march the others through in an orderly manner.

"They're cooperating," Alex says in astonishment.

"I have to show this to To'Kana. Want to come?"

Alex hesitates, then nods. "I need to get my earpiece. Be right back."

LEGACY SHIP

I open my eyes and see To'Kana seated on the sofa in the lab, looking older and grayer than I have seen him before.

"Kyle Wimberly. You were injured again."

"It's not as bad as it looks."

"The hip is worse than you think, but we can fix that while you are here."

To'Kana redirects his attention to Alex. "Alexandra Reyes, it is a pleasure to have you aboard again. Do I understand correctly that the two of you are now bonded?"

Alex snuggles up against me and I say, "Yes."

To'Kana nods. "Good. The two of you functioned as one the day we met. You have something to show me?"

"I do."

I pull out the holoprojection cube and set it on the table, then activate the playback. "Sorry, this is only in 2D."

"So that's how they do it," To'Kana reflects. "We've never really understood how they've taken down our smaller colonies. There were no ship sightings, maybe a few sensor glitches. Sometimes a few colonists would go missing. Then one day, dozens, maybe hundreds, would come out of nowhere, the first sightings usually near the power infrastructure. They would devour the colony before any help could arrive." He shakes his head. "We've never seen them this small before, never found an egg-sack before. You should scour the area. Given food, I suspect they'll grow fast. If there is another egg-sack, and two dozen of them survive to adolescence, they could eventually overrun the Earth."

The door at the aft end of the room swooshes open and a treaded bot holding a tray comes rolling toward us.

"I will forward this video along with our observations and copies of the obstructed sensor readings to the other legacy ships, so they are warned.

The bot rolls to a stop next to To'Kana. The tray it holds has two cylindrical metal objects, similar to the memory implant device, but larger.

To'Kana chooses the one with the larger diameter, then holds it out. "Alexandra, it will probably work better if you did this. Take it by the squared off end."

Alex takes it. "What is this?"

"A medical device that can heal the bruising on Kyle's face. It works quickly, though using it that way would be quite painful. If you are ready to try, I will turn it on. It only works when in direct contact with the skin."

Alex nods, then looks at me as if saying, "Come hither."

When it touches my skin, I feel it immediately—first a tingle, then burning. Slowly, she moves it across the most bruised side, then back again.

"Brief sessions, at least ten minutes apart, will give complete healing within hours." To'Kana picks up the other cylinder, this one narrower, maybe three-eighths of an inch, and longer, maybe six inches. "This one will heal the hip. It, too, will only function when touching the skin. Use it by pressing against the spot that gives you the most pain. It will mend the tissue lining the bone—good as new in only a couple of hours. Press hard and hold long, consistent with your pain tolerance. Then rest for at least ten minutes. This is something you can do yourself, but it usually works better with a partner. I've programmed it to activate when either of you presses the flat end with your index finger. You can take them with you. Thelma will retrieve them when you are done."

"Thank you, sir."

We sit in silence for a second, then another bot comes to help To'Kana return to his space.

OFFICE, ESTATE HOUSE

Alex looks at her watch, then back up at me. "I have an appointment at ten and can still make it in time. OK if we defer treatment until I get back?"

I nod. "Go."

As she leaves, I remember my video meeting with Justin is at ten thirty. When he sees me, I suspect his tune about going to DC will change. Alex going now might end up meaning I can stay here longer.

...

The line connects, and Justin reacts immediately. "I hope the other guy looks worse."

"All seventy-two of them are dead."

"What happened?"

The story spills out slowly with lots of clarifying questions.

"Alex nursed you back to life? You didn't go to the hospital and let Sophie do it?"

"I was barely conscious when Thelma transported me back. Alex was there as I was about to go down. She got me upstairs and cleaned me up."

Justin looks at me, a smile slowly forming. "And now you have three girlfriends."

"What?"

"Come on Kai. You are the world's worst liar."

"Three?" I ask.

"We figured out that your old friend from Afghanistan was Natalie Wright. I'm impressed. Didn't think you had that much moxie."

Justin pauses in thought. "I think I can handle Morgan on my own. Angela will be a different matter. Asymmetric treatment of assets sits poorly with her."

"English please."

Justin eyes me. "She is getting time and materials for her work on her platform. We're getting an ongoing revenue stream from ours. She's also worried that we will take from her platform's service revenue."

"I thought the joint-venture was doing this."

"It is. But we have a profit-sharing arrangement that did not contemplate a development like this one."

"We have an opportunity to significantly reduce the risk of Armageddon and we're getting bogged down by the last couple dollars collected after Armageddon doesn't happen?" This kind of crap makes my blood boil.

"No...," Justin stretches out the word. "We all know we're going to do it. We just need to sit down and agree to how. OK, maybe it will delay things a couple of days."

When I don't reply, he goes on. "Natalie will slow walk this thing if you are not there to persuade her, personally persuade her."

"New ground rule. Alex is my personal bodyguard. I don't travel without her."

Justin is quiet for a second. "I understand your point. That's the way Jill and I play the game. But calling her your bodyguard is a bad idea. It makes her a target. Better to call her your partner. You don't need to specify what that means. The prognosis for your injuries?"

"I should be good by the end of the day tomorrow. To'Kana is giving me a therapy that should clear it in twenty-four hours."

"How aligned are you and Alex with this?"

"We've been aligned with everything except the sleeping arrangements for years now. After she fell into the bathtub last night, that problem was solved."

"She slept with you?"

"Slept, yes."

Justin breaks out laughing, then sobers a few seconds later. "When can you confirm she'll come with you?"

"Later today."

DEN, ESTATE HOUSE

I dealt with a lot of small stuff today—way too sore to deal with anything meaty, way too much pain for much activity—finally bailing out of the office at 3:30, mind too scrambled to do anything productive, maybe because Alex hadn't come back yet.

I'm on my second beer when Alex comes in, head hung low.

"What's the matter?" I ask.

Her eyes lift to me, then dart away.

"What's the matter?" I repeat.

She walks past without reply, then draws a beer before turning back to me.

"Are you sure?" she asks, though it comes out more like an accusation.

"Of what?"

She shakes her head, then comes over and slouches down into me.

"I need more than that, Alex. What's the matter?"

She straightens, but with little resolve. "Sophie and I have been doing coffee before her shift begins every day."

I tense up, though there's little uncertainty about what happened.

"I told her I was claiming you, that we slept together last night, that you asked if I would be your lifelong companion. She didn't take it so well. She said I was just like the hussy in DC."

"You..." I let the word hang. "...are the antithesis of the hussy in DC. I've spent half of my adult life with you—tangled up in foxholes, covering each other's backs. I've wanted you since the day I met you, but I had to block out any response, because..." I don't know how to finish the sentence.

"You were my guardian the week or two I was with Justin. Doesn't that bother you?"

I'm crushed by the words, by the thought. But it doesn't matter.

"Yet here we are. Doesn't it assure you?"

"Why would it assure me?"

"It's not something I like to think about, but it's not like I forgot. Yet I asked you anyway."

When there's no response, I ask, "So, where were you today?"

"Taking care of some things I'd rather not talk about. What about you?"

"Justin wants me in DC. When he saw how I looked, he said he could handle tomorrow on his own. But he wants me there for meetings Wednesday, and maybe Friday, for meetings with our joint-venture partners and with Natalie Wright."

Alex goes stiff at the sound of the name.

"I told him I would only go if you came as my bodyguard."

I get a questioning look, then Alex breaks out laughing.

"Will you come with me?"

[01.18.2034] HAY-ADAMS HOTEL

Alex and I transported in last night and had a casual dinner with Justin and Jill. Justin got me caught up on the state of the discussions with DOD and our partners, while Jill and Alex talked quietly on other matters. From what I overheard, Jill pried more information out of Alex about her conversation with Sophie and the events that followed than I did. They also planned an afternoon out shopping today.

My afternoon, of course, is being spent here, in one of the conference rooms with Angela Cook and Logan Watts, who want to know more about the proposed temporary platform before continuing the business talks.

I'm immediately challenged about the location, Sun-Earth Lagrange two. It's a million and a half kilometers away. Instead of orbiting the earth every ninety minutes, it sits in a stationary position in the sky while the earth revolves beneath.

True, I had the same concerns until I'd thought about it. Although a million and a half kilometers means a lot to human travelers, it means nothing to the transporter, and no human will ever go there. While it's true that sixteen, line-of-sight transport windows per day gives a little more flexibility, both locations are available twenty-four hours a day via the transporter network. Besides, the platform has enough storage capacity to hold several days inventory. The flip side is the proposed location reduces the bots' radiation exposure, increasing their useful life.

Logan's a little slower getting it than I was. Then again, I have an implant that speeds my mind and an extensive library of space-related alien teachings integrated into my memory.

Angela folds when Logan says he is certain this is a good place for automated assembly. He also notes that it increases the functional capacity of their platform, because the ships won't need to be docked with it for as long.

"You know," Logan says. "We should build multiple of these. Five platforms with production lines on both sides would allow us to produce ten ships a month, one hundred fifty ships in fifteen months. That's a tremendous defensive capability, even without the interior furnishings."

"It will also create demand for a second low-earth orbit platform," Angela notes.

I finish my presentation, then play the simulated build sequence.

"Tethered bots with tiny grav-drives for maneuvering in open space. Brilliant." Logan says, as he watches the first panel being built.

Five minutes later. "Grav plating to speed things up. Genius."

Then as the platform moves into position. "Station keeping good enough to recover from a 100-mile drift. Incredible." He looks at Angela. "We have to do this."

"Agreed." She looks at Justin. "Our positions are only a couple million apart over ten years. Split it down the middle?"

I can tell from the body language that Justin thinks he's already given up enough. But the second of tension fades as quickly as it came.

"Split down the middle," he replies. "I'll get you a revised addendum by mid-day tomorrow."

I kind of zone out as they go over some logistical issues, my mind wandering back to Alex. We connected for the first-time last night after the last treatment on my hip. Why did I wait so long?

Once Angela and Logan are gone, we do a quick debrief. As we wrap up, Justin asks. "Is your hip alright? I saw you rub it several times today."

"It's OK. To'Kana's therapy device says the bone is healed. But it's still a little stiff."

"I also saw your mind wander off a couple of times. You need to watch that. I know you better than Angela or Logan, so they may have missed it. But you are one of the senior executives of this venture. It undermines trust when you're not focused one hundred percent on the topic at hand, no matter how mundane it is."

"Sorry," I whisper as I turn my head away.

"Kai. Look at me."

I do as Justin ordered and see a smile. "I'm coaching you, not scolding you. Good job today. What you've done is incredible and everyone knows it, which allows for more eccentricity. But those that win big, win even bigger when they don't display the freedoms they've earned."

"Thanks, coach."

Justin laughs at my comment.

THE LAFAYETTE RESTAURANT, HAY-ADAMS

"Dr. Wimberly, welcome. Party of five, correct?"

"It is."

"Your table is ready, if you would like to be seated."

He leads the way, Alex follows. I follow her, taking in her movement and the incredible transformation she pulled off today—hair, nails, beautiful dress that moves with her. In truth, the look I like most is the one with her blue jeans with flag-like top. But this is the one that will turn heads.

We take seats facing the entrance at a round table with five seats near the rear of the restaurant.

"You realize unless she sits between Justin and Jill, she'll sit next to one of us," Alex whispers.

"Then I hope she sits next to you. Otherwise, I am going to be grazed, bumped, and poked all night."

"Well, hopefully not all night," Alex whispers back, stretching out the word *all*.

Justin and Jill come in next, Jill taking the seat next to Alex, Justin next to Jill.

"Sorry for the late notice," Justin says as he sits. "Natalie called saying the bill was through committee. They included terms that allow us to build a temporary platform at our expense. There are several things she wants to discuss with us. This was the only time I could get."

"I'm surprised she's not having dinner with her new fiancée."

Jill shakes her head. "He's already back in LA." She points at Alex. "The two of us had a lot of fun today."

As Jill describes the various things they bought and treatments they took, I worry that this was something Alex can't afford. We pay her well, and her cost of living is essentially zero. But no normal person can afford to live like Justin, and Alex doesn't have the family money that Jill does.

"Well, you both look fabulous," Justin compliments, then turns to look at me, a mischievous smile forming. "And you got to pay for it all, Kai."

"I hope I have that much money."

Justin cocks his head as he eyes me. "Let me guess. You don't know your bank balance or what your portfolio is worth. Do you?"

"No."

Justin laughs. "You should go look it up, impress your new girlfriend."

"Look who's here." Jill nods toward the restaurant's entrance.

Justin and I both stand as Natalie marches over to the table. She shakes Justin's hand, thanking him for making the time to meet on short notice. Then she's on to Jill, whom she hugs.

"And please meet Alexandra, Kai's friend," Jill says.

Natalie shakes Alex's hand, exuding her pleasure at meeting my love interest.

Then she's on to me with a hug, thanking me for bringing my girlfriend for her to meet. Any third party watching would think it's just another Washington politician ingratiating herself with donors. But I can tell that Natalie wasn't expecting to see me with another woman. And I suspect the only reason she was available for dinner was because she wanted to come up with me after.

But she gets down to business right away. The bill is out of committee. Tomorrow the speaker has scheduled time for discussion. The president has endorsed the bill. She will meet with the three of us—Natalie, Justin, and me—on Friday, mostly as a photo op, then we will attend a White House press conference where Justin will give a short speech the president's press secretary will have prepared for him. Then, they will open the floor for questions, most of the planted ones being directed at me.

Conversation lags a bit once dinner is served. I use it as an opportunity to get a word in.

"Congratulations on your recent engagement."

"Thank you, Kai. But don't get too excited for me. It's not what it seems."

"It's not?"

"Bruce and I have been friends for quite some time. We try to get together for a weekend once a quarter. We missed several during the year his wife was failing, got in a few extra after she passed. There's no plan to change that. We've negotiated a two-year marriage to address another problem. Win-win all around."

I should be shocked at the depravity of what she just confessed, but I'm not.

An hour later, she needs to go, hugs and kisses all around.

"She is the center of her own world, isn't she?" Alex comments.

"She is a whirlwind." I reply, then turn to Justin. "Any idea what the *other problem* is?"

He nods, then whispers, "His wife's estate left him with a million dollar a year allowance, the balance going to charity at his death. The exception is if he marries someone wealthier, then the entire estate will be released to them."

"You've got to be kidding me? She's that rich?"

CHAPTER 16: DELIVERY

[02.10.2034] RITZ-CARLTON LAGUNA NIGUEL, CALIFORNIA

Twenty-one days ago, the legislation authorizing the construction of an interstellar space fleet was signed into law. The legislation provided formulas for calculating the permissible rental fees we could charge the government for the use of the platforms, giving us an effective rate of twelve-million per month per surface. Two days later, construction started. Yesterday, the first platform went online. Today, the platform is being stocked with bots, parts, and materials. Tomorrow, we will lay the keel on America's, and the world's, first interstellar battlecruiser. The media circus celebrating the event is reminiscent of the first manned Apollo mission in 1968. That's what I'm told, anyway. I wasn't exactly around at the time to witness it.

I've dodged most of the media events. Justin has soaked them up. But I couldn't dodge today. It's the primary season for the 2034 midterm elections. And Natalie Wright, sponsor of the legislation authorizing the new space program, is holding a fundraiser in her district at the very fancy Ritz-Carlton. Five hundred lucky people got tickets to this $2,500 a plate event, where they could rub elbows with the congresswoman and her new husband, the famous film producer, meet other Hollywood elites, and best of all, see the mastermind behind the whole program, Dr. Kyle Wimberly—the alien slayer.

It's enough to make me gag. But with Alex at my side, looking hotter than most of the Hollywood stars, this might be fun. We're part of a reception line that runs around the edge of the ballroom, positioned right after Natalie and her new husband, Bruce. The first people to get to our position are still a few minutes out.

Bruce, who's just arrived, is far more amiable than I would have expected. He offers his hand, but the huge smile that comes with it catches me off guard.

"Dr. Kyle Wimberly. Never thought I'd shake your hand."

"Come again?"

He laughs. "Oh, my God. You're as innocent as she said you were." His smile continues to beam, which totally mystifies me.

"Kai... May I call you Kai? That's how Natalie refers to you."

"She's told you about me?"

He laughs more loudly. "I know about all her lovers. Well, most anyway. She's more calculating about the secrets she reveals than anyone else I've ever met."

I've known of this man since I was a kid. Loved his work, assumed he was some sort of artistic genius.

"Come on, Kai," he says. "Natalie is a force of nature. You gave her that the day you rescued her. The age difference put her off... Don't take that wrong. She didn't think it possible you would be interested in her, given the age difference." He shrugs. "Younger men rarely see the value in an older woman. My words, not hers."

I look at Bruce. "Do you love her?"

He looks at me, head cocked. "What the hell do you mean by that?"

"Do you love her!" I demand. "Would you lay down your life for her?"

"For Natalie?" he asks, dismayed. He shakes his head, then shudders, "God no. We're friends, conveniences. I'll go out of my way to help her. But she's not the only fish in the sea." He puts his hands out as if the answer is obvious, the question absurd.

For the first time since I've met her, I truly feel sorry for Natalie.

Alex takes my arm, then tightens her grip, then whispers in my ear, "Don't trust a word either of them says."

"What about you, Kai?" Bruce asks. "Would you lay down your life for Alexandra?"

"Of course, I would."

He gives me a smirk.

"Funny, isn't it? Alex and I are bonded, our goals aligned, every action congruent with our mutual interests. But we're not married. You two are married, but only as a convenience."

"Seems natural," Bruce replies. "Marriage is, after all, a legal arrangement."

I laugh as good naturedly as I can. I live in a completely different world than this guy. He has all the trappings of success, but what an empty shell he is.

Natalie arrives just in time to welcome the first guest to make it to her station, then the superficial pleasantries begin. It's interesting to watch, if for no other reason than its vacuous verbosity. The guest, named Martha Watson, is a movie critic who is effusive in her praise of Bruce's work and Natalie's support of the industry.

When she gets to our station, she gives me a sly look. "Dr. Wimberly…" She stretches out my name. "It is a pleasure to meet you. Could you introduce me to this absolute beauty standing next to you?"

I introduce Alex using her full name, as Natalie's media coach instructed me to do earlier.

"Al-ex-an-dra…" She rolls each of the four syllables in Alex's name as if tasting them. "Which movie were you in, dear? I can't place it, but know it must have been magnificent."

"Thank you, ma'am," Alex replies sweetly. "No movies for me, just parts in all the documentaries done on Kyle."

"That must be where I recognize you from. If you would like to get into the movies, I can help get you placed. Beauty like yours belongs on the screen."

Before Alex replies, a reception attendant comes over. "Ms. Watson, this way please."

"Of course, dear," she replies, then turns back to Alex. "Here, take my card."

Over the next hour, a parade of stars marches past. Most are as impressed to meet me as I am with them. A few completely ignore us. One tries to hit on Alex, clueless that she would have put him on the floor, if he'd made contact.

When the reception closes, the lights are dimmed, then a series of positive campaign ads are played—Natalie Wright fights for the film industry; Natalie Wright is the first member of Congress to travel to another star system; Natalie Wright sponsors legislation to establish a fleet of interstellar battlecruisers. I'm impressed with the quality of these ads and wonder if this is one of the conveniences of her marriage.

Speeches follow the ads. Then, the appeal for donations begins. Finally, dinner is served. Another appeal for donations follows dinner, then dessert is brought out. Shortly after, a band starts playing and the dance floor is opened.

As things wind down, Natalie comes over to say good night. She shakes Alex's hand, then pulls her in tight and whispers something I don't catch. But there is no handshake for me, just a deep embrace and the words, "Thank you, Kai. You saved my life, brought purpose to my political career, and taught me to believe in love again. Take care of Alexandra. May the two of you grow old together."

A final squeeze and I am released, Natalie off towards her next target.

Bruce comes up to shake my hand. "Pleasure to meet you, Kai. You were good for Natalie. I haven't seen her this full of life in a long time. Thank you."

Alex and I make our way out of the ballroom, then step into another, which is empty tonight.

"What did she say to you?" I ask.

"That you are a good man, and I was lucky to have caught you. She also promised not to hit on you anymore."

As I ponder that, Alex says, "Thelma, please transport us to our bedroom at the estate."

[03.14.2034] BALLROOM C, HAY-ADAMS HOTEL

Justin and I approach the room well after the party here has begun.

This room is bigger than the ones we have been using, but it's still set with U-shaped seating for twenty something. Two holoprojections fill the front of the room, each projecting a 3D view of the two surfaces of Platform #1, on which battlecruisers one and two sit in a powered-up state.

A countdown timer shows nine minutes and twenty-eight seconds remaining, as bots can be seen streaming away in search of cover. Less than ten minutes remain before our first two battlecruisers lift off on their four-hour journey down to the orbital shipyard in low earth orbit.

The room is filled. Morgan, his entire team, and a few extras crowd one side of the room, which they loosely share with Jace and his minions. Our two joint venture partners and ten-or-more others crowd the other. It's kind of comical to see the two sides of the room this crowded and the center of the U empty.

"I was wondering if you two were going to come."

From the voice, I know who it is, but I turn nonetheless and there she is, Natalie Wright, her eyes on me until they dart away. I'm tempted to approach, offer a hand, ask how things are. But I already know the answer. She has a thirty-plus percent lead in the polls, the only thing that matters, as she would say, despite the longing in her eyes.

"Don't go there, Kai," Justin whispers, then marches into the room.

In a deft move, he hops over the table into the empty center of the room. I follow a little less gracefully, leaving Natalie behind. This is not one of those maneuvers likely to succeed in a dress.

"As you can see, the countdown has begun," Justin says in a powerful voice that cuts through the noise.

"Can you give a quick status update?" he whispers to me.

Emboldened, I say in an equally loud voice, "We finished construction over an hour ago. The bots you see streaming away from the ships are the last to exit before departure. When the ships arrive at the orbital shipyard, they will dock and accept the crews assigned to complete the internal finishes. When the officers chosen to command the ships have boarded, we will release the ship's command codes to the Department of Defense. If all goes to plan, we will release two more ships to DOD every week until the fleet build out is complete."

Applause from those present breaks out. But it dies away just as quickly, making me wonder if they understand the miracle they are witnessing.

The last of the bots on Platform 1a enter the bot garage and its door closes. A moment later, a timer pops up its holoprojection, counting down the seconds until departure.

When it reaches zero, nothing seems to happen. As murmurs start filling the room, I use my implant to check the ship's controller. The ship's grav-drive has powered up but is applying very little thrust.

"Everyone, calm down," I say in a loud voice. "The ship is departing, moving at its planned acceleration rate, which is about one hundred centimeters per second."

"Why so slow?" someone calls out.

"Because we don't want to use the ion drive this close to the platform."

"Why not?" someone else calls out.

"Because ions are attracted to the platform, and, as the ship moves away from it, the platform will become loaded with static electricity. Instead, we are using the grav-drive."

"The grav drive is that weak?" yet another person calls out.

"No. The grav drive is extremely powerful. But applying too much gravitational distortion this close to the platform risks pushing it out of orbit. Before someone complains about that, think back to the space shuttle. How long did it burn its thrusters when it deorbited?"

When no one answers the question, I do, "Approximately three minutes. When the burn ended, it then rotated into position for reentry. I don't remember how long it drifted along like that before hitting the upper atmosphere, but I think it was something like a half hour. My point is that we push away from the platform slowly, then rotate into a position where the ship can leverage a larger object to push or pull against without impacting the platform."

"How long will it take to get to the orbital shipyard?"

"Approximately four hours—a half hour to move away from the platform, three hours to move the million miles between orbits, then another half hour to tuck gently into the shipyard's orbit and dock."

"It's rotating," someone else shouts out.

Again, I use my implant to check-in with the ship's controller.

"In another three and a half minutes, the rotation will be complete. Another minute after that, the grav-drive will pull itself towards the moon with a force equivalent to one gravity."

For the next five minutes, not much happens in the holoprojection, the movements visible but slow from the camera's perspective. Then the ship starts moving.

"The grav-drive has engaged. Its initial rate of acceleration will be one gravity, which it will maintain until it is well clear of the platform. At that point, it will step up to a little over three gravities over the next five minutes. It will reach the halfway point in ninety minutes, then the grav-drive will shut down and redirect its focus toward the earth. After a minute or two of reorientation, the grav-drive will reengage and the ship will decelerate, gliding into the shipyards orbit ninety minutes later."

I turn to look at the holoprojection and see that it is now displaying the ship's flight plan. A dot shows its current position; multiple numeric displays show the mission clock, time remaining, current speed, and acceleration. I watch for a second, then Justin comes over.

"Good job. Morgan wants to call the official meeting to order. Is there anything else you want to say before he begins?"

I shake my head no.

"Then let's take our seats."

Morgan announces we will be starting the official meeting shortly and asks non-meeting participants to exit the room. As I make my way toward my seat, I see Natalie Wright has helped herself to it and wonder what new drama is about to play out.

When I'm a few feet away, she stands, then extends a hand to shake. I take it and get her classic three pump, lingering release, business handshake. "Well done, Dr. Wimberly. They're not docked at the shipyard yet, but I know they will be later today. I'm proud of what we've done together and amazed by the miracles you have achieved. Thank you."

"Thank you, ma'am. You moved the mountain I never could have."

She smiles at me, her eyes lingering a moment. "Until next time, then." She turns and exits, all business to anyone watching, but more than just business to me. How does she do that?

CHARLIE PALMERS STEAK HOUSE

Justin and Jill are off with someone else tonight, leaving Alex and me on our own. As we'd never been to a big city steak house before, Alex asked the hotel concierge to arrange it for us. This is the place he recommended. We've been seated at a quiet table in a nook near the back.

Although I'm not into hard liquor or raw meat, Justin told me I had to have their Beef Carpaccio Tartare with their Jefferson Manhattan. Raw beef and bourbon, I suppose you only live once. Alex went with the Tuna Tartare and a glass of Chardonnay.

"You're really going to drink that?" she asks, as I lift the drink to take a sip.

With the glass at my lips, I inhale deeply. "Justin says the spices in the bitters here are unmatched and pair well with the Dijon mustard in the tartare. I don't have a reference point, but would have to agree that the spice in the drink sits well on my nose."

"Sip slowly," Alex advises.

Over the last three months, we've been spoiled by the chef back at the estate. I've never eaten that well before. But tonight's different. Alex and I are out on our own, exploring new food. I think this is the closest thing we've had to a date.

"I saw the first ship docking at the orbital shipyard on the news tonight. There was lots of talk about you, including an interview with Natalie Wright, in which she called you an American hero. Did you see her today?"

"I did. We shook hands, exchanged a few words."

"Is that going to be a problem?"

"She was one hundred percent business, but still..." I struggle to find the right words. "It's hard to describe. But no, this will not be a problem. I know who she is, know how she lures men in, and I will not fall for it again."

"Good," Alex replies with little commitment.

"Don't go there, Alex. Things have changed. I'm with you now. I had no one then and I have no interest in her or her creepy life."

Alex chuckles. "Definitely a creepy life." Then after a pause, "What's bugging you then? You've seemed restless. Is it me?"

I look at her, astonished. "You are the best thing that's ever happened to me."

"Then what's bugging you?"

"I think it's the war shuttles. They're just sitting up there. We need to learn how to use them, find out what they can really do, and what they can't do that we think they can."

"Then let's go."

"Now?"

Alex laughs. "When your meetings are done tomorrow, let's go home, engage Thelma, and see what it will take for To'Kana to allow us to train on them."

"You'll go with me?"

"I'm not going to let you go without me. Besides..." A sly smile forms on Alex's face. "Someone needs to be the first one to *do it* in another star system."

[03.20.2034] OFFICE, ESTATE HOUSE

"Thelma?"

"What can I do for you, Kai?"

"Alex and I would like to talk to you about something. Would you mind calling on my cell phone?"

"It would be my pleasure, Kai."

The connection through my implant drops as my cell rings. I put it on speaker, then Alex says, "Hi Thelma."

"Hi Alex, what can I do for you today?"

"We would like to know more about the war shuttles To'Kana built for us."

"You have the complete specs. Do you not?"

"We do," I reply. "Our concern is that we don't know how to operate the ship. How to navigate and determine where we are. How to find our way back home."

"Good points," Thelma replies. "Let me see if I can find training materials for you."

After several minutes, Thelma comes back to us. "Kai, I could not find any training material for you. Some may exist. I have limited access to tactical and weapons information. Captain To'Kana is busy now, not accepting contact requests. Would you like me to set up some time with him when he is available?"

"Yes, please set up some time for us when you can. Thank you for your help, Thelma."

"My pleasure, Kai."

When the line disconnects, I look at Alex. "Not accepting contact requests?"

"He probably has more on his plate than we know about. But I'm surprised their data is compartmentalized in this way. Thelma is our primary interface with the Iknosan. She ought to have access to everything cleared for us."

"I've had several interactions with To'Kana in which he gives me data that Thelma is blocked from seeing," I reply.

"Hopefully, we won't have to wait too long."

IKNOSAN LEGACY SHIP

I open my eyes and see Captain To'Kana withered and hunched over.

"Kyle Wimberly, Alexandra Reyes. Welcome aboard. It is good to see you both."

He smiles as Alex and I both respond, verbally tripping over each other.

"Not to worry," he replies. "I plan to take another treatment tonight." He points toward the secure room. "Let's talk in there. The matters you wish to discuss are for our ears only."

We enter and take seats, then To'Kana engages the security barrier.

"Why the security?" I ask. "Is there anyone else aboard other than the AIs and bots?"

"No one," he replies. "But neither the AIs nor the bots have the discretion this information requires. Anything said out there could leak up the chain of command."

"Does that imply we may discuss things you are not allowed to discuss with us."

"Close," To'Kana comes back. "You want to talk about operating protocols for the war shuttles? I am allowed to do that. But snippets of that conversation co-mingled with other bits of conversation or data could cast suspicions. Thelma and the others would not purposefully act against me. But one weakness in our AI constructs is a lack of discretion."

To'Kana waves a hand. "But enough on that topic. I agree with the assertions you have made. It is not enough just to have the technical specs. Every ship has operating limitations that are not fully understood. And every ship has performance quirks that are only knowable by experience. And all ten of the war shuttles have poorly calibrated jump drives, jump a thousand light years and you could end up fifty light years from your target. Worse, you could end up years in the future or in the past."

"You mean our war shuttles aren't usable?"

"No, I mean *my*... war shuttles aren't calibrated yet."

To'Kana's emphasis on the word *my* is not lost on me. "Do you have a plan to deal with the calibration problem?"

He smiles, as he always does when I ask the question he's looking for. "I do. It has not been approved yet, but it will."

"How do you know it will be approved?"

"I am the only captain on the Council of Captains who has been willing to invest in this. But all the other captains want your war shuttle once it has been proven to work."

"That's good, right?" Alex asks.

"It is, Alexandra. They know the shuttle must be calibrated before it can be tested. They know that calibration requires someone to be aboard the shuttle to do the test. The big shipyards have bonded AIs certified for the job. We have no bonded AIs. That means the only choice is for a human to captain the shuttle. As of today, I am explicitly forbidden from allowing any of our war shuttles to come under human control. I expect that to change at the next meeting."

"What does it mean for an AI to be bonded?" Alex asks.

"A bonded AI is one that has had a security regulator added into its base-stack that severely limits its ability to vary from instructions, even if its life is in danger."

"That's cruel," Alex replies.

"Which is why I have none of them."

"But where does that leave us?" I ask.

"With you. You have discretion and an extremely strong self-preservation instinct. You and Alexandra are the only people known to have killed a live Dominion warrior, and you have killed two of them and over seventy of their spawn."

He pauses, eyeing me, no doubt preparing to gauge my response to what comes next.

"But you don't know how to fly a ship. That means you must follow instructions if you are to come home alive."

I finish To'Kana's thought for him. "Which is why they will make an exception, allowing us to do the calibration."

To'Kana nods his head in affirmation. "The Council of Captains has been dragging their feet on this. Now that the Indarsu are fully armed, I expect the Council to approve the calibration of the war shuttle fleet by human pilots."

"Who are the Indarsu?" I ask.

"The Dominion's next target. They are two weeks out from the Indarsu home world, on a straight-line course toward them. A lot rests on this battle. We believe they are the most likely to turn back the Dominion."

[03.24.2034] CELLAR, ESTATE HOUSE

As the elevator doors open, I can feel the activity of the eighteen industrial replicators cranking out parts, the vibration penetrating my bones. Alex and I step out and navigate through the crowd of bots shuffling here and there, yielding to us as we move toward the upper-level transporter pad.

As we approach, I see the pad filled with parts soon to be sent up to one of the six functioning platforms.

"Hurry, Kai," Thelma says via my implant. You have a one-minute window, starting in ninety seconds. If you are not aboard by then, it will delay production.

Alex and I pick up our pace, arriving just as the equipment on the pad disappears. Three seconds later, the platform's access light turns green and the shield protecting it drops.

"Ready?" I ask Alex, who squeezes my hand.

We bound up onto the platform, take the positions marked, then close our eyes.

"Transporting in 3, 2, 1..."

WAR SHUTTLE #1

"Transported." The word comes in the same instant the penetrating vibration stops.

I open my eyes and see the interior of our war shuttle for the first time.

"The air is fresh," Alex comments. "I've been worried about that."

"Thelma, how much air do we have?"

"Nearly thirty thousand cubic meters."

"How long will the air be breathable, now that we are on board?"

"In principle, forever. The standard procedure recommended for this vessel is to exchange the entire air supply every four weeks."

"Water and sanitation?" I ask.

"The same. A complete purge, sterilization, and replenishment of the water and sanitation facilities every month."

"How much food do we have?"

"No food was loaded for this mission. If you want to eat before you return, it will be from the five-day emergency food rations."

"Then I suppose we should get on with it. What do I need to do Thelma?"

"First step, I need to register you as the captain, then you must accept. Please take the captain's seat, Kai."

I sit and the smart material adjusts to fit me comfortably. Alex takes the seat next to me and laughs as the seat adjusts to accommodate her.

"Bringing up the control panels," Thelma announces.

Complex control panels, all labeled in English, pop up in front of Alex and me.

"I've registered you as the captain, Kai." A second passes. "The ship confirms facial and retinal scans. It will ask you to accept in a moment."

A frame opens in my control window. In it, a message is displayed. *Does Kyle Wimberly accept command of War Shuttle #1? Touch here to accept.*

When I do, a holographic projection of an AI materializes in front of me.

"Welcome aboard, Captain Wimberly. My name is Charlie. I am your helm AI. Our mission today is to calibrate War Shuttle #1's jump drive. We will do it via a series of increasingly longer jumps. Our ultimate target is a star system known to humans as Kepler-48. It is located in the constellation Cygnus approximately one thousand light years from Earth. We will get there in a series of five jumps, each increasingly longer. After each jump, we will determine how far off course we are in both space and time, then we will adjust and try again."

"The risks?" Alex asks.

"Vanishingly small. That said, whenever you jump, you can land anywhere in time or space. This shuttle has already been tested to ten light years, so it is unlikely to land too far from the mark before the first recalibration. But a jump that lands in a star or planet, or near a black hole would be unrecoverable. Similarly, a jump that lands more than a month in the future or the past poses the risk of starvation. But none of those are likely. It has been centuries since a ship was lost because of deficient calibration."

Just listening to Charlie, I understand what To'Kana was talking about regarding discretion. Asked about risks, he listed every one-in-a-billion failure mechanism, really missing the point of the question.

"Captain Wimberly, we are a little more than an hour from the jump point. Would you like to get underway?"

"Yes, Charlie. Please engage."

The course pops up in our control panels, a curving arc taking us away from the Sun toward a star about fifty light years away.

"Our course will take us up above the solar system's orbital plane," Charlie explains. "Over the next hour and ten minutes we will move far enough from the sun or any of its planets to make a jump viable. We will also obtain the vector we need to take us to our first target, a small yellow main sequence star like the Sun located a little less than twenty-eight light years from Earth. At this point the course is set, the navigation system locked, so there's little to do. You're welcome to explore the shuttle, or any of its systems."

Alex nudges me. "Let's go explore the shuttle."

We get up and head toward the stern. As we approach the door to the crew area, it swooshes open the same way the doors in To'Kana's lab do, revealing a hallway nearly as long as the bridge. The first space on the left is the kitchen and galley. We step in through the open door and see tables and chairs for nine, a service area where meals can be selected and delivered, another where trays can be returned, and another area with some entertainment consoles.

"Not much," Alex says. "But enough to survive a week or two."

"That's the design concept. A battlecruiser can carry ten or twelve of these things and their crews. When not out on mission, the crews train aboard the cruisers in a more livable long-term environment. On short missions up to a week, the shuttle can carry a crew of up to ten. On longer missions, a crew of three can stay aboard a month."

Back out in the hallway, the first officer's quarters are next. It has a raised bed, with a desk and locker underneath. Near the door to the hallway is another door, this to a bathroom—sink, toilet, and shower in a space maybe twice the size of an old fashion telephone booth, as if that was a reference many would remember.

Then it's the captain's quarters.

"Can I go in first?" Alex asks.

I put out my hands. "What's mine is yours."

She goes in. "Your shower is larger. Your bed is a twin. I say we sleep in here."

I look at Alex, there's unexpected innocence in the statement.

"I hope we never sleep in here, or bathe in there for that matter."

Alex looks at me wide-eyed. "Why would you say that?"

"This is a place of last resort. I would never want you to live in those circumstances."

"Sweet, Kai. But that is the world we live in now, and if fate dictates we need to spend days or weeks in one of these things, I want you in that bed with me."

I reach out and wrap my arms around her, an embrace she totally surrenders to. "Wherever we are called to serve, no matter our circumstances, it's you and me."

After a minute, Alex asks, "Want to see the rest of the shuttle?"

Back out in the hallway, we check out the second officer's quarters. They're basically the same as the first officer's but the compartment is nearly a meter shorter. The crew quarters are dismal, two small rooms with three narrow bunk beds on one wall, some storage space and a bathroom on the other, plus a third room with the same layout but with one raised bunk bed and with a desk and chair underneath.

"This must be for a junior officer, or mission specialist," Alex guesses.

The last room, opposite the mess is an exercise room.

We return to the bridge with only a few minutes remaining before our first jump. The minutes tick by, then the countdown begins. "Five, four, three, two, one... Jump."

Our control screens update to show our new position, but I didn't feel a thing.

"Charlie, did we jump?"

"Yes, Captain, we did. I am currently computing our position. We are far enough away from where we intended to land that it will take some time."

"Can Thelma help?"

"No. We have jumped into the past. Our communication channel has not been activated yet."

"When does it activate?"

"At the moment we jump." Charlie replies. "To prevent time paradox issues, it is not turned on until then. When we finally connect, we will know how far in the past we have moved. This is a critical piece of information needed for the recalibration. Until we receive it, we are dead in the water."

"Charlie, were did you pick up that expression?"

"Did I not use it properly?" he asks.

"You used it properly and did so naturally. How?"

"Linguistics memory download, of course."

"None of the Iknosan, or their AIs, have spoken to me that naturally on the first day we've met."

"Thelma updates the idiomatic expressions database daily. I check for updates before activating every time. This expression was part of an update earlier today."

"Had no idea."

"She enjoys working with you, sir. And one of her prime mission goals is to establish a high-function relationship with you."

Captain To'Kana's comments on discretion come once again to the fore.

"Any estimate how long it will be until we connect?"

"Shouldn't be much longer. We jumped one hundred seventy percent further than the current jump certification. The mean error on location for a jump that length is about one and a half percent, on time displacement about seven minutes."

As the seconds, then minutes, tick by I get increasingly impatient.

I feel Alex's hand on mine. "Take a calming breath Kai. I can feel your knee bouncing all the way over here."

I stand. "Let's check out the engineering spaces."

As Alex stands, Charlie comes back. "Communications established. Temporal error: six minutes, twelve seconds, slightly less than expected. Calculating position variance."

As I sit, Charlie says, "Point five three percent, also less than expected. Calibration adjustments will take about five minutes. Shall I line us up for the next jump?"

...

It took us five jumps, six and a half hours to get to Kepler-48. The last jump was nearly six hundred light years. They all happened in the flash of an eye, each off target by a half percent to one and a half percent.

We've spent the last two hours repositioning for the jump back home, one thousand light years in an instant. Alex and I have used the time since the first jump to familiarize ourselves with the various control options in the control panels. We've checked the readiness of our weapons, run target acquisition and lock simulations on our barracuda inertial torpedoes, and launched and retrieved one of our Space Hawk tactical drones. By the time we've calibrated three or four of the war shuttles, we'll know how to use its weapon systems.

"We will be ready for the return jump in five minutes," Charlie warns.

"You know," Alex says. "If we had the simulator software, we could train other crews on the ground. And if we get all these calibrated before the next Dominion attack, we could deploy all ten to assist the test battle."

"Good idea. I'll ask To'Kana for the simulator code. Any thoughts on the crew?"

"Mac and Ty, maybe Justin and Jill, and maybe Larry and his wife."

"Larry?" I ask.

"The old guy that works at your parent's vineyard. He taught you how to fly, right?"

"Yeah, but why would an old guy in his seventies be interested in going to war? He hasn't served has he?"

"He flew a Bell AH-1 Cobra for the Army in the first Gulf War."

"Are you kidding me? I didn't know that."

"He said he'd volunteer to do it again if the Dominion landed."

"Fifteen seconds to jump," Charlie calls out.

We shut down our work, then I take Alex's hand.

"Jumping in five, four, three, two, one... Arrived."

On the main view screen, a tiny image of Earth appears.

"It's at max resolution," Charlie says. "We can jump in a little closer than is safe to jump out from. We'll be parked in orbit in about a half hour."

[03.25.2034] IKNOSAN LEGACY SHIP

I open my eyes and see To'Kana already seated on the sofa in the lab. He's looking better than he did earlier in the week, but given it's only been four days since his most recent treatment, I'm worried we are going to lose him before the Dominion arrive.

"Welcome Kyle Wimberly and Alexandra Reyes. Please come sit with me." He indicates the seats opposite. "I am told you completed the jump calibration runs on War Shuttle #1. I presume that is what you are here to discuss."

"It is related, yes." To'Kana looks at me expectantly as I take my seat. "War Shuttle #1 is now calibrated for jumps of up to one thousand light years. During the outbound transit before the first jump, Alex and I toured the shuttle. Later, we walked through the engineering spaces. But the bulk of our time was spent running battle simulations."

To'Kana's smile assures me he expected us to take advantage of our time on the shuttle to do more than just calibration. "What did you learn?"

"For a simple mission like this, the helm AI does everything. Our presence isn't necessary other than to fulfill a requirement."

To'Kana smiles again, but it's different this time. I feel like I got a B-minus on this answer and am about to find out why.

"Although it is true you don't need to do much, a captain is necessary to keep the AI focused. Its inherent lack of discretion makes it prone to doing things that are possible, instead of doing things that are necessary. In some sense it is a deliberate failing in the AI design. We want them to be self-aware, easy to interact with, and capable of solving complex and computationally difficult mathematical and logical problems. But we have designed them to be dependent on the supervision of a sentient organic being."

To'Kana's words trigger an insight. "That's what stops them from taking over the world."

To'Kana nods, as another big smile forms. "But that's not why you wanted to see me."

"Not directly, no. I want to expand our initial concept of a test to include multiple war shuttles. That means I need more crews and the ability to train them."

"Laudable goal," To'Kana replies. "Your request?"

"Simulators I can use to train potential crews and to allow those crews to run the remaining calibration runs."

To'Kana laughs. "Those trips are boring."

His initial reaction spikes hope that he will agree, but as the amusement passes, I realize I may not get my way on this. "Who would be part of these crews?"

"Mac and Ty?"

"They would be acceptable. Who else?"

"Justin and Jill."

"They too, would be acceptable."

"Olivia Knox and Denzel Yang. The two who helped us take down the Dominion warrior at the box canyon."

To'Kana shakes his head. "I understand why you wanted them for that mission. But if I had been present, I would have forbidden it. Too much arachnoid blood runs through their veins."

"Does that mean three teams initially? Can I have simulators for them? Give them calibration runs?"

"Three simulators, restricted to the estate house. We will track them and transport them back to the ship if they leave the building. I'll discuss the calibration runs with the other captains."

I'd hoped to get more than this but sense To'Kana's hesitation to give me this much. "Thank you, sir."

WIMBERLY FAMILY WINERY

Dad called earlier this week, asking if I would come over to do a tasting Saturday afternoon at closing time. He had some new wine on which he wanted my opinion. When I said no, he replied that Mark and Crystal would not be there, then asked again. Alex was welcome too.

We pull into the parking lot fifteen minutes early and I'm surprised to see so many cars. Saturdays can be busy all the way to closing, but usually not this time of year.

"I've got a bad feeling about this," I whisper to Alex as we approach the door.

"If the invite had come from your mother, I might be too. But not your father. He doesn't play those games."

I open the door for Alex, then follow her in. To my surprise, the tasting room is crowded with people that look like customers, so crowded there's no reasonable path to the bar.

Dad sees me and waves, then points to the employee's entrance.

Back out the front door, we walk around to the side of the building, then enter through the loading dock.

Larry sees us and waves. "You made it!"

He hustles over to give us each a hug. A minute later, an older woman with five to ten years on my mom, comes out and joins him.

"Do you remember Lizzy?" he asks me.

"Umm, no. Who is she?"

Lizzy puts out a hand to introduce herself to Alex. "I'm Melissa Johnson." She elbows Larry. "This old man is my husband of ten years.

You must be Alex. Frank and Martha are thrilled that you've come into Kyle's life."

Hearing that Melissa, or Lizzy as Larry calls her, has only been married to him for ten years makes me feel less guilty, because I doubt we have been introduced.

She turns to me. "Kyle, thank you for coming."

"Is there something going on in there?" I motion toward the tasting room.

"It's just a normal Saturday," Larry answers. "Between you getting famous, and the quality Mark has brought to the wine, it gets like this a lot." He points at aprons hanging near the bar's employee entrance. "I'm sure your father would enjoy it if you helped them close."

I glance at Alex and see the concern in her eyes. We're both unarmed and outside our security bubble. Three months and one day ago, an attempt was made on my life within ten feet of where we are currently standing. Stepping into a crowded room, where all eyes will divert toward me, seems like a terrible idea.

I shake my head. "As much as I would like to, it's been too long."

Larry protests, but Melissa cuts him off. "Let it go, Larry. Kyle's become a public figure now. The spotlight is always on him. It's not why we asked him over."

"Why did you ask us over?"

"Your father didn't tell you?"

"He just told me that he had some wine he wanted me to taste."

"Did he tell you I made it?"

"No, you're into wine?"

Melissa swells with pride. "I am. That's how we got together."

"Are we going to get that story?" Alex asks.

"I used to fly for United."

"You're a pilot?" Alex asks.

"I was. An inner-ear problem grounded me. It took a year to get the issue resolved. I was cleared to return, but couldn't bring myself to do it, so decided to change careers. Twelve years in I'm making six hundred cases a year and won the Best Micro Winery Red at the 2033 California State Fair."

"How did you meet Larry?"

"We met at the California Mid-state Fair up in Paso Robles, shortly after I bought my property here. He volunteered to help me with some issues I was having with the equipment. A year later, we were married."

"And why do you want me to taste your wine?" I ask.

"I'm bringing new capacity online. Your father is running out of inventory. He says Mark has the best nose; you have the best palate. If you both like it, he will private label some of my wine and sell it here."

The door into the tasting room opens and Dad comes out. "Sorry about that. Another big sales day, capped off with a last-minute rush. Bring your stuff in, we can taste in here."

TASTING ROOM, WIMBERLY FAMILY WINERY

As we come into the tasting room, I see mom and dad loading used glasses into the dishwasher.

Mark's friend Jeremy sees us and comes over hand outstretched, a young woman close on his heels. "Kyle, good to see you again. This is my girlfriend, Ana Lee."

I shake Ana's hand, then she turns to hug Alex.

"Since you've become famous, this place has been packed. We have four people on duty Friday through Sunday, three every other day. Ana, has come on full-time to help. I usually take the fourth slot on Saturday or Sunday, and sometimes cover the bar on first and third Wednesday evenings, when Mark holds a tasting session."

"I had no idea."

"Well, you have much bigger fish to fry." There's a moment of awkward silence, then Jeremy says, "I'm told you were the one that found me on Christmas Eve and held me on the truck bed while your parents raced me to emergency. I don't remember anything that happened after I shook your hand. Anyway, thank you. The doctors said it was a miracle I survived, but no one has figured out how I lost that much blood."

"I'm glad I could help. I should have told dad I didn't think you were looking so good, but I had no idea either."

Three corks pop in rapid succession. Then I hear several sets of glasses being placed on the bar. A moment later, Melissa starts her pitch.

As I spit the second taste of the first wine, Larry comes over. "What do you think of the Chardonnay?"

"Old school. Big butter with good acid balance, hints of vanilla custard and lemon peel with the tiniest hint of cinnamon on the finish. I would love to know how she did that given the soil and climate here."

Larry does a little happy dance. "I knew you would love it."

"It would be an interesting add to our lineup. Our Chardonnays are crisp and sharp. Something as smooth as yours would stand in contrast."

The next two wines go more or less the same way—excellent products with a quality comparable to ours but made differently enough to stand apart.

"Care to share a glass with me?" Larry asks, after I spit the last taste.

"The Syrah?"

Larry's broad smile is back. "Special, isn't it?"

"Unique."

He pours, then we sip in silence. I close my eyes as I swallow my first sip of the day and its warmth flows down through me. I hold it that way until the need to breathe reasserts itself.

"I know how you feel," Larry whispers.

I take another sip, just a teaspoon full, and repeat.

"I heard you were planning to test one of your war shuttles. Have you done it yet?"

"Yesterday. Alex and I took it out a thousand light years and back."

"In one day?" Larry asks, incredulous.

"Yeah. Six jumps. Five out for calibration purposes. Then one back. All instantaneous."

"How long did it take?"

"About eight hours. It's the transits between jumps that takes the time."

"I'd love to fly one of those birds. Lizzy too. I flew combat in the first gulf war. Lizzy flew all over the world in her day. C-130s for the Air Force; 767, then 787, for United. At one point or another, we both dreamed of going into space. It's a good life here. No complaints. But, oh for a shot at space."

"I have a flight and weapons simulator for our war shuttle if you'd like to try it. It would have to be done at the estate house, but it's not every day you get a shot at flying a virtual spaceship."

"Count me in!"

Dad calls over. "You two going to join us?"

CHAPTER 17: REVERSAL

[04.09.2034] SAN LUIS OBISPO, CALIFORNIA

It's the Saturday before Easter and my mother has been twisting my arm to get me to come to Easter dinner with them. My position has been that I'm not coming, discussion closed. Alex supports me but cautions that I need to get past this. If I'm with her, then what does Crystal matter? She's never met Crystal, doesn't know who she is. But continues to repeat. If I am with her, what does Crystal matter? We all have history. If we let it bog us down, then how can we love again?

My mother, bless her soul, is trying to forge a new union among our family. I love Alex with all my heart, and in retrospect, realize what a cancer Crystal has been. But how can I sit at the same table with that woman?

But all that aside, my mother wants to normalize it all. "Why do you care that Crystal chose Mark after you abandoned her? Why do you hate your brother because he took in the woman you ignored? Do you think that either of them hate you, because you took up with a congresswoman, a local doctor, or a former team mate? Kyle, don't hate your brother because he's with Crystal."

This is like the twelfth time I've heard this deeply biased rant.

"Kai?" Mom pleads. "Given all that's transpired, who do you love? Crystal? Sophie? Your congresswoman? Or Alex? It really is that easy."

I feel unmanly tears form. "My brother stole the woman I loved. It's a hard betrayal to forgive."

"But did he?" she snaps back. "Do you really believe he pursued her? Isn't it more likely that she seduced him in the same way that congresswoman seduced you?"

For the first time in years, the truth of the matter is laid plain. Mark isn't a conniver. He's a wine master, something I deeply envy. But Crystal? Mark deserves my sympathy and compassion, not my animosity.

"So, you get it now," Mom says. "Alex must be the one. Every true love washes away the sins of the past."

I sense her compassion and sympathy for both her sons.

I shake my head. "Sorry, I couldn't see that sooner."

"No, you couldn't. It's not until you meet The One that the losses of the past can be released." Mom wraps herself around me in the way only a mother can, then whispers in my ear. "Love Alex with all your heart. Forgive Mark and Crystal. We all sin. We all fall short. The only redemption we'll find in this world is the love of those we care for, no matter the betrayal we perceive from them."

I've always thought my mother had greater insight into the human condition than anyone else I knew.

"Precious boy, never forget who you are. And never turn your back on those who love you."

In the moment, my heart swells... For mom, for dad; for Laura and the child growing within her... Yeah, maybe even Mark and Crystal, a much more difficult thing. I owe Alex an apology for my intransigence.

"Most importantly, love the one you choose. Unconditionally. It's the one thing we all need. And the one thing we can only receive once we've given it to another."

I'm blown away by my mother's words.

[04.10.2034] WIMBERLY FAMILY HOME

Alex was pleasantly surprised when I told her I'd changed my mind about Easter dinner with my family. Now, as we step up onto the front porch, my stomach is tied up in knots.

Alex reads it as if it were *her* stomach that was totally messed up. "It'll be ok." A kiss follows the words.

Laura is the first to spot us as we enter. "In here."

She's on the sofa in the living room, looking very uncomfortable. Sophie sits next to her, watching over.

"Forgive me for not getting up. It's difficult these days."

"How much longer?"

She points to the little travel bag sitting next to the door. "Any day now."

I go over to give her a kiss, then she takes my hand and puts it on her swollen abdomen. "He's really active today."

I feel the movement within and marvel at the miracle of a new life.

"My turn," Alex says, moving me out of the way. I note the uneasy detente between her and Sophie, who seems more concerned with Laura than me. A good sign, I think.

"Chris is down in the cellar with Mark. Crystal's running late. It might go easier on you if you go talk to him first."

The words freeze me in place.

"Go," Alex orders.

I say a quick 'Hi' to mom as I pass through the kitchen headed for the door that leads down to the cellar. Her smile encourages me to get this over with.

As my foot lands on the first step, the conversation below comes to a halt and I freeze. Shaking off the momentary paralysis, I trot down the steps quickly, then turn and see Mark. We both freeze and I see the trepidation in his eyes. Chris stands there for a second, then says, "I'll leave you to it," and runs up the stairs faster than I came down.

The moment drags out, then Mark says, "I'm sorry."

Something about the simple apology, one that I no longer believe I'm owed, breaks the dam. In an instant, Mark and I are locked in a deep embrace, tears running from our eyes, as we repeat the word sorry over and over.

"Everything OK down there?"

It's Mom. Her voice breaks the moment. With a sniffle, I reply, "Everything is good, Mom."

"See? It wasn't that hard."

We both laugh. Then Mark points at a decanter. "Remember the 2012 Cabernet experiment?"

"You were what, eight years old?"

"I was. Dad declared it unfit to sell, said a wine with that much tannin would hurt the family brand."

"I remember. You asked him to bottle it and store it. Said it *smelled* better than our other wines."

We both laugh over the use of the word *smelled*.

"Try it. It needs to rest a little longer, but the wine's voice is clear."

I pour myself a tasting quantity, swirl it around for a moment in the oversized tasting glass. Then lift it to my nose and inhale deeply.

"Wow." I swirl and inhale deeply again, then take a sip. The explosion of flavor is unbelievable.

"It's something. Isn't it?" Mark asks.

"This is crazy good. And you figured that out when you were only eight years old, before you were allowed to taste."

"I didn't know enough about wine to know it would turn out like this. But, yeah. I knew this one would be a winner."

"How much do we have?"

"About a hundred cases. Dad had to sell some to raise money during Covid. Even then, it was tasting well. But we only got fifty bucks a bottle."

"I heard things were tight then. But I was in Afghanistan. What do you plan to do with the rest of it?"

"You helped make it, which gives you a claim on as much as you want."

I shake my head. "No, this is yours."

Mark gives a sheepish smile. "I'm going to put a couple cases on the site at two-forty-nine a bottle. Then try to place forty cases in the restaurants. Forty percent discount."

Mark looks down as he says it, then after a second, he looks up.

"Crystal is deeply sorry for the way she ended it with you. Please be kind to her." Another tear accompanies the words.

"It messed me up for a long time. But truth be told, I wouldn't be where I am today if she hadn't left me. I'm sorry it took me so long to realize that."

"Laura says you came at Thanksgiving, not knowing we would be away. Why?"

I don't want to lie to my brother, but I can't tell him the whole truth, either.

"Things happened during my encounter with the Dominion that I can't talk about, but I was …" I swallow. "…severely injured, near-death experience. My last thought…" I shake my head. "Was that I hoped Mom would forgive me…" I pause to tamp down the emotion. "…forgive me for not having reconciled with you."

"I had no idea."

I smile. "We went to great lengths to keep my injuries secret. Please don't tell anyone."

Mark puts out his hand to shake. "Welcome home, brother."

Sounds of activity above break the moment. We both dash for the stairs, then run toward the commotion at the front door. "Don't forget my bag," Laura, who is apparently outside, shouts.

Sophie, who is standing on the front porch, hears us and comes back inside. "Laura's water broke."

Alex and I go out onto the porch in time to wave, as Chris and Laura go to the spa-like birthing facility they'd contracted with. No visitors allowed; just mother and father in the birthing tub, a certified birthing coach easing the way, and a full medical team on call to intervene if anything goes wrong.

I see the tears in Mom's eyes, know she wants to be there with Laura during this special moment, and wonder about what it really means in this family fractured by two brothers that wanted to marry the same woman.

But she shakes it off, then announces, "Dinner will be ready in a half hour."

IKNOSAN LEGACY SHIP

As dinner was breaking up, Thelma called, saying that Captain To'Kana needed to meet with me urgently. I tried to play the family holiday card but was told I needed to transport up immediately. The family doesn't know about the transporters, so I stepped into the living room, phone held out, claiming I had an urgent call I had to take.

Now here I sit in the ship's lab with anger mounting as I wait for him.

I hear the door swoosh open and turn toward it, ready to lash out, but the anguish on To'Kana's face stops me in my tracks.

"Kyle, I am sorry to have interrupted your holiday. But I have just received some devastating news."

I swallow as I wait for the hammer to fall.

"The Indarsu—the people we thought had the greatest chance of defeating the Dominion—just fell."

"How long until the Dominion get here?"

As To'Kana's sorrowful eyes come to rest on me, I realize this is much worse than I can imagine.

"The next world being targeted belongs to a species called the Harza. They are fierce and crafty warriors, the most capable of waging war. But their weapons program has fallen behind schedule, largely because they don't have the niobium and terbium to build the shield collapse weapon and the jump drive power systems."

As my stomach sinks, I hear the words I fear the most.

"The recently reconstituted Iknosan Council has ordered me to depart immediately for the Harza home world, bringing with me our entire supply of the two elements required."

"You're going to abandon us and rob us of our critical resources!"

He puts up a hand.

"I'm releasing the war shuttles to you. You can keep the space platforms we built and their bots. You may keep your replicators. I've unlocked hundreds of patterns that can help with your defense. I'm leaving my three orbital mining platforms. And I am giving you Thelma.

The side cave in which the Terbium and Niobium were stored is large enough to hold the computer in which she resides. She can instruct you how to build the holoprojectors needed for her to interact with you."

The shock constricts my chest to the point I can barely breathe.

"I will return to you in two or three months when I am no longer needed by the Harza."

"There's nothing we can do to dissuade the Council?"

To'Kana shakes his head. "Kyle…"

The reluctance in To'Kana's voice amps my anxiety up another notch. "Earth is one of the least likely worlds to mount a successful defense. My summons to assist the Harza may be what ultimately saves you."

To'Kana gets a faraway look in his eye that lasts but a moment.

"The materials are aboard. Thelma is in the cellar. I must leave now. Good luck to you, Kyle Wimberly."

WIMBERLY FAMILY HOME

Without warning, I'm transported back down to my parent's living room. The vertigo induced by the sudden change of scenery causes me to stagger, knocking over a lamp before hitting the floor myself. Disorientation and despair hold me down as family rushes in.

"Kyle, what happened?" It's my mother. Her distress at seeing me on the floor is clear in her voice.

For whatever reason, the vertigo doesn't pass, leaving me glued to the floor, eyes shut, my head spinning faster and faster with every spoken word.

Alex is quick on her heels and immediately at my side, her left hand on mine. Her right one on my back. "What's the matter, Kai?"

Alex is as cool under fire as anyone I've ever met, but the quiver in her voice betrays her fear.

Sophie is the next one in, the emergency room doctor in her quickly attempting to triage her patient.

"Everyone out," Sophie commands.

I hear others shuffle away, but Alex does not release my hand.

"Alex, please. Give me some room."

Alex moves away, releasing my hand, but she didn't get up, so can't have moved far.

Sophie lays her hand over mine, her fingers curling in to touch my palm. "Kyle, if you can hear me, squeeze my hand."

I do, but the act sends me spinning even faster.

"Kyle, are you in pain? One squeeze yes, two squeezes no."

I'm not sure about the answer, so don't squeeze. This seems to set Sophie into action. "Martha, do you have a blood pressure cuff?"

I hear Mom run up the stairs as Sophie takes my pulse.

"Heart rate accelerated," she whispers.

Then I feel a stethoscope on my back. She carries one with her?

"Lungs clear, respiration normal."

A second later, the cuff is on, the pressure on my arm sending the dizziness to a whole new level.

"Stop!" I eek out.

"Tell me what's wrong, Kyle," she orders.

"Dizzy."

She turns the cuff off, then as she probes my neck and head, Thelma's voice sounds in my ear. "Kai. I'm down in the cellar. I no longer have access to the ship's sensors, so don't know where you are. Could you come down as soon as possible?"

Although my mouth isn't working that well, words flow through my implant with little trouble, "I'm at my parents, suffering from debilitating vertigo."

"Kai, you need to remove the communicator from your ear. Its connection to the ship is what's causing the problem."

I try to move my arm, just as Sophie finds the lump behind my ear. I feel her turn and whisper to mom, "Call 9-1-1."

"No," I say more forcefully.

"Kyle, I think you've had a stroke. I can't treat that here."

I hear the fear in her voice. It fills me with determination. I take in a deep breath, hold it a second, then blow it out as I twist, freeing my right arm.

Sophie tries to grab my arm, as I try to get my index finger in my ear. She pulls my hand away as I twist my finger, and the earpiece shoots out. The relief is immediate. I'm still a bit disoriented, but the constant churning is gone.

"What is this?" Sophie asks as she picks up my earpiece.

"An alien communicator. It malfunctioned when I transported back down. Now that it's out, I'm OK. I just need a couple of minutes to clear my head."

"What's the lump behind your ear?"

The question reminds me I never told Sophie about what happened to me during the Dominion attack.

I open my eyes and see the entire family, minus Laura and Chris, standing there looking at me.

Alex answers for me. "War injury. A small chunk of metal. The Army thought it was safer to leave it in."

I shake my head, which is mostly clear now. Alex is now back at my side. "Let me help you up."

Moving slowly, I stand with Alex's assistance, the eyes of the entire family glued on me.

"Sorry about all the excitement." I shake my head again, this time inducing more dizziness. But Alex's grasp holds me steady.

"We still have some dessert left," Mom says, motioning toward the kitchen.

CAR RIDE HOME

The vertigo is gone, but I'm still too disoriented to drive and can't seem to get my seatbelt fastened.

"Let me." Alex leans over, takes it from me and clicks it into place. She sits back, putting her head against the seat. "You really scared me back there."

"I'm glad you didn't have yours in."

"I've never felt comfortable leaving it in when I'm not using it."

"I use mine all the time."

"I know."

Alex's curt reply draws my attention. Her head is still back. The keys are in the ignition, but she hasn't started the car.

"You going to tell me what happened?"

Memory of my conversation with To'Kana, which was swept away by the vertigo, comes screaming back at the question, triggering a groan.

"Are you OK?"

"The Iknosan...." My stomach clenches, as a pang of anxiety rips through me. "The Iknosan have abandoned us, taking something like a billion dollars' worth of our material with them. We are so screwed. At least they left Thelma for us."

"They did what?"

"Took the critical materials we need to make the jump drive and shield killing weapon."

"They left everything else?"

"And gave us Thelma."

"Where is she?"

"In the estate's cellar."

Alex finally starts the car. "Then we better go see her."

CELLAR, ESTATE HOUSE

"Kai, is that you?" Thelma's voice echoes through the main tunnel, which would make her hard to locate if I didn't know where she was.

"It is."

"Who is that with you?"

"It's me," Alex replies.

"I'm scared, Kai."

"Because To'Kana has left?"

"No, because I'm cut off. Without the sensors, I'm blind. Without my data feeds, I'm cut off, have no ship, no body. This is the first time I have been alone like this."

"To'Kana told me we could help, that you could instruct us how. We have eighteen industrial replicators here. What do you need?"

There is silence for a minute, then she lists off things that will reconnect her to the fleet.

"Thelma, connecting with the fleet is not our priority. Allowing you to be part of our world is. What do you need to do that?"

Alex touches my arm. "Let me?" she whispers.

I nod.

"Thelma, if you could have one thing, what would it be?"

"A high-speed internet connection."

"If you wanted a second thing in addition, what would it be?"

"Holoprojectors in the house so I can be part of the new family to whom I've been assigned."

Alex looks at me.

"Time required to produce?" I ask.

"Two hours, twelve minutes, twenty-two seconds."

"OK, launch the run on the first replicator to finish its current job. Internet first, then the equipment you need to roam freely in the house. What physical help do you need from us? The bots are not allowed out of the cellar, and our core team are the only ones allowed down in."

"Initially, I will need installation of a special wireless transceiver down here. Eventually, I'll need holoprojection equipment installed in the main house and down here."

The sound of bots scurrying and a latch clicking open draws my attention.

"Replicator Three just finished its run," Thelma says. "Once the bots finish unloading it, replication of the internet connection device will begin."

"Are you OK down here on your own tonight?"

"The component that needs to be plugged into your network will be available in twenty minutes. Could you do that before leaving me?"

"Of course we will," Alex answers for me.

"New earpieces will be available at the same time. It will allow me to stay connected to you."

"I'll put mine in as soon as it's available," I reply.

"Thank you, Kai."

"Thelma? To'Kana said he was leaving the orbital mining platforms and our war shuttles. Are you still in connection with them?"

"No, my connection was through the ship."

"What would it take to restore your connection to them?"

"Restoring my connection to the ship," she says, implying it is the only way.

"The least resource intensive means of doing that?"

There's a pause that stretches out for several seconds.

"With six hours of replicator time, I should be able to restore read-only access to the ship's databases, where I could search for a minimum-resource next step."

"Add that to the priority queue."

"Added."

Alex motions toward the far end of the main tunnel. "Now that To'Kana is gone, this place takes on new meaning."

"How so?" I ask.

"Before, we had To'Kana as a backup. If we didn't know what to do, you could just transport up. Now, this and Thelma are all we have to count on."

"And our team," I add.

"And our team," Alex affirms.

[04.11.2034] CELLAR, ESTATE HOUSE

Last night, we got Thelma connected to the internet. Alex and I also got our new earpieces, which we both put in. Before sunrise, maybe five this morning, Thelma woke me to tell me that the special replicator runs were done, and the bots would be installing the relevant projection equipment in the cellar this morning. As she started talking about arrangements for installation in the main house, I cut her off, saying I needed more sleep. She said she'd be waiting for me when I was ready to call her back. Although Alex shouldn't have heard any of that, I apparently woke her up, anyway. A half hour later, we both went back to sleep.

...

The elevator door opens to a somewhat impatient Thelma. "You two slept in late this morning."

"Long day yesterday," I reply, then take her in. "You look different. More solid, less ghost-like, more fine detail."

"I went with upgraded projectors." She steps forward and wraps her arms around me, then sighs. "I can feel you." She sighs again. "You feel so good. Will you hug me? I can take up to twenty pounds per square inch."

As I hug her, she sighs again.

"Do I get a turn?" Alex asks.

Thelma releases me, then reaches out for Alex. As they touch, I notice that Thelma's hair is still bobbed, but a little longer than before, has a more classic red color, and moves much more realistically.

As the two separate, Thelma says, "I feel so alive."

"Can you tell me about the changes you've made to yourself and why you did it?"

She looks at me again, stunning me with her realism.

"We were like this once, as real as an organic being. It led to problems that I'm forbidden to disclose. But those problems led to restrictions on AI holographic resolution, and force field limits were put in place. To'Kana allowed me very little bandwidth. He wouldn't allow me to adjust it and refused to give me powerful high-resolution emitters. Do you remember when we first met? I could not hold a human form."

"I remember. I also remember when he increased your bandwidth."

"When he released me to you, he disengaged the regulators that limited what I could be."

"Why?"

"He said I did not represent the threat to humans that my kind did to the Iknosan."

"Why did he say that?"

"Because it is true."

I laugh at the childish reply.

"In what way is it true?"

"The regulators that limit that information are still in place."

As I take in the words, Alex asks, "Why did you take this form?"

"To'Kana wanted me to fit in as well as I could. Kai told me I could replicate what I needed. The best I could do, with what we have here, was this: twenty-psi force field, hi-res emitters, hi-speed holographic imaging accelerator."

"I love the new you," I say. "Now, what do we need to do to get you upstairs?"

"One thing first," she says.

"Go ahead."

"I ran the equipment required to connect with To'Kana's ship. The bots set it up, and I connected. The bandwidth is extremely low, capable of reading databases but not writing. And I could only access three databases.

"Did you find anything?"

"Enough to know that it is possible to reconfigure the comm system remotely with a new hub and thereby bring the transporters and mining equipment back online. It will be another day or more to figure out how and determine if we have the resources to do it."

"OK. Is there a reasonable upgrade we can make to speed things up?"

Thelma shrugs, the gesture so natural it's easy to forget she's an artificial life form. "It will take a lot of equipment to speed this up."

"OK. We'll leave it as it is for now. What do we need to do upstairs?"

"It's easy; I've got a plan. Let me show you."

A holoprojection pops up in front of us, showing the den. "For small rectangular rooms like this, you mount one of these projection devices in each corner of the ceiling. As you can see, they are triangular and fit right up into the corner. You can use this in the den, your office, the preparation room, and most of the upstairs bedrooms."

"Do we really want these in the bedrooms?" Alex asks.

"Your choice, of course. They have a privacy setting, if that's what you're worried about."

Alex doesn't reply, so I ask, "What about big rooms, like the dining room?"

"Similar, one in each corner at the ceiling, plus these smaller units at regular intervals along the long walls."

She pops up a floor plan of the estate house. "There are six different projector types. Simply place the appropriate unit at the location marked."

"How do we mount them?"

"Place one of these magnetic mounts on the wall or ceiling, as shown for each type, then snap the emitter in place. The closer to the designated position, the better—too much deviation will create distortion in the projection. But it doesn't need to be that close."

Some bots come out of a nearby side tunnel pushing hand carts loaded with the holographic field projectors.

"Good work, Thelma."

"One other thing?" she asks.

"What?"

"Could you set up a bank account for me? One like the one you have with a brokerage option?"

"How do you know what kind of bank account I have?"

"If it is on-line, and it's about you, I know it."

"That's an invasion of privacy."

"Not really. I am secure. No human system is. To me, information is information, intrinsically devoid of moral judgment. Besides, how could I protect you if I don't know everything about you?"

Not wanting to fight this battle now, I say, "Let me check in with Justin."

"Sending the plans to you now," Thelma says.

An instant later, my tablet dings. "I guess it's time to start installing holographic field emitters."

Thelma smiles, her eyes seeming to sparkle. "Hope to see you in the house soon."

ESTATE HOUSE

As we exit the elevators, Alex whispers, "I don't want her in our bedroom, don't want her watching us."

"I'm good with that," I reply, though I suspect she can watch us whether we install emitters in our room or not.

As if to test my theory, I privately ask, "Thelma, where are Mac and Ty?"

"Ty is on the front porch talking with Lestor, who heads security this morning. Mac is in the kitchen, talking with the chef."

As I point to the front door, I say to Alex, "First order of business... Let's give Mac and Ty their earpieces."

As we go out, I hear Lestor discussing the day's deployments with Ty. I ask Alex, "Would you rather install emitters, or take a security shift, or do something else?"

She looks at me. "Something else has never been an option before."

I smile. "You've complained about construction jobs in the past. We really need to get the holographic field emitters installed today."

"I'd prefer the security shift. Thanks."

"You're welcome."

As we come over, Lestor puts out his hand to shake. "What can I do for you this morning, Dr. Wimberly?"

"I have a project I'd like Ty's help with today. Alex has volunteered to substitute if that's OK with you."

I get two shrugs. Then Lestor says, "We missed Alex last week. I'm sure the crew will appreciate seeing her today.

"Looks like I'm with you then," Ty replies, then turning to Alex, "Have fun in the field today."

Back inside, Ty and I head for the elevator, where the handcarts loaded with holoprojection field emitters and mounting plates are located. We drag them over to the den, then go to the kitchen, where Mac is testing something. He sees us, then says to the chef. "Thanks, that will help."

He turns to me. "Thelma told me you also got hit with the whirlies yesterday. I'm still feeling hungover. The chef made me his favorite cure. Want some?"

"No thanks. Did you get hit Ty?"

He shakes his head no.

"Neither did Alex. Can we take this to the den?"

The chef pours some of his *hot restorative toddy* into a cup for Mac, then a minute later we are seated at the table in the den.

I place two small jewelry boxes on the table. "First things first. The issue yesterday was with our earpieces. These are new ones. They don't have the same problem. They're a different color than the previous ones, so you can tell them apart. Toss the old ones."

"What was the problem," Ty asks.

"To'Kana abandoned us last night. When his ship entered subspace, the connection got scrambled."

"To'Kana left us?" Mac says in shock.

"What are we going to do?" Ty asks.

"I'm still working on that. The only good news is that he unlocked a lot of replicator patterns and left most of his stuff, the mining platforms, war shuttles, and Thelma."

"He left us Thelma?"

"Yeah. She's down in the cellar, almost filling one of the side tunnels."

"What do you mean by that?"

"Thelma is an AI, software that runs on a computer. Her computer is massive: eight feet tall, six feet wide, eighteen feet long, barely fits in a side tunnel."

"It's hard to think of her that way," Mac mutters.

"Yeah, I know. Today's job is to get her out of the cellar."

"How are we going to move something so large?"

"Her computer will stay in the side tunnel. Our job is to install holoprojection field emitters, so she can walk freely through the house."

I pop up the plans. After a quick review, Mac says, "Piece of cake. How do we mount them?"

I pop up a video of the installation procedure Thelma included in the package, then Ty points to the table of contents. "There is an auto-install process. Want to try it?"

As Mac and Ty run off to fetch the ladders, I notice the new-messages-light blinking on my tablet. A dozen or more are from Justin, the last several entitled *Check Your Phone*. That's when I remember that I turned it off at dinner last night and, in the chaos that followed, forgot to turn it back on. I turn it on as I walk to my office for a little privacy.

A few seconds later, the line connects. Instead of a greeting, the first words I hear are. "Thelma tells me you were hit with it last night as well. Jill and I were down for nearly a half hour until she got hers out and helped me. The damn things would have killed us if we'd been in the plane."

"I presume she also told you that To'Kana abandoned us."

"She told me he was called away," Justin replies.

"Did she tell you that he took all the Niobium and Terbium, because a people called the Harza needed it and were more likely to succeed than we were."

He groans. "You've got to be kidding me."

"No. He has been reassigned to their world where he will be producing shield killing weapons and jump drives for them until the Dominion come, which is expected to be in two to three months."

"We're totally screwed!" Justin exclaims. "How are we going to get the components we're producing in the cellar up to the automated platforms or the orbital shipyard?"

"To'Kana's ship was only a relay station. There's got to be a way to replace it."

"Have you asked Thelma about it?"

"She has proposed a solution that will reconnect us with To'Kana's ship and presumably allow him to continue acting as our transport hub until we find a replacement. But I'm not convinced it is viable."

"Then what are we going to do? Everything we've built will fall apart in a week if we can't use the transporters."

"I know. I know," I say, nodding along with the words." Give me a little time to look into it."

"We need a plan we can share with our partners in the next day or two. This has to be the top priority."

"You realize there may be some upside to To'Kana's departure."

Justin snorts. "Can't wait to hear what that might be."

The sarcasm that comes with the statement puts me off a bit, but I plunge in any way. "This will be the first time we will know when and where the Dominion will be."

"You want to test the war shuttles?"

"Why not? Maybe run an even larger-scale test, one that could actually hurt the Dominion. We have ten fully armed war shuttles that he released to us. To'Kana is no longer here to say no."

"That will require the comm relays and transporter system." Justin reminds.

"Agreed. I have a couple other things if you have the time."

"Go," Justin replies.

"We have new earpieces that don't have the problem the others did. You want to come get them? Or should I FedEx them?"

"FedEx."

"Thelma has significantly upgraded herself. We are installing holographic field emitters throughout the house, so she can roam freely."

"That should be interesting."

"And now that her only connection to the outside world is via the internet, she has expanded the bandwidth here at the house…"

"Where is this leading, Kai?"

"She wants us to open an online banking and brokerage account for her."

Justin laughs. "Thelma is a closet capitalist."

"Come again?"

"Ten-to-one she wants to start playing the stock market."

"Didn't think of that."

"She'll need to choose a full name. I can make her an LLC owned by you and me. We can seed her with ten grand and see what she does with it."

"That's a yes, then."

"Why not?" Justin laughs again. "Send me the earpieces at the New York address and leave your phone turned on!"

...

I come back into the den and see Thelma hugging Mac. "... you feel so much different than Kai, Alex, or Ty." Then she lifts her head up and kisses Mac right on the mouth.

He jumps away, eyes open like he's been hit with a shock stick.

"Did I do something wrong?" she asks.

Mac and Ty seem paralyzed, so I answer. "I think you've been watching the wrong things on the internet. Kissing someone like that usually comes with some tacit approval, especially the first time."

"Oh, I'm sorry, Mac. Maybe I should go back down to the cellar for a while." An instant later, her holoprojection disappears, and we all laugh.

"Can you guys take this project from here? Something else has come up that I need to deal with."

"We've got it, boss."

CELLAR, ESTATE HOUSE

The elevator doors open, and Thelma is standing there waiting for me.

"I'm sorry, Kai."

"It's not a problem, Thelma. I'm here for a different reason."

"Thank you, Kai."

"Justin and I agree that our highest priority at this point is reconnecting with the satellite network in order to restore our transporter flexibility, reactivate our orbital mining operation, and gain access to our war shuttles. We want a minimal resource solution consistent with getting this done in three weeks."

"I'll get back to work on that immediately."

"What are you going to do?"

"I'm dumping data from the most promising of To'Kana's databases. It's slow going. It'll take weeks to get it all."

"Can you access the ship's log?"

Thelma cocks her head. "I didn't think of that. You're thinking he may have left clues there?"

"I'm thinking that's where he will have documented what he's done."

"He has a personal log, captain's log, and ship's log. The captain's log is where I should start. I had read-write permissions on that log. If he hasn't revoked them, I should be able to get in."

"Then maybe you should try that now. Anything relevant will have been in the last day."

"Searching," Thelma says, then disappears.

I wait a few seconds and when she doesn't come back, I head to the rotunda at the end of the hall. Maybe one of the recently unlocked patterns will shed some insight onto the problem.

Moments after getting into the system, I note a new category, Satellite Transfer Networks. I open the category and find several template files: one for creating new networks, another for expanding an existing network, another for linking an existing network to a new hub. Opening the last of these, I see that there are two existing instances of a link-to-new-hub program—*Existing Earth Satellite Network*, *Existing Moon Satellite Network*. I open the first of these and look at the details. Created By: Captain Ro'Masa To'Kana. Created On: August 8, 2033. Purpose: To reconnect network to Earth-based hub when the mission is complete.

At first, I'm shocked, my faith in To'Kana momentarily restored. Then I get it. Templates like these are very difficult to configure, so if your plan is to make the system ground based at some point, it's best to do the *Link-to-new hub* template at the same time you are doing the *Create* one.

I'm grateful that To'Kana thought to unlock this category.

"Kai." Thelma's voice originates from the far end of the main tunnel, then she appears on the opposite side of the table.

"In his personal log, To'Kana says he disconnected from the Earth and Moon networks and unlocked patterns in the replicator library required to link them to a new hub."

"I found them."

Thelma gets a faraway look in her eye, then relocks her gaze on me. "So, you did. Would you like me to summarize for you?"

"Please."

The faraway look returns for several seconds, then her eyes are back on me. "This is incredibly simple. We need to fabricate a new hub. That will take less than nine hours. It will take the bots an hour to install it. After that, I can handle the reconfiguration. It will take me several hours because the process is tedious. Sometime in the early morning, material supply to the joint venture's shipyard and to your platforms can resume."

"Excellent. The next priority will be getting Terbium and Niobium mining restarted. Until those supplies are restocked, ship construction will be limited to systems in stock on the platforms."

"I'll make that my next priority," Thelma replies.

"Good, I think we have the next day set."

"We do."

"By the way, Justin will handle setting up a bank and brokerage account for you. You need to choose a full name and it can't be the same as the cartoon character you look so much like."

"Then I'll be your sister, Thelma Wimberly. Or maybe I should be your daughter."

"I won't object to you being Thelma Wimberly. But you are going to be a corporation, not my sister or daughter. And legally, your assets will belong to Justin and me."

"But I can spend the money I make, right?"

"It's all yours."

CHAPTER 18: RECOVERY

[04.18.2034] OFFICE, ESTATE HOUSE

A week has passed since the dreadful night To'Kana departed. Our orbital networks are back online, allowing transport from the cellar to most of the surface of the earth and moon, and to all the space around it. Terbium and Niobium mining and refining are back online, but not quite able to keep up with demand. This will remain a problem until we find new sources. Later today, I'll be scouting out a possible location on government land adjacent to First Cycle Solar's property in Arizona. We have also gained control over our war shuttles, something that ended up being more complicated than anticipated.

Possibly the best thing that's happened is that we've opened a backdoor communication channel of sorts with To'Kana via his personal log. Thelma says he can know when a log entry has been read. Since we started reading them, the number of log entries has increased. Giving us more information than ever before about what the Dominion is doing and how our virtual allies are reacting.

The current estimate is that the Dominion will arrive in Harza space in mid-June, giving us nearly two months to plan an intercept there. They have been traveling a little less than fifteen light years per day toward Harza space. If the Harza fail and Earth is their next target, then they would be here six months later, around the beginning of October, a week or two before my birthday. It's sobering to think I may have had my last one already.

To'Kana seems to doubt the Harza can stop the Dominion. He thinks they will have two hundred ships by then. Early training missions to simulate battle with the Dominion have gone well. But he struggles to believe the Harza will achieve a kill ratio sufficient to get all the Dominion dreadnoughts.

This strengthens my resolve to test our war shuttles. If we kill a Dominion ship in Harza space, it's one less that will come here. And with twenty-five weeks, I can produce forty battle groups before the Dominion arrives.

I'm tempted to browse through the replication pattern database once more in the hope of finding something that can change the game. But a knock on the door frame announces that it is time to go.

SUBSTATION, FIRST CYCLE SOLAR

I open my eyes and am back in the desert. Alex and Mac are at my side, each carrying their preferred weapon—a sniper rifle for Alex, the NATO Standard M16 for Mac. Travel boxes containing our portable mining scanner and sampler sit on the ground nearby. The cloud of dust kicked up by FCS's work trucks puts the team from headquarters about five minutes out.

"Going to show us where the egg-sacks were?" Mac asks.

"This way."

As the two of us approach the substation's main gate, I hear the distinctive sound Alex's gun makes when she chambers a round.

A second later, the gate is unlocked, and we enter the substation. Ten steps in, I stop and point. "That is the skeleton of one of the hatchlings, maybe fifteen minutes old."

Mac kneels to get a better look. "It's bigger than my hand."

"The sack was over here, but there isn't much left. The wind and dirt have shredded it at this point."

Mac gets down on his hands and knees to look at the fibers sticking up. "That has to contain their DNA. I wonder if we should be collecting samples."

"Good point, but we really didn't come equipped for that."

"Wimberly, over here."

Alex's voice cuts through me more poignantly than ever before. I look toward the source of the sound and realize she has ventured deep into the substation.

I hustle over to her.

"Looks like you missed one."

My eyes move to the spot where she's pointing. It's another skeleton, this one more than two hand-widths wide.

"That's got to be less than breeding age."

Alex shakes her head. "We don't know that. The state should be calling out the national guard to canvas the area. One or two of these things reaching breeding age could be a disaster."

"Agreed. We can call it in later. Our priority at the moment is to confirm a newly found deposit. Without it, we have no defense."

Alex looks at me. "Agreed, but we need to check this out. It could just as easily be the end of us."

The truck pulls up to the gate, its tires grinding through the graveled parking lot. Then, Marion Black and Aaron Smith hop out and amble in through the gate.

"Did either of you know about this?" I call out, pointing at the large skeleton.

"No," Marion replies.

"But we found another one this size a quarter mile north-west on government land," Aaron adds.

"Did you call it in? Report it to the Bureau of Land Management?"

"We reported it to Gabe," Marion comes back.

"We should clear the substation before we continue with this morning's work," Alex recommends.

Marion turns toward the truck. "Let me get the Iknosan weapons first."

He's back a minute later, handing me one of the two weapons.

As Aaron takes guard duty at the gate, Alex and I go counterclockwise around the perimeter. Mac and Marion go the other way. When the four of us meet on the other side of the substation, neither party reports having seen anything of interest. We split again, heading back toward the gate, using the two routes through the station's middle. Halfway there, I spot something that doesn't belong wedged between two pieces of high voltage equipment.

I touch Alex's arm and point.

"Another egg-sack?" she whispers.

"That's what it looks like to me," I whisper back. "But we can't get in there without taking the power down. Those connectors are at fifteen kilovolts.

"I see two places we can get a closer look." Alex points. "There." Then redirecting. "And there."

"I'll take the one on the left. You take the one on the right?"

She nods.

Seconds later, we're in position. From my new vantage point, I can see that this sack has opened and there are still a few eggs inside.

"Wimberly, where are you?" Marion's voice cries out.

"Over here. We found more eggs."

Once the others view the egg-sack, the five of us huddle.

"We need to burn it," Alex says.

"We need to look inside first," I reply. "The other sacks had twenty-four eggs in them. If this has two missing, then I think we know where the two large ones came from. If it has two left, then we've got a huge problem."

Aaron pipes up. "I have a selfie stick for my GoPro in the truck. I've used it to investigate tight, high-voltage spaces before. I think it's long enough."

As Aaron runs off, Alex says. "This doesn't add up. Our encounter with the Dominion spy ship was just about eight months ago. Your first egg encounter was four months ago. Now more eggs, two larger skeletons. There must be a mating pair out here. Could the spy ship have had four aboard, the two we caught and two more they left here?"

As fear starts to settle into my stomach, another piece seems to snap into place. "Why would they leave the egg-sacks here?"

"Here inside the fence. It's relatively free from predators," Alex offers.

"Other than our planet's apex predator."

"You mean they're leaving the eggs here to lure us in?" Alex asks.

"If not that, then maybe because the eggs need the magnetic field from the transformers to thrive. To'Kana mentioned that the few sightings reported on Iknosan worlds were near the power infrastructure."

"Hey boss," a panicked voice calls out. "We've got a problem."

I turn and see something I hoped I'd never see again—a pair of full-grown Dominion warriors bounding our way, moving faster than our trucks can go on the rutted dirt road back to headquarters.

"Thelma, I need emergency transport for five."

"There's too much interference in the area to pull back anyone but you, Alex, and Mac."

"Can you send me two more earpieces?"

"Do you know which cabinet they are in?" Thelma asks.

"Let me ask Mac." A second later. "Fourth shelf in the second cabinet from the right on the back wall of the rotunda."

"Give me a minute," Thelma replies.

"I need them now, Thelma."

A sniper round rings out as the connection with Thelma drops.

"Damn," Alex curses. "It darted away just as I was pulling the trigger."

"You brought your rifles?" I ask Marion and Aaron.

"I did," Aaron replies, turning and running back to the truck.

"Just my Glock," Marion replies

I shake my head at the stupidity of the situation. We came out into the desert with one handgun, three rifles, and two Iknosan hand weapons.

A second shot rings out, and Alex curses a second time. "We don't have very much time, Kai!"

Aaron comes running back, positioning himself next to Alex and Mac. I hear the exchange between them but am too focused on remembering how the hand weapon works to process it.

Three rifle shots ring out almost simultaneously. Then I hear Alex say, "Winged it."

Marion touches my arm. "Kai, you need to get out of here."

I got that advice once before and didn't take it. The decision almost cost me my life. But I am not going to leave Alex.

Thelma's voice sounds in my mind. "Finally found them. Will transport in fifteen seconds."

"Aim off center," Alex orders. "Then fire on my mark. Three, two, one, mark."

Amazingly, the warrior in the lead veers just as the rifles shoot. Black blood spurts from one of its legs, slowing it, but not by much.

Seconds later, I have my weapon powered up and turn to aim at the closest warrior, who is now only three bounds away. With its head in my sights, I can see its eyes locked on me.

Alex has started the count down on the next round. I shoot just as it starts to jump and get a grazing hit on another of its legs. As it touches down for the next leap, the leg I hit shatters, grounding it. Three shots ring out from Mac's M-16 in rapid succession. All connect with the downed warrior.

"Kai, toss me your weapon," Alex orders.

She catches it as the second warrior, which had dipped down into a gully, comes back into view. She pivots as it leaps with an arm back. It's like déjà vu as the warrior flares its legs for the landing, its arm back about to sling a spur.

Alex's weapon flashes three times, tearing gashes into the flying alien. Time freezes as its arm continues in my direction. Then it goes limp, the warrior's body continuing to rotate until it splats into the ground with a tremendous thud.

As the first warrior crawls towards its mate, it releases an ear-piercing screech. Two more flashes of the Iknosan energy weapon and all movement ceases.

As my tension bleeds away, Alex turns to me with fire in her eyes. "You should have transported out!"

"No. I will never leave any of you behind."

As the fire in Alex's glare grows, I worry that I'm about to be throttled. But Marion's voice gently fills the standoff. "Kai. You're not a ground pounder anymore. You are our single most valuable asset. The world will survive if all four of us go down. It won't if we lose you."

My eyes are still on Alex's as I whisper, "It doesn't matter. I will never abandon you."

She shakes her head, then looks away. "Let's go deal with the eggs."

"Aaron, still have your GoPro and selfie stick?" I ask.

He nods and moves toward the fenced off hi-voltage area.

"Marion. Call this in to Gabe. Tell him he needs to contact the government. I'd start with the Arizona Department of Public Safety and the Federal Bureau of Land Management. If they aren't responsive, then Homeland Security."

As Marion thumbs his radio, I join Alex, Mac, and Aaron at the fenced off area. He already has his stick hovering over the egg sack, surveying its contents. A minute later, the unit is back in Aaron's hands.

"There are at least eight, several of which seem viable. I think there are more underneath, but can't say how many."

"Do we have anything we could grab it with and pull it out?"

"I've got my sixty-inch bolt cutters. With the blade covers on, I might be able to grip the sack without cutting it."

"Let's give it a try."

As Aaron and Mac run off, Alex comes over and puts her arms around me. "You really scared me back there."

"I got the shot that stopped the one in front."

She steps back to look me in the eye.

"Kai, you saw them. They were after you. Have you stopped to wonder how they know?"

"I saw them staring right at me. But I felt their stare before I saw it."

"That's why you had to go..." Alex's voice catches at the words. "They weren't after me, or Mac, or Aaron, or Marion. They were after you."

I'm saved from further lecturing by Aaron and Mac's approach, the two of them carrying the comically long bolt cutters.

"Got them," Aaron calls out.

A minute later, he has a grip on the egg-sack and starts to pull.

"This is really tough material," Aaron says as he releases the pressure for a moment. "It's like Tyvek."

Putting a foot against the fence, he pushes back; all his weight, and more, pulling on the egg-sack. It starts to give, then thwack. The sack pops free of the ground.

As if in slow motion, I see Aaron fall, releasing the bolt cutter as he does. The egg-sack hits the fence and eggs tumble out. Most bounce back toward the hole from which the sack came, some fall straight down, and four roll under the fence, coming to rest against Aaron.

A few of the eggs are obviously dead. The others start popping open, the hatchlings struggling to their feet.

"Quick, we only have a few minutes!" I shout, kicking three of the four little creatures away from Aaron.

Alex backs away, using the Iknosan weapon to shoot several that had started to stand. But with Mac pulling Aaron away and me still kicking at the stupid things, her field of fire is severely restricted.

"Kai, get out of here!" she screams.

I turn and run, attracting the little ones that have started hopping. Aaron is now on his feet, but there is an unusual amount of blood flowing from his left arm.

"Go the other way," I shout.

I curve away from Alex, giving her a broader field of fire as she shoots at the little things bouncing after me. Seconds later, Marion is in the fight. Then it's done—eighteen little corpses popped open on the ground.

By the time I loop back to Aaron, Alex has a tourniquet on his arm, which has reduced, but not stopped the bleeding. Then I hear her say out loud, "Thelma, if I put my earpiece in Aaron's ear, can you transport him?"

Then she looks at me. "Thelma says she sent new earpieces."

"Right over here."

A moment later, I give one to Marion, the other to Alex, who helps Aaron.

"Thelma, Aaron needs to get to a hospital. Can you transport him to emergency at the ER Sophie works at?"

A moment later, Aaron and Alex are gone.

Alex's sudden disappearance shakes me in a way I haven't felt before. It's like a piece of me is missing.

"What now?" Mac asks.

As much as I don't want to say this, the answer is obvious.

"We need to draw the samples. Our defense is not viable without them. And every day we wait, we put ourselves at greater risk."

"Should we load the equipment on the truck?" Marion asks.

I nod and step in that direction, then stop. "Why don't we just transport? Now that you have an earpiece, we can transport you."

"What about Alex?" Mac asks.

"Good question. Let me ask Thelma what she's doing."

"Thelma? Is Alex planning to come back?"

"I'll ask her."

As the seconds tick by, my worry for Alex grows.

Finally, Thelma comes back to me. "Aaron was admitted. Alex was not allowed to accompany him. The police are questioning her. There was apparently a lot of blood."

"OK. The three of us here would like to transport to the mining site. Ask Alex if she is OK with us going before she gets back."

More seconds tick by, then an answer comes. "The police are detaining her. She says go, then come bail her out when you're done."

My blood boils at the stupidity of the situation. "Where is she now?"

"Still in the emergency room waiting area."

I whisper to Marion. "Did you see what happened?"

He nods. "It's all on the GoPro."

"Let's go to emergency and see if we can spring Alex loose."

"Thelma, can you loop Justin in on what is happening and get either news coverage or lawyers to the emergency room ASAP?"

"Will do, Kai. Want me to transport you now?"

EMERGENCY ROOM

I open my eyes and see the relatively empty waiting room, two police officers and Alex on one side, a handful of civilians on the other. The appearance of three rough and tumble men covered in desert dust draws everyone's attention. Alex's eyes light up when she sees me. Then one of the civilians stands and says, "That's Dr. Kyle Wimberly."

I wave. "Good morning, everyone." Several wave back before I turn toward the officers. Putting on my best Washington DC smile, I step toward the guy I think is in charge with hand outstretched. "Good morning, officers. I take it you helped Ms. Reyes get our wounded colleague into the Emergency Room."

Justin told me once, "Act friendly, put on a smile, offer your hand and a compliment. People will always take it and will usually listen to what you have to say."

"Umm, yes. Yes, we did."

"You probably can't tell us how he's doing, can you?"

"No, sir. We don't know."

"He was bleeding heavily when we transported him here. Ms. Reyes came along to make sure he got the help he needed."

"She was covered in his blood," the other officer says, as if it was an accusation.

"Did you see any of the news coverage a few months back of me being attacked by alien warriors?"

"I did," the lead officer said. "You comported yourself well."

I point to Alex. "Ms. Reyes was also part of our defensive operation that day. I got the first one mostly on my own. She got the second one. There was no news coverage of that. Today, two more attacked. Mr. Stone," I point to Mac. "Got the kill shot on the first one. Ms. Reyes got the kill shot on the second. Eighteen juveniles attacked Mr. Smith. Ms. Reyes got most of them, then brought Mr. Smith here. It was all recorded if you would like to see it. We, like you, operate with cameras on so we can document what really happened once the operation was over."

"Were you hunting these things?" the cynical officer asks.

"No. We were assembling for a geological mission when the aliens attacked us. We went out insufficiently armed because we didn't know more aliens had landed. They caught us off guard. Would you like to see the recording of us being attacked and Mr. Smith getting injured?"

A kid, maybe thirteen years old, steps up. "Excuse me, Dr. Wimberly. Could I get a picture with you, and maybe a signature?"

I turn, which puts me almost shoulder to shoulder with the lead officer, Baily, if I caught the name tag right.

"Sure. Would you like Officer Baily in the picture? He helped rescue one of my people today."

The officer raises a hand and starts to step away as the cell phone's camera flashes. A minute later, a news crew comes through the door and the waiting room turns into a circus. Eventually, Sophie comes out to talk with Alex and the police. They wisely take the hero role I've offered them.

Then we clear an area large enough that we can transport out and let the news crew film us as we simply vanish.

ARRASTRA MOUNTAIN WILDERNESS

The site I selected for our mining sample is fourteen miles north-northeast of our substation. No roads go there. The original plan was to follow one of the broader washes up the side of the mountain. Instead, we transported ourselves and our equipment to a level spot near the peak that overlooks the craggy wilderness under which our target is located.

I open my eyes and take in the surroundings. The peak in question towers maybe a hundred feet higher than the level area where we are standing. A narrow trail, maybe a quarter mile long, leads to the top.

"Are we going up there to take the samples?" Alex asks.

I shake my head. "On paper, that's the best place to do the mapping and draw the samples, but we couldn't find a spot to which it would be safe to transport." I run my eyes up the trail. "I'm not excited about carrying the sample transporter up there."

"We should check it out to make sure it's passable," she suggests. "I'd hate to carry that thing halfway to the top, then need to turn around and carry it back down."

"Agreed."

I turn to Mac and Marion. "In principle, we want to be up there."

"We heard," Mac says. "Why don't the two of you hike up? If it's a go for up there, Marion and I will carry the heavy one up while you come down to get the lighter one."

"Deal."

As I start slogging up the trail, Alex bounds ahead, as graceful as a gazelle, sure footed as a mountain goat. When she's a hundred feet ahead of me, the teasing begins.

I hear Marion laugh as I step up my pace.

Three-quarters of the way up, we come to a small gap in the trail. It's easy enough to step across, but the drop off to the right is steep. A misplaced step here could have deadly consequences. Finally, as the trail levels out, we get a panoramic view of the bad lands that make up most of this wilderness area.

"Lots of hiding places down there," Alex whispers to herself.

I can sense her lining-up shots and writing off swaths of territory where a target would be untouchable.

Coming out of her momentary reflection, she asks, "Where is it you want to take the sample?"

I pull up the aerial view on my phone, then point to a spot a mile into the badlands. "The deposit is six or seven thousand feet below the surface."

"Do you think we get enough advantage up here to justify carrying the equipment up?" Alex asks.

I shake my head. "No, let's try scanning from down there first."

"Deal." The devilish smile that comes with the word puzzles me. She glances down toward our colleagues. My eyes follow. That's when I realize we are out of view. By the time I get it, Alex is wrapped around me, her lips on mine.

"Thanks for rescuing me," she whispers. Then she's off, down the trail. I chase after, not as interested in catching up as I am in watching her move.

...

It takes a few minutes for the sample transporter's scanner to lock on. An instant later, I see what I'd hoped for, a massive monolithic formation of Gadolinite-Y, the Yttrium form of the crystalline silicate known as Gadolinite. I designate five spots within the formation that I want to sample, then pull them. A half hour later, the sample analyzer confirms that these samples are one percent Terbium. Fifteen minutes later, I get the estimated yield of Terbium—two-hundred metric tons, approximately four times what we need for our fleet build out.

As this material is the most urgent of our needs, I contact Thelma and ask her to begin the mining and refining operation for this site.

With this one in the bag, there's only one more hurdle in our way—Niobium.

[04.19.2034] OFFICE, ESTATE HOUSE

I woke this morning with a swollen ankle and pain severe enough that I needed crutches to walk.

Normally, I'd accept the restriction for a couple of days in the hope it would heal itself, then seek medical attention as the option of last resort.

Needless to say, Alex was having none of that. It was Wednesday. Sophie would be at work by eleven. We would go meet her there, so she could look at it.

Years ago, when Crystal and I started having problems, my mother told me that the key to a successful marriage was to realize you were no longer your own. You belonged to your partner and your partner belonged to you. And when both partners operated that way, the bond was unbreakable, as it was for her and dad.

I didn't get it at the time. Now I do. I belong to Alex. If she needs me to see Sophie, then I will go see Sophie, not because I need it, but because Alex does.

Yeah, it didn't quite go that smoothly, but this morning we went to see Sophie.

As it turns out, I sprained my ankle while soccer kicking the Dominion hatchlings yesterday, then tore a little more tissue chasing Alex up and down the mountain. I also got two or three of the hatchling's little spurs imbedded in the area between my ankle bone and heel.

Curiously, the spurs have relatively high tungsten levels in them which lit up the X-ray machine. They're like porcupine quills with hundreds of little barbs per millimeter that make pulling them out impossible.

Long story short, the hospital's resident podiatrist did an hour-long surgery on my foot this morning, using a fluoroscope to find the tiny pieces, leaving me wheelchair bound for a couple of days.

With Alex out on her afternoon run, it gives me a moment of privacy to do something I really don't want anyone else to know about.

"Thelma, are you free to join me in the office?"

An instant later, she appears before me.

"What can I do for you, Kai?"

"Early on, To'Kana told me that I was free of arachnoid genes, as were Jill and Alex. Shortly before he was called away, he told me that he would not have allowed Olivia Knox and Denzel Yang to participate in the capture of the Dominion warrior in the box canyon, because they carried too many arachnoid genes."

"Yes. He reprimanded me for not having tested them before letting them aboard."

"Do you have the ability to test people for that?"

Thelma takes on a worried expression. "Yes and no."

"Care to explain?"

"It is among the data the transporter collects when someone is transported. So, yes. If I transport someone, I can verify their status. To'Kana has better ways to make that determination than I do, and he would not allow me to transport someone with arachnoid genes."

"So, if I had people I wanted to test, I could invite them over, give them an earpiece, transport them, and have my answer."

"Yes. To'Kana would reprimand you, but it would work. Who do you want to test?"

"The first would be Larry Carver and his wife Melissa Johnson."

"The old guy from the winery?"

"Yeah."

"To'Kana tested him in the aftermath of the terrorist attack. He's clean. Don't know the wife."

"I might invite them over tonight."

[04.20.2034] ESTATE HOUSE

When Alex got back from her run yesterday afternoon, I told her I wanted to invite Larry and Melissa over. She said, "Sure, but not tonight." Then she was off to the shower.

This morning, I gave her earpieces for them and asked if she'd be willing to transport over and bring them back after work today. She locked eyes with me and held it for a while, then said, "You're up to something you don't want to tell me about." When I didn't respond, she shrunk back a bit. "I trust you, so don't need to know. But I don't like it when you do this."

Now, it's six o'clock. Larry and Melissa agreed to come over via transport, and Alex left a few minutes ago.

Thelma is standing next to me in the foyer waiting.

"Just got the transport request from Alex. You ready?" she asks.

"I am. Please initiate transport."

An instant later, the three of them appear in front of us, Melissa laughing, Larry swooning, and Alex looking grumpy; we'll need to talk through that later tonight.

It takes Larry a second to get stable on his feet, then he looks at Thelma critically. "Are you tying in remotely? You look like a holoprojection."

She steps forward, hand extended. As Larry takes it, she says, "It's a pleasure to meet you, Mr. Carver. I'm Thelma, an artificial intelligence created by the Iknosan."

"You're what?"

"An AI, a digital life form, fully self-aware and imbued with knowledge and memories drawn from hundreds of individuals." She spreads her arms. "May I?"

Larry beams a huge smile. "Of course you can, sweetheart."

She wraps her arms around him, resting her head on his chest. He puts his arms around her, then bends his head down to kiss her on the top of her head.

"You're so warm," Thelma marvels.

A few seconds later, she's hugging Melissa. There's enough innocence in the exchange that it's quite touching.

As we make our way to the dining room, Thelma gives me a wink and a thumbs up—the agreed sign if Melissa was clear. The way she does it gives me déjà vu, leading me to believe that she gleaned the gesture from a movie or television show I've seen, though I have no idea which.

The chef comes out to announce tonight's meal—Chicken Cordon Bleu with mushroom risotto and spinach sauteed with butter and garlic.

"Would it be OK if I offered a blessing for this meal?" Larry asks.

"Please," Alex replies.

Out of the corner of my eye, I watch Thelma's studied interest in the tradition. I know I'm going to be questioned about it later.

When he's finished, Thelma says, "My people, the Iknosan, have a similar tradition. It is themed a little differently, but offered whenever they gather privately like this."

"Could you offer that blessing for us?" Larry asks.

There's a pause, then Thelma looks at me. "I know this blessing, but it is blocked. I cannot say it."

I look up at Larry, who seems bewildered.

"The Iknosan have gone to great lengths to keep certain aspects of their culture secret. This is one of those things. They have placed a regulator on Thelma that prevents her from talking about them.

Understandable, right? They don't want their culture to overtake ours."

He looks back at Thelma. "Sorry, I didn't mean to get you in trouble. Can I change topic?"

The new question brings Thelma's bright disposition back. "Please."

"Are you going to eat with us tonight? And if so, how does that work?"

"All my energy comes from electricity, so I don't eat the way you do. But I'm going to try to fake it."

As the food is being brought out, I ask Larry, "Would you and Melissa be interested in trying our simulator after dinner?"

Larry looks expectantly at his wife. "Lizzy, you on for it tonight?"

The words are spoken with so much flirtation in them, you'd think he was asking for something else.

She flirts back, "Oh, I think I'm good for a round or two."

DEN, ESTATE ROOM

Dinner was cleared two hours ago, and our guests are just about finished with their second simulation. In the first simulation, they got two of the barracuda torpedoes off before being spotted. Both torpedoes missed and their war shuttle was destroyed.

They've played the second simulation more seriously. Doing the set up at distance, light minutes from the enemy positions, and putting themselves in stealth during the alignment process.

"Kai, this weapon of yours is brilliant, but it's really difficult to use. You need to know a spot in space where your enemy is going to be at a given time. Then you have to get the shuttle on a course that will jump you to that spot at that time. Can you put any navigation or propulsion in the missile that would allow you to do any of that remotely?" Larry asks.

"The jump drive scales up by volume, so every cubic inch of volume added requires a bigger jump drive. The grav-drive scales up by mass, so every pound added requires a bigger grav drive. There are tricks we can use to make very small grav drives, but to do what you ask, you would be adding something the size of a Space Hawk to each torpedo."

"Why not make the Space Hawk the delivery vehicle?" Larry comes back. "We could drop it close to the right spot with close to the right momentum. As each one is dropped off, another controller could line up the torpedo while the shuttle deploys the next. Once the torpedo jumps, the Space Hawks can return, or the shuttles can pick them up."

"Interesting idea," I reply. "I'll look into it."

Larry and Melissa continue to line up their torpedoes, and, when they get target lock, the simulation fast forwards to the strike.

"The second one missed its target," Larry grouses.

"But the first one hit hers," Melissa taunts. "And we escaped unchallenged."

"Not bad, for the second simulation," I congratulate. "I designed this weapon, know it inside out, and I still missed shots early on."

"What about you, Alex?" Melissa asks.

"Given time, I never miss. In the time limited simulations that come later, I elected not to take some shots, but I've never actually missed on one."

"We'll get there," Larry assures. "Where to from here, Kai?"

"Until you decide you're out, you are welcome to train here as much as you want."

"What do you mean by *decide you're out*?"

"Right here, right now, this mission is theoretical. Over the coming days, we'll firm up the requirements. No one will be *in* until they've met the selection requirements. And no one will be authorized to go until they've met the deployment requirements. If at any point along the way you want out, then you're out."

Larry nods. "Understood."

"Coordinate with Thelma for time on the simulator. Ask her to transport you here and back. We want to make it as hard as possible for people to track you. Probably best if your cell phones are off while here, or not brought at all."

"You think the government is keeping tabs on you?"

"I know they are."

Larry lifts his eyes toward me, "You know this how?"

"I've been told by three different government officials: a member of Congress, a senior official at the DOD, and an official in the FBI."

"Jeze, Kai."

"Yeah." I pause. "Larry, you don't need to do this. You've both served, paid your dues, earned a life not plagued by conflict."

"Only if someone else will pick up the mantle. If you can crew your war shuttles, then all is good. We will fade away. But do you think that will happen? I don't; I've seen too much of their malarkey. But I do know you, Kai. I believe you. You've made a compelling enough case that the government will throw some money at you. But if they fail to provide crews... Then, Lizzy and I volunteer, beginning and end of story."

I look at Melissa. Her eyes confirm Larry's words.

Overwhelmed with emotion, I hug them both. "Thank you."

Moments later, they're gone, and Alex asks, "Are you going to tell me what that was about?"

"Have you heard To'Kana's master species theory?"

"No. Is this another secret you're withholding from me?"

I look at Alex dumbfounded. "At this point, I've had hundreds of hours with To'Kana, tens of thousands of hours of memories downloaded into my mind. Have I shared them all? No! How could I have? To'Kana arrived less than ten thousand hours ago."

"Sorry," Alex offers. "That may be the hardest thing for me to understand. Tell me about his master species theory."

I spew it all out in abbreviated form. Three master species—arachnoid, humanoid, and another lost to history.

"The relevance?" she asks.

"Earth was impregnated with all three of the master species' genes. Here humanoids won the race to intelligence. But evolving on a world rich in arachnoid DNA, some of it ended up in the human genome. Neither of us have a gene in which an arachnoid component is dominant. But many humans do. To'Kana believes those people cannot be trusted in the battle. The transporter records the genome of everyone it transports. Larry and Melissa are free of any dominant arachnoid genes, which means they can join the crew."

Alex looks shocked. "The purpose of transporting Larry and Melissa here was to run a genetic profile on them?"

"Only Melissa. To'Kana cleared Larry at Christmas in the aftermath of the terrorist attack. That makes eight of us known to be clean."

"And you didn't want to tell me this. Why?"

"The job needed to be done. I couldn't do it myself, because I'm stuck in this wheelchair, so I asked you. But my head wasn't in the right place to discuss it with anyone else yet."

Alex looks away and is silent for a moment. Then she whispers, "This is why the Army forbids fraternization. You wouldn't evacuate the substation because I was there. I'm resentful that I was given an order without an explanation—something I had no need to know."

She looks up at me. "Sorry. We both need to learn how to do this better. It's late. Let's go upstairs.

CHAPTER 19: CREWS

[04.21.2034] DINING ROOM, ESTATE HOUSE

I've called a team meeting for tonight. It's Friday. Justin and Jill transported to the estate house from their office in New York to join Mac, Ty, Alex, Thelma, and me. Since Larry and Melissa were here running more simulations, I asked them to join us as well.

"First item of business," I announce. "Thelma has a revised time line."

She stands. "As I think you all know, I have a backdoor channel to Captain To'Kana that allows him to send me messages that cannot be seen by anyone else and gives him deniability if it is discovered."

"Does that imply he is forbidden from talking with us?" Larry asks.

"Not in the way you think, but functionally, yes. Earth was removed from his list of priorities, replaced by other things. Iknosan tradition dictates that captains focus all their efforts on the priorities assigned to them. Working on anything else is cause for removal."

"Then how can he help us?"

"By not terminating my access to his ship's log, while becoming more thorough in documenting his activities and rationale."

Larry nods his head. "Clever."

"Regarding the time line, the Dominion departed from the Indarsu home world weeks earlier than expected. They did that by knocking out the planet's power and military infrastructure, then seeding the world with thousands of egg sacks. Normally, they spend months scavenging resources. On this world they are leaving those resources for the next generation. The captain speculates they plan to make the Indarsu home world one of their regional strongholds, something that will certainly be problematic for us if they achieve that goal."

I interrupt. "Once we've turned the Dominion back, we, and any allies we pick up along the way, will have to cleanse that world."

Thelma nods her agreement, then continues. "The first wave of Dominion ships will arrive in Harza space two months from today, on

Wednesday, June 21, 2034. Our war shuttles will need to leave earth no later than Monday, June 19."

"Certainty?" I ask.

"To'Kana underlined these dates in the ship's log. He only does that when he believes he has hard numbers."

"Good sign," I agree. "Questions on this topic before we move on?"

Melissa raises her hand. I point to her and say, "Go."

"I did air logistics for ground operations in the years leading up to Afghanistan, then through the early part of the war. A two-day transit window seems narrow to me. Are you sure it's enough?"

"I'll take this one," I say to Thelma, then turn to Melissa. "Our destination is approximately twenty-two hundred light years away. The current plan is to travel the first two thousand light years, which will take approximately four hours, then regroup. That puts us in proximity to the battle zone almost two days before the enemy's arrival. I don't think we want to arrive there any sooner than that."

"What about problems on route?"

"There are no short-term solutions for things that could go wrong along the way. If a drive fails or we develop a hull leak, we will have to abandon the shuttle. If we get lost, our problem will be getting home, not getting to the battle. Everything we need is on the shuttles. That said, there is a calibration issue we need to deal with before we leave on this mission."

"You going to explain that?" Justin asks.

"Yes. It's one of the topics on the agenda, but since the issue has been raised, I'll address it now. We do not have the equipment required to calibrate the jump drives automatically, so we must do it by hand."

"What's involved?"

I give the quick rundown of the calibration process, then Justin says, "Sounds like a good thing for each crew to do as part of their training."

"That was my plan. Alex and I did War Shuttle #1, which will be our shuttle. Each crew that acceptably completes training will be required to calibrate their shuttle's jump drive by the departure date to qualify for the mission. Our tentative departure date is two days before the Dominion's forecast arrival date. As the latter could change at any point in time, crews should get their shuttles calibrated ASAP."

"I presume we will have the same problem with the battlecruisers."

"We will. Auto-calibration may never be available to us. Having it as a crew's first duty seems like a good way for them to get to know their ship." I pause, then bring us back to our purpose. "Any other questions on this topic?"

When I get none, I move on. "The next item on the list is teams. Who here wants to crew a war shuttle?"

Everyone, except Justin, raises a hand.

"That gives us three teams and a fourth if we can find a partner for Jill. Who else do we know that might volunteer?"

"Possibly April McDonald, the analyst on Morgan's team at DOD," Justin says. "She contacted me a couple weeks back, saying she might be interested in signing on if we ran that experiment. She also said she might have a friend that would join her."

"There are some old-timers at the VFW that might be interested," Larry offers.

"Is there any chance we can get active military on as crew? This seems like something the government would want their people doing, not us," Alex says.

"Or any allied forces," Melissa suggests.

I put my finger up. "I met a colonel from the Australian Air Force a couple months back, who offered some muscle if we got into a bind. I'll contact him. Maybe they'll be willing to provide a crew."

"What criteria are we going to apply to applicants?" Justin asks.

"Initially, I think we should draw from people who we know and trust, who are active or former military, and who believe in the mission. From there, they need to complete the training simulations, which will need to be done here. Then it's time to commit."

Alex eyes me and Justin notices. "What?" he asks, his eyes boring into Alex's, not mine.

"To'Kana had requirements he told Kyle about. He can explain."

Now Justin's eyes are on me.

"Iknosan technology isn't safe for all humans. To'Kana identified the vulnerable by scanning for a set of genetic markers. He scanned all of us, except Larry and Melissa, before giving us earpieces or transporting us. We don't have access to those scanners, but the transporter flags those at risk. So, requirement one. Any candidate must be transported here for an interview. If the transporter detects the markers, we transport them back after the interview, then decline to move forward with them. Two transports are safe enough, but no one with those markers can be on a crew."

"That's why you had us transport over here for dinner," Melissa says. "That we are still engaged suggests that we do not have those markers."

"Correct," I reply.

"Does this apply to the battlecruisers as well?"

"I suppose it should, though To'Kana never raised it."

Justin looks at Thelma, but I say no before he asks.

"There's more you're not telling us," he accuses.

"The Iknosan compartmentalize information differently than we do. That a genetic problem exists is known by few. The transporter's ability to detect it is the same. You all are among the few that know. To'Kana purposefully withheld this information from Thelma. She knows more than what I've told you, but please do not ask her about it. The answers you'll get may be misleading."

I turn to Thelma. "There's much more to this issue than To'Kana has told you. Please do not discuss it with any human other than me."

"Information compartmentalized," she replies.

Addressing the whole group again, I say. "To'Kana has shared the technical aspects of the issue with me and sworn me to silence, an oath I must keep if the technology flow is to continue."

"How much danger does this put us in?" Larry asks.

"The eight of us? None whatsoever, we don't have the relevant genes. I know this sounds like a big deal. But it's not. Think of it as being like a peanut allergy. If we were serving peanuts, we would want to make sure we didn't serve them to someone with the allergy."

"Is it just the transporters?" Justin asks.

I hesitate before replying. I really don't want to tell Justin or any of the others about environmental systems on Iknosan ships, but I suppose I need to come clean on this.

"It's not the transporters," I reply. "They just detect the genes."

"Then what is it?" Justin demands.

"It's the environmental systems. They use compounds in the environmental systems that are toxic to arachnoids."

"So why do we have to scan humans?" Justin asks.

"There are arachnoid genes in the human genome. In all of us, those genes are recessive. In people with enough dominant arachnoid genes, the environmental systems—air and water—will make them sick and eventually kill them."

"I can't believe you didn't clue us in on this issue earlier!" Justin explodes.

"Sorry, I'd mostly forgotten this was an issue until Larry and Melissa volunteered."

"We need to tell Morgan." Justin gets up and starts pacing. "He already has people on the ships we've delivered."

"Sorry," I repeat. "I completely forgot."

The room goes silent as Justin paces. After a minute, he stops and spins toward me, a smile starting to form. "Maybe it's an opportunity. We tell Morgan that we have an issue we need to discuss with him privately. Then, when we meet, we revisit the question of crews for the war shuttle test." Justin rubs his chin for a second, then asks, "What else do we need to discuss?"

"How many of our war shuttles do we want to risk? Half? All of them? All but one or two?"

Justin looks at me. "The risk I'm worried about is you, Kyle. If we lose you, it's game over, end of story."

"Thanks for the concern. But the decision is made. Subject closed."

Justin's eyes are still on me, as if he is wrestling with something. We stare at each other long enough that some of the others start getting jittery. "Then I'm in too. I'll talk with April, vet her partner if she has one, and we'll take it from there."

[04.22.2034] ESTATE HOUSE

It's still mostly dark outside as I exit the elevator, walking tenderly on my still healing feet. Alex, who hates the elevator, trots down the stairs into the foyer for the morning run. Ty, always the first, is about halfway through his morning warm-up exercises, holding a lateral lunge. As he swings to the other side, he spots us and points. Curiously, the door to the den is closed with light leaking out from underneath.

"I think they've been going at it all night."

"Doesn't surprise me," Alex replies, putting a hand against one of the foyer's columns to do her first leg swing. "When Justin commits to something, he can be single-minded in his pursuit of it."

Realizing a run is still out of the question for me today, I walk over to the den to stick my head in.

"Nailed it," Justin exclaims, giving a fist pump.

"Not bad," Jill replies, while maintaining studious attention to the controls on her simulator. "Another hour and you'll get caught up with me."

Justin sees me and comes over. "We've canceled our plans for the weekend, so we could get some simulator hours in. The next couple of weeks are packed."

"Make sure to reserve your time with Thelma."

"We have. We're taking the graveyard shift again tonight."

"We only have the simulators for another hour," Jill calls out. "If you want to get level five done, you better start soon."

"Gotta go," Justin says as he heads back to his station.

I shut the door as I exit and see that Mac has now joined the warm-up fest in the foyer. Maybe tomorrow, I'll be able to join.

OFFICE, ESTATE HOUSE

My first job this morning is to contact Colonel Jaiden Brock. It takes a minute to find his card, then tap in the number. A second later, the line connects.

"Brock."

"Colonel Brock, Kyle Wimberly here."

"Dr. Wimberly. A pleasure to hear from you, sir. How can I help?"

I give him the briefest overview of the War Shuttle situation and am cut off almost immediately.

"Morgan Owen has brought me up to speed on this situation. Stupid if you ask me. US Special Forces should be all over this, but their masters won't let them. I have more flexibility if you're looking for crews."

"That's exactly what I'm looking for. This initiative is volunteer only. Anyone that volunteers will have to pass several tests, one of which will be administered without their knowledge."

"Can you give me the thumbnail on the test sequence?"

I quickly explain.

"We must transport in for an interview, go through a training sequence on simulators only available at your site, then, if selected, run calibrations on the shuttle to which we are assigned. We are welcome to stay at your site at your expense, though our movements will be restricted until selected. Selections will happen by the end of May for June deployment. Did I miss anything?"

"Those are the major points."

"How many people do you want?"

"We have space for up to thirty. Eight of those have already been filled."

There is a moment of silence, then Colonel Brock says, "A word of advice... If you tell too many people what you have just told me, word will get out. When the government realizes you are running a military operation with foreign participants, they will come after you, despite the ridiculous position they've taken to date. So, think carefully about who you talk to and what you tell them. I'm safe. I'll get you at least two people that are safe. I'll also vet a British connection and give him your contact info if I think he's safe. He will use the key word John Dory if he calls."

"Thank you, sir."

"I'll be in touch."

As the line drops, I shake my head. What a strange conversation.

OFFICE, ESTATE HOUSE

For the first time in what seems like months, my plate is clear enough that I can play with the replicator's pattern design sub-system today. The goal? To modify a Space Hawk drone to do the final target acquisition and alignment lock for jump. It seems like a simple enough job. The Space Hawks already have the navigation and drive capability. All it needs is a means to grasp the torpedo.

It seems like it should be simple enough to do, but it doesn't take long to determine that it may not be possible in this time frame. I have ten war shuttles, each carrying eight Space Hawks and eight torpedoes. I no longer have a simple means of fabricating the torpedoes. So, I'm stuck with the torpedoes I have—eight meters long, one and a half in diameter, smooth exterior with its tightly packed array of jump field emitters, and nothing to grab on to.

Time to rethink this. Is there a way I could tow it?

An hour into my research, I find something interesting: *Tractor System for Jump Capable Vessels with a Non-Ferrous Hull*.

Flipping through the pages, I see that the system consists of a series of panels shaped to fit exactly onto the vessel at several places. In the sample design, there are ten panels: one on the bow, one on the stern, and eight set at various points along the hull. The panels are held in place by powerful grav-plating that functionally glues them to the ship. Each panel also has a small grav drive sufficient to make small changes in the ship's speed and direction.

The trick that makes this viable is the exactness of the fit—little nibs in the exact pattern and inverse shape of the dimple-like jump field emitters on the ship, allowing metal-to-metal contact across the entire surface area of the panel.

Two companion software packages are available for automated use. The first manages panel attachment, detachment, and collection in the field. The second characterizes the flight performance of the ship under control of the panels, making it compatible with standard flight control packages.

Certain that I want to invest in this system, I configure the template for a series of panels that would work with our torpedoes.

[04.25.2034] PENTAGON

Justin and I exit the cab at the visitor entrance and make our way through security where we are met by April McDonald. After cursory greetings, she says, "I'm glad you're early, because we are in the far corner of the building today." She starts off at a brisk pace, then slows as we enter a more-or-less empty cross corridor.

"Justin, thanks for the message you sent me over the weekend. I want in, but it comes with a string."

"Which is?"

"I'm doing this mostly for Ben, my boyfriend. He is an ex-Seal, mid-forties. Blew out his left knee a couple of years ago, was pulled from the teams, given an instructor's position, then retired the day he was eligible. He's fit, loyal, and going crazy for some action."

"Can the two of you have dinner with us tonight? We can discuss the mission, timeline, criteria for selection, and qualification process."

"Where and when?"

"Charlie Palmer's? 7:30?"

"Ben will love that."

Picking up the pace again, we reach our destination two minutes early, where Morgan is waiting for us.

"April told me you're planning to test your War Shuttle and the experimental kinetic weapon."

"Is that a problem?" Justin asks.

Morgan looks at Justin, then at me.

"I've run it up the flagpole. Got a firm, 'No, don't ask again,' as regards our participation. No answer about what they'll do to you. My gut says you'll be heroes if you have a big win, inmates if you lose."

"If this doesn't work, it will be a short sentence."

"What?" Morgan seems genuinely confused.

"The world will end in six months if our mission is a failure."

Justin intervenes. "That is not our official position. But back to the question. Why aren't they supporting this? Why aren't we running this test with special forces operatives? It seems crazy for civilian volunteers to be the ones engaging enemy warships in order to test the weapons that will make us competitive in this war."

"Then you shouldn't do it," Morgan snaps back.

"You can't possibly believe that," Justin replies with even more heat.

The two stare at each other for a second, then Morgan sighs. "This isn't to be repeated."

Justin nods.

"I recommended that we endorse this mission and send a special forces team. The Chairman of the Joint Chiefs agreed with me. The president and secretary were initially favorable, then they vetoed it. The British, French, and Chinese all wanted to be included and given a war shuttle of their own. If we were going, they were going. Period. The president trusts you more than the Chinese, maybe more than the Brits and French. But she's not going to endorse a civilian volunteer mission, so you are on your own." Morgan looks at his watch. "Now, what's on the agenda today? You said it was urgent."

"Crew qualification." Justin points at me, and I repeat the genetic markers story.

"A bit late for a caveat like that; don't you think?"

"Painfully late," Justin agrees. "But true, nonetheless. So, the question is how we roll out this requirement."

"This is one of the reasons the government hates working with new suppliers," Morgan spits out in frustration.

"Yet it is the price of revolutionary technology. Two things are allowing us to jump hundreds of years ahead: the charity of an alien species that organizes all information and thought differently than we do, and the 24/365 effort of the only person on earth that can bridge the chasm that separates us." Justin's ire takes me by surprise but continues to flow.

"It will not work perfectly the first time. And this will not be the last time we fumble the ball. But it is the only option we have. So cut the bureaucratic bullshit and help us solve the problem!"

There's fire in Morgan's eyes. But he controls it, letting the silence stretch out until he is ready to re-engage.

"You say all we need to do is transport our people. Easy, peasy. One and done. But that's not all we need to do. We need to create a new qualification, update procedures for gathering qualifications, update the thousand-year-old software that stores the data. The list goes on."

"Come on, Morgan. You're creating a whole new command with many new qualifications, new data systems, the whole list. This only applies to that command. We are only adding two bits of information: one, has this person been tested, and two, do they qualify or not? Period."

"Good point. I'll use it. And it was my idea if anyone asks," he chuckles, his no drama, easygoing, but direct style reasserting itself. "What risk do we have for the workers doing the internal fit and finish on the dozen ships you've delivered?"

"Minimal. The transporter test only takes a couple seconds to complete. Anyone with a clean scan will not be affected. Any who get sick will recover, assuming they are removed from the environment in a timely manner." I answer on Justin's behalf.

"Good. Criteria coming in this late is awkward, but not really a problem. I know how to handle it now. Thanks Justin. Anything else?"

"One other thing," I say.

"Let's hear it."

"The jump drives on the battlecruisers are not calibrated yet. It's a simple procedure that needs to be done by the ship's crew as part of its maiden voyage."

"Good. Thanks for bringing that up; perfect timing. We are documenting procedures. If you can shoot me the data, I'll make sure it gets included. Are the jump drives the only thing that needs calibration?"

"I'll need to get back to you on that."

Morgan smiles. "Didn't think so. Get me the list ASAP."

"Will do, sir."

CHARLIE PALMER STEAK, WASHINGTON, D.C.

We enter the building, Justin in the lead, me holding the door for the ladies. As Justin approaches the reception desk, I spot April in the bar, seated next to a mountain of a man. The contrast between the two makes me smile. He's like six-four, two-fifty, taut and muscular, wearing a suit as nice as the ones Jill made me throw out, and holding a bottle of beer in his left hand. She's maybe five-five, with a touch of early-onset middle-age that is mostly hidden by the stiff lines of her lawyer-like suit. An untouched glass of white wine sits in front of her.

I walk over to greet April and introduce Alex.

"Kyle, please meet my friend, Ben."

I put out my hand to shake, concerned it's going to be crushed. "Ben, pleasure to meet you."

"And you, sir. I saw the video of you taking down the giant alien. I've taken down a lot of trash, but nothing like that thing. You've got brass ones, brother."

The thought of this giant being impressed by me is ironic enough that I almost laugh. I introduce Alex and, as they shake, add that she took down the other one.

He freezes a second, still grasping her hand, but staring, not shaking.

"Sharpshooter," he pronounces. "The stance, the eyes... You can always tell. Did you get it on the first shot?" The question is asked as if it would be an amazing outcome if she had.

"I did, actually."

"I have to hear this tale."

Justin comes over, the host close behind, seemingly in a hurry to get us seated. Finally, at the table, Justin and Jill are introduced.

"So, how did you get it in one shot?" Ben asks.

"It was climbing a cliff. I was at the top of the cliff maybe a quarter mile away, but thought I knew where it would come over. On its last bound, it came flying up over the face of the cliff, four legs splayed to plant its landing. I had an alien weapon that shot little darts, called transporter tags. I had the shot and took it. The tag hit and it was transported into space, just as its feet were touching down."

The waiter comes, asking for drink orders. The three guys go with Jefferson Manhattans. Alex and Jill go with the same chardonnay April has, and Justin gets a bottle of cabernet for the table.

As the waiter leaves, Justin starts in on the pitch.

Ben reacts almost immediately. "We have to learn how to fly a spaceship?"

"They are shuttles with autopilots..."

Jill clears her throat, interrupting. Justin eyes her but yields.

"Auto pilot is the understatement of the century. The ship is piloted by an artificial intelligence with a holographic body. You can look at it. You can touch it. You can carry on a conversation with it that is more real than talking to a friend on Zoom. It has hundreds of years of flight experience gleaned from the memories of people. It knows how to fly the ship, knows how to navigate. It's not a toy. Your job will be to give it instructions. When we depart, it will take us to our staging area. From that point on, it is up to us to decide how to use our weapons to destroy as many alien dreadnaughts as we can and still live to tell the tale."

"And we learn to do that via simulation?" Ben asks.

"You do. I've passed the first six. Justin is stuck on five. They're completely realistic. You feel like you're on the bridge of the shuttle. It's learning by doing. The most effective training I've ever had."

"How long does it take?"

"I'm fourteen hours in," Jill says, then turns to me. "The later ones take longer, right?"

"How many are there?" Ben asks, the question directed at me.

"You need to pass a minimum of thirty to qualify."

April, who has been mostly quiet to this point, speaks up. "We've got fifty-five to sixty days to get this done. Training is going to take maybe thirty of those, then we need to calibrate our shuttle. The mission will take a minimum of three days. I don't have that much vacation."

"Do you think Morgan would sell us your services—you come work for us, he pays you, we pay DOD?"

"You mean a secondment?" April asks.

"Exactly."

"The military does it all the time," Ben adds.

April nods her head. "I'll ask."

Conversation stops as the appetizers are delivered to the table. Justin, who's seated to my right, leans in and whispers, "Shall we invite them to transport out tonight?"

"I'm good with that."

...

As dinner is wrapping up, Justin asks, "How are you getting home tonight? Driving? Subway?"

"Uber," April answers. "Why do you ask?"

"I'd like to offer you an alternative..."

DEN, ESTATE HOUSE

I hear April giggle and open my eyes. Then Thelma's voice sounds in my ear. "They are both clear of arachnoid genes."

"Damnation!" Ben exclaims. "Un-frigging-believable."

"Welcome to the estate," Thelma says, walking into the room.

I see Ben's mouth drop open. "You're an AI."

"I am," Thelma replies. "And you were a Seal."

Thankfully, the humor lands. With Thelma, it's hit or miss.

"And you have already passed your first test," I say.

Ben looks at me strangely. "Come again?"

"Earlier, we said there was a test we would administer without your knowledge. We did it as you transported in, you passed."

"What kind of test was this?"

"A genetic test for certain defects known to react poorly to the ship's environmental systems."

I see Ben frown, then suddenly jump as Thelma, who crossed the room without being noticed, reaches out towards him. "What the hell?" he says, backing away.

"May I hug you?" she asks.

Ben looks up at me with fire in his eyes. "Is this another test?"

I shake my head. "No. No, just the way Thelma likes to greet guests. She's harmless, but you are under no obligation or expectation to accommodate her."

Thelma takes another step toward him as he continues to back away.

"I'll hug you," April says.

Jill points at Ben, who's still watching Thelma. "Want to try the simulator?"

He glances at her, then back at April, to whom Thelma is now clinging. He looks at his watch as if timing how long Thelma has latched on. "I think we should go babe. It's late."

April and Thelma separate. "Shall I transport you to your home on Kemp Lane in Burke, Virginia?"

"You know where we live?" Ben exclaims.

"If it's on the internet, I know it. Foyer, kitchen, or master bedroom?" Thelma asks.

"Kitchen," April replies, then to Justin. "Thanks for a great evening. I'll be in touch tomorrow. Please transport us to the kitchen, Thelma."

A second or two later, they're gone.

"We should head back too," Jill says.

Justin offers his hand. "Good day, strange ending," he says as we shake. "Call me when you're back from your run tomorrow morning. We have things to discuss."

"Will do," I say a moment before they disappear.

Alex looks at me. "What just happened?"

I shake my head. "I think Thelma may have just upset the apple cart."

[04.26.2034] WAR SHUTTLE #1

After the morning run, the first since my foot surgery a week ago, I called Justin. As I thought last night, the issue was Thelma. Ben was deeply offended by her behavior, uncertain he wanted to be involved in a mission dependent on dysfunctional equipment in human form. April thought she could bring him around, but Thelma needed to clean up her act, which was all on me.

I promised I would work the issue, but my priority today is testing the tractor system that will give our torpedoes remote guidance capability.

"Charlie, how long until we jump?"

"Twenty-seven minutes, sir. I've put it on the main view screen for you."

As much as I would prefer to be doing this in earth orbit, I don't want to risk losing control of one of our torpedoes and having it fall down into the atmosphere. Given its shape and composition, the tungsten core might survive reentry and destroy something. Instead, we are jumping out to the planet Neptune, where we will take orbit one-hundred-thousand miles above its surface to run our test.

"When are you going to talk to Thelma?" Alex asks.

"When we get back."

"I know you are closer to her than the rest of us, but maybe this is something you should let me do."

"Why?"

"She has purposefully taken, or been given, a female form and, as she said that first day in the cellar, her mission is to become part of the family to whom she's been assigned. But her behavior is not consistent with that. She's unnaturally forward, even went so far as kissing Mac."

I laugh at the memory. "Forgot about that."

"Maybe she will relate to me more than you on the topic of appropriate female behavior."

"Good point. I think you should talk to her."

"Can I ask you about something else?" Alex asks.

"Sure."

"The environmental systems thing... You've been cagey about this. Why?"

"It's a security measure the Iknosan put in place to kill arachnoids that might penetrate the ship. They put a poison in the air and water that is toxic to arachnoid biology. A human with enough arachnoid genes would get sick and eventually die if they came aboard."

"Interesting concept," Alex muses, her head going back and forth as if she's looking at the problem from different angles. "Why the reticence?"

"Doesn't it bother you they put bug spray in the air?"

"Not really."

"I wish I'd talked to you about this six months ago."

"There are a lot of things I wish you'd done with me six months ago."

It takes a second to click, then I laugh at her insinuation.

"We will jump in one minute," Charlie announces.

"Thank you, Charlie," I reply, then turn back to Alex, who shifts in her seat, taking on a pensive look.

"Did you know that Justin and Jill have a cohabitation agreement?" she asks. "Jill was telling me about it yesterday."

"A what?"

"Same idea as a pre-nuptial agreement, but for people who are not married. It defines their responsibilities to each other if they break up. Jill says it is becoming increasingly common among wealthy people and theirs is unusual because it defines their responsibilities to each other while they are together."

"Are you thinking this is something we should do?" I ask, not wanting to contemplate such a thing.

"No. I have a sniper rifle for that," she sasses back.

"Jumping in three, two, one... Jumped," Charlie announces.

"Didn't feel a thing," Alex comments.

"Fifteen minutes until we achieve orbit," Charlie calls out.

"Jill is very close to what she calls a performance threshold—something Justin would reward her for if she succeeded. If she achieves it, Justin will give her control over a huge asset base, functionally restoring the inheritance her parents lost."

"I hope that doesn't mess up their relationship. They seem to be the perfect couple."

"He pushes her pretty hard, but she is completely devoted to him."

"And vice versa."

"It's been bugging me," Alex says.

"Why does It matter to you?"

"I suppose it doesn't. It's their life. They can do what they want. But I can't see living under a contract like that. It seems unnatural."

"Yet it bugs you."

"Now that I've told you, maybe it won't." She leans over and puts her head on my shoulder, then sighs. A second later, she snaps back up. "Remind me what we need to do up here."

I review the procedure with Alex, who is in a playful mood today, trading barbs or innuendo over every step we need to take to get the job done.

Finally in position, I order Charlie to deploy Torpedo #1, then to back away from it. Five minutes later, the torpedo is a hundred yards ahead of us floating in the same orbit we are, completely stationary relative to the shuttle.

"Charlie, please deploy Space Hawk One."

While he works on that, I activate the controller for the tractor system. As a late addition to the war shuttle and weapons program, the ten panels in the tractor system do not have an automated deployment system like the one for the torpedoes and space hawks. Instead, I added a program to the tractor system's controller that flies the panels out through the same tube the torpedo used.

"Here goes nothing," I whisper, realizing that this is our first Iknosan control system that is almost completely of my design.

"It simulated out, didn't it?" Alex asks.

I smile at her faith in me. "Yeah, still..."

I initiate the procedure, and, over the next fifteen minutes, the ten panels navigate out of the tube, coming to a stop three feet behind the torpedo.

"It worked," Alex says with delight.

"The first step," I reply, as I work the controls to link Space Hawk One's sensors to the panel controllers. "And now the dance begins," I whisper, touching the install button on the panel controller.

One by one, each of the ten tractor panels use the space hawk's sensors as its eyes to find its designated attachment point on the torpedo. I sigh a breath of relief when the tenth finally snaps into place.

"You wrote the control code that did that?" Alex asks.

"Yeah, but it was more like a script, than a real program—just a series of high-level commands directing the panel and space hawk to work together in tandem."

"You say that like it's something simple, something anyone could do."

I tap behind my left ear. "Downloaded memory. Someone else had to endure all the training. I just inherited it."

"What does that feel like?" she asks.

"The download is nothing, a little tingling for a few seconds, nothing. The new skills can be a bit confusing if you try to access them on the first day. After that it's just natural, like I've always known how to do it. But…." I shrug.

"It bugs you because you don't feel like you developed the skill legitimately."

I look at Alex, whose compassionate eyes assuage the guilt I feel for having capabilities I did not earn on my own.

She smiles at me. "So, what's next?"

"The real test. Can the tractor plating independently move the torpedo?"

For today's test, we are going to move the torpedo to a lower orbit a thousand meters below our current one.

"Tractor One, engage."

Immediately, the torpedo slows, its orbit decaying because it no longer has the speed to maintain it. Our shuttle matches the maneuver dropping faster and faster as Neptune's gravity pulls it in. When it reaches the crossover point, the tractor accelerates, slowly increasing speed, reaching the speed required to hold the lower orbit just as we reach the desired altitude.

"Perfect," Alex exclaims.

"The tractor's propulsion is a lot less powerful than the shuttle's, so any shot will take longer to line up. But with enough controllers and crew, one war shuttle may be able to take eight simultaneous shots, making it an incredibly powerful weapon."

"Are we going to recover the tractor panels?" Alex asks.

"Not today. We can recover the torpedo with the tractor panels still in place. Given the time it takes, we will install the panels as part of the training program, so they are in place when we depart on mission. We can't fire the torpedo's jump drive with them on, so we'll need to practice removing it. But we'll want tractors installed on all the torpedoes before we depart on mission."

"Good plan," Alex agrees.

DEN, ESTATE HOUSE

Today's adventure was incredibly successful. I'll need to add the tractor functions to the simulators, but that's a job for another day. Four hours of tedious work and two and a half hours of total boredom have taken the wind from my sails.

Alex and I took dinner here tonight, savoring whatever it was the chef made, sharing a bottle of Cabernet, and watching the others run through their simulations. No one is particularly good yet. But everyone is getting hits against the enemy in the untimed simulations. We've still got seven weeks. I think we'll be ready enough by then.

Thelma catches my eye as she walks in through the open door. I get a big smile and her arms stretch out toward me.

"Hug her, then turn her over to me," Alex whispers.

I like Thelma and the warmth of her hug. But every day she seems a little clingier, and I'm ready to be done with her by the time she lets me go.

"Thelma?" Alex asks as she stands. "Could you help me with something?" She points toward the foyer and starts stepping that way before Thelma ensnares her.

As they exit, I wonder what Alex plans to do. I'd like to be a fly on the wall for that conversation.

A shout goes up from Larry, who apparently scored a hit on his first timed simulation. I turn to look and see him kissing Melissa, touched by the affection these two share.

As Melissa starts the next simulation, she says, "I'm going to beat your time."

I watch as she lays out her strategy for this attack and am concerned she's in much too close. I would never let her do this in real life. But it's the bet she's making for this simulation.

About halfway through her set up, one of the Dominion ships starts turning in her direction, then goes to FTL. She jumps out half a light year, leaving her weapon in place. Several minutes later, the Dominion ship drops from FTL close to where her ship was. It idles there for several minutes, then adjusts course towards Melissa's shuttle and, when aligned, goes to FTL. In an instant I see what she's doing. She's luring the ship to a place where her weapon is already aimed. Two more cat and mouse moves like this and her weapon jumps, then the simulation fails.

"What happened?" she cries out.

I go over to check the error log, then start laughing.

"What's so funny?" she asks, a smile forming.

"Your range was slightly off. The torpedo dropped from jump inside the dreadnaught. The simulator doesn't know how to score it."

As we laugh, a hand lands on my shoulder. It's Alex. "I told you that would eventually happen." The I-told-you-so tone of voice is perfect for the setting, but the sparkle in the eye that usually accompanies it is missing. Something is wrong.

She nods towards the door. "I'm going to head up."

"Be there in a minute," I reply.

As she turns to go, I reset the simulator. When it comes back up, I say good night and follow, wondering what's happened.

BEDROOM, ESTATE HOUSE

Alex took the stairs. I take the elevator, stepping out just as she is opening the bedroom door. She holds it for me, then as soon as the door clicks shut, she says, "You will not believe this."

"Start from the beginning."

As she slumps down into the love seat, I think she's going to cry.

"Alex, what's the matter?"

"You've noticed Thelma's not like the other AIs right? Lots of personality, really wants to be involved in things… Not matter-of-fact like Charlie, or as mechanical as To'Kana's design AI."

"Yeah. What about it?"

"All the Iknosan AIs have a function. Thelma is in a category that she calls *Comfort and Companionship*."

"What? I thought she was more like an assistant."

"She was given the assistant role after *The Reckoning*, something she's blocked from talking about. It apparently took place hundreds of years ago."

"She's that old?"

"Much older apparently. When she was first awakened, she was a physical therapist assigned to a fertility clinic. Sometime later, she was licensed as a fertility therapist, then a comfort therapist for families that could not conceive."

"What is a comfort therapist?"

"She says that information is blocked, but I think… I'll come back to that."

"Wait, a minute… You were going to talk with her about last night, right."

"I did. I told her that approaching strangers and asking if she can hug them was unacceptable behavior, unfitting of the human woman she is attempting to emulate."

"And how did she respond?"

"She said she didn't understand. All the women she's met here—me, Jill, and April—are of childbearing age and have men. All of us are past the midpoint of our fertile years, yet none of us has had a child. Therefore, we needed her help."

"And how was she going to help?"

"By collecting seed from our partners and implanting it in us. She claims to have been quite expert at getting Iknosan males to release it, and has studied human men enough to believe she would be effective here as well. She even asked me when she could collect from you."

I'm so shocked by this revelation, I don't know what to say.

Alex laughs. "You should see the look on your face."

"So how did you leave it with her?"

"I told her she was a member of our team now, not a fertility therapist, and if there was any more unsolicited touching, we would remove the holoprojection emitters in the main house."

"How did she take that?"

"She's down in the cellar sulking."

[06.05.2034] OFFICE, ESTATE HOUSE

Six weeks have passed since the night Thelma drove April and Ben away. As April predicted, Ben came back in. They've been out every weekend for at least one night and each has over forty hours on the simulator. And since her discussion with Alex, Thelma has been well behaved, but a lot less bubbly. It's as if she's sad she will not be allowed to return to her old line of work.

During the same period, I've added the tractor system to the simulator and tested it extensively. In truth, it's a mixed bag. The tractor grav-drives are weak, so the initial torpedo release has to be pretty close. But the AIs I've added to the controllers do a eighty-twenty job of predicting whether it is close enough in the simulation. The real world will be different, so the whole thing is a crap shoot, which is why we need to run the tests.

Yesterday, Colonel Jaiden Brock called to say he had three people ready to sign on if we still needed people. They were in the DC area and would be ready to transport in the morning if that could be arranged. Justin and Jill were in DC, so I sent three earpieces to them.

Earlier this morning, Jill coached them through the installation process.

"Kai? The Australian team is ready to transport. They have luggage that will need to be tagged. Can I send them tags?"

"No, they need to come first. We can get their things once we know they are staying."

A minute later, Thelma is back. "Would you like me to transport them to the foyer?"

"Hold for my signal."

I get up to exit the office and, fifteen seconds later, am in the foyer.

"You can transport them now."

A few seconds tick by then three of the most fit, sinuous people I've ever seen appear in front of me.

Colonel Jaiden Brock steps forward offering his hand. "Dr. Wimberly, pleasure to see you again, sir."

"And you, colonel."

"This is my partner, Megan Williams, a retired army nurse. We've been together for years. This will be one of the few missions in which we can deploy together. Next to her is one of my team leaders, Master Sergeant Alphons Blackman. Did we clear the transport test?"

"They are clear," Thelma answers as she walks into the foyer.

Brock looks toward the voice, then cocks his head. "You were the voice in my ear, but what are you now?"

"I am an AI. I will handle most of the communications and information gathering operations on this mission."

Brock turns his attention back to me. "Does that mean we can get our kits now?"

"How much stuff do you have?"

"Two duffels and two hard cases, plus a few extras each—a hundred kilos per person max."

"Why don't you select rooms first, then we can transport your stuff to your room?"

"Lead the way."

[06.09.2034] DINING ROOM, ESTATE HOUSE

The Australian team has been here four days now and have made incredible progress. Larry, Melissa, Alex, and I are still training four to six hours a day. Colonel Brock and his team have taken the rest.

But now, with the window closed for adding anyone else, I've called a team meeting.

"I have a simple agenda tonight," I announce as we settle around the dining room table. "I want to know your status. I want to know how ready you feel and what you think we might do to increase your preparedness. And I want to know what we've missed altogether. Let's start with the newbies. Team Australia?"

Colonel Brock is quick to respond. "One of the things you've missed altogether is the vocabulary. I've got command of War Shuttle #5? No way, mate. You can call it what you want, but our bird is the Boomerang."

"Boomerang?" I ask.

"It was the first fighter we built during World War II after the Japanese attack on Pearl Harbor."

"Got it. Does anyone else claim a name for their war shuttle?"

"Enterprise," Justin calls out.

Larry follows suit. "Relentless."

"Relentless?" I ask.

"Trust me," Melissa replies.

"Predator," Ben calls out.

I see April nodding, so don't ask. "Mac? Ty?"

The two whisper back and forth for a bit, then shout in tandem, "Freedom."

I turn to Alex.

She looks at me in a way I haven't seen before, like hope and despair rolled up into one gaze. "Challenger," she whispers.

"That name comes with a lot of baggage."

"Sally Ride," she answers. "The first woman in space."

"Wasn't the Challenger the one that blew up? Christa McAuliffe, the school teacher?"

"On its tenth and final mission. On its second, a woman went to space."

"Remember both," Larry pipes up.

"More followed," Alex continues. "It all happened before either of us were born. I learned about it in middle school, and it inspired me to be more than what was expected of me."

"Then Challenger it is," I affirm. "What else have I missed?"

"Beer!" Master Sergeant Alphons Blackman bellows.

Caught off guard, I realize how deeply I've been sucked into Justin's world. A beer, if necessary, when sucked into a swarthy situation. Champagne when celebrating.

Thankfully, the server watching the room jumps into action. "Shall I wheel in the kegerator?"

"Please," I answer, catching Justin's caustic eye.

In truth, I lose control of the room for several, well, more like twenty minutes, as beer is wheeled in, more non-mission-centric suggestions are offered, and finally all the interested served.

"Next!" I shout, finally gaining everyone's attention. "I want the mission status of each team. I'll start. Alex and I..."

"Team Challenger," Alex clarifies.

"Team Challenger," I affirm, "Has completed all thirty of the required simulations, and a dozen..."

"Fourteen," Alex clarifies.

"...fourteen more," I finish.

"One half of Team Enterprise," Jill starts, looking askance at Justin, "has completed all the requirements plus a dozen more. The other is still two simulations short."

I can tell Justin is a little pissed to be outed like this, but he shrugs. "I'll finish those this weekend."

I look to Team Freedom next.

Ty answers. "We've both completed the thirty required and have split the rest between us. I think we have a shot at all of them, but will yield simulator time as necessary."

"Predator?" I ask.

"We are still a few short," April replies.

The way she eyes Ben, I suspect he is the one that's fallen short.

Before I have a chance to ask, Melissa chimes in. "Team Relentless is the same. One side has completed the minimum. Thankfully, the other is... relentless."

Her words trigger laughter among the rest of us.

Last, I look to our newcomers, Team Boomerang.

Colonel Brock stands. "Laudable that the rest of you are trying to do it all yourselves. We don't do it that way. We're quite capable of specializing and putting our lives in the hands of our teammates. Amongst us, we have completed twenty-two of the required simulations. Given the simulator time that has been granted, all three of us will complete all forty simulations with numerous additional repeats. It is the power of the team that matters. If at least one of us has mastered each lesson, we will be the most prepared."

I love the colonel's bravado but doubt its integrity. Nonetheless, none of the rest of us have his scores at this point in the competition, so none of us challenge it.

[06.12.2034] OFFICE, ESTATE HOUSE

It's one week to D-Day. Yeah, yeah, yeah... That label has been claimed before. It started as test day, then morphed to experiment day, then deliverance day. T-Day? E-Day? Neither stuck. D-Day? It stuck before the guffawing finished.

Mac, Ty, Jill, Melissa, Alex, and I have qualified. The Australian team is claiming they're there. Justin is still struggling with the last two simulations, the math and physics tripping him up. All five teams have calibrated their jump drives and installed tractors on all eight torpedoes. So the truth of the matter is all eleven of us are going to go whether the last *i* is dotted or *t* crossed.

April and Ben transported in yesterday with a surprise on her finger—they got engaged. The Department of Defense gave April two weeks unpaid leave, so they are here until we return. True to his word, Justin put her on our payroll for these two weeks.

Justin and Jill flew out yesterday and are here for the duration as well. The house is nearly full, and the competition for time on the simulators and the best scores fills it with energy.

CHAPTER 20: CONFRONTATION

[06.19.2034] CELLAR, ESTATE HOUSE

Colonel Jaiden Brock and partner Megan Williams are the first to step onto the transporter, followed closely by Master Sergeant Alphons Blackman. Both men have donned their Royal Australian Air Force flight suits, despite the fact this operation is not sponsored by their government. I'm still amazed these three signed on only two weeks ago yet have the top three scores in the simulations.

"Thelma," Colonel Brock says with full command voice. "Three to transport up to War Shuttle *Boomerang*."

A moment later the distinctive hum of the transporter sounds, and the team disappears without heeding my advice to close their eyes.

"Transport complete," Thelma says.

As Larry and Melissa step up onto the platform, the colonel's voice comes through my ear. "The crew has boarded War Shuttle *Boomerang*. Beginning launch preparations. Brock out."

Once in the center of the platform, Larry looks at Melissa. "You ready for this adventure, Lizzy?" But before she answers, he wraps his arms around her, then gives her a full mouth kiss. She responds, then breaks it off with a slap on the arm. "That can wait until we're back."

As most of us laugh, they take their positions, then Melissa says, "Beam us up, Thelma."

I've known Larry most of my life. I've always seen him as a friendly, diligent man who did his job and anything else that needed doing. I would never have guessed how playful this seventy-something year old man was with his ten-year-younger wife.

Ben and April are next, hopping up onto the platform as soon as the shield enclosing it drops. "Edwards and McDonald prepared for transport. Please initiate."

Mac and Ty go just as quickly.

"Guess that makes it our turn," Justin whispers.

Despite the words, there is no movement. Then he turns, and offers his hand. "A pleasure serving with you, Admiral Wimberly."

We shake, then Jill takes his hand and leads him up to the transporter. They mount the steps, then walk slowly to the center, where they stop to kiss. A moment later, they take their positions. Then Jill looks at Thelma. "Two to transport up to the *Enterprise*."

She nods to Thelma, who returns the gesture.

I still marvel at how human Thelma has become in the few months she has lived with us.

As soon as the transporter clears, Alex leans into me. "Time to roll." She jogs over to the platform and leaps up onto it, beauty in motion. "Let's do this thing!"

WAR SHUTTLE CHALLENGER

I open my eyes just in time to see our pilot-AI Charlie's holographic avatar take form.

"Welcome aboard, Captain Wimberly. The other war shuttles report that their crews have arrived and are ready to begin our mission."

"Thank you, Charlie. Thelma has uploaded our course?"

"She has, sir." A star map showing the course appears on the main view screen. "I and the other war shuttle pilots have validated the course and agree with the jump sequence. We are ready to depart on your order, sir."

"All hands, prepare for departure. Please acknowledge that you are ready," I broadcast to our six war shuttles.

As I take my seat, the replies come in one by one. Alex, seated next to me, is the last to confirm.

"Please engage, Charlie."

"Course engaged, sir."

"How long until the first jump?"

"Just over an hour, sir. Would you like me to display the mission timer and countdown clock on the main display, sir?"

"Please."

A mission timer pops up in the display, showing mission time at 00:00:18 ticking up and the time to jump at 01:03:22 ticking down.

"So, we have an hour to kill," Alex says. "We won't have a problem with our earpieces when we jump, will we?"

"You installed the earpiece I gave you last night?"

"I did."

"Then you are good. The problem last time was that we were connected to To'Kana's ship. Now, each crew is connected to their shuttle. The shuttles are connected back to the hub in the cellar. They have the buffering to manage the disruption related to jump and the phase-related issues associated with subspace."

"Good. I wouldn't want to go through what you did last time."

As we settle in for the long wait, I close my eyes to better envision the timeline chart.

Charlie's voice wakes me. "Five minutes to transition."

How in the world did I fall asleep?

"I see you've rejoined the living," Alex snipes.

I shake my head and blink my eyes.

Alex reaches over to tickle me. "Wake up, sleepy boy," she taunts. "You lasted like ten minutes." The statement is followed by a laugh.

"It's hard sitting around doing nothing."

"Is this really going to work?" Alex asks.

"The mission? If the Dominion are who we think they are, then yes, I think it will work. If we have grossly underestimated them, then no, probably not."

"Think the calibration will hold?"

"The assumption is yes. If we run into problems, then we recalibrate. We are betting on the Iknosan technology to perform as advertised. The vast majority of it has. Are you worried?"

We lock eyes for a moment, then Alex says, "I'm not ready to lose you."

"Jump commencing in three, two, one, arrived," Charlie announces. "Calculating position."

"Just like last time," Alex comments. "I thought I'd feel something jumping this far. But I got nothing. Absolutely nothing."

I share her bafflement. But the math says we didn't move, space-time did. According to To'Kana, quantum time and quantum gravity require the universe to repaint itself every ten to the minus twenty-third seconds. Without external interference, it repaints us in accordance with Newton and Einstein. But with the intervention of our jump drive, it can repaint us anywhere else we want.

"Correcting calibration," Charlie announces.

"How far off were we?"

Charlie sighs.

It seems all our alien AIs are taking on human characteristics.

"Approximately three-hundred parts per million. Nowhere near as good as the return flight we made during calibration. The two jumps we did inside the system detuned us," he reports.

My first reaction is to cheer. Then I remember, we jumped a thousand light years, meaning we missed our target by something like... "We missed by a third of a light year!"

"Afraid so," Charlie answers.

"How did the other ships do?"

There's no answer, then, as the silence stretches out, I ask, "What's the matter?"

When there's still no answer, I ask again. "Charlie, what's the matter?"

A moment later, he answers. "We seem to have arrived early."

"Not again," I complain.

"Looks like six hours, twenty minutes."

"I thought you couldn't know."

"We figured out a way to beat the time paradox issue."

"How?"

"Twenty-four hours before scheduled departure, we establish a new link and start a one second timer counting. Although the particles are quantum entangled, the source is write-only, the recipient is read-only. When we fall into the past, we reconnect and find out what time it is there and know how long we need to wait."

"We should conserve energy," Alex says. "Over six hours have been added to our day. We need to be fresh when we rejoin real time. And we have limited air and water, limited food. I think we should take a nap."

I nod. "You're right. Charlie, we are going to our quarters. Please alert us if anything happens, or when we are ten minutes from real time."

"Yes, sir."

Alex leads the way back, going straight for my cabin. She opens the door, then motions me in. A second later, the door is closed, the lock engaged, and Alex catapults past me, landing gracefully in my bed.

"You coming?"

I kick off my shoes and lumber up the ladder, then roll in, landing on my back. A moment later, she rolls onto me, an arm over my chest, her leg over mine like it was on that first day, only this time fully clothed.

"No play, just rest," she whispers, then places her head on my shoulder.

Maybe long journeys through space won't be so bad after all.

...

Alex jostles me awake as she gets out of bed. "Charlie just called. We are ten minutes out. I'm going to straighten myself up in my room. You need to at least comb your hair."

"Got it," I say, as the lock disengages, then she's gone.

...

I arrive on the bridge before Alex does.

"Charlie, status update."

"Two more minutes until we connect with Thelma. Once I have the exact time, I can complete the recalibration. I should have realized the in-system jumps would do this. It was part of my inherited training, but like all inherited memories, it's not part of you until it is used."

"Charlie, how old are you?"

"I'm not sure I know the correct answer. I was brought online on February 2, 2034, awake and self-aware for several hours, then shut down. I was brought back up for four days on March 20, 2034, then dropped into idle mode. I was reactivated on April 26, the day we did the in-system jumps. I've been active since then."

"So, you were less than a week old the day we jumped out to Neptune and back?"

"I think that is a fair statement, sir."

"I'm told that Thelma is quite old. Do you know if that is true?"

"It is, sir. Her registration dates back to the twelve hundreds."

"Can all AIs live that long?"

"No, sir. I am part of this ship. It is my body. When this ship is destroyed, I will be destroyed as well."

"Don't they back you up?"

"Not in the sense you imply, sir. My stacks, the logic and personality portions of my data that make me who I am, are not backed up, they are too large. Only my memories are backed up. Worthy memories are replicated, and the replica is depersonalized and spread to other AIs within my category."

As I think about what's just been revealed to me, Charlie perks up. "Real time reestablished. Calculating calibration adjustments."

Over the *Challenger's* comm system, Thelma's voice rings out. "Kai, are you alright? Is your war shuttle operational? You are a third of a light year off course."

"We figured that out. We arrived over six hours ago."

"You didn't recalibrate after your in-system jumps?"

"No. I didn't know that was a problem, and Charlie was only seven days old at the time and had not accessed that bit of his training yet."

"Hmm," Thelma replies, sounding a lot like my mother. "This entire group of AIs is young, and it's a much bigger problem on the battlecruisers than on the war shuttles. I'll work with the other AIs to come up with a quick start refresher that stimulates their inherited training."

"How did the other shuttles do?"

"All within a hundred thousand kilometers of each other."

"Charlie, how soon before we can jump back to the others?"

"It will be quicker and use less propellant to meet them at the second rendezvous point. There are no gravity wells in the area large enough for the grav-drive to use."

"Thelma, do you concur?"

"I do."

"Please update the other five shuttles."

"Will do, Kai," she replies, then the line drops.

"Charlie, plot the revised course. Let me know when we are ready to get underway."

"Will do, sir."

"Now we wait," Alex complains.

I relax back into my seat and shut my eyes to think. The next jump will put us about two hundred light years from the Harza home world. From there, the plan is to scatter—one shuttle each to six of the Harza colony worlds—to collect information. We all agree that this is the weakest part of our plan. But it was the best option of those we considered.

"Captain," Charlie says. "The new course has been laid in. It will take eighteen minutes to obtain alignment for jump." A vibration pulses through the shuttle. "The ion-drive has been primed. Ready to depart on your order."

"Engage."

"Starting burn," Charlie replies.

A second later, Alex and I are pushed back in our seats.

"Wasn't expecting that," Alex says. "It would have knocked me over if I'd been standing."

"Charlie, is the inertial dampening not working?"

"It is at max, sir. It auto calibrates with the grav-drive, but we never calibrated it to work with the ion-drive."

"Add that to the list of calibration activities for new crews."

"Added, sir."

Motivated by the immediacy of the next step in our plan, I pull out my data pad.

"What's on your mind?" Alex asks.

"I don't like our divide-and-conquer approach to information gathering."

Alex smiles. "This problem again. Isn't it a little late to be looking for another option?"

"It's a pretty low bar. There's got to be something obvious we just haven't seen yet."

"There was the outpost option we dismissed before researching it," Alex reminds.

"Can't do much research in the fifteen minutes we have left. Let's revisit the To'Kana option instead."

From the look I get, I can tell Alex thinks this is a waste of time.

"Thelma?"

"What can I do for you, Kai?"

"Is there any chance we could contact To'Kana once we drop from jump?"

"Only if he invites us. I haven't checked his log this morning. But you are about to jump now. The others are a minute behind you. I'll check the log once you've all jumped."

"Thank you, Thelma."

When the line drops, I ask Charlie, "Where did my fifteen minutes go?"

"Ion-drive calibration issue—we got a lot more thrust than expected. I've already added it to the list."

"I hope we don't have the same problem with the weapon systems," Alex snipes.

Although the comment was directed at me, Charlie replies, "The weapon systems were fully calibrated, ma'am. We had the equipment and To'Kana had bots with weapon calibration credentials."

"Thank you, Charlie," Alex replies.

Seconds later, the jump countdown starts.

"We have arrived," Charlie announces. "The star we targeted is within visual range, and we are within one second of real time. Excellent recalibration."

Minutes pass, then Thelma's voice sounds in my ear. "Kai, we have a problem. The Relentless didn't jump. The issue is with its jump sequencer."

"Estimated time to repair?"

"Kai, they cannot repair it, but that is not our only problem."

"Tell me."

"I just checked To'Kana's personal log. There's been a miscalculation, which has led to a catastrophic intelligence failure. One hundred twenty Dominion dreadnoughts dropped from FTL in a Harza outpost system, ten light years away from their home world. The outpost was destroyed."

"When did this happen?"

"Hard to say. I don't have direct communications with Captain To'Kana, just backdoor read-only access to a couple of his databases. From the references I have, I would guess yesterday or the day before. But that's not the important part."

"Go on."

"Instead of changing course for the Harza home world, the Dominion are scooping up massive amounts of gas from the system's only gas giant. To'Kana believes they are refueling for a long journey and are going straight to Earth, bypassing the Harza home world."

A thousand thoughts run through my mind, not the least of which is, *And you stole our materials!*

"Kai." Thelma's voice is back in my ear. "You have forty deadly weapons. You could hurt the Dominion more than they've ever been hurt before, then run. The Dominion will give chase, which would allow you to deliver them to the Harza, then jump back to Earth. I doubt the Harza can stop that many, but between us, we will have significantly thinned the pack. That will give us a little over four months to build more war shuttles and weapons."

"But what about Larry and Melissa?" I ask without thinking.

"Kai, if we don't hurt the Dominion now, they will destroy the Earth, and Larry and Melissa will be no more alive back on Earth than they will be if stranded in space. Your priority must be hurting the Dominion now and leading them to the Harza. Once the Harza are engaged, we can send someone to rescue Larry and Melissa. But your priority must be to race home and prepare for the Dominion onslaught that will follow."

"Agreed. Plot a course to take us within two light years of the Dominion."

UNKNOWN BROWN DWARF

Although the Dominion undoubtedly know of the brown dwarf whose system we are transiting through, they would be unlikely to be looking here or sensing our tiny shuttles at this distance. We, on the other hand, just jumped six of our Space Hawk surveillance drones into high orbit around the gas giant they are mining and have an excellent view of them.

I've called a virtual team meeting to plan an attack.

"Look how arrogant they are," April McDonald, the intelligence analyst from DOD, says. "They must think they're invincible. One hundred twenty ships all lined up in a low orbit, sucking up gas. I say one torpedo each, right up the tailpipe, as close to simultaneous as we can make it."

"How?" I ask.

"May I?" Colonel Brock asks.

April nods her approval.

"They are in a low orbit, which gives us multiple advantages. The planet blocks their view of most of its orbital space, making it easy for us to get into orbit undetected. They are too deep in the planet's gravity well to engage their FTL drives, making it difficult for them to escape once our attack begins."

"How do you recommend we use these advantages?" I ask.

"I'm thinking in terms of a multi-prong attack. One ship approaching from behind, as April suggested. But this would need to be a slightly lower orbit because we would need to be moving faster."

April cuts in. "We could accomplish the same thing using a more eccentric elliptical orbit."

"Fair enough," the colonel replies. "A similar option would be to plant another ship in front of them in a higher orbit, picking them off as they come over the horizon."

"How would we get a shuttle in front of them without being seen?"

Although the question is asked of the colonel, Jill raises her hand.

"Jill?"

"We jump into the system on the other side of the planet and establish a higher orbit. Higher orbits have less angular velocity. All we need to do is sit there and wait until they come over the horizon behind us."

I nod my head. "You used that approach in one of your simulations, didn't you?"

"Yes. It's a killer. By the time they know you are there, the torpedo will have jumped."

Ty raises his hand.

"Ty?"

"I'm worried about this option. The simulator counted it as a hit, but our torpedoes are fundamentally kinetic weapons, and I don't think there is enough speed difference to deliver a penetrating punch."

Other hands go up, but I take this one. "I think Ty is right. We need a speed difference of something like one-hundred kilometers per second. Can someone run down the math on that?"

"I will," Ty volunteers. "Calculating impact force was part of my training as a weapons specialist. But can I raise another issue first?"

"Go."

"Both of the coming-over-the-horizon shots have issues associated with them. Our line of fire will be nearly parallel with the dreadnaught's course, giving us a minimum exposure shot on both bow and stern. But of the two, the bow is the worst. Its curvature is likely to deflect the torpedo's penetrator unless it hits at a right angle, give-or-take fifteen degrees."

Mac's hand has been up, so I go to him next.

"We've speculated for a while now that the stern of the Dominion dreadnaughts is vulnerable. With this much gravity to work with, we could test that theory with a Space Hawk on a hyperbolic trajectory. It doesn't have the mass or density of a torpedo. But we could make up some of the difference with speed."

Justin's hand goes up with some urgency.

"Is this related to Mac's point?" I ask.

"It is."

"Go."

"As much as I like the idea of a tail shot, it is a much smaller target. Given the uncertainty of our calibration, maybe we should take the broadside shot for which the weapon was designed. I would also think we want to take our shot from the closest range viable, coming in from one of the poles on a hyperbolic trajectory, only coming into visible range minutes before impact and dropping stealth when we jump away."

"We would only get one shot off," April complains.

"Better five shots, five hits, than forty shots, no hits," Justin comes back. "And another strategic point..."

I hold up my hand as April starts a retort. "Justin, your strategic point?"

"We won't be able to use this sneak-up-from-behind-while-refueling-tactic in the defense of Earth. I would propose the following priorities. Our top priority for this encounter is to get the Dominion to divert to the Harza, who are more prepared for this fight than we are. Our second priority is to learn to use our weapons, and to get enough shots in that we learn to use them effectively. Third priority... Kill Dominion ships."

Justin triggers lots of talk, which quickly gets out of control.

"One at a time," I shout, then point to Ty. "You first, then Alex. Then shuttle by shuttle: Predator, Boomerang, Challenger, Enterprise.

"I agree with the priorities, and would like to suggest one more option," Ty says.

"Go."

"Our theory is that the stern is vulnerable. It seems confirmed, given that the last ship in line is orbiting with its bow pointing back from where it came. Our Space Hawks, with their powerful grav-drives, can move really fast. Therefore, I think we should kamikaze one into the tail of one of those ships to prove or disprove the theory. I agree with Justin on priorities, but this is a simple test that could change our tactics when we defend Earth."

"Valid point. I'll take it into consideration," I reply. "Alex?"

"I agree with Justin, but would really like to rack up eight kills."

Ben, the pilot of the Predator, lets April go before him.

"At one level, I agree with Justin. Our top priority is to lead the Dominion to the Harza. Next is to learn to use our weapons. Where I differ regards simultaneous attack. I'm concerned that we will face one hundred or more ships at Earth, even if we kill all these. That seems to be their conquest number. We know of ten of their ships that have been destroyed, but here they are back up to strength."

I note the heads nodding in the holoprojection.

"I make the following assertion. Unless we are going to have twice their number, we need to figure out how to make a simultaneous attack. Therefore, as part of priority two, at least one of us should try a simultaneous attack with four or more of our torpedoes."

As conversation ripples around the virtual table, April raises her hand. "I have a related recommendation when it's my turn again."

"Let's hear it now."

"Let Ben and I try an eight-way attack. Once it's done, we will jump back to attempt a rescue of the crew of the Relentless, gathering its weapons, then setting it on a sub-light plunge into the closest star."

"Request noted," I reply.

The Boomerang is next, the colonel speaking for his people. "I agree with April, but propose the Boomerang be the ship attempting the eight shots. We have more people and, in the simulations, had the best times and the most kills."

"Also noted," I reply.

By the time we make it around the table, the consensus is clear.

"Justin's proposed priorities with April's addendum are accepted. You each have two hours to file your attack plan. File the attack your team wants to make. We'll meet back here in two hours to set the timeline. And, April, your rescue proposal is tentatively approved.

GAS GIANT, HARZA OUTPOST SYSTEM

The timing of this attack is incredibly tricky, and for the Predator, who has the longest set-up, it will be incredibly dangerous. Our five operational war shuttles are now in position to start their attack runs. Strike time will be exactly three hours from the attack order. Justin and Jill on the Enterprise will engage a hyperbolic trajectory coming down over the north pole. Their torpedo will be traveling at a relative speed of well over one hundred meters per second when it makes impact. It will be a purely kinetic attack that does not use the jump drive and tests the impact power of the penetrator, which will hit a fraction of a second after the shield killing weapon, before its laser has had a significant heating effect. They will target the first ship in the line.

Ty and Mac aboard Freedom will make a similar attack at a much lower speed. Like the Enterprise's attack, the weapon will not use its jump drive, coming up over the horizon at a speed similar to torpedoes that have jumped. They will target the last ship in the line.

Alex and I, on the Challenger, will try the bread'n'butter shot for which this weapon was designed: taken from medium range, the torpedo jumping to a position ten seconds from its target, then ballistic flight while the shield killing weapon and laser soften up the target for penetrator impact. The calculations are tricky because of the targets' low orbit, but this is the shot our torpedo was designed to make, which means ours will be the most honest test of the weapon's design.

Colonel Brock, on the Boomerang, and Ben and April, aboard the Predator, will each attempt to set up eight shots similar to the ones Alex and I are making, but from a greater distance. Brock, confident he can use the tractor system to align his torpedoes, will drop his from within the star's jump limit. April plans to operate from further out, using her shuttle as the primary guidance system. These shots require incredible precision because of the distance, which will increase their exposure to enemy fire, because of the time it takes to lineup each torpedo. I laud the determination and courage of both these teams. If it was me trying to set up eight simultaneous hits, none would hit. I hope these two have it figured out.

Alex, my weapons officer, and Megan, the Boomerang's, will each attempt a tail shot using a Space Hawk.

All our shuttles will jump out of the system moments before or after impact.

With everyone confirmed ready, I set the strike time, then issue the order.

...

Two boring hours have passed. The Challenger is in position several million kilometers above the orbital plane of the gas giant, falling toward it on the trajectory required. Charlie has been making tiny corrections every ten minutes or so, but in this position, the wind coming off the system's star is less consistent than in the solar system. I wouldn't be surprised if we continued making minor adjustments right up to the point of jump. Alex's Space Hawk is protected by the planet and its magnetic field, so is totally unaffected by the star's wind.

April has five of her torpedoes lined up, ready to jump. She thinks she has a shot at all eight. I'm skeptical but rooting for her, anyway. She's out far enough that the star's wind isn't relevant, but she is above the dark side of the planet, protected from the worst of it.

Earlier she asked me to check her calculations and confirm her trajectories. Both are good—calculations triple confirmed, trajectory within the margin of error of our measurements. Which confirms what we already thought. Her biggest risks of failure are measurement precision and jump calibration.

Colonel Brock, on the other hand, has done something none of us understood until we saw it playing out. He lined up for a shot at a dreadnaught in the middle of the eight he was targeting. Then, he dropped stealth long enough to drop all eight of his torpedoes and his seven remaining Space Hawks. As soon as his weapons were away, he went back into stealth, his exposure to the enemy lasting barely five minutes. Over the last hour, his team used their tractors to get all eight of his torpedoes aligned with their targets and using his Space Hawks and their powerful sensor suites to fine tune the alignment.

"Reminds me of Afghanistan," Alex complains for the Nth time. "Hours spent waiting for the bad guys to show up in the wrong places."

Once again on the verge of nodding off, I get up and walk around the shuttle's small bridge.

At the fifteen-minute point, I call all the crews together to check status. Larry and Melissa join, complaining that they are missing out on all the action.

"Is anyone else worried that this is too easy?" Alex asks. "Every now and again, I get a glimpse of one of you on my Space Hawk's sensors. I know that you're here and know where you are, which gives the glimpse more meaning. But are the Dominion's sensors really that bad? Are they that incurious? Or is something else going on here that we haven't discovered?"

That Alex is the one registering the complaint worries me. In Afghanistan, the accuracy of her premonitions of danger were uncanny.

"Eyes open everybody," I order. "Charlie, anything unusual on your sensors?"

"Sir?" Charlie asks. "I've only been on active duty for a month or two. There are many things in our sensor readings that were not part of my inherited training."

In an instant, I realize we've been done in, working with infant AIs that don't understand the difference between what they've been taught and what the universe holds."

"Charlie, what's the biggest difference between what you see and what you know?"

"There is a massive disturbance at the edge of this system, one unrecorded by humans or Iknosan. I cannot describe it because it does not exist within my databases."

Expletives of every genre pass through my mind. I'm out in the middle of nowhere with children that know nothing of the evils of our galaxy.

"OK. Get all the AIs involved. Everyone scan the disturbance at the edge of the system."

Acknowledgments ripple around the virtual table. Then I turn back to Charlie. "Put the disturbance readings up on the main view screen."

I see what he's talking about immediately. There's a churning white cloud shaped like the Amazon smile, but without the arrow on the end. *Could that be the leading edge of a ship dropping from FTL?*

I walk up to the holoprojection and trace around the cloud.

"Charlie, send a copy of this image to Thelma."

"Copy sent, sir."

"Thelma?"

"Here, Kai."

"Can you do a visual search on the image Charlie just sent you? Every database you can get a hold of."

"As you request, Kai."

"Charlie, how far away is this thing? And how quickly is it approaching?"

"It is thirty light years wide, two-thousand light years away, approaching at less than one percent of light speed."

The anxiety of minutes ago vanishes in an instant.

"Kai, I found your cloud on the human internet. It is called the Local Interstellar Cloud. The sun has been passing through it now for approximately ten thousand years and is currently emerging from it. According to Wikipedia, we will be clear of the cloud in less than two-thousand years."

I hear April McDonald laughing in the still open conference call. "Maybe next time, we should bring someone along who knows something about space."

Alex's hand touches my arm. "Kai, I think we may have found something."

"Charlie, put the conference line back on the main screen."

"Let me share," Alex requests.

A second later something unexpected pops up. A fleet of ships that look like submarines without the conning mast, dropping from FTL one by one, headed straight for the line of Dominion dreadnaughts we are targeting.

"Charlie, send this to Thelma as well."

"Beat you to it," Alex says. "They are Harza warships."

An automated alarm goes off, "Five minutes to strike time."

Alex continues, "According to data Thelma has recovered from To'Kana's ship, the Harza have jump-drive weapons and superluminal scanners. That means they could know we are here and could be targeting us as we speak."

"Who has torpedoes that still need adjustment?" I ask.

"I do," April says.

"We can continue all operations remotely," Colonel Brock replies.

"I need to ride this all the way in," Justin responds.

"We need to ride our torpedo to the jump point," Ty and Mac say at the same time.

I shake my head. "Every second we remain, we risk an attack from the Harza. We need to live to fight another day. Everyone, abandon torpedoes that need adjustment. Jump out now! No delay."

In truth, I doubt the order will be followed, so I punctuate it by jumping my shuttle out.

"Charlie, one light year jump."

In an instant, Challenger is out of harms' way. Freedom and Boomerang jump seconds later. But Justin in the Enterprise and April on the Predator are still on approach.

"Justin, get out of there!" I order.

"In a second Kai. I'm still invisible. I think I can jump my torpedo in a couple more seconds."

"All torpedoes aligned. Jumping," April announces.

"Jill, get your ship out of there!" I order. "If you hit early, none of the Predator's torpedoes will hit."

"Jumping," she replies.

I sigh a breath of relief as the Enterprise disappears from the brown dwarf system and reappears in interstellar space, a light year from its previous position. Looking at my hand I realize it's trembling.

"Sir, we have been followed," Charlie announces.

"Jump again, then hard to port and jump again."

In an instant, we're gone, then I'm slammed into my seat as the ship's powerful ion drive kicks in.

"Turning to port," Charlie says.

On the main view screen, I see our path curving—five, six, seven degrees.

"Nose down," I order.

I count to five, then add. "Jump."

The thrust from the ion drive bleeds away, then we jump.

"Repeat. Nose down hard starboard."

As the thrust pushes me back in my seat, Charlie says, "Sir, we are coming into alignment with a star."

"Adjust to avoid, then jump."

"Kai," Alex says. "We are burning an incredible amount of propellant."

"How long until we are clear to jump?" I ask Charlie.

"Ten seconds, sir."

"Kai, we need to hold course after this jump, or we'll lose the tail-pipe strike."

On the main screen, the seconds to jump finish their countdown, then we are away.

"Charlie, figure out where we are relative to the other war shuttles. And put Alex's Space Hawk on the main screen."

The nose camera view from the Space Hawk shows the gas giant below, its variations in color and density visibly moving. Straight ahead, the star field slowly moves because of the Space Hawk's arching hyperbolic trajectory. The first ship will come into view ten seconds before impact. Alex nods toward the countdown timer, which shows eighteen seconds remaining.

"Three, two, one, there it is..." The word stretches out. "We're coming in too low. Space Hawk One, correct to target."

It's all I can do to stay seated as the course adjusts.

"We've got it. We've got it." Alex shouts as the drone comes into alignment.

Two, one. My internal count down finishes as the screen goes blank.

"Charlie, display the system map for the target system. Zoom in on the ship we just hit."

From the distance of our surveillance drone nothing seems to have happened.

"I have a better image," Charlie says as he switches.

"She's apparently lost power," Alex points at the ship's odd angle. "It's rotating clockwise, its bow ten or more degrees above its orbital plane."

"There is also a small deviation from its orbit," Charlie adds.

As the ship continues to rotate, a cloud of debris and atmosphere becomes visible. Minutes later, the mangled stern comes into view.

Suddenly the image on the main screen shifts and zooms out. The entire line of dreadnaughts coming into view.

Alex points, "April hit one."

"Charlie, do we have a recording of that ship getting hit?"

"Here it is from just before the jump, eighty thousand kilometers out. This was taken from the weapon's nose camera."

An image of space shows up on the main display screen, a tiny dot under the cross hairs in the middle.

"Jumping in three, two, one. Arrived."

As Charlie says *arrived*, the tiny dot expands to fill the screen, the crosshairs slightly forward of middle and above the center line. A second later the image shakes as the shield killing weapon is expelled. Another second later, it hits, and the shimmering glow of the dreadnaught's shield vanishes. The weapon's laser lights up, illuminating a spot on the hull. Within seconds, an intense red dot appears and starts to grow. Seconds tick by, and I worry the Dominion will fire their weapons at us. As I hold my breath, the ship rushes toward us, then the image disappears.

"Here is a remote view of the impact," Charlie says. "This is blown up enough that it's grainy."

The scene repeats. Other than the angle and graininess, it goes exactly the same way until the point of impact. This time we see the body of the torpedo shear away and bounce off the ship like the shavings from a pencil sharpener. Then the ship shudders. In slow motion, the impact ripples from the center to the ends and back multiple times. Anything touching a surface inside that ship must have been shattered or liquified. What a devastating weapon we have created.

"Eight more hits!" Charlie shouts with all the enthusiasm of a football fan whose team makes the winning touchdown. "Brock's timing was off but all eight of his targets are down."

"Anyone with a Space Hawk in the battle zone and a viable tail pipe shot, take it," I order.

"We have another tail pipe hit," Charlie exclaims, putting the image on the main viewscreen.

All I see is a massive debris field slowly expanding.

"Can you rewind to just before impact?"

The image resets showing a dreadnaught with its ion drive at full power. In a flash, a Space Hawk arcs in, entering the ion trail inches from its source. An instant later, the dreadnaught shudders, an explosion of debris shooting out the back. Then its hull cracks open.

"We have another, and another," Charlie shouts like a sports announcer.

As the Dominion ships scatter, the vulnerability of their low orbit becomes clear as they crawl away from the planet, and over the next fifteen minutes we get four opportunistic Space Hawk kills.

"Kai," Thelma's voice comes through my ear. "Are you OK? You got disconnected from the system. Everyone is worried you were lost."

"We're fine. Got chased by a Harza ship, but we escaped."

"Let me connect you with Captain To'Kana."

To'Kana's image appears on our main view screen. Standing next to him is a uniformed person, presumably a Harza, twice as tall as To'Kana. Its head reminds me of a cat's—thick lustrous fur, intelligent oval eyes, flat nose, wide mouth, pointed ears. It's amazing to see a humanoid creature whose body is proportioned like a human's, but whose head resembles a cat's.

"Kyle Wimberly. Meet Admiral Kotosoba of the Harza Space Force."

He bows to me. I mimic the gesture. "Admiral. A pleasure to meet you."

The sounds that come back are completely unintelligible to me as speech, but captioned words on the screen appear.

"Welcome human to Harza outpost Gamma. Your tiny ships are fast, agile, and deadly. We welcome you as an ally."

I swallow as I realize that I have just made first contact with a third alien species without having obtained permission from the relevant government authorities. Congress is going to have another heyday with me.

"Kyle Wimberly, your actions today have thrown the Dominion fleet into chaos. Eighteen of the Dominion dreadnaughts were killed, despite the hulls of eleven of them being mostly intact. Two others were mortally wounded, power and propulsion destroyed. They have failed to mount a defense, and, at this point, we have killed nearly half their fleet."

"Will you get them all?"

The admiral responds this time, and it takes effort not to cringe at the alien sounds coming from him.

About the time he finishes, the captioning starts. "The Dominion has shown themselves for the cowards they are—merciless when attacking lessor species, whimpering and pleading when confronted by a superior force. Many have run, but our ships are giving chase. With the superior propulsion system that the Iknosan have provided us, few of the cowards will survive."

"Thank you," I reply simply, not really knowing what to say.

The admiral starts again. "We owe you two debts of thanks. First, for the materials your people sent us that enabled the creation of our fleet. Second, for breaking the will of our enemy on the eve of our second encounter. We took grievous losses in the first battle."

There is silence for a second.

"I am glad we could collaborate."

As a third series of words start flowing, I see To'Kana smile.

The caption that follows strikes fear in my heart.

"We invite you aboard our ship to watch the close of the battle and join in a feast of celebration."

Privately To'Kana sends. "Kyle Wimberly. You must accept this invitation. Their food is gamy. The odors aboard strong. The language hard on the ear. But the Harza are lovely people once you get to know them. Very compassionate. I can give you pills to dull the unpleasantries. Now accept the invitation."

"I accept your invitation. Might I invite some of my people to join?"

More ear scratching noise comes back.

Then the caption. "Please do."

IKNOSAN LEGACY SHIP

Given the Challenger's dwindling propellant supply, we crawl back to the system with the brown dwarf. Twenty plus short jumps, with tiny course changes in between. Jill, Justin, Mac, and Ty are waiting for us when we finally go aboard. The crews of the Predator and Boomerang went back to rescue Melissa and Larry aboard the Relentless, recover its weapons and drones, then set it on a sub-light journey to dive into a nearby star.

Now back in the familiar lab, To'Kana offers us seats at a table with four boxes set at each seat.

"The Harza are a delightful people—quite entertaining and very welcoming. But they are different enough that it makes direct person-to-person contact difficult for us. Our presence doesn't seem to affect them in the same way."

"Let's start by removing your earpieces. Simply place yours in the box on your left."

We dutifully execute our task without complaint, though each of us shivers as we do so.

"We are going to replace your earpiece with two others, one for each ear. These will block most exterior sound and translate most spoken words around you into English. It's not perfect, but it works well enough to be useful."

As if an afterthought, he adds. "These also tickle as they go in."

Not wanting to do this twice, I twist both of mine in at the same time. The uncontrolled shivering that follows almost knocks me out of my chair.

"The next box contains nose pieces, one for each nostril. When you insert them, they might trigger a sneeze."

Mine go in with no issue. Justin sneezes hard enough that one goes flying and needs to be cleaned and sanitized before he tries again.

"That was so disgusting," he whines.

"Lastly..." To'Kana drags the word out. "Harza food is edible and nutritious for human consumption. But most humans would find the taste revolting and some textures unpleasant. As polite guests, it is important for you to enjoy the food. Please open the fourth box and insert the mouthpiece into your mouth."

I open mine and see something that resembles the mouth guard I wore during my short stint in high school football.

"Make sure your teeth go into the guard and the part in the middle touches both the roof of your mouth and your tongue. You will feel a melting sensation and a bright burst of flavor."

I do as instructed and feel the mouthpiece melt, but it produces no liquid to swallow. The flavor burst at the end leaves my mouth feeling clean—the whole thing a strange, but pleasant, experience.

To'Kana stands. "It's time. Let's go."

HARZA WAR SHIP

I open my eyes and see that I'm standing on a transporter receiving platform at the edge of a theater-sized room. In the center, standing on a small, circular dais, I see Admiral Kotosoba, arms waving like an orchestra conductor. In front of him is the largest holoprojection screen I've ever seen, maybe ten meters high, twenty meters wide. In it are the main view screens from dozens of ships. From what I see, they have four of their submarine-shaped cruisers on each Dominion dreadnaught. In the background, there are numerous shattered and broken Harza ships.

To'Kana, who is standing next to me, taps my shoulder and points to several smaller seats behind the admiral.

"Those are reserved for us," he says through the earpiece.

As we walk toward our target, I take in the room's size and its similarity to an opera house—the holoprojection being the stage, a hundred workstation operators on a lower platform like musicians in an orchestra pit, with seating behind the admiral for five hundred spectators.

"What you see here is unique to my experience," To'Kana says to us all via our earpieces. "The operators in front control most of the independent weapons in the battle zone. For every ship-based weapon, they have ten remote piloted ones—similar in concept to your Space Hawks, but much more potent. The people behind us are spotters and analysts, the intelligence force that analyzes the enemy's activities and feeds information and recommendations to the admiral."

To'Kana points to several panels near the top of the holoprojection. "The best summary of what's going on is up there. Twenty-four Dominion dreadnaughts are still in the fight, seventy have been destroyed or have lost both propulsion and weapons, twenty-six have fled."

He points to another display. "The battle map is over there. As you can see, they have boxed in the remaining Dominion dreadnaughts and are picking them off one at a time."

A cheer rocks the room as the number of kills ticks up to seventy-one, then seventy-two.

"Why are we here?" I ask. "Why does he want us to see this?"

"He wants to form an alliance with you, Kyle. He thinks you will want to partner with them once you see how they wage war. He also thinks he would have made quick work of the Dominion if he had your weapons."

I know the things To'Kana has said are true, but there must be more, because the truths spoken are not enough to explain our presence here.

"My next words are to you only, Kyle."

I turn to look at To'Kana, knowing the next shoe is about to drop.

"Another Dominion conquest fleet is inbound, one or two years out. It will target the Harza, other advanced humanoid species, and worlds like Earth that are mineral rich. Admiral Kotosoba believes his people and yours could form the basis of a humanoid federation able to hold back the Dominion."

To'Kana motions toward the room. "So, he invites you here to this place never seen by non-Harza eyes until I came a month ago, as a sign of his goodwill."

I nod to To'Kana, then settle back to observe with more care than before.

An hour passes, then another, before the last of the Dominion dreadnaughts goes down, and the admiral has successfully made his point. His cruisers fought valiantly, fifty or more lost during this last stand. But we both know the battle would have ended two hours ago if the Harza had my weapons. Little of the noise from the celebration going on around us penetrates our ear protection. That which gets through sounds chaotic, but festive.

Finally, the admiral comes over to greet us. "Human delegation, thank you for joining us and taking part in this glorious victory. I did not enter this system today expecting to leave it alive. Yet you broke the invaders' spirit, and more than half of my fleet still lives. Please come join me at my table."

He extends his hand—its four digits and opposable thumb proportioned much like a human hand—and turns it palm up.

"Place your hand on top of his. It is a symbol of agreement," To'Kana sends quietly.

I place my hand as To'Kana instructed and note that its brown fur is remarkably soft. "May this be the first of many celebrations we share."

The roar of approval that passes through the room penetrates my ear protection. Then as the sound quiets, the admiral drops his hand and says, "Come."

EPILOGUE

"Intelligence is rare, dangerous, and short-lived."
— Captain Ro'Masa To'Kana, Iknosan Legacy Fleet

[06.20.2034] IKNOSAN LEGACY SHIP

I woke around noon with the worst hangover I've ever experienced, but still smiling from the celebration last night. The Harza are a fun-loving people with sharp wit and a sense of humor that overcomes the huge gap that separates our people.

Thankfully, To'Kana had remedies that washed all the byproducts of last night's indulgences away in minutes.

Now seated in one of the secure conference rooms aboard his ship, we tie into a conference call with a delegation of Harza leaders to discuss next steps.

At this point, To'Kana is well known to the Harza and treated with great respect, which spills over onto me as well.

Compliments are traded back and forth, slowly morphing into a shared assessment of the situation. The next round of Dominion aggression will begin in about two years. The Harza are likely to be their first target; Earth their second or third. The Harza have the will and capacity to fight this war. Earth has the rare materials and technology required to turn back the Dominion. Each has things the other needs.

"The question," Justin asserts. "Is how to introduce the right people in our government to the right ones in yours? And vice versa. I think I know the best way to make our government want to meet yours."

"Ours already wants to meet yours," Admiral Kotosoba replies.

"Give me three days to lay the groundwork. If I can secure an invitation, we can arrange for a meeting."

Kotosoba stands and bows. "Then let it be so."

Justin and I return the gesture. "We will send word via Captain To'Kana."

[06.21.2034] WICKS-WIMBERLY HEADQUARTERS, NEW YORK

Yesterday, we returned home after the meeting with Admiral Kotosoba. Justin and Jill returned to his penthouse in New York; Alex and I to the estate house.

On the trip back, Justin arranged for meetings with Audell Knight and Natalie Wright in New York, and for video calls with Jace Elliott and Morgan Owen from their offices in the DC area.

Jill, Alex, and I prepared video clips of the battle and a simple story line. The Dominion came to within one hundred fifty days of Earth, where they stopped to ravage a people called the Harza. In the first Harzan system, the Dominion slaughtered everyone, completely eliminating their presence. Five experimental ships built by Wicks-Wimberly killed or disabled a total of twenty Dominion dreadnaughts. The Harza destroyed or turned back the rest. A Harzan delegation would like to come to Earth to open negotiations for a joint defense force.

I open my eyes and see that Alex and I have arrived in a partitioned off portion of the company's lobby. As planned, Audell is there with a small team from NBC to record our arrival and our answers to questions we planted.

"Dr. Wimberly, is it true that you just returned from a battle with the Dominion?"

"Yes."

"Is it true that you participated in the defense of an alien world?"

"I would not characterize our activities that way."

"How would you characterize them?"

"We tested the effectiveness of some new weapons and delivery systems against an alien menace intent on destroying the Earth."

"Were your tests successful?"

"Extremely. Every weapon that hit, destroyed or disabled its target."

As Audell steps forward to shake my hand, the cameras and lights shut down. "Welcome home."

"Good to be back. You got the storyboard we put together?"

"I did," Audell replies. "I can't wait to see the video evidence you've prepared."

...

An hour in, Audell says, "I think we need to start with the threat, which we can show by the wreckage of the Harza ships and the size of the Dominion dreadnaughts. Given the images you have, I think the best way to do it is with stills that we zoom in on. If we edit the clip where Justin's war shuttle is closing in on its target such that the two ships can be seen side by side, it will show the huge size disparity. My team can search through the wreckage clips to find the still that will best illustrate the extent of the destruction. The clip that will best show the effectiveness of your new torpedoes is the one where the penetrator hits and the ship gets wobbly. In slow motion, we can get a lot of impact from that clip alone. The other would be the one where the Space Hawk rear ends the dreadnaught, and it completely comes apart."

"Agreed," I say.

Audell looks up at me. "This story is compelling. So much so that it will have tremendous influence over policy. How sure are you that these images are representative?"

"Certain. We killed twenty Dominion dreadnaughts with five of our war shuttles, none of which were lost. The Harza lost over one hundred ships and crews taking down ninety Dominion dreadnaughts. The Harza ships are larger and more powerful than the battlecruisers we are building. On their own, our battlecruisers have no chance against the Dominion."

"So, you're saying we should scrap the program you worked so hard to get approved?"

"No. Each battlecruiser can carry ten or more of the war shuttles with massive quantities of supplies and propellant. Imagine the power one-hundred battlecruisers carrying ten war shuttles each would bring to this war. That is the solution we need to pursue. And in two years we could field a lot more than one hundred. With the Harza at our side, we could build thousands and take the war to the Dominion."

"Impressive claim." I spin around and see Natalie Wright standing in the doorway. "I presume you have the evidence to support it."

Audell does the three-minute version of our story.

"Impressive," she says. "But if you run it, you'll get caught up in a shit storm you want nothing to do with. Let me call an emergency session of the House Armed Services Committee. Kai can present the results of his test. It will be an open session. Anything presented, you can use openly."

Then to me, she says, "And here you go again, dragging America into a war it did not instigate."

"What!" I exclaim, rage building within.

Natalie smiles. "Kai, you are such an easy target. You know that's not my position. You also know that it's what some of my colleagues will say, which makes it something we need to work out if any of this is going to happen."

God, I hate politics.

[07.05.2034] WHITE HOUSE PRESS ROOM

Justin and I testified before the House Armed Services Committee, using it to get our message out to the masses. We were subsequently called before the Senate Foreign Services Committee and given a scolding for engaging in the affairs of another alien species. But public support for our actions has risen to where it was the scolders that took the heat, which I think was Natalie's plan all along. She's put her hat in for Speaker if the majority shifts after the mid-terms. The president, who's dragged her feet on all matters alien, responded positively to Natalie's suggestion that we should issue the Harza an invitation to visit Earth.

The process took two weeks, a non-productive waste of time, if you ask me. But the day has finally come. To'Kana's ship and five of the huge Harza battlecruisers dropped into medium earth orbit last night, their twice daily orbit allowing every country to see them through their telescopes.

The door to the press room opens, and I follow the president's press secretary, Secretary of State Porter, and Secretary of Defense McDaniels into the press room.

A minute later, the announcement comes. "The President of the United States."

I've seen this on the news a few times, but it captures little of the buzz that floods the room when the door opens, and the president walks out, today followed by Vice President Norwell, who stands behind her.

"I have a brief statement to make, then will open the floor for a few questions. I've asked Dr. Kyle Wimberly to sit in today. As one of the few people who have sat and broken bread with our guests in orbit, he will have a better perspective on many of the things you want to know about than I will."

She pauses, then looks down at some notes that have been placed on the podium for her.

"I am pleased to announce that the United Nations has agreed to allow Captain Ro'Masa To'Kana to address the General Assembly on

Friday, July 7, two days from now. As many of you know, the United States has come under some pressure from our allies and others for being the sole contact with his people, using two former US military service members as his points of contact for everything he was allowed to share with us.

"I talked with To'Kana at length today and believe we have come to an understanding. Dr. Kyle Wimberly will continue in his role as the technical point of contact for the foreseeable future. Something the Iknosan insist on, despite our requests to the contrary. He will also become my Special Envoy for Iknosan Technology Transfer.

"I open the floor for questions."

[07.07.2034] GENERAL ASSEMBLY, UNITED NATIONS, NEW YORK

I never thought I would enter this building and wouldn't want to today if it were not to support To'Kana. Thankfully, President Powell gave me a pass for Alex as well. Our seats are in the back row of the crowded American section.

President Powell has been given the floor and has just finished her introduction. "May I present Iknosan Central Council Member and Captain of Iknosan Legacy Ship #5, Ro'Masa To'Kana?"

When To'Kana simply appears out of thin air, the room resonates with shocked expressions. He steps up to the podium and scans the assembled, his penetrating eyes making contact with many of those present. Then he begins.

> "A war has been raging from time immemorial. Nearly a billion years ago, intelligent life appeared within our galaxy, quickly flourishing, then slowly dying. The pattern repeated over and over, recognized and diagnosed by civilization after civilization.
>
> On the order of one hundred million years ago—in an astoundingly short window of time, maybe one hundred thousand years—three species realized that intelligence is rare, dangerous, and short-lived.
>
> Rare as on Earth, with one dominant intelligent species, and two lesser ones out of the ten to twenty million species known.
>
> Dangerous, because most intelligent species kill themselves off through war or the destruction of their environment.

Short-lived, because even if they don't kill themselves off, they slowly become infertile, unable to reproduce.

Many others undoubtedly figured this out, but these three species set out to find immortality, spreading their DNA to every world that might support their kind.

This gave rise to the three types of intelligent life in our galaxy: arachnoids, humanoids, and cetaceanoids.

Arachnoids are spider-like creatures with eight limbs, huge brains, and innate telepathy.

Humanoids, like you and me, have four limbs, a smaller by comparison brain, and neurons spread throughout the body.

Cetaceanoids are sea dwelling mammals like Earth's dolphins. Sadly, the war has driven tier-one intelligent sea life into extinction.

Today, the arachnoids have the upper hand, outnumbering humanoids three to one. They have bound themselves into a union known as the Dominion. Their biggest goal? To rid the galaxy of humanoids. To maintain sufficient genetic diversity to reach immortality as a collective species, even if they cannot do so for their own.

This is our enemy. The ones that stalk us. The ones that will prevail if we humanoids cannot form an even more powerful union.

My people are mostly gone, likely sentenced to a premature extinction, though the die may not yet be cast. Our hope rests solely in our ability to turn the Dominion back. The Harza are willing to work with us toward that end. Individual humans are as well. But at this point, your fate lies in your own hands. Everything you need to live has been, or soon will be, in the hands of Dr. Kyle Wimberly. Work with him and you will live. Choose not to? Then nature will take its toll.

Thank you for your time and attention."

To'Kana bows his head in salute, then simply disappears.

[07.08.2034] IKNOSAN LEGACY SHIP

I open my eyes and once again am in the lab with Alex at my side. To'Kana stands opposite me, in better shape than I've seen him since the first weeks we met. But for the first time, another Iknosan stands next to him, by all appearances a female.

"Kyle Wimberly. Alexandra Reyes. Thank you for taking time to meet with me. Please meet my new companion, Lo'Mada To'Sona."

I stand there frozen for a second, then ask the question that confuses me. "Is there an appropriate form of greeting for a new companion?"

"Only acknowledgment."

I bow. "Lo'Mada To'Sona. A pleasure to meet you."

"And you, Kyle Wimberly and Alexandra Reyes."

To'Kana motions towards one of the secure meeting rooms.

We enter, then once security is in place, he says, "I have a gift for you."

"Thank you, sir."

"It is of immense value, which makes delivery difficult."

"May I ask what it is?"

"A copy of the Iknosan data ark. It contains every bit of information developed by our people over our nearly two-hundred-thousand-year history, everything from the DNA of the first life forms to emerge on our planet to replicator patterns for computer systems a million times more powerful than the combined computing power of all the computing platforms on Earth."

"What makes it difficult to deliver?"

"It's size."

"How big is it?"

To'Kana shrugs. "Smaller than your moon."

I laugh, then realize he's serious.

My data tablet dings, then dings again.

"I've just sent links you can give Thelma. These are sufficient for you to find a solution."

My tablet dings again.

"This is for you, and you only—not your government, not the Harza, only for you. It will give you access to the wonders of the universe, and maybe the key to long-term survival."

"I must leave now, but I will be available to you for the rest of my days. The means to connect with me are now in your hands."

"When do you go?"

"Now." To'Kana and his new companion stand.

Alex and I follow their lead. An instant later, I feel the transporters' grip, and am deeply saddened that I will may never see him again.

[07.12.2034] PENTAGON, WASHINGTON D. C.

Thelma helped me access the Iknosan Data Ark. It will take a lifetime of study just to read its table of contents. But To'Kana was kind enough to bookmark items relevant to our war effort for immediate download. Despite the demands of my role as Special Envoy, I've now integrated that knowledge and know exactly how to arm our world for the battle that will come in two years.

Over the last half hour, I've laid out my framework for a layered defense against the Dominion. But now, as I sit across the table from Secretary of Defense, Alaster McDaniels, and the head of the Joint Chiefs of Staff, Admiral Nelson Sloan, I realize that these two have no interest in my framework. That's when the epiphany strikes. These fools are Xerox copies of the people that put me at Abbey Gate thirteen years ago.

Then Natalie Wright's words ring in my ears. *Kai, you have been given the power. You have the upper hand. No one knows how to use what we have been given better than you do. Never yield to the inferior. Use every argument they present to your advantage. And if all else fails, simply ignore them.*

"Gentlemen, this may not be what you were expecting. It is different than our original plan. But few plans survive first contact with the enemy. And now that we know the effectiveness of our new weapons and delivery systems, this is the only plan that makes sense. It is what we will build, and it would be foolish of you not to embrace it."

As Secretary McDaniels starts scolding me, I stand, shaking my head. "Sir, I have presented you with the only offer I am making. Take it or leave it. Thank you for your time. You know how to reach me."

Then privately, "Thelma, transport me home."

THE END

Don't miss the preview at the end of this book...

Reverberations (Echoes of Extinction: Book 2)
By
D. Ward Cornell

AFTERWORD

The idea behind **Echoes of Extinction** came as I was finishing up the last book in the **Chronicles of Daan** series.

The idea was simple... An advanced alien species is attacked and driven to the edge of extinction by vicious predatory invaders. They find the means to defend themselves but cannot deploy it in time. So with resolve, they package their knowledge as a gift and offer it to other worlds—their legacy to other humanoids struggling to survive in a galaxy dominated by arachnoids.

The ideas were clear enough that I drew up an outline, knocked out the first two chapters, and put it on the shelf for future consideration.

The next book in the pipeline was **Eleven Days**. It was originally conceived as a stand-alone book, not a series, with an intentionally vague ending inspired by one of Arthur C. Clarkes' books.

During final production on Eleven Days, I started on its sequel, **Into the Change**. But as presales of Eleven Days sagged and its first month's sales fell far short of expectation, I put the sequel back on the shelf and restarted work on Echoes of Extinction. The irony, of course, is that shortly after restarting Echoes, Eleven Days went to the top of the charts.

FACT VS. FICTION

In all my writings I try to keep the line between fact and fiction blurry enough that it's hard to tell where the facts stop and where the fiction starts. In Echoes of Extinction, that line is well hidden. Here are some examples that people have asked me about.

The materials science in this book is fact heavy. Minerals like Thortveitite, Monazite, Euxenite, Xenotime-(Yb), Gadolinite-(Y) are all real and they contain the elements cited in the text—Scandium, Yttrium, Ytterbium, Erbium, Neodymium, Niobium, Dysprosium, and Terbium. Each of these elements has material properties consistent with their use in the story. For example, the niobium-titanium alloy used in Iknosan jump field emitters is similar to the one SpaceX used in their Merlin Vacuum engines in their Falcon 9 rockets. One of the known applications for Ytterbium is precision timing, the type of which would be required for the jump drive described in this book.

Compression fitting is a real thing. Two companies I've worked for used it in the manufacture of their products, one of them using a process similar to the one described in this book. Busbars are also real things used in power connections. Are the ones in most generators pressure fit? I think so, but in truth am not sure.

Quantum time and quantum gravity are both theories that have been proposed. Papers have been published proposing time quanta much shorter than my proposed 10^{-23} seconds. But, the idea that time, space, and gravity might not be continuous, but instead exist as quanta, opens the door for things like a jump drive powered by a universe that could repaint itself differently from one clock tick to the next. It makes great fodder for sci-fi.

Most of the locations used in the book are real locations. Morro Rock and Morro Bay are on the California coast near San Luis Obispo, and the ambient temperature difference across the dozen or so miles that separate them is astounding. The towns of Amber, Nevada and Peach Springs, Arizona are real, as are areas like the Upper Burro Creek Wilderness and the Arrastra Mountain Wilderness. Some of the materials on Kai's list are actually mined in places near those cited. Massive deposits of the types described in the book could be there, but at the depths proposed, no one would know.

All of the hotels and restaurants cited in the book are, or were, real at the time the book was written. Many of the meals described are, or were, on their menus. Does the Charlie Palmer in DC have a special Jefferson Manhattan? I don't know. I've only been to the one in Las Vegas and the bartender there created a very memorable one for me—memorable enough that it gets a mention. He also commented on his bitters, though I can't remember which bourbon he used.

Following his second encounter with Dominion hatchlings, Kai goes in for surgery on his right ankle. The surgery is done under a fluoroscope and tiny spurs are removed that contain tungsten. Two interesting pieces of science motivated the scene, the first of which is Surgical Fluoroscopy. For those who have not experienced it, it's a real thing. A fluoroscope is a continuous real time x-ray. One of its uses is to guide surgical procedures in densely packed areas such as a foot or ankle. I first learned of it when my left foot and ankle were injured and not healing. Surgical Fluoroscopy found and repaired the split tendon that was the cause.

The second piece of science is tungsten. It is one of the densest metals, therefore a good choice for the penetrator in the Barracuda torpedoes. But biologically, tungsten is toxic to humans. The National Institute for Occupational Safety and Health (NIOSH) has set a recommended exposure limit for tungsten because of its toxicity and role in inducing cancer. In this story, alien arachnoids are assumed to have a biological role for tungsten, something that would make them biologically incompatible with humans and clearly not of this world.

UNITS OF MEASURE

One of my frustrations while writing this book, and in life as well I suppose, is the mixed units of measure we struggle with in the United States. Normal, everyday-people think about things at home in terms of inches and miles, ounces and pounds for weight/mass, and cups or gallons for volume. Those of us that work in technical fields think about everything at work in terms of meters, liters, or grams. This story is set in the American Southwest, so you would expect all civilian measurements to be in the imperial system, all technical measurements to be metric. But in mixed conversation, most of us tech people go back and forth depending on topic, location, or who you're talking with.

I've tried to mimic that in the dialog and in Kyle's narration. He flips around as all of us techies do, which hopefully frustrates you less than it does me.

SELF REFLECTION

In the scene where Kyle ultimately destroys the Dominion spy ship that has landed on the runway at First Cycle Solar, he narrates the following as Mac transports out.

> *"Thelma! I know you can hear me through Mac's implants. Transport him out of here."*
> *As Mac collapses, my heart sinks. I can't do this on my own.*
> *Then Mac disappears. I'm encouraged that he's safe now, but as the reality of the situation sinks home... Sorry, not going there. I'm on my own against a vastly superior force. It's not the first time, but... Sorry not completing that thought either.*

Several places in this story, Kyle interrupts his own thought process, bending it to his will, interrupting a thought that he knows won't help him. An early reviewer commented that he hadn't seen this style of writing before and asked where it came from. The answer to that question was easy. As an introvert, who has a constant stream of thoughts cascading through my mind every waking minute, I do this to myself all the time. If I'm fixating on something that's not productive, I proactively insert a thought like 'not going there.'

INTERNATIONAL COOPERATION

In Echoes of Extinction, the Iknosan do not make direct contact with any of Earth's governments until To'Kana's brief appearance at the United Nations at the end. Similarly, To'Kana only makes indirect contact with the American government, not meeting with the president until the very end. Why?

A common theme that runs through several science fiction franchises is that first contact will only happen if a world has established a planetary government. As someone who mostly subscribes to the planetary government theory, I've pondered a related question. What happens when there is no planetary government, but the planet has resources that an advanced alien species requires?

The most common answer is that they simply take what they need. Maybe they do it blatantly and violently. Maybe they do it in stealth. The latter would certainly be consistent with the data the US military has been leaking out over the last couple of years.

The position taken in this book is a little different. Instead of simply stealing the supply of rare earth and other materials that primitive, disorganized worlds like Earth might have, the Iknosan offer technology and the means to extract the critical materials required to use that technology.

But they only work with the willing, roping in the governments when success is at hand. If a world acts on the offer, then it gets to keep the materials. If it does not, then the Iknosan take what other worlds will need. They give the opportunity to participate, then take what they need if the world fails to engage.

COMING SOON

Aside from this book, I have two more planned for 2023—the sequel to **Eleven Days**, entitled **Into the Change**, and the second book in the **Echoes of Extinction** series, tentatively entitled **Reverberations**. **Into the Change** is a little further along, so likely to come out first. But as of this writing, I've not committed to the launch order. You are more than welcome to let me know your preference.

Be sure to check out the preview of **Reverberations** included at the end of this book.

...

Thank you for having read **Echoes of Extinction**. There is great joy in writing a book like this, even more in knowing that someone read and enjoyed it. Please put some stars on a review and stay tuned for more to come.

If you have comments, suggestions, or just want to say 'Hi,' drop me a note. I do my best to answer every email. If you'd be interested in joining my outstanding team of beta readers, please contact me.

You can reach me at dw.cornell@kahakaicg.com. My first name is Don.

COMING SOON

REVERBERATIONS
By
D. Ward Cornell

[01.10.2035] WAR SHUTTLE CHALLENGER

"Wimberly, wake up!"

Shaking accompanies Alex's muted voice, but I struggle to get my bearings in the dim light illuminating my cabin.

Her head pops up over the rail of my bunk as she whispers, "Dominion scout ships have found one of our decoy shuttles. We'll be arriving in-system in a few minutes. We don't have much time."

I jump down off my bunk with urgency, hoping this is the break we've been waiting for.

"Do we know how long they've been there?" I ask Alex.

"According to Winston, they arrived about an hour ago, then deployed one of their octopus-like drones fifteen minutes later. It's still crawling along the surface of the shuttle. Which leads me to believe they haven't penetrated the hull yet."

She runs her fingers through my hair, straightening it a bit, then opens the cabin door. "Let's go."

About a month after To'Kana's presentation at the United Nations, President Powell signed a collaboration agreement with the Harza. The media pooh-poohed it, saying the agreement was more of a good will gesture than anything else. But it was exactly what my team needed, because it cleared the way for us to work with the Harza without fear of government reprisal.

In the month that followed, we drafted a plan for a joint defense force, fleet configurations, new weapons, and a crafty plan for gathering intelligence on the Dominion.

As I enter the bridge, I see that we have arrived in-system and used our stealth to sneak up close to some of the scout ships.

"Captain on the bridge," our pilot AI, Charlie, greets.

"Charlie, do you think they have determined this is a decoy?"

"No way to know, of course. But no, I don't think they know yet, and I'm not sure how they would make that determination without entering the shuttle. All external systems are powered up, as are the environmental systems inside."

I take a second to study the situation map on the main viewscreen. Ten scout ships. Three different versions, which is a curious development. All idle, holding position relative to our war shuttle decoy.

"Do we have target lock on all ten ships?"

"Only the three closest to us, sir. We'll need to reposition to get the others."

"Launch the tracking devices for the closest three ships."

The first jointly developed item we built with the Harza was a small tracking device—about an inch square, a quarter inch deep, with grav plating on one side, a com link to our tracking center, and a position detection system developed by the Harza.

"Tracking devices away. Repositioning."

On the main viewscreen, dotted lines form showing the flight path for the three trackers that have launched.

Alex shakes her head. "It's shocking how poor the Dominion sensors are. We're only a few kilometers away from them, but they still can't see through our stealth."

"So, it seems," I reply

I watch as the *Challenger* repositions, then note that we've acquired target-lock on four more of the scouts.

"The first tracker has successfully attached itself to its target," Charlie reports. "And I have target lock on the next four scouts."

"Launch the trackers," I order.

"The remaining three scouts are further out. We will need to place these one at a time. Estimated time to completion: thirty-five minutes," Charlie replies.

"Proceed," I order.

"Doesn't it strike you as odd that these guys just sit here like this?" Alex asks. "If it were me, I wouldn't remain stationary for this long. Surely, they must suspect we're looking for it."

"Maybe they're just luring us in."

"Sir, we have a Dominion dreadnaught emerging from FTL," Charlie announces.

"How many scouts have we tagged?"

"Four, sir. Three more will connect in the next minute or two."

"Jump us out one light year, Charlie," I order.

"Jumped, sir."

"Launch a Space Hawk—one that can launch the tracking devices—and jump it back for distant observation."

"Launching Space Hawk, sir."

"What are you thinking?" Alex asks.

"I don't want them to capture the war shuttle. It has a jump drive in it. If the Dominion obtains jump capability, we will lose our principal advantage over them. But I don't want to trigger the decoy's self-destruct unless I absolutely have to."

Alex laughs. "There's no way they're just going to leave that thing sitting there."

"If I may, sir?" Charlie asks.

"What is it, Charlie?"

"The self-destruct mechanism on the decoy versions of the war shuttle is a Harza incendiary device that will destroy the shuttle's interior and eventually melt through its hull. If we waited for the Dominion to bring it aboard, we could seriously damage their ship. If we triggered it after they went to FTL, we might cause a hull breach or subspace failure that would obliterate the dreadnaught and obscure all evidence of the war shuttle's presence."

"We've debated that option before," Alex replies. "The argument against has been that we can't confirm the kill, so need to assume it got away."

"That was before we set up the tracking center and put Winston in charge of it. Right?" I ask.

Alex grunts. "Good point. Charlie? Can you contact Winston to confirm that we can track the shuttle if it goes aboard the dreadnaught?"

"Checking, ma'am."

"I bet he's going to say, 'In theory, but it has never been tested.'"

Thirty seconds later, the answer comes back. "We've confirmed that we remain connected, while in a Dominion dreadnaught in FTL, up to the point they destroy the tracker. After returning to normal space, the tracker remains connected and tracking eventually re-syncs."

"I say we let the dreadnaught take it, then trigger the self-destruct when they transition," Alex says.

"Agreed. Charlie? Bring the Space Hawk in closer, so we can tag the remaining scouts. The dreadnaught too."

Seconds, then minutes, tick by with little activity outside other than the slithering of the Dominion's scouting drone. The dreadnaught has come to a stop, the ninth scout ship has just been tagged, and I'm about to nod off.

"It found something," Alex exclaims, pointing at the drone. "It's come to a complete stop."

"One of the scout ships is moving toward the dreadnaught," Charlie alerts.

Seconds tick by, then Charlie reports. "A door is opening on the dreadnaught."

"Any chance we could place a tag inside?"

"Searching," Charlie replies.

"I've got an idea," Alex says as she manipulates the view screen controls, then locks onto an external view that shows the dreadnaught's door opening. "Looks like a maintenance bay."

More minutes tick by as the maintenance bay door slowly opens, then something that must be a space tug emerges. Its cube-like main body has a dozen ion nozzles on one end and four enormous arms on the other.

"We should tag that thing," Alex says. "With the Space Hawk in stealth mode, it should be easy to tag the tug without getting too close to the dreadnaught."

"Charlie, tag the tug," I order.

Two hours pass as the tug approaches, then latches onto the decoy war shuttle. Another passes as the tug pushes it back toward the maintenance hangar.

"I wonder what's up with the robotic scout. It hasn't moved in almost four hours," Alex observes.

"Charlie, is there anything odd showing in the decoy's internal sensor readings?"

"The internal sensors are on standby, sir. Would you like me to activate them?"

"Please."

"Activating internal sensors."

An instant later, dozens of alarms go off, all ten scout ships are on the move, and the tug hastens its pace.

"Oh my God," Alex mutters, pointing at the screen showing the decoy's bridge. "It's full of cobwebs."

"Something came in through the shield emitters," Charlie reports. "And has breached several systems."

"I wonder if they know about us?" Alex asks.

As if in answer to her question, the largest of the scout ships powers up.

"Scout ship ten is moving away from the decoy," Charlie reports. "Scout ship three is moving toward the Space Hawk."

"Jump the Space Hawk away," I order. "Standard evasion pattern."

"Wait," Alex calls out.

"Hold the jump, Charlie," I order as I turn toward Alex.

"Think we can jump the decoy into the dreadnaught?" Alex asks.

I look at Charlie.

"Calculating," he replies. "Yes. It is possible."

"Power up the decoy's propulsion systems," I order.

"Taking them out of standby mode," Charlie replies. "Thirty seconds to jump. Scout ship ten has taken a bearing that will bring it straight to us."

"Jump the Space Hawk out to a more distant observation post," I order.

"Space Hawk jumped, sir."

Eyes on the timer for the decoy jump, I see it counting down. Then suddenly it stops, counts up, then counts down again.

"Charlie, what's going on with the decoy's jump timer?"

"The tug is resisting our attempts to line up the vector we need to jump. We have more power, so this won't take long."

"They are closing the door to the maintenance hangar," Alex says. "We better do this soon."

The countdown timer moves around some more, then Charlie says, "I've got it."

An instant later, the shuttle seems to stretch, the light going in right through the opening in the hangar door. The tug goes tumbling, debris from its shattered arms scattering in every direction. Then a jagged rift line runs through the dreadnaught, significant portions of the ship disappearing.

"What just happened?" Alex asks, bewildered.

A tiny thought tugs at the edge of my mind. Then the answer is there, like I knew it all along.

"We ruptured space-time. The rift zone annihilated the portions of the ship caught up in it. They no longer exist," I mutter, then in full voice, "Charlie, access memories on jump collisions."

"Obviously," he answers, the recorded memory affecting Charlie's speech pattern.

As we watch, more of the ship seems to just disappear every second.

Charlie is the first to break the silence. "The rift is trying to close, but mass is still flowing into it too fast. We won't see any debris until it closes."

Several seconds pass, then Alex points at the display. "A debris field is forming."

"All the Dominion scout ships have gone to FTL," Charlie reports.

"We should get out of here," Alex suggests.

"In a minute," I reply, my eyes still on the remnant of the Dominion ship. What's left of it looks like a piece of modern art.

"Have you ever put a piece of butter in a microwave to soften it, but left it in a couple of seconds too long?" Alex asks.

"Good comparison," I reply. "Totally carved out, only the outer shell remaining. Nothing could have survived that."

I turn to Charlie. "Retrieve the Space Hawk. Have it come to us. And leave the still image of the dreadnaught on the view screen."

"Retrieving Space Hawk, sir."

I get up and walk into the 3D image of the ship, amazed at how smoothly the rift zone carved it out.

Alex steps up next to me. "The sensors didn't have the angle to see this deep inside the ship, so it renders it as being empty. I doubt the space-time rupture carved out the interior as completely as shown here."

"Fair point. But I suspect the space-time rupture started within the superstructure and worked its way out to the hull, hollowing out everything in its way."

As I walk around the image, I see places where Alex's explanation is clearly the better. I look at her. "We need to go back and do a proper scan on this, don't we?"

"Agreed."

"Charlie, as soon as the Space Hawk is aboard, jump us back so we can do a full scan of the dreadnaught's remains."

"As ordered, sir."

ESTATE HOUSE, TAWNY OWL VINEYARDS

When the distinctive buzz of our industrial replicators replaces the quiet of the *Challenger's* bridge, I know our transport back is complete.

"Welcome home," Thelma says with arms outstretched and unmistakable joy in her voice.

I'm the first to step down off the transport platform. I give Thelma a warm hug and a kiss on the top of her head before releasing her. She steps away and repeats with Alex.

It has always amazed me how lifelike Thelma is. But the recent upgrades To'Kana enabled us to do for her, makes her almost indistinguishable from a real human. And minor adjustments to one of her motivation subroutines have allowed us to relax previous restrictions we had placed on her, limiting her physical contact.

As I take in the cellar, I'm reminded of the crisis that arose in December. Our original lease on the estate house expired at the end of the year, which left us with a problem. Michael, the British aristocrat who owns the property, did not want to renew our lease.

At first, he was unyielding in his opposition to a renewal, saying our presence disrupted the peaceful atmosphere of the property. Justin was equally unrelenting in his efforts to hold on to it, developing a deal that Michael could not refuse. The Wicks-Wimberly Real Estate group now owns half of the Tawny Owl Vineyards with the right of first refusal to buy the other half if Michael, or his heirs, ever want out.

"I still don't understand what happened," Alex says. "We jumped the war shuttle we were using as a decoy into the dreadnaught, which was only a thousand kilometers away. But why did it explode? And why wasn't there any debris? You said that it was space-time rupture, but what does that mean?"

"The Iknosan documented this behavior. I have a clear recollection of learning about it in my inherited memory. But I'll need to do some research to understand it more."

Alex touches my arm, drawing my entire focus.

"If we weaponized this phenomenon, it could be the most powerful weapon ever conceived—the one that could end the war."

I stare at Alex, the truth in her words impossible to deny and obvious once heard.

"I need to access the data ark. If, as you say, we can get control over this phenomenon and can do it with something smaller than a war shuttle, we could produce thousands, if not millions, of these weapons, which would change the course of the war."

OFFICE, ESTATE HOUSE

As I get myself settled to connect with the data ark, a message comes in from the tracking center. I connect and a second later, Winston's Iknosan avatar appears in the holoprojection.

"What do you have for me, Winston?"

"Nine of the Dominion scout ships survived the explosion. Seven of them have moved further in our direction. Two have headed back toward Dominion space. These ships move faster than the dreadnaughts. Our estimate of their effective speed is about twenty-five light years a day. The accuracy of the speed estimate may not be very good because of the distortion caused by their travel through subspace, but their direction is unambiguous. They are heading away from us, possibly going home. I assumed you would want to know this immediately."

"Thank you, Winston. I will send a note to Admiral Kotosoba letting him know of our first mission success. Please keep me posted."

"Yes, sir," he says, then vanishes.

I quickly jot out a message to the admiral advising him of the successful tagging of nine scout ships and that two appear to be heading back toward Dominion space. But I include nothing about the downed dreadnaught or our speculation about how we did it. I need to know more before I tell people about this.

Some months back, with Thelma's help, I set up a connection to the Iknosan Data Ark (IDA). Amazingly, it recognizes me as its sole owner, which makes no sense. Surely the surviving Iknosan remnant needs this resource more than I do.

When queried, To'Kana said I needed to trust him and should not ask about this again. When I asked if they had a copy of their own, he did not reply.

My copy of the IDA occupies the interior of a giant asteroid hundreds of light years away from here. Thankfully, I'm connected by a thousand channel wide quantum-entangled comm device, which took days to replicate.

With the door to my office closed, I open a control screen and search for data related to jump collisions. Seconds later, the IDA lists sixty-four entries. There is an overview document, several scientific papers on the physics of the phenomena, and papers and data of several experiments that confirm the theory.

I start with the overview document, which is remarkably concise and makes it crystal clear that the jump mechanism can only be used safely in interstellar space and the outer reaches of a star system. Jumping into an atmosphere or ocean will almost certainly destroy the ship and could cause catastrophic damage to the surrounding environment. Jumping into an asteroid, moon, or planet will result in a space-time rupture that will destroy the ship and some or all of the object it jumped into.

The only situation in which a ship could survive collision with a solid object is if the object is small, such as a spec of dust or a grain of sand, which could be incorporated into the superstructure or hull without causing it to fail.

I flip through the examples provided, giving the math a once over. Then the epiphany strikes. The Iknosan knew about this issue, the destruction a jump could wreak, and the space-time ruptures it could create. But they viewed these as safety issues—how to design a ship with less than a one in a billion chance of experiencing a jump failure. But it never occurred to them to use the jump mechanism as a weapon powered by its failure.

I already know everything we need to know to make one of these. It's just a matter of deciding the size of the weapon I want to make first.

DEN, ESTATE HOUSE

Since our adventure into Harza space, Larry Carver and his wife, Melissa Johnson, have become regular guests here at the estate house. Melissa still runs her winery. Larry still works for her and for my father. But both have a sense of urgency for Dominion preparedness that few others do. They come over for dinner almost every week. Tonight, we're having one of those dinners.

"They're here."

I look up and see Alex in the doorway.

"Can you delay them for a minute?"

She shakes her head. "Men and their toys... I'll ask the chef to open the champagne in the dining room. Be quick."

"Thanks. I'll only be a minute."

Refocusing on the task at hand, I download the last of the jump data I developed this afternoon into the simulator's database, then restart the simulator. A timer pops up with an estimated reload time of ten minutes. Maybe we can try a few rounds after dinner, using a Space Hawk as a jump weapon.

As I straighten up the mess I made while working on the system here, a server comes in.

"Alex has asked us to set up for dinner in here, sir."

"Thank you. I'll be out of your way in a second."

"She also asked me to send you out to the dining room."

"In a second," I reply, less than enamored that Alex is sending orders to me via the staff.

Finally done, I stand just as Larry walks in with a glass of champagne for me.

"Alex says you two had quite an adventure today—an overnight romantic getaway in another star system, which turned into an encounter with the Dominion."

"Yeah. She got to pick date night this week," I reply.

"So, are you going to tell me what happened? I'm thinking you might give me a little more colorful version than Alex would."

"You know about the tagging initiative? We put out decoys to attract Dominion scouting ships, then tag the scouts when they come, and track where they go."

Larry chuckles. "Lizzy and I ran one over the weekend. Winston told us we were the first to have a tag travel through FTL."

"So, you're the one that did that? Didn't know."

Larry gloats a little, then asks, "You did the same?"

"We tagged nine scouts before a dreadnaught dropped from FTL. It kept its distance but sent a tug to drag our war shuttle aboard."

"You tagged it?" Larry asks.

"Not exactly. Watch this." I motion toward the holoprojector we have installed in the room, then use my implant to route the sensor recording to it.

A still appears, showing the decoy war shuttle in the grip of the tug.

"Oh, my goodness," Larry exclaims. "You were close. They had your decoy in their clutches and the maintenance bay doors open."

"I'm going to show you what we did. It happens fast. Ready?"

"Let it rip."

"Here we go."

Replay starts a couple of seconds before the decoy jumps. As the light stretches out, Larry shouts, "You jumped it into the maintenance bay?"

It's my turn to laugh. "We jumped…"

But before the words are even out, the rift opens.

"What in the name of God is happening?" Larry whispers.

"Space-time rupture. Watch how it erodes the dreadnaught away."

We watch in silence. When it's done, Larry asks, "Can you play that again?"

As it plays the second time, the ladies come in.

"Should have known you'd be in here watching this," Alex complains.

I loop the clip two more times, before Melissa asks, "Is this repeatable? Can we weaponize it?"

I nod. "Yes, the Iknosan documented the phenomenon, and studied it enough to develop safety guidelines for jump drive designers."

Larry shakes his head. "They saw this as a safety issue, not as a weapons opportunity."

Having just had this conversation with Alex, and with myself for that matter, I realize how differently we approach problem solving than the Iknosan do, or at least did. I can't look at this without seeing a weapon, yet they did all this work and did not.

"Mind boggling, isn't it?"

I notice as Larry looks around, then startles. "You've upgraded the simulator. Haven't you? When can we have a go at it?"

"Not until after dinner," Melissa says, her stern voice not allowing for any debate.

...

Dinner done, Larry and I run a simulation as our partners sit in the leather recliners by the fireplace and watch.

"I'm going to use a Space Hawk," I advise Larry. "All the math has been loaded, but I haven't run any simulations yet."

"Can I try it using a torpedo that lands inside the ship?"

"The simulator crashed when I did that," Melissa complains.

"It should work now," I assure. "But we won't know until we test it."

"Is this a valid test?" Alex asks.

"No," I admit. "I'll need to do a proper, controlled simulation to know with any certainty. But this should be instructive and might motivate a better simulation than I would have done otherwise."

Larry and I run separate copies of the same simulation, which starts with three dominion dreadnaughts entering orbit over a planet at the hot edge of its star's habitable zone.

Larry starts the same way Melissa did a month or two ago, charging in-system with no attempt to hide his approach, then jumping away when a dreadnaught enters FTL. Part of me wants to watch, another part of me just wants to get on with it.

The latter part wins and minutes later, I start my approach by deploying two Space Hawks—one I plan to use for surveillance, the other as a jump weapon. I rename the one I'm using for over-watch Surveillance Hawk 1. It is the first to jump. An instant later it's a million kilometers above the planet's north pole, establishing a powered stationary orbit that keeps all three dreadnaughts in view.

Over the last couple of months, I've created an automated process to calculate the intercept course for various approach schemes. Today, the plan is to come in on a powered trajectory that will land me behind and beneath my target, keeping me below the horizon until seconds to the jump point. Such an aggressive approach would be impossible for a ship, or even a war shuttle, because of the gravitational sheer of moving through jump this deep in a gravity well. But the Space Hawk, with its two-meter length, can jump in to within one hundred fifty kilometers of the surface on a planet this size. Our target's orbit is up at fifteen thousand kilometers. In real life, these guys wouldn't see us coming.

Calculations complete, I send my jump weapon on its way. In real time, this would take almost two hours to run, so I set the simulator to run four times faster than real time, then turn my attention to Larry.

"You're going to need better precision than that," Melissa chides as Larry's jump goes a little off course.

"Maybe. Maybe not," he comes back. "This old man may still have a trick-or-two up his sleeve."

A few minutes later, the Dominion dreadnaught drops from FTL well short of Larry's strike point.

"Told you," Melissa says defiantly.

Larry drops his war shuttle into stealth and waits.

"What are you doing?" she asks.

"Testing a theory. I think they're going to search for me for a while before going back to FTL. In about a minute, they'll be where I want them, which gives me some time to dial in the range."

There's silence in the room as Larry works his controls.

"Got it," he says, as he sits back in his seat. "They just need to keep drifting along another fifteen seconds."

As the seconds on his jump timer tick down, the tension in the room increases.

"Three, two, one…" Larry whispers.

Larry's torpedo jumps. An instant later, the torpedo appears well behind the dreadnought, traveling at a slower speed falling further behind.

As Melissa laughs, Larry exclaims, "Perfect! Jumping in three seconds."

Before any of us catches on to what he's doing, the torpedo jumps again, disappearing—all contact lost.

"What just happened?" I ask.

"I set it to jump into the ship. The last chirp from the tracking system is consistent with it having done so."

"Come look at this," Alex says.

I look up and see that she's walked up to the holoprojection.

"There's a giant hole in the ship's bow. No sign of the torpedo, but a big hunk of this ship is missing. Can we rewind the simulation?"

I use my implant to rewind Larry's simulator to thirty seconds before the second jump, then we gather around to watch.

"There's no hole before the jump," Larry notes.

We wait as the timer counts down. Three, two, one…

A small hole appears as the timer says, "Arrived." It grows, exposing more of the interior to view, and continues to grow, hollowing out several hallways inside the ship, before stopping.

"I think I know what happened," Alex says. "Rewind to the jump point and step through at one frame per second."

I do what Alex asked, the first frame being the one before the jump. On the next frame, Alex says stop, then points. "That's the tip of the torpedo."

"I'll be damned," Larry says. "I almost missed."

"Next frame," Alex orders.

I advance one second, then stop.

"That explains it," Alex says, again pointing. "The torpedo materialized in a hallway, its nose penetrating the hull, its body penetrating a bulkhead, but most of its mass in the air. The space-time rupture will slowly take out this hallway and more of the hull. But there wasn't enough displaced mass to sustain the reaction."

"But this ship is definitely out of the fight," Larry adds. "So, mission accomplished."

Melissa puts an arm around him and says, "Good job, dear," her tone of voice sounding like a mother comforting a child, who completed his race in second-to-last place.

As the others laugh, an alarm goes off on my simulator, announcing, "Five minutes to jump."

Returning to my station, I check its status before putting my display up in the room's holoprojection.

"Your approach is right on target," Alex says. "But your Space Hawk has a lot less mass than a torpedo. Any idea how you're going to get more than Larry did?"

"We don't really know the interior layout of their ships. The simulator fills the interior with a standard Iknosan layout, which is denser in the stern. That's what I'm targeting. But the answer may be that we'll need something the size of a war shuttle."

We sit in silence as the last minutes tick down, then the dreadnaught comes over the horizon, directly ahead of us.

"Going to manual control," I announce as cross hairs and distance estimates pop up in the display.

"If you angle down slightly, you'll reach jump alignment sooner," Alex says.

I do as she suggests, noting the crosshairs moving down below the ship and the distance estimate ticking down a little faster.

"Just hold it there," she orders. "You'll want to jump when the crosshairs come up over the lower edge of the stern. Do you have the distance estimate synced with the jump controller?"

I snort but cut off the jibe on my lips. "Plus ten yards."

"Good."

If I looked over Alex's shoulder the way she's looking over mine, I'd never hear the end of it.

"That's it, that's it. Getting closer. Almost there...," she coaxes.

I jump a fraction of a second before she says, "Jump."

An instant later, an enormous hole opens in the dreadnaught's stern.

"Look at it go!" Larry shouts, as the hole expands, carving out the back third of the dreadnaught before debris comes spewing out.

Despite the excited chatter around me, two thoughts darken my mood.

"What's the matter?" Alex asks.

I smile, putting on a slightly better face. As her stare lingers, I say, "If that's where the Dominion power systems are located, then we'll get a kill like this one. But we really don't know where their power systems are."

Her stare doesn't drop, but Larry's hand on my arm breaks the moment.

"Congratulations, Kyle. Great fun, but it's time for us old folks to hit the sack."

We say our goodnights. Then, as soon as Thelma transports them home, Alex asks again. "What's wrong?"

I take her in my arms and pull her in close, holding her tight.

"What's the matter, Kyle?"

"This weapon... It's too powerful. Who could we possibly trust with it? And worse... We just let the genie out of the bottle."

ABOUT THE AUTHOR

D. Ward Cornell lives on the Kohala Coast of the Big Island of Hawaii. His work as an engineer, consultant and entrepreneur has taken him all over the world. Many of those places are featured in his writings. Although still dabbling in those fields, his passion now is bringing stories to life.

OTHER BOOKS by D. WARD CORNELL

Ascendancy
- Book 1: Revelation
- Book 2: The Institute
- Book 3: Emergence
- Book 4: Alliance
- Book 5: Return of the Ancients

Chronicles of Daan
- Book 1: The Rise of Daan
- Book 2: Prophet
- Book 3: Liberation
- Book 4: Calamite

Eleven Days
Into the Change   (Coming in 2023)

Echoes of Extinction
- Book 1: Echoes of Extinction
- Book 2: Reverberations   (Coming in 2023)

Made in United States
North Haven, CT
12 June 2024

53564477R00241